The Dog That Talked to God

"Jim Kraus has written a funny, heartfelt novel in the tradition of Garth Stein and John Grogan. For a long time dogs have been man's best friend. It only made sense one would finally come along to save our souls."
—Rob Stennett, author of *Homemade Haunting* and *The Almost True Story of Ryan Fisher*

THE DOG THAT TALKED TO GOD

Jim Kraus

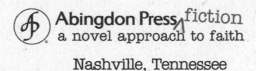

Abingdon Press fiction
a novel approach to faith
Nashville, Tennessee

The Dog That Talked to God

Copyright © 2012 by Jim Kraus

ISBN-13: 978-1-4267-4256-9

Published by Abingdon Press, P.O. Box 801, Nashville, TN 37202
www.abingdonpress.com

Library of Congress Cataloging-in-Publication Data

Kraus, Jim, 1950–
    The dog that talked to god / Jim Kraus.
      p.   cm.
    ISBN 978-1-4267-4256-9 (book - paperback / trade pbk. : alk. paper)
    I. Title.
    PS3561.R2876D64   2012
    813'.54—dc23

2011044545

Printed in the United States of America

2 3 4 5 6 7 8 9 10 / 17 16 15 14 13 12

To Rufus, a noble dog

1

Born in the wealthy enclave of Barrington, Illinois, in late autumn, Rufus was the smallest pup in a litter of four—black with white highlights, white eyebrows and chest. The breeder, a precise woman with a lazy eye, said that as an adult, he would most likely remain on the smallish side. That's a good trait for a miniature schnauzer. He had the look, even as a seven-week-old, of a polished, professional dog, holding a practiced dog show stance—legs back, chest forward, eyes alert—all inherited traits, genetics at its best.

But she said nothing about Rufus talking. Not just talking, but talking to God. In dog prayers, I imagine.

Though, in her defense, I would guess that she was unaware of this unusual talent.

And, also in her defense, if she knew of his abilities and had mentioned, "Oh yes, Mrs. Fassler, and the runt of the litter—the dog you want—well, he talks, and he claims he talks to God." I mean, honestly, if she had said that, or anything remotely like that, then odds are that the good dog Rufus would not be sitting in the chair opposite me right now, watching me type.

Perhaps if Rufus had been adopted into another home— a home with an owner who wasn't lost and confused and didn't need to be returned to the awareness of the existence of God—he would not have bothered speaking at all, except to bark at the door to be let out. Even Rufus is not sure of that possibility.

"I don't ask foolish questions, Mary," Rufus answered when I asked him about the odds of him spending his life with me, rather than some other, more spiritually healthy person.

But I digress.

I did not mean to cavalierly hurry past the most compelling element of this story: the fact that Rufus talks to God. And he talks to me—Rufus, that is, not God. Sometimes.

It's hard to be nonchalant or blasé about such an ability, I know. But I cannot leap into this tale without returning to the beginning. You need to know how all this came about. You need to know the origins of the story. After all, what would the Bible be without Genesis and the garden of Eden? Confusing, to say the least, and most likely incomprehensible. Imagine the Bible as a movie you walk into during the middle. You can make up your own backstory, but it would all be just a guess. Admit it: without that opening scene, not much of the rest would contain any internal logic.

As a child, I used to do that—walk into a movie theater whenever, and watch the film, sit through the ending, and wait for the opening reel to start again until I would say to myself, "This is where I came in." It was easier years ago, before the age of googolplexes and corporate theater chains. Back in the day, each theater had one screen and would play the same movie over and over, with only a cartoon and previews to separate one screening from another. Once I got to that point of having seen a particular scene before, I would leave, satisfied that I saw the entire story. I remember doing that to *The Time Machine* with Rod Taylor, a movie star without much reason to be a star. Seems ludicrous to me now. I had constructed my own narrative as to how Rod got to whatever point in the future he started at, which then altered my imagined story as the true narrative unfolded. With that movie, I was close to guessing the actual story and plot. Close, but, as they say, no cigar.

As a child, reconstructing a complicated narrative was child's play.

It is not so easy today.

Throughout my youth, my family owned pets. *Owned*, I suspect, is now a pejorative term. I mean, do we really own a dog? Or do we merely cohabit in the same spaces? The latter, I am now certain. My father, an impetuous man with a generous heart, once bought a squirrel monkey from Gimbels Department Store in Pittsburgh, Pennsylvania—when department stores, I surmise, could sell squirrel monkeys.

A monkey proved to be a pretty interesting pet, but if you fed it something it did not like, it would simply heave it out of the cage. Neatness is not any monkey's most endearing trait.

I remember growing up with a mutt, the family dog, a loyal animal who became as much a member of the family as I. As a teenager, I stood beside her in the vet's office when he administered the oh-so-humane and oh-so-lethal injection to a lame, sick, dying dog. I remember her eyes, just as they went dark. I remember weeping all night over that loss.

In my forties (midway, if I am feeling honest) I found myself alone again. I was pretty certain I needed a dog. Christmas was coming and I did not want to be alone.

Before—well, before my current losses and tragedies—the parameters of a dog purchase became the topic of long conversations among Jacob, John, and me. It had been decided that hypoallergenic was a necessity; preferably non-shedding, small, with minimal genetic health concerns, loyal, good with children, non-nippy, benevolent, artistic, and kind. Just kidding about the last three, but we did have a pretty substantial list of preferences. The miniature schnauzer breed met all of our qualifications.

But we, as a family, never had a chance to fulfill that dream.

Alone, now, I decided to take action—and taking action was something I did not do lightly. Unlike me, the schnauzer, according to the breed books, had decisiveness bred into its genes. A good watchdog, the books insisted. A barker, but not a biter. Since I live in a relatively safe suburb, a barker would be sufficient.

I made a few calls; I looked on the Internet.

A friend advised against getting any dog. "They're all the same—stupid, hairy, and only interested in food. Trust me," she had said. "You will get companionship, but it will be stupid companionship. Like a blind date who you find out later cheated to get his GED, and who is five inches shorter than he claimed."

She owned an Irish setter, a truly small-brained animal. I say *she* owned it since she did all the dog upkeep in her family—feeding, walking, feeding, letting out, letting in, feeding, washing the muck off of it. The rest of the household liked the dog, but as is often usual for families, the mother remained stuck with all the dog duties. And to complicate things, her dog could not be described as smart—not even close to smart.

It ran into the same glass sliding door every morning of its life. Like a chicken, it appeared to wake up to a new world every dawn. A pleasant dog, for certain, but, as noted, not very smart. And it often smelled wet. Most of us know that musty, yeasty, heady, nearly unpleasant aroma of a wet dog. Like wet newspaper. What they have in common is beyond me.

"But I'm looking at a smaller dog. Something that I can pick up if I have to," I told her.

It took two people to lift my friend's Irish setter, or a single person using a hospital patient lift—and where was one of those when needed?

"Jacob always wanted a schnauzer. Sort of like fulfilling a promise, you know?" I added.

My friend shrugged, apparently resigned to my choice, to my fate.

After all, how do you argue with one of the last wishes of a dead man?

There were a few AKC breeders near where I live who specialized in miniature schnauzers.

And when I was ready, only one breeder—the precise lady in Barrington with the lazy eye—had a litter with an unspoken-for puppy.

"I have a litter of four. The two females are spoken for. The larger male is going to another breeder in Florida. That leaves one male puppy. He's the runt of the litter. But he's healthy."

I attempted to make arrangements to complete the purchase.

"It's not that simple," she said, a slight note of caution in her voice. "Before you come, I have some questions. Save you a trip. I don't sell my dogs to just anyone."

"Of course not," I said, thinking it was a poor method of marketing puppies, but I played along. "I completely understand."

"Do you live in a house or apartment?"

"A house. It's too big for me," I said, telling this stranger more than she needed to know. "I plan on selling in a year or two, and moving to a smaller house. More manageable. But a house. A house, yes, not an apartment or a condo. I don't think I would do well in an apartment anymore. Odd noises and someone is always cooking with too much curry. So, yes, I have a house. I will have a house. Now. And in the future."

"Does the house have a yard? Will the new house have a yard?"

Don't all houses have yards?

"It does. And the back is fenced. It's pretty big. The landscapers bill me $40 a week to cut it . . . so there's a lot of room for a dog to run. And if I do move, that house will have a fenced yard. Keeps out the riffraff dogs, if you know what I mean."

Her silence probably meant that she didn't.

"Do you work?"

No . . . I thought I might pay for the puppy with food stamps.

Sorry. That's just me being snarky. Sorry.

"Yes."

"Are you gone all day? Will the dog be alone all day?"

Oh . . . now I see why you're asking.

"No. I work from home. I write books. And I edit some. And I publish a newsletter for writers. But I'm home 95 percent of most weekdays. I do go out to Starbucks sometimes to write. There's something about having to block out other people's conversations that makes me concentrate more effectively. But that's only once a week. Maybe twice, if I'm stumped by something."

The precise lady waited, then spoke carefully.

"I wouldn't sell this dog to a single person who worked outside the home all day. These puppies need companionship.

They'll get neurotic without a person—or people—around. Nothing worse than a neurotic dog."

She said nothing about dogs that had delusions of grandeur. Would I describe Rufus as . . . delusional? Or would that just be me?

"Any small children in the home?"

I waited a heartbeat, as I have done now for these last few years, until that small scud of darkness passed.

"No. No one else. It's just me."

The precise lady must have been thinking "divorced," or "widowed," or "never married." I did not volunteer further information. She did not ask. Often, when even thinking about the past, even to myself—still—I would get teary. Buying a dog is no time to get teary.

"Well, why don't you come up this Saturday? The puppy won't be ready to leave for at least another three weeks. You can see how you'll get on with him. We can talk."

I hung up the phone thinking that I need to make a good impression on this woman, or else I'll have to find another breeder and the next closest—with puppies available—was in Ohio. I did not want to drive to Ohio. Not just yet. Maybe not ever.

I arrived at the breeder's home early—a lifelong trait. To me, being on time is fifteen minutes early. The setting was not exactly rural, but I estimated that I was a good ten minutes from the nearest Starbucks—or a Texaco station selling chilled bottles of Starbucks Iced Coffee. So I sat in the drive and waited. I would have really liked a coffee. Caffeine settles my nerves.

I rattled in the car, more than a little nervous.

The breeder was exactly as I had pictured: precise, wore her hair short, trim, with practical glasses clipped to a gold chain around her neck; with that one eye slightly off-kilter to the other. She may have been wearing Earth Shoes. I was unaware if they had made a comeback; hers looked sensible and organic with a leather strap. I admit that I am far from being style-conscious. I buy good clothes, good outfits, designed to last. I haven't purchased a new outfit in years . . . well . . . since before the accident, I guess.

She extended her hand for a firm handshake, and escorted me to the basement. I could hear scuffling and yipping as we descended. In a large, airy room, with French doors leading to the outside, now closed, two adult schnauzers were in a large pen with what appeared to be a large, single mass of wiggling puppy. The room smelled of dog—but that inviting new-dog smell.

"Sit down," she said, and for that second I was not sure if the breeder meant me or the dogs. I realized that I should sit.

I sat on a plastic chair—one of two in the enclosure.

The two adult dogs sniffed the air, not in fear, but in exploration, in greeting. The larger one trotted over to me, placed its front paws on my knees, and stared hard into my eyes.

Schnauzer eyes are dark, or mostly dark, so the iris in their eyes is all but indistinguishable. They are like cartoon eyes—all one color—so it is difficult to see emotion in them. And schnauzers are not smilers. Some dogs—like labs, for example—can pull their lips back and offer a grin, with a lolling tongue. (I have since discovered that labs aren't that happy. They are simply manipulative.)

The larger dog, apparently satisfied with what it was looking for, hopped down.

The smaller dog walked toward me, with what I took to be deliberate steps. It too placed its paws on my knees and stared.

"That's the mom," the breeder said, not using the word *mom*, but the breeder word for a female dog—a word, incidentally, that I have never liked using, either in anger or in scientific dog-calling. She was Rufus's mother after all, though the name Rufus would not be decided for a few weeks.

She stared deeply, as deeply as a dog can stare, without being distracted by the yelping of one puppy or the whine of another. She stared, just stared, for the longest of moments. Longer than most dogs stare at anything, with the possible exception of an empty food bowl. (This I have learned recently as well.)

I didn't know what to do, so I gently covered her paws with my hands—like offering a manner of assurance that I was a good person who would treat her offspring well.

After what seemed to be a long time, she sort of gave a nod, like she approved, or found me acceptable, or knew her one special offspring was exactly the puppy I needed, then dropped back to the ground, sniffed my leg and shoe for a moment, and walked back to the big ball of puppies in the corner. This was not her first litter, so she obviously knew the routine. Puppies grow up and move on in the wild, and they do the same if they reside in urban domesticity.

The breeder walked over, reached in, and extracted a small furry lump of wiggle, mostly black, with some white. She handed it to me.

"This one will be yours if you want."

I held the small wriggling bud of puppy cupped in my two hands with plenty of room to spare.

"The pup can't see real well yet, so all it sees is your hands."

I stroked the little face with a finger, gentle, but not overly gentle. It was a boy puppy, after all. The puppy seemed to like that, and promptly fell asleep in my hands.

"That's a good sign. Some dogs just stay all riled up—being picked up, carried, strange scents—they'll struggle to get away. Apparently, he thinks you're a safe place."

He was the most beautiful puppy I had ever seen.

And he fell asleep. My heart began to sing, just a little. After such a long silence, it startled me at its ability to do so.

This was indeed the puppy that I needed to have in my life.

More surprises came later.

———— ∞ ————

The breeder gave me a list of things to do, and to have them all accomplished in the three weeks between the initial meeting and the final handoff—Rufus's adoption, as it was. The list was not extensive, but it was twice as long as I had anticipated.

"I can't visit your house, so you have to give me your word that all of it gets done. Okay?"

It was a command that I could not say no to.

"Of course."

I could see why she was good at training dogs. I really wanted to please her.

A dog crate; dog carrier for the car ride home; puppy food— one of two preferred brands—a water dish; collar, two leashes; one retractable, one a strong tether; the name of the dog's veterinarian; a picture of the fenced yard; an appointment set for a puppy class. The list ran on for nearly a full page.

Obtaining all the necessary documentation and supplies was not that difficult. The cage—sorry, the *crate*—fit into the alcove of a desk built into the kitchen layout. (I had been told that *cage* was pejorative, *crate* was preferred by most breeders.) I never used the kitchen desk, except as a temporary storehouse for receipts, mail, and magazines waiting to be evaluated before becoming recyclables. The top drawer held in the neighborhood of a thousand pens and pencils, all halfway to being thrown away because none of them worked, forcing me to take telephone notes with a huge felt-tipped sign marker on legal pads, the ink soaking through four sheets at a time.

I have to get better organized. I mean it this time.

The cage—rather, the crate—fit snugly in the kneehole of the desk. I added two sleeping pads, the top one a leopard print, to ensure a soft rest. I took a picture of it. I would show the breeder all my preparations.

No one prints pictures anymore. All they do is show others the back of their camera or cell phones. I miss passing actual snapshots around, but I didn't think I needed a permanent record of a dog crate and food bowls and the like, so I carried my camera with me.

I'll probably never delete them from the memory stick, though.

I wasn't sure about the crate situation. I never had a crated dog before. The family dog had the run of the house. Looking back, I don't remember where the dog slept. Did we have a dog bed somewhere? My mother, the sole surviving parent, resided in a nursing home, and while she had only begun to wade into the shallow, yet troubled waters of dementia, for now she would resent being asked inconsequential questions like "Where did the dog sleep?"

She would become agitated a little, and wave the question off as if it were a pesky mosquito. "How I am expected to remember foolish things like that?" she would snap, prickly as she had ever been. Some things do not change over the decades.

I would want to say that I did not expect her to recall the details, but that we were simply making conversation. Instead of asking a follow-up question about how the family had decided on a dog name, I would instead sit back, and watch *Wheel of Fortune* with my mother. She could not hear worth beans and had no use for gadgets like hearing aids, so the volume would be turned up to a painful level. Virtually every television in the Ligonier Valley Nursing Unit remained turned to the same level. I don't understand how the nurses and aides tolerated it. It would be like working in a tavern that featured heavy metal music. Or working in a steel mill. Here, all televisions, except the one in the main visiting lounge, had to be turned off by eight in the evening. Then silence rolled down the halls like a tsunami.

The breeder said that the prehistoric dogs lived in dens, so a crate, which she was careful to call a crate, fulfills their ancestral urges of being covered, protected, and easily defended. I draped a thin blanket over the top and sides. I planned to swap the thin one out for a heavier one in colder weather. The door latched easily. The crate provided plenty of turnaround area. The padding looked, and felt, pretty comfortable as well.

I had not purchased the Kuranda Dog Bed—patented, orthopedic, and chew proof. It certainly looked comfortable in the pet store, nearly as expensive as the new mattress I had purchased for myself eighteen months earlier. That was a necessary purchase; a deluxe dog bed could not be considered in the same category.

I had an assortment of puppy food, puppy chews, puppy toys, and assorted puppy diversions.

Even before I handed the breeder a check, this dog purchase had become expensive.

Do friends ever give puppy showers? My initial reaction was a strong no, with a wishful yes right behind.

I was ready. I was prepared.

Yet nothing could prepare me, really and truly, for what was to happen in a few short months.

The breeder actually looked at every picture I took of my purchases, my preparations, my supplies, my complete photo essay of my backyard. She even checked the photocopy of the medical license of my intended veterinarian.

"I've never heard of him," she said, "but he went to Cornell. Best vet school in the country."

"She. She went. The B. T. stands for Barbara something or other," I answered.

The breeder brightened.

"Good. I've always found female vets to be more compassionate—and intuitive. Good choice."

I felt proud of what I had accomplished. It was a feeling I had missed in recent months.

She presented me with the puppy's papers and AKC registration—a thick packet of documents that displayed his lineage back to the *Mayflower*, apparently. I had assured her that I had no interest in showing the puppy, or dog, as it grew. I promised to have him neutered; perhaps breeders do not want more competition from unskilled amateurs like me. "Neutered makes for better pets," she declared. I knew, for certain, that his papers would be filed in my office at home, and then lost in less than six months.

I'm not going to sell the dog for a profit, like flipping a foreclosed house. He's not going to procreate. Why would I need to know his great-great-great-grandfather?

I handed her the check. The dog was now mine.

"What are you going to name him?" the breeder asked.

I shrugged, apologetically.

"I'm not good with names . . . or book titles. I let my publisher pick titles. But with the dog, I thought I might see what sort of name fits him after a day or two."

"Don't wait too long. Puppies get imprinted with whatever you call it—especially if you use it a lot when they're young."

He lay down in the middle of the pet carrier, not frantically trying to escape or cowering in the corner. But in the middle, like that is where he was supposed to be. It did make it easier to carry, since the weight was evenly distributed.

I had been nervous concerning the ride home, worried about a whining, yelping puppy carrying on so much that I would have to stop. I'd imagined him chewing wildly at the door, scrabbling to escape his new and probably evil owner. But there were no histrionics, no puppy on the edge of puppy craziness. Just a very calm puppy, supine, staring out through the wire mesh door.

I pulled into the garage, stopped the car, and carefully took the carrier from the car.

"Show him his bed, his food, and the door you'll use to take him outside. Take him out on a leash right away and start his bathroom training," the breeder instructed, touching on the three most important elements in a puppy's small world.

I followed her instructions to the letter.

He dutifully sniffed at his crate, stepped inside, sniffing, looking at the cushion, then up at the top of the crate—like people do on all the HGTV shows when they enter a new room. I have noted that potential homebuyers invariably look at the ceiling, as if to make sure the house has one. Why do people do that? It's a plain ceiling. Look to see how big the closets are first, and if you have good water pressure. No one checks the water pressure on those shows. I have yet to see a single buyer flush a toilet. There might be a lot fewer home sales if people flushed toilets or ran showers.

The puppy completed his examination of the crate. I led him to his food dish and water bowl—both filled with fresh supplies.

He sniffed at both.

I snapped a leash onto his collar and led him to the . . .

Wait. What door am I going to use?

The back door led to a back deck, a second-story affair. A puppy this small would not yet be able to climb stairs.

I'll have to use the front door.

We stepped outside through the main door, and his sniffing became a bit more earnest. It took him fifteen minutes to sniff his way around the front yard. I was cold by the time he completed his inspection. There were other dogs in the neighborhood, so he took some time getting acquainted with their calling cards.

I am told that dogs can tell the size and sex and temperament of other dogs by the scent they leave. Seems a crude way of doing it—but if you can't talk or write, I suspect it is the only way.

He actually relieved himself out there, by a bush toward the side of the house—a bush I didn't really like, so if his ministrations killed it, I would not be upset. It was some sort of weedy looking shrub that had been billed as the bearer of fragrant flowers. The flowers lasted all of three days; the rest of the time it simply looked weedy. I praised him, as I had been told to do.

We walked back into the house. I unclipped his leash.

"Keep him in the kitchen at first. He'll be overwhelmed if he has too much space to explore."

Two doorways led into the kitchen: one a pocket door to the dining room, easily closed off; the other archway could be cut off by opening the basement door, leaving a gap of only an inch or two. The bigger problem was the wide arch between the kitchen and the family room.

The puppy seemed to be a cautious type, so my initial solution employed two lengths of white clothesline rope, strung at two inches off the floor, and the other at six inches, and affixed to the molding with adhesive-backed Velcro. If the puppy ran into them at full force, which he gave no indication of doing, the ropes would give way. More important, if I ran into them, stumbling toward the sunroom with the first coffee of the day and with my typical morning slit-eyes, then I would dislodge them as easily, without tumbling down and scalding myself with hot coffee.

The puppy sniffed the ropes, and made no attempt to cross the barrier.

It appeared effective. Maybe I could market this idea.

The puppy stared up at me.

No. How hard would it be to duplicate this? Not very.

I sat on the floor, my back to the wall, and invited the puppy to play. He slithered over with a wiggle. I imagined that he looked happy. I couldn't tell. This was the start of a long process, learning how to read the moods of this small animal.

He crawled into my hands and began a gentle nibbling on my fingers. His breath smelled healthy, like milk.

"Don't let him bite you," the breeder had scolded me. "Bad habit for a dog to have—biting."

But chewing is what a puppy does. As long as he did not bite in anger, I would tolerate a dog-to-owner chew every now and again.

After thirty minutes, the puppy crawled down from my leg and sat on his haunches, looking as tired as a . . . well, a puppy.

"Go into your crate," I directed and pointed at the open door to his den.

The puppy stared at my finger for a moment, as if my finger was the object he should focus on. "No," I said, as I pushed my finger forward into the air, gesturing toward the door. The puppy appeared to scowl, or furrow his brow as if in thought, then turned his head toward the crate. He lifted himself off the floor and walked with a surprising deliberateness toward his den, his crate, climbed over the two-inch frame, walked in, circled three times, then laid down, his head on his paws, his eyes facing me.

"Tired?"

He blinked, and let his head fall farther onto his paws.

"Can I get some coffee? Will I keep you awake?"

He did not answer. I am not sure, in the retelling of this episode, if he understood me at that young age, and simply waited to speak until the right time, or if he was in the process of trying to understand my speech. I think the latter, though I have not asked him. It doesn't seem to be that pertinent a question, in retrospect.

I sat in the upholstered chair in the bay window in the kitchen, sat with my coffee, watching The Weather Channel with the sound muted, sipping as quietly as I could manage, watching the puppy fall into a deep, untroubled sleep.

2

I named the puppy Rufus. I wish I had an interesting story behind the name. I don't. There was a King Rufus of England, I think, and a Rufus King, an American politician back in the 1800s (that fact I looked up), a minor biblical character, and Rufus Wainwright, a singer—but none of them had any bearing on my selection. Like with a new baby, I opened the *Baby Names* book to find an appropriate moniker. I had done this only once before, and I had, in the years between then and now, never, ever imagined that I would be doing it again. When I found the *Baby Names* book on a bookcase in the basement, it took me three days to open it.

I scanned the pages, eyes avoiding certain letters, then settled into the "R" chapter. The name Rufus appeared halfway down on a left-hand page. The name means "red." The dog wasn't red, nor would he ever be red, but the roundness of the name sort of fit perfectly. I knew no one named Rufus. I don't think I had ever been introduced to anyone with the name Rufus. There were no Rufuses in the neighborhood, so if I were to stand on my back deck and call the dog's name, there would be no confusion. Nor would I feel foolish—like shouting "Mr. Wiggles."

The puppy sat a few feet away, still in the kitchen, gnawing politely on a very small chew toy. The long rays of an autumn sun streamed through the bay window and the puppy sat in a warming pool of sunlight.

"Do you like the name Rufus?"

The puppy stopped chewing, and looked up at me. I had no idea what was in his eyes, save that it was a wide-eyed look up.

"Rufus. Should I name you Rufus? It sounds sort of dog-like, doesn't it? I don't like when people give dogs a real people name—like Mike or Paulie or something like that. Confusing to everyone, I think."

The puppy waited, the chew toy gripped between its forepaws.

"Rufus," I said with some authority. The puppy's ears perked up, as if he had heard the word and was now trying to remember it.

"Rufus," I said again a little louder.

This time, the puppy laid the chew toy down, stood up, and scampered toward me.

"Rufus," I said again, and by this time he stood at my feet, then on his hind legs, front paws on my legs. That meant he wanted to be picked up. Or to go outside. Or his stomach was empty. This time I interpreted it as wanting to be picked up. I cradled him my arms, not like a baby; that gets weird when an almost middle-aged woman starts treating a dog like a real human baby. No. I resisted that urge and held him like a dog should be held as I sat in the easy chair in the kitchen. Then he sort of stood on my stomach and made a beeline for my face. He did not try to nip at my nose. It had become a favorite game of his. Instead, he stopped mid-chest, and stared up.

"Rufus," I said, more softly this time, with as much quiet solemnity as I could muster.

He sat back and stared. I knew he had to be internalizing the sound of the name. I hoped that was what he was doing. No one could have told me with assurance that he wasn't doing exactly that. "Rufus. That's your name. It fits your face. You look just like a Rufus is supposed to look. A little beard. White eyebrows. A perfect Rufus."

He waited another moment, and then leaped at my nose. I caught him mid-jump. His teeth were sharp enough to draw blood and I did not want to spoil this sort-of-almost-hallowed moment of bestowing a name. I held him in both hands, while he squirmed happily.

"Rufus. From this day forward, noble dog, you will be known as Rufus."

Then I held him close to my chest and tried not to cry, remembering too much from the only other naming ceremony I had been party to.

This one was much different. Happy. But so had been the time before.

And as had happened in my only previous naming ceremony, moments later the newly named fell asleep in my arms, the sun bathing his perfect features, outlining every color and fold, every centimeter of a dog's personal topography in immaculate clarity.

I would remember this day forever, too, feeling a tiny heart beat close to mine once again.

I know I should tell something of my past. I have been avoiding that story every time I've felt the slightest nudge to let it unfold. Sometimes, that dark night seems as if it stands decades in the past; other times, it lies within a hand's reach.

I will tell you what I can, what you need to know at the moment.

I am forty-three, nearly forty-four years old. I am a widow. My name was . . . is . . . Mrs. Jacob Fassler. I think that was the proper terminology. Now I sign my name "Mary Fassler."

Obviously, this means that I had once been married. Until three years ago.

I am now living alone. Well, now with Rufus here, sitting in the office chair, staring out the window, watching me from the corner of his eye, I am not quite totally alone.

My house is much too large for one person and a small, well-mannered dog. The house was much too big for my husband and me. It was much too big for my husband and son and me.

I will soon get myself organized. I will clean the clutter out of this office. I will go through their clothes. I will donate them to the church's resale shop. I will find the golf clubs, the very old lacrosse equipment, and the electronic games and give them all away.

My heart is beating faster. I do not want to tell more of this story. I do not think I can.

I am alone. I don't like being alone. I wish things were different. I wish they had never headed east and had never crossed into Ohio.

I have stopped typing. I cannot stop weeping—softly, silently, without tears really—just a heaving of the chest and a near strangling tightness in my throat. I have never before—in the space of the last few years—put any of my story to paper or computer screen. Now that I have, it comes back in a flood and I am forced to stop.

That's when I see Rufus standing at the edge of the chair. He is too small to jump down by himself, but that is clearly what he wants to do. I had to help him up into the chair earlier. I take him down from the chair and he runs at me and attempts to scale my leg, thankfully clad in denim this afternoon. He makes it up my shin before he falls back into a heap. I stop wallowing in self-pity and pick him up. He burrows and climbs and attempts to get to my neck, and once there, in the crook of my neck, he nuzzles against it, pushing his damp, cold nose against my skin. It is almost a shocking feeling, and my tears leave me, my throat unsticks.

And that's when Rufus settles down as well. I sniff once more, and my stifled tears stop, and the puppy is obviously happy that I am no longer so unhappy.

⸺∞⸺

Rufus lived in the kitchen for two weeks. He hid toys under the pair of upholstered chairs in the bay window and circled the bottom skirt, pretending the toys were rabbits in hiding, then lunged under the flap of fabric, pulling a plush animal out into the open. He did not attempt to dismember any of his toys. He nibbled at them ever so gently. He would circle his domain ever so often. He would stop at the rope barricade, look out into the family room and the sunroom beyond, never once trying to break through the flimsy and mostly symbolic gating. He slept in his crate at night, with the door closed.

I agonized over that first night. I placed him in the crate, patted him on the head, closed the door, and told him, "Good night." He looked back up at me with those impervious eyes— not with sadness, but something more akin to resignation. Too small to climb the steps to the second floor anyhow, he had to sleep somewhere safe. I expected a long night of whines and barks, but I got nothing. Not a single peep. The next morning, a bit earlier than usual, I hurried downstairs. Rufus sat in the middle of the crate, not smiling, but waiting for me. He jumped out of the crate into my hands and began his puppy-nibbling.

We happily went outside. Rufus needed to know what dogs had come calling during the night. He tried once more to kill the shrub at the corner of the yard. He had found his spot.

At the end of those two weeks, I took down the ropes separating the family room from the kitchen. Rufus waited until I coiled them up and placed them in a drawer, then he took off with a joyful bounce and ran, full tilt, through the family room and into the sunroom, sliding on the polished hardwood floor, and crashing into the pair of hassocks, rolling, paws akimbo in the air, as happy as I had yet seen him. He had been looking at this route for a long time, and now he was relishing his first chance at experiencing in a joyful, headlong charge.

You had to admire both his inscrutable patience and his joyful verve.

He was almost big enough to scramble up into one of the chairs or onto the sofa in the sunroom. I spent little of my time in the family room—the room that lay between the kitchen and the sunroom. The room had seemed to grow too large, too uncozy, despite my best efforts of adding warmth. The acoustics were odd as well; the vaulted ceiling swallowed up dialogue on the television, and I did not like turning up the sound to the volume in my mother's nursing home. So, even on the chilly days, I usually had my morning coffee in the sunroom. Well, with the exception of these past few weeks. I would have felt guilty about abandoning poor little Rufus in the kitchen, all by himself for breakfast as well.

So I sat in the sunroom again, my back to the sun. Rufus snuffed and sniffed his way around the room, then sat at my feet, looking up. We had been outside, and he had noisily eaten kibble for breakfast, so I assumed that he wanted up.

I placed him on the sofa with me and he explored each cushion. Then he placed his paws on the back of the sofa, as if he wanted to climb up. The sofa had a wide back, with plenty of room for him to navigate. I picked him up and placed him there. He paraded back and forth once, then sat near my shoulder, staring out into the back yard, growling ever so slightly when he caught a glimpse of a squirrel in the trees that grew along my back property line.

In the future, that would become Rufus's favorite daytime resting and/or sleeping spot. He could watch out over his world, be close to me, and nap peacefully as the sunlight flowed, diffused by the slate, through the wide wooden blinds.

***

Friends came over to visit that first month, after hearing I had acquired a dog. They oohed and aahhed over the puppy, picking him up, with some planting kisses on his head. I had determined not to be the sort of semi-crazy pet lady who would do that. I have to say that human-to-pet smooches simply look wrong. Weird. I am pretty sure that Rufus did not like the forced smooches either, but he had no forearm with which to wipe off an unwanted kiss after being bussed on his forehead. Worse yet was the occasional trace of lipstick that remained afterward in his white eyebrows that I had to clean off when the over-affectionate guest departed.

Over lunch at a local fish house (a restaurant I could never go into by myself because it just felt too much like a couples place) one of my friends asked what was going on in my life. I appreciated that; most friends felt uncomfortable delving into my personal life and its tragedies and found it easier to chatter on about gardening or the upcoming house tour for charity or their exercise classes at the YMCA.

"I'm doing . . . okay," I said. "It doesn't get any easier. But maybe I'm just getting used to the way things are now. And the dog helps. Somebody in the house to talk to."

Beth pushed her blonde bangs from her eyes. (The blond was not natural, but then, what in today's world is totally real and unadorned?)

"No . . . I mean how are you really doing? You don't come to church anymore. Or hardly ever come. No one from our Sunday school class ever sees you. I've asked. We're worried about you. Or . . . well, I'm worried about you. You only come out when somebody calls you for lunch."

For a moment, I felt sad that I disappointed so many people. Then a moment later . . . no a second later . . . I grew angry. Why do I have to answer to so many other people about how I spend my Sunday mornings? Is it any of their business? I think not.

I decided to lie. I decided to smile and lie. Once more. It was just so much simpler than the truth.

"I'm fine. Really. It's hard to go to church. I see so many familiar faces, and I keep imagining that they either pity me or are waiting to pounce on me, offering some off-kilter advice. Or set me up with their third cousin on their mother's side who is way into comic books or is a *Star Wars* or *Star Trek* fanatic. Trekkies do not make for good potential dates."

The best defense is a good offense, they say. Put the blame on others.

Beth smiled. I know she knew what I meant about the match-makers in the church. Then a more serious look appeared in her eyes. "Mary, are you sure? Maybe it's time to find another church, then."

I took a deep breath. Of course I had considered that option. Every Sunday since the accident, I guess. But I couldn't. He . . . Jacob . . . grew up in this church. His father had been an elder for decades. If I left now, people would talk. His parents were still here—for the summers, anyhow. Mesa, Arizona, for the winter. (Cubs training camp was their version of Lourdes.) How would I explain to them why I was leaving the family church? I couldn't. They were not what I would call generously spirited people. They waged a letter-writing campaign when the new pastor started taking his tie off for the summer services. Personally, I don't see how a few feet of expensive fabric makes a man more devout or righteous or reverential—but there it was.

It's where our baby had been baptized.

That's all I need to say. There could be no leaving.

And, at the moment, there could be no going either.

I did attend—maybe monthly. Or thereabouts. I slipped in the back after the service began, and slipped out a split second after the benediction and hurried into the narthex before the final "Amen." I ran into more people than I wanted to even at that.

So I still attended. Just on my own terms. Abbreviated, to be sure, but it was all I could handle right now. Maybe, in the future, in a year or two more, I would start full power again. I would join the Ladies Bible Study. I would volunteer in the nurs . . . no, not there. I would volunteer in the library. I would begin to go back to Sunday school. I would begin to reintegrate my life with the family of God again.

But not now. Not now at all.

"No, that's silly. I'm just healing a little more slowly . . . than I expected."

Beth pushed her hair back again.

Why didn't she get a different haircut? I want to smack her hand every time she does that.

"But you are healing? Right? You're not simply fading away from . . . you know—church and Jesus and all that, are you? I mean, that would be a shame."

"No, I'm fine. Or getting to be fine. Really."

Beth reached over and patted my hand, like an aunt does to an unruly seven-year-old niece. "It will be okay. You know, things happen . . ."

DON'T SAY IT! DON'T SAY THINGS HAPPEN FOR A REASON. DO NOT SAY THAT!

I forced myself to take a deep, cleansing, calming breath. Beth seemed to sense the possible impending eruption.

If I hear once more that "all things happen for a reason" or "God wanted them in heaven" or "You're young—you can marry again—start over" or "Everything works out in God's perfect plan . . ."

My life has not happened according to God's plan! The accident was not part of God's merciful plan to draw unrepentant sinners to him. How could that be? Why take those two people, God? Why? Maybe they are in heaven—no—they *are* in heaven. But I'm here. I'm left here. I'm alone. There is no reason for that. I'm sad and miserable most of the time and alone. There is no part of this that would fit into God's master plan. It does not make sense. Don't say it!

". . . you know that little things happen, like not going one Sunday, and then it happens again, and pretty soon, you don't go at all and it's for no real reason."

Beth smiled as if she had dodged a plummeting chandelier. Or an angry bullet. I think she knew.

"It's not that. Well, maybe it is, a little."

I decided to let her off the hook. She meant well.

I speared the last of my tilapia. It was covered in a lemon *beurre blanc* sauce with a light, flavorful cream, probably made with really good wine, for sure, and some topping made with something crunchy and nutty and extremely delicious. I missed having good fish and refused to smell up my kitchen for days as I overcooked some nearly fresh halibut filet from the grocery store. This tasted much, much better.

"Beth, I know you're concerned. And I appreciate that. I do. You have no idea. I'll tell you what: this Sunday, I'll go to church with you. We'll sit together. Like old times."

Except one of us—two of us—won't be there like old times.

"Well, then," she said brightly, "that's the old Mary I know. Call me on Saturday then. We'll figure out where to sit."

"That's a promise," I said, smiling a bit too broadly, happily knowing that I had three full says to come up with an excuse for why I could not be there.

Three days is a long time.

I once wrote half a novel in three days.

Not my best work, but—surprise, surprise—it was one of my best-selling efforts.

Go figure.

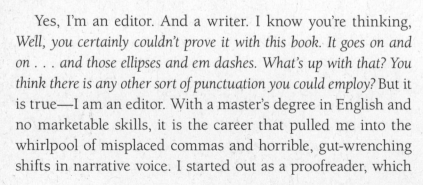

Yes, I'm an editor. And a writer. I know you're thinking, *Well, you certainly couldn't prove it with this book. It goes on and on . . . and those ellipses and em dashes. What's up with that? You think there is any other sort of punctuation you could employ?* But it is true—I am an editor. With a master's degree in English and no marketable skills, it is the career that pulled me into the whirlpool of misplaced commas and horrible, gut-wrenching shifts in narrative voice. I started out as a proofreader, which is the publishing industry's fancy word for underpaid editor. I told friends that I enjoyed it, but not really.

I proofread, correcting spelling and punctuation, and gritted my teeth over horridly florid descriptions of women's clothing and their dramatic, breathy sighs over Bradford, a lost love, who miraculously turns up in Chapter 18 with amnesia, a scar, or rich. For three years I worked at a publishing house whose management team specialized in collecting tales of how they almost signed the next Stephen King or Tom Clancy. I heard the same tales over and over of how they missed signing the latest writer du jour because they offered a measly $100,000 advance, or because our acquisitions editor laughed like a hyena. But the team managed to get a few base hits, and they kept the doors open and the proofreaders paid.

At the end of my first three years as a glorified proofreader (and this years before I met Jacob), I received an offer from another publishing house. They were located in the Loop in Chicago, which meant a longish train ride or a nightmarish car ride or a move, relocating to somewhere closer to downtown. The money was better, but with the added costs, I probably would break even.

I suspected, after the interview, that I would have to start over with my wardrobe. While none of the women at the downtown publishing firm wore expensive couture designer garb, really, they all seemed to specialize in Bohemian Expensive— odd, off-kilter apparel that must have been purchased at eclectic, off-kilter boutiques in Lincoln Park, where the sales personnel wore black lipstick, had multiple piercings, and wore berets indoors without the slightest hint of pretension.

I might have mentioned before that I am semi-unstylish.

I made the mistake (which proved to be a wonderful serendipity) of mentioning the new job offer to my closest work friend—two cubicles down, single, master's degree in English from DePaul, aspiring author of children's books—and she related it to the proofreading supervisor, who quickly became apoplectic. It seems that our corporate culture frowned on losing staff to competition.

The supervisor hurried into my office . . . cubicle . . . sat down, breathless, I guess, from the seven paces it took to get there from his office, and drew the uncomfortable guest chair close to my desk.

"I heard about . . . your situation, Mary."

He said it with such earnest compassion that I thought I might be pregnant or have cancer.

"We don't want to lose you. I like your work. You're really good."

This was all whispered, since, after all, we were in an open cubicle. I had to lean forward to even hope to hear correctly.

He might have been coming in to tell me that people were talking and saying we were having an affair—that's how close and whispery he was.

"I want you to stay. I'll promote you to associate editor. *A little better paid, and you could actually change a writer's horribly mangled syntax now and again.* With an office. And I am prepared to offer you a raise in this amount . . ."

He took a folded slip of paper from the breast pocket of his short-sleeved dress shirt, which he wore with a tie—a fashion abomination if there ever was one. He placed the slip of paper on my desk and slid it forward—all of three inches.

His eagerness and excitement plainly evident on his face, he watched me open it. I was surprised: four hundred dollars a year more than the downtown offer.

"If you need some time to think about it, that's fine," he whispered.

I am a terrible poker player. Or I would be a terrible poker player if I played poker.

"I'll take it. When do I start?"

He looked surprised. He would have stuttered had he started talking right away, which he didn't.

"Next week. Please, let's keep this confidential until HR signs off on who has to move. Or who doesn't get to move."

There was an empty office, smaller than my cubicle actually, but it had a door. The previous editor had a baby and told everyone she would be coming back and then we never saw her again. All the single women in the editorial group wondered if they would do the same. A number of proofreaders were silently vying for the coveted room with a door and a window, jockeying for the most favorable position. I figured that I had no chance, so I had not participated in the maneuvering.

That's how I became an associate editor. A year and two pregnancies later—not mine, of course, but those of other newly married staff—and I became a full-blown editor.

I realize that this seems off target based on the title of this book. But I need to tell you a little of how I became a writer and now manage to stay home and do my work in my pajamas.

I never do that—work in pajamas, that is. I hate the feeling of it being 10:00 a.m. and I am still pajama-clad. I can't do it now that I have to take Rufus out for a morning walk, anyway. It's up and change clothes and go out into whatever the weather is. Rain, cold, snow—the dog needs to go outside, and that means I need to go with him. Yes, I could boot Rufus out the back door and let him handle things on his own. But if I did that, when would I get any exercise? So, unless there is lightning in the sky, Rufus and I head outdoors. My neighbors marvel at our consistency.

The neighbor to my right uses a service that cleans up their yard after their dog, so it may be faint praise. A truck comes once a week and the poor serviceman walks back and forth over their lawn, looking for the leftovers from a dog. How I pity that poor man. I know he gets paid fairly well to do what normal people would consider a really, really unpleasant occupational choice. Not much in job prestige, either. "I pick up dog poop for really lazy people and get paid for it," would not be the most effective pick-up line in a trendy singles bar.

So, there I am, an editor. And that role, I must admit, I am born to do. I can see the weeds and chaff in a writer's work, and usually have the kindness and tact to get writers to allow me to prune their work. Or more truthfully, they encourage me to do the pruning.

After editing and helping rework a few novels that actually sold pretty well, several of those authors began to ask for me by name. Our publishing company is all too happy to oblige them. Anything we can do to edge the competition is smiled upon by management—most of whom don't really understand what it means to edit a book. So I get a lot of smiles. I suspect that I should have parleyed those smiles into a better salary—but that sort of savvy horse-trading is not part of my nature.

And you know what was strange in all this? After a few of our authors hit it large—not big, but large—the company's editorial team seemed to take great relish in disliking them and their work. Familiarity breeds contempt, I guess, and a large number of our best-selling writers were not corporately beloved best-selling writers—at least among our editorial cubicles and tiny offices packed to the gills with free books.

We seemed to like them a lot for their first and maybe second books, then they all morphed into being pains in our collective necks. Not so much me, since I have a pretty high level of tolerance for unknowingly sadistic, insecure, and inept writers. And who could blame authors for being needy and requiring constant attention? You slave and write and rewrite and worry and agonize over a book for six months or a year or all your life up to that point, and then you hand it over to a nameless, faceless editor who doesn't tell you a thing until that person sends the manuscript back to you, filled with so many red slashes and cuts and suggestions and deletions and addendums and slings and arrows of outrageous fortune. And then she asks—urgently—for you to make your changes and get it back to her in three days because she has a printing deadline to meet.

The horror, I know.

So, there I am, in my mid-twenties. Well, late twenties, but no single woman ever says she is in her late-anythings. I have many friends at work, some closer than others. There is a group of us single women who do things socially—dinners, movies, even host a party now and again. Some of us attended a large, almost mega-church, whose singles group is large and notorious for being a Christian singles meat market. As much as I pooh-poohed the image before I attended, I discovered that it was exactly that—attractive, stylish single men eyeing the new women with a critical tilt of their heads, and you could see them dismissing the ones, out of hand, who did not meet their criteria. A small contingent of less-attractive men—with less attractive haircuts and who shopped at Target and did so badly, who had a lower standard—looked for women who were at least breathing and if they were lucky, semi-sentient.

And occasionally a woman from work—one of the single ones—would meet a man, start to date, then get married. Go figure. It did not happen for me, and while I was not nervous about it, I did think about such things. I heard the echo of my mother, when not as close to dementia as she is now, telling me not to be so picky. I would have argued with her; I'm not picky at all. There just weren't that many men who orbited about me to be picky over.

That was until Jacob Fassler joined the company. He worked in marketing—smooth-talking, glib, always with a ready smile. You know, one of those marketing types. And he was handsome, in a Bohemian sort of way. He stood a few inches taller than me—and in flats, I was an even five feet, five inches tall. He had an almost dark look about him, dark hair with waves that he sort of pushed back from his forehead with a calculated insouciance that made it look as though he had just stepped away from the beach. I would have wagered that he smelled of salt water. He had dark eyes—deep, expressive, more brown than any other color—in contrast with my Nordic-looking blue eyes, my blond hair in a limp bob. He had a dangerous look to himself, opposite from me and my gingham-and-lace-apron aura. I could wear a leather jacket with leather chaps and studs in my nose and ears, and someone would ask me where the Sunday school social is being held. I have that sort of nice, nearly angelic face. I'm not that way, really. I can be bad. Seriously. I have done bad things.

Sort of.

Well . . . not really bad. Maybe *naughty* is a better word. *Mischievous* perhaps.

So Jacob joined the company, and he became the talk among the single ladies—or shall I say, single girls, or single women—in the company for weeks. He was a safe subject because none of us women had actually talked to him. And I am pretty sure that, in the deepest, darkest, remotest part of our hearts, we all figured that we had no shot at him.

He was that handsome.

Most of us in editorial did not lack intelligence, but we did lack self-confidence.

I would have considered my situation, my chance with Mr. Jacob Fassler, as long of a shot as shots could go—until that one fateful Saturday.

I tend to do my editorial work quickly and usually left work at the official quitting time. There were other editors who always worked late, and my opinion is that they simply worked slower. To me, desk time had always been less important than a job well done.

But, owing to the neurotic behavior of our latest good-but-not-great-selling author, his deadline had been shredded. He had held on to his manuscript six weeks longer than scheduled, the edits were more extensive than usual, he became more anxiety-ridden as he worked through the suggestions, and now it fell to me to get the final manuscript ready for typesetting by the end of the following week.

That's why I worked in my tiny office on Saturday. I was there because I knew I could work faster there than at home, where I would be distracted by my roommates and the availability of cable television and mah-jongg on the computer.

Midway through a particularly confusing shift in voice and tense in the manuscript before me, I heard a voice from the end of the hall.

"Anyone here? Anyone know how to fix this machine?"

There was a copy room at the end of the hall. It used to hold the fax machines as well—and most of those have long since disappeared.

I stood up and sidled around my desk. That's how you had to do it—sidle past it. I told you my office was small.

I stepped into the doorway of the copy room.

There stood Jacob Fassler in all his dangerous glory. He wearing a white T-shirt and worn jeans—actually worn, and not just purchased new and worn. He had on sneakers—white Converse high-tops. I had, up to that moment, considered high tops to be an affectation on anyone but actual basketball players. But on Jacob, they looked good.

His hair was slicked back more than usual; it appeared as if he had just come in from working out.

"How do I fix this thing?" he asked, holding a sheet of paper in his hand. "Is it turned on?"

I nodded. "It is. But it's temperamental."

"Do you know how to fix it?" he asked.

"I don't," I said. "Usually when it stops working, I sneak out of the room and go to another floor, looking for a copier that works. Eventually someone shows up who knows what to do—or they call the service guy."

Jacob smiled at me, a knowing secret smile.

"That's what I'm doing. The copier in the marketing area went down, and I'm wandering about the building looking for another that works."

I liked it that he smiled at me.

"I don't think anyone else is in the office today," I said. "The finance person—Rita, the lady who pays the bills—she came in here earlier. But I don't think she turned on the copier in her area."

"Rats," said Jacob.

"Is it important?"

He offered a half smile, half grimace.

"No. It's just a . . . a recipe that I promised I would get for my landlady. I can do it Monday, but I happened to be in the area."

He cooks. And I don't think he's married. No ring. And married people don't usually talk about landladies. And the temp in HR said he wrote "single" on his employee file—but no one can trust a temp.

"Hi, I'm Jacob Fassler. Marketing."

He extended his hand and I took it. It felt warm and firm, but not painfully firm like some men I have met who make it their mission to cripple others with their Gigantor Death Grip.

"I'm Mary Knopf. Editorial."

"Like the publisher?" he asked.

"I wish. Well, yes, like the publisher, but no relation. At least not that I've been able to ferret out so far. If I turn out to be a long-lost cousin or daughter of Alfred Knopf . . . well, you won't see me again. I'll move to New York and edit books while looking out over Central Park."

Jacob laughed, his laugh melodic and not monkeylike, as in some men I have met.

And from there, I am not sure where the conversation went. *Dreamy* would be a word I would use if I ever used the word *dreamy*—which I don't. All I know is that twenty-five minutes later, we were in the Starbucks down the street, both with small lattes—"I hate ordering a small coffee as a tall"—and sat there and talked for another two hours.

That's when he asked me out to dinner and that's when I accepted.

And that's the night I fell in love with Jacob Fassler.

3

I'm a novelist because of that same Jacob Fassler.

I have always been a writer, I suppose. Back in fourth grade, I wrote an essay about what I did over the summer vacation that so impressed my teacher that she had me read it aloud in the fourth grade class—and after I finished, they all applauded. Of course, that has never happened before or since then—the applause thing, I mean—but that started my writing career. I wrote for school newspapers and the school's overly dramatic "literary" magazines. I, of course, was just as guilty of emotionally overreaching back then as any other pubescent writer. I believe I have matured some since then.

An avid reader, I often blustered at bad novelists, sputtering to anyone in the vicinity that I could do better than what I'd just read.

I blustered that way to Jacob one day, in a Starbucks, my ire fueled by a second small latte.

"Then write something better," he said. "I mean—you do work for a publishing company, you know. If anyone has an inside edge to finding a receptive editor, it would be you."

He was charming when he said that, and I should have reacted differently, but I recall scowling at him. We were at that point in our relationship where one or the other could offer a pretty-much-fake scowl in response to being called on something.

"Well, maybe I will then."

A few sips passed. Silence.

"What do you think I should write about?" I asked.

Jacob shrugged. He was reading the fifth article on the most recent Chicago Bears' loss. Why anyone would need to go into such great depth over a stupid game—a game that they lost by multiple points—was beyond me. You would think that losing would be suffering enough. No, they had to revel in the gory, painful details of just how they lost and who they could hold responsible for the latest loss.

I am not a sports fan. Obviously.

Jacob looked up from his coffee.

"I dunno. Something about somebody who's Amish? Or doesn't want to be Amish anymore? Maybe somebody who wants to become Amish again? Amish seems to be a hot genre."

He resettled into the sports pages, his glum eyes fixed on the grading system for a bad team in a death spiral, I guess.

"Amish?" I replied.

I sat there, mulling over his words, and the story came to me, just like that: a beautiful woman who grew up in a traditional Amish farm family has to leave the faith—or better yet, abandon her culture—to go to New York to be a model because she's so beautiful and models spectacularly well. She makes a lot of money, gets famous and into *People* magazine, finds the modeling/famous people world horribly shallow and degrading, seeks to return to her roots and find a husband, and live a quiet life, but she meets great resistance from everyone on both sides until she discovers the kindness of Kurt Franz, a bachelor Amish who's semi-outcast because he's sort of a rebel. They find love and eventually are reaccepted by their Amish community and everyone lives happily ever after.

Really. That's the story. It came out of my head, that well formed, in as much time as it took to type the paragraph. Her name . . . was Gretchen—uh—Gretchen Stolz. That sounds Germanish.

By the end of the next day, I had written twenty-three pages of the novel, done a two-page synopsis, and the company agreed, by the end of the week, to take a chance and publish it.

Go figure.

It did not sell huge numbers out of the gate, but it got reprinted six times.

And with that, I became an editor *and* a novelist.

Being a mid-level novelist (and I'm being generous with the grading system here) pays about the same as you would get if you worked the same hours at the local 7-Eleven, except at the 7-Eleven, the hours would be better and you probably get benefits with it. And all the Slurpees you care to consume. The company graciously signed me to a three-book contract after the first one came out. I became their go-to Amish writer.

And the truth is, I didn't know all that much about the Amish. I was born in western Pennsylvania and our family visited the Pennsylvania Dutch country several times—before it morphed into a family-friendly tourist attraction. And I saw some old movie on TV with Tony Perkins playing Quaker a few years ago. And I read a lot. My research may not be encyclopedic, but it has been said that my dialogue was "very believable" and that my characters "face true-to-life problems" and that my plots "keep you guessing to the end." The last praise is both wonderful and quite flawed, because in gentle Amish fiction, one seldom has the hero or heroine dying before they communicate their love for each other. Endings are usually pretty happy affairs for all concerned.

I don't mind writing those sorts of books. I guess I never considered myself a serious novelist. A serious modern novelist is one whose books leave you really depressed at the end. A truly great, modern novelist is one who leaves you wanting to kill yourself at the end of the book. I am a popular modern novelist. People who read my books know pretty much what they are getting, and I deliver a finely crafted, and mostly intelligent, novel. I write believable stuff—the truth, I call it.

Jacob said he loved the cover of my first book. He took me out to a very expensive restaurant to celebrate the publication.

"Did you like the book?" I asked him, just before the crème brûlée arrived.

Jacob seldom looked to be at a loss for words. But at this moment, his tongue appeared to be tied.

"You did read it, didn't you?"

He looked away.

"I will," he said in a very small voice. "I planned on it. I just got busy." We both knew that he was a terrible liar. "I'm not much of a reader."

"But you work at a publishing company," I countered.

"I work in marketing," he replied. "We don't have to read books to sell them."

I narrowed my eyes and said as drily as I could. "Really?"

He squirmed. "Some of us do, I think, read them. Or some of them, I guess. But reading takes a lot of time. We sell a lot of books. Other people said your book was really, really good. Much better than any other Amish stuff on the market. I trust them. I bet it's great. And I really liked the cover. That woman is hot—even in the goofy bonnet and all that."

And that's when I knew I would marry Jacob Fassler. He told the truth when a lie would have been so much easier—and more productive, if you know what I mean.

I knew Jacob would marry me after one particular moment during our first spring together. That's when I knew he loved me. He really, really loved me. I had come down with a cold, or the flu, or dengue fever. My eyes puffed, my nose turned red, I went through an entire box of tissues in one evening. My hair ratted into a Medusa-like do. I felt wretched and looked every bit a wreck.

I awoke, just after 5:00 p.m., to hear my front door squeak open. Jacob called out to tell me it was him. He had an "emergency" key—just for situations like this. He called up and said he would be upstairs in a few minutes. I heard rattling and clanging from the kitchen, but could not rise out of bed under my own power.

The noise stopped. And in my doorway, Jacob appeared, carrying a tray. He closed his eyes.

"Are you decent?" he asked softly.

"No, but I am clothed," I responded with a sneeze.

He carried in a tray with a glass of orange juice. (He must have brought it with him, because I never bought the stuff.) On a plate was a grilled cheese sandwich. And a pot of hot tea, with a freshly sliced lemon.

Jacob had a red beach towel wrapped around his waist. He saw me staring at it.

"These are good pants," he explained. Then added by way of further explanation, "Your stove spatters."

I had to smile, weakly and sickly.

He placed the tray on the bed, helped prop me up, helped feed me the grilled cheese sandwich—overdone on one side (the side he placed face down on the plate) and a bit light on the other side.

"You don't have Velveeta. How can you make a grilled cheese without Velveeta? It's un-American, I think."

He helped me drink the tea, now strong and hearty, sweetened with honey.

He sat beside me on the bed as I nibbled. He scooped the tray away when I finished, came back up—without the towel this time—and sat with me, holding my hand, until I managed to fall asleep.

I staggered out to the kitchen the next morning and found him asleep on my couch.

"I didn't want to leave you alone," he said, wrinkled and groggy.

How could I not marry him after that?

Jacob and I were married by the Fox River, west of Chicago. Neither of us had any strong ties to the river, except that autumn had come and the foliage along the river would provide a good backdrop to our wedding pictures.

The day before the wedding, a storm passed through, with high winds and thundering rain, and when the sun peeked through the following morning, virtually every tree along the river had been denuded of all its colorful leaves. We could have just as easily gotten married in somebody's backyard for all the scenic beauty the river provided.

Despite that, the wedding and reception were lovely— another word I do not use often. Here I was, a plain, semi-attractive woman, edging toward the end of my prime, almost mousy, snagging the best, most attractive man our company had seen in years.

You might be wondering how I managed to do that.

I asked myself the same question. And often.

I didn't do it with a "come-hither" look, nor smoldering sex appeal or sexual antics, I can assure you of that. I mean, I was super attracted to Jacob, in every way, and I mean that both literally and figuratively. But we were both brought up by very strict parents with horribly strict interpretations of the moral depravity that marked premarital relations—thus, we maintained a fairly pure dating relationship.

There were moments, however, when the spirit and the flesh were very weak. Or would that be willing?

But as we edged toward whatever abyss we were edging toward, one of us, or the other, would draw back, take a deep breath, push away, and say something inane, like, "We need to slow down."

And we did.

The waiting and self-denial did make for a wild honeymoon, however. And incredibly satisfying.

The wedding was wonderful, but coming back to work, quite problematic. The company had no rule about two married people working at the company, but there were those sidelong glances that followed us—as if what I did could help Jacob's career or vice versa.

I suppose that Jacob could steer more advertising dollars toward my books, but he did not set budgets.

I submitted my resignation a few months after the wedding.

And no, I had not become "with child"—although that would have been more easily accepted and understood as a reason for my departure.

As I think about how we fell in love, which warmed my heart, I also considered the question of why we fell in love.

People have asked that of me on occasion, and I do not think I provided a good answer.

But here's an attempt at the truth of why it all happened.

I have no idea—save for a best guess. I could make him laugh, and vice versa. He's always funny . . . *was* always funny and always game for any adventure. I thought things out more, and acted a bit more analytical, so I guess we balanced out. He said I was pretty. He never said beautiful—except on our wedding day—and other than that day, I wouldn't have believed him if he had said "beautiful." He always said "pretty." And he said it in a wistful, yearning manner, as if he really and truly meant it. He said that he had dated a lot of women, but there was something lacking at their core—the beautiful ones he'd dated, that is. He once said that some really attractive women know, deep down where they hide their own painful truths, that their beauty is always in the process of fading. Of course, beautiful young women sometimes turn into beautiful old women—but for someone who has savored the wine at the acme of its taste, any reduction in clarity and power will be viewed as a slippage, a step into the abyss of looking merely nice, or sort of attractive. It was a slide that some of them did not want to endure; their fight against it made them brittle and hard at the same time.

Me, on the other hand—well, I was a ray of warm sunshine by comparison. I knew that I had not started at the mountain-top, so my personal slide into being a little less pretty was far less steep and nowhere near as frightening.

He didn't phrase it so crassly or harshly, but that is what he meant.

And that was enough.

We did make each other laugh.

And we both believed in God.

He did up to the end.

Me? Now I am not so sure.

———✖———

This is where the good dog Rufus makes his entrance onto the main stage of my life—the play in motion was the tragedy of my most recent years. I get maudlin at times, and wallowing in self-pity seems to be my second-favorite form of exercise.

Rufus, now in his second year, is full grown, and as large as he will ever get, plus or minus a pound or two and an inch or two.

Even though the breeder said that as an adult, he would be smallish, she had been mistaken. The runt grew up to be a big dog, by miniature standards. We run into another schnauzer during our evening walks—a distant cousin of Rufus, actually, due to the fact that they came from the same breeder. I haven't looked at his papers to see if they actually are related, but they do look alike. Go figure—they are both schnauzers. The other dog is exactly the same as Rufus except for Rufus's size. He is a big miniature schnauzer. Taller than his cousin by several inches and a good half-dozen pounds heavier. I don't mind at all; it simply means that he will never be a show dog. And he couldn't be, actually, since he was "fixed" a few weeks after I got him, and such dogs aren't allowed to participate in dog shows.

I don't know why.

Well, actually I do know why, now that I've looked it up, but it still doesn't make sense to me.

4

I snapped on the leash to Rufus's collar and we headed outside. The air had grown cutting and brittle, a hint of winter to
come, and any wind, at night, found its way through the weak
defenses of my coat and hat and scarf and gloves. The complaint from the dog during winter months came from walking
in newly fallen snow, the wet kind of thick snow, like chilled
oatmeal. It would ball up between his toes. The snow balled
up and he would stop every so often to try and chew it out.
Or look at me with a supplicant's face and silently request my
help. He was small last winter, and we only caught the tail
end of winter, and we did not travel as far during our walks.
Winter had never been my favorite season. It was to be Rufus's
second.

The moon slipped up over the horizon out, and the winter
moon seemed whiter, more ashen, than normal, the pale light
at the bare tree limbs, spiking shadows along our path.

Rufus stopped to investigate a particularly interesting bush.
Sometimes, I let him have free rein on the time we're out; other
walks, when I am either cold or impatient, I will snick at the
leash to get the small beast moving again.

This night I waited.

I pulled a dog snack out of my coat's breast pocket. I buy them in bulk at the local pet store. They look like Styrofoam, in yellow and brown and tan, supposedly representing the flavors of chicken, beef, and peanut butter. Rufus loves them. He considers them almost as desirable as table scraps.

Almost.

I took one and broke it in half, the snap of the snack crackling loud in the cold air.

Our vet said he might be a pound or two heavy for his size, "but nothing to worry about. He's in good health."

I slipped the half-snack back into my pocket and bent down and gave Rufus the other half. He accepted it with gratitude and chewed as noisily as he could.

We both began to walk again. A dozen paces later, Rufus stopped. He did not look at me directly, nor did I look at him. He stops all the time during our walks.

"Why do you break my crunchy in half?"

I heard the voice, his voice, Rufus's voice, as clearly as I have heard anything in my life—maybe clearer than most.

Have you ever seen any of the Walt Disney animated Winnie the Pooh cartoons? Do you remember Eeyore, the sad-faced donkey with a tacked-on tail? Do you remember his voice? A very slow, deliberate, bass voice—not stupid by any means—but as if his words were being very carefully chosen and formed in his mouth, like chewing a large amount of gummy food. The voice, not stupid, just slow, as if each word had to be slowly measured out and scrupulously selected to be the most correct.

That's what Rufus sounded like.

Wait.

That's Rufus I am talking about.

And Rufus is a dog.

Bewildered isn't the right word for how I felt. *Frightened* isn't the right word, either. *Nonplussed*, maybe. I don't know. I never trust anyone who claims that they don't have the right words to describe something. We think in words—right? Use them. But tonight . . . tonight, I really did not have any words to use, no words that could properly describe what I was thinking.

The conversation, such as it was, simply felt . . . normal. Just everyday normal. Sorry, but I did not have a thesaurus handy.

So normal that I remained standing—rational and standing—and slowly formed a reply.

"I . . . I don't want you to get fat," I said, as I would to a friend whom I tried to convince from taking a third piece of pie at an all-you-can-eat buffet after breaking up with her cad of a boyfriend.

At that specific moment, his question and my answer seemed altogether, totally normal. I think I already said that . . . but it all felt . . . normal.

Rufus sort of nodded, as if digesting the information, and began to walk again, only to stop a few paces later. He turned his head ever so slightly toward me like he might be dreading the next question.

"Am I fat?"

What do you do when your dog asks you a perfectly linear, logical question?

In the cold dark of a winter night.

You answer him.

"No. You're not fat. Dr. Barbara, you know, your vet . . ."

Rufus nodded.

"She said that you could lose a pound or two. No big deal, she said. So . . . I thought I would cut back on these treats. Just a little."

Rufus waited a heartbeat or two and then continued on our walk.

"Okay," he said as we turned the corner on Glencoe and headed for home.

∽∾∽

Several hours later, in bed, well after midnight, I sat bolt upright, wide awake.

It was 2:15 a.m.—exactly the time I received that phone call three years earlier. The phone call that shattered everything.

Sometimes the night terrors would overcome me.

But this was no night terror.

I had awoken from a hallucinogenic dream—where up was down and light was dark and dogs could talk.

Rufus lay at the corner of the bed. He slept there, not always, but when he did, he positioned himself at the corner, on a diagonal, so he could see the window and the bedroom door at the same time. His guarding instincts were deep in his being.

He must have heard me sit upright, or felt the movement. I snapped on my light.

He blinked, his eyes trying to adjust to the brightness.

"Did you really talk to me, Rufus? Or am I just widow-lady-crazy, with a horribly overwrought imagination?"

He did not speak, but I saw his eyes. The dark color seemed to deepen in understanding. He lowered his head, then looked back up, as if sheepish about not responding.

He nodded. At least I am pretty sure that he nodded.

Then he lay his head back down on the comforter and closed his eyes.

I took a series of deep, cleansing breaths, learned from the three yoga lessons I took at the YMCA until I dropped out because I couldn't stand the soft-talking instructor.

My dog talks to me.
Is that my life now?
It is and was.
Go figure.

∞

The moment Ava touched my doorbell, Rufus both fell and jumped off the sofa in the sunroom, his claws scrabbling for purchase on the polished hardwood floors, his back legs looking like a cartoon, where the animated animal in question spins its legs in a furious circle for a moment until it finds traction. Rufus was like that, at least on the hardwood. On rugs, he took off like a shot, right away.

And the doorbell was the only device I had found that drove him completely insane. I suspect the guarding instincts, buried under hundreds of generations of domesticity and civility, were not so buried after all. Rufus slid through the kitchen, like a stock car on a clay track, his rear legs pumping furiously, barking with every step, barking louder and more frantically as he drew near to the front door, the pitch of his barking escalating with each step, until it sounded like he nearing an explosion from a paroxysm of the squealy-bark-squealies.

But as soon as I opened the door and deemed the visitor welcome, Rufus would revert, like an iconic Jekyll and Hyde, into a tail and hindquarters wagging machine, with yips of joy and lots of happy whimpers and squirms, reveling in welcoming whoever had come calling. So far, we had never encountered a person I did not want to be there. Some people, Rufus liked more than others. But with Ava—well—he really liked Ava. As soon as she took a chair in the kitchen, Rufus attempted to climb onto her lap. He almost made it, and she grabbed at him to pull him up, only to have him yelp like he was in excruciating pain. A small spot at the end of his rib cage elicited this sort of response.

The vet—our vet, I suppose—Dr. Barb, had found nothing amiss when I told her about it. She had poked and prodded a bit.

"My best guess is that he just doesn't like being touched there," she had said. Now, when I pick him up, I try to avoid the area.

Ava recoiled as if she had caused permanent damage, and nearly dropped Rufus to the floor. But he clawed his way back onto her lap and, with a raised paw, demanded that she pet him.

She obliged, of course, and scratched and petted him for the better part of twenty minutes, until I made coffee and brought out cookies. Rufus could not beg from her lap, so he took his standard position at the foot of the chair, staring at me, then Ava, wondering who would first give in to his plaintive staring.

I usually was the one to weaken, but today, Ava snapped off a corner of a tea cookie and slipped it to a grateful Rufus, who did not chew, but swallowed it relatively whole.

"So, life has been good?" Ava asked.

Ava has been a long-time friend, a friend before Jacob came along. She worked with me, at the same company, for a year. She left to return to teaching and got married—and divorced—all before the accident. Her life was neither simple nor turmoil-free. Now we were both single again. Commiserating with her felt good, sort of therapeutic. We both lived at the same level. Lonely. Addicted to sympathy.

"It's been okay," I replied.

Ava popped most of a tea cookie into her mouth. "You're a bad liar."

She could get away with saying things like that because . . . well . . . she sort of always told the truth. She pushed an errant wisp of brown hair from her face. She had added red highlights to her hair a few weeks earlier, but they came out more purple than red.

"Just like when you lied about my hair. You said it looked 'striking,'" she said, mocking my tone, her self-amusement lighting up her face. She was a pretty woman when she smiled—wide mouth, full lips, with cheekbones that made makeup almost unnecessary.

"It is striking."

"It's hideous. Like it had been attacked by a wine-soaked stylist-in-training, after a particularly trying day. Without her glasses. Or a mirror. Or directions. While I lay deep in a coma."

I laughed, almost spitting out a mouthful of coffee. I didn't because I would have spilled it over the upholstery that I tell other people to be careful of. She was right. As hair goes, it indeed could be classified as hideous, but in an avant-garde sort of way. I don't think Ava considered herself avant-garde.

"Well," I said after composing myself, "the color will fade soon enough."

I really liked Ava. She made me laugh. We made each other laugh—though I know her job of amusing me was much more difficult than mine.

"I do get second looks from the young hoodlums at the car wash and the 7-Eleven on Main Street."

"Ava," I said in my best schoolmarm scolding voice. "You are terrible."

"No. I mean it. They think I'm an older degenerate—just like they want to be in twenty years. Like flies and honey. I could have been asked to the fall dance at the high school a hundred times, if I had wanted to. Just have to pretend to be more accessible, if you know what I mean. Dress the part more. A little more cleavage."

Ava acted as a tonic for me. She lived so far from the traditional suburban woman—if there is really such a person. Her almost abrasive, semi-caustic sort of personality could shock people. I guess I liked that quality in her.

"So how are you and Dr. Tom getting along?" I asked. She was three months into a relationship with Dr. Tom Wakley, a twice-divorced podiatrist with a large practice the next town over. He was fit, bald, and drove a Lincoln.

"He's not a doctor. He's a podiatrist," she answered.

"They go to medical school. That makes them doctors."

She shrugged. "When is the last time you heard of someone dying from toenail fungus?"

I stifled a laugh again, gulping down the last half swallow of coffee.

"I'll call him a real doctor when my TV has a doctor's show featuring a staff of podiatrists," she smirked. "Like that will ever happen."

Rufus trotted off once our cookies were consumed.

"Me and the podiatrist . . . well, we're doing okay." She toyed with her empty cup, tilting it back and forth. "I guess. He's a nice enough guy. A bit of an ego problem. Not a deal-breaker. Not the best sense of humor, but he can be funny on occasion. You know . . . it's okay, most of the time. It is nice to have someone to hold hands with . . . if you know what I mean." She arched her eyebrows, as if unwilling to say out loud what "holding hands" meant. Maybe she didn't want to shock Rufus.

I did know what she meant, which marked a huge difference between myself and Ava. Some things she did, I could never do. At least, I think I could never do.

She poured herself another cup of coffee.

"I would be having a better time if this were wine."

"Ava—it's three in the afternoon."

"So? Wine is illegal in the afternoon? Not like I'm operating on a bunion later today."

I walked to the refrigerator and took out the half-and-half. In all honesty, I had always been relatively addicted to coffee, so multiple cups in the afternoon were pretty much standard operating procedure.

"And how goes it with you, Mary? You're always asking the questions—and never answering any."

"I'm a writer. I observe."

Ava offered a twisted smile.

"You steal truths from other people's lives, that's what you do."

"Do not."

"Do too," she countered. "Remember that character in that book of yours—the rebellious Amish farmer who wanted to move to . . . where . . . Montana or someplace?"

"He wanted to learn to ski."

"Yeah, that's the one. He was the spitting image—a duplicate—of Ronald Weerset. Remember him?"

We both knew Ron Weerset as a single man from our shared work experience some ten years earlier. I will be kind and say that he could be classified as odd. A socks-with-sandals sort of guy, a gentle spirit I suppose, but given to long-winded explanations of just about everything, and hair that looked as if he cut it himself.

"He was not. Ron was not that handsome."

"But his characteristics. His mannerisms. They were like twins."

I hesitated in answering. She was right. I had copied that poor man's characteristics. And I didn't offer him a dime in royalties for the usage.

"Okay. I'll answer a question. Ask away."

Such an offer did not occur often with me. I seldom had ever volunteered to provide personal information—even to a friend.

I am pretty sure that having Rufus in my life had broken down some of my personal walls, my protective shell, just a little. I was getting used to talking to him during the day. After three years, almost, of silence during the day, for the most part, I now yakked—a lot. Jabbered, actually. Rufus would fall asleep sometimes even in the middle of a particularly impassioned diatribe. However, he never talked back during the day—or had not so far. Instead, I would chatter on and on to him.

And I would never admit this to anyone, not even to Rufus, at least not now, but before Rufus came into my life, I would walk about the house, and talk to the various pictures of Jacob that I still had on display. Some of the pictures—pictures of me with my son—I removed, stored safely in a cardboard box, taped shut, securely taped, labeled IMPORTANT PICTURES.

There were still three pictures of my son on display: one in the sunroom, a small one, his face nearly hidden by the hood of his sweatshirt; one in the bedroom that used to be his, a group picture of his friends at a church day camp the summer before I lost him; and one in the formal living room, a horrid picture of the three of us, taken for the church's pictorial directory. Jacob in a tie and a jacket nearly luminescent in the harsh lighting and my hair looking more wispy and flyaway than usual, with John serene and happy between his mother and father.

Jacob was represented in a handful of pictures, spread out over the house.

Furtively, I would walk about, usually late at night, after dusk for sure, and talk to the pictures, asking my husband, my late husband, about things in my life and what I should do about the insurance for the house and if I needed to roll over his IRA into something else. I would ask him about what color I should paint the family room and if I should highlight my hair, and if the plumber who quoted replacing the leaky toilet in the guest bath could be considered honest or not.

I talked and talked and talked and tried not to be a crazy lady. I tried to avoid talking directly to the picture, you know, talking while staring at a dead man's face. I was shy, even circumspect about it. But I did it. A lot. And I waited to hear an answer.

Sometimes, I would get a very strong, nearly visceral feeling. Unmistakable.

Like the question about the plumber. I heard . . . felt . . . and came to the conclusion that the plumber I considered operated on the up and up. And he did the job quickly. There were no leaks. He cleaned up after himself. And he charged me less than he quoted. I think he realized I was a widow and took pity on me.

That's how Jacob talked to me. Not like Rufus. No . . . their communication styles were very much different. One . . . maybe one I made up. The other one was real.

One . . . I wanted. The other . . . came to me, came upon me, without my looking for it.

There is a difference. A big difference.

Since Rufus arrived in my life, I have talked less to the photos of Jacob, though I still do so, once in a while, in a quiet hiss of a whisper, in the fading light of day. I wait for the nudge from beyond.

Sometimes it happens . . .

Ava snapped her fingers.

"Mary? Are you listening? You said you would answer my question."

I blinked.

"What? What did you ask again? I guess I was thinking about . . . something else there for a minute. A book problem, I think."

Ava placed her hand on my forearm.

Funny how much communication is done without words through the simplest of gestures—like one person's hand placed on another person's arm. I have lived now for years with little human contact—skin to skin touching, that is.

Oh, there is the quick, shoulder-to-shoulder hug at church, or at the supermarket. There is the handshake from insurance salesmen and car dealers.

But there is little discretionary touching in my life.

That's why widows go to the beauty parlor every week. It is the human touch they crave, without knowing it. No one needs their hair cut and styled on a weekly basis. With the possible exception of the queen of England, perhaps.

Ava's hand on my arm got my attention. A connection—a physical connection—grabbed me. The intimacy—even that slight touch—got to me like no words could ever do.

"Are you ready to start dating?" she asked.

The words registered, but I think I must have looked shocked, or puzzled, or gobsmacked. (Don't the English have such great words?)

"Well? It's a legitimate question. I waited a year after my divorce. Healing time. And it has been lots longer for you, Mary. It's time, right?"

I struggled to find a word, or words, to answer her with.

(I have discovered recently that most grammarians, the modern ones anyhow, now say that it is okay to end a sentence with a preposition. I don't think I have ever been a stickler for not doing so, but now, when it happens, I no longer worry that an aggressively proper copy editor will flummox my sentence construction to prevent ending my words with a "with" or a "for.")

"No."

"No?"

"No."

"Why not?"

"Because."

"That's not an answer.

"It is too."

"It's time, Mary. You know it's time."

"It's not."

"You're young. Sort of, anyhow. And you—and I—neither of us are getting any younger. You need to. Date. Really."

"I don't. Really. It's too soon. Much too soon."

But I did crave that touch. Not sexual, I think, but just touch. Hand in hand. A hand on my forearm or bare shoulder. How wonderful it would be to be held by a man with strong arms . . . protecting me . . . enveloping me.

"It is not. You know it."

She glared at me for a moment, then tilted her head.

"You're thinking about it, aren't you?"

"I am not."

"Rufus," she said, trying to recruit my best friend to her side, "doesn't she need to go out? It's time, isn't it?"

Rufus sauntered over, looked at me, then put his paws on Ava's knees and looked back at me in a pretty snide dog manner.

They had ganged up on me.

"I'll . . . I'll think about it. That's all I can promise you."

And I was determined to get back at Rufus for siding with my other best friend.

<hr>

Later that evening, after Ava had left, after she made me promise, again, to think about what she had said, twice, I gathered my coat and Rufus's leash. I was still smarting from his cozying up with Ava, as if he thought that chumminess wasn't obvious to me. He took her side on this dating thing.

I shivered when the word came into my mind.

Dating? Good grief.

Ava was right. It had been a long time. And there were those times when I nearly ached for the touch of a man. I did not admit that to anyone—not to friends, not to Rufus, and certainly not to the pictures of Jacob.

But dating? Another man? A stranger? Kissing some other man? Wouldn't that amount to cheating? Adultery, even?

Yes, there were a few earlier attempts to entrap me into dating—all of them at church. What is it about churchgoers who seem to think it is unnatural for a woman to be alone? I know, there are those verses that say something about "better to marry than to burn with lust."

I wasn't burning with lust, exactly, though I did miss all that went along with lust. In the good, married sense of the word. Please. But what I missed more than all that biology and anatomy was being held, being wrapped up in someone's arms. I missed being connected by touch.

Hugs are hard to do without.

Rufus bounced and wiggled as he always did, making it difficult to attach the leash to his collar.

"Rufus, stop wiggling," I barked at him, my voice not at all kind and gentle.

He stopped and looked back up at me, as if my harsher tone was unfamiliar and unsettling.

We stepped out into the cold. I could see my breath form in the shadowy light of the streetlight at the end of my driveway. Rufus sneezed once. He sneezed a lot. Dr. B. ruled out allergies. "He sneezes. It's what he does. No big deal. He's a snouty sort of dog."

We hurried to the corner, then turned south. We would take the route that included the sidewalk that ran alongside the small retention pond behind the big houses. The pond lay on private property, and one homeowner plastered her fence with stern NO TRESPASSING and PLEASE CLEAN UP AFTER YOUR PET signs. Not a welcoming attitude. The sidewalk was community right-of-way, but we always hurried past the pond. It was darker, not dangerously darker, but it was less traveled at night. Streetlights lit most of the rest of the way.

As we stepped into a pool of darkness, halfway between streetlights, I stopped.

"Why did you side with Ava?" I asked Rufus, and immediately realized how delusional I sounded—expecting a dog to answer me.

"I don't know. What's dating, anyhow?" he replied.

"Dating? Well, it's when two people go out together so they can get to know each other better. Dinner. Coffee. Movies. That sort of thing."

Rufus stared across the waters of the pond. During the summer, a large egret lived along the shore. It swooped over us once, taking off and spooking the bejeebers out of both of us. Now Rufus kept an eye out for it. He was not a dog that liked being spooked.

"Do dogs date?"

How do I answer that?

"No. They don't. But people do. They have to get to know each other before they . . . get married or move in together."

Rufus pulled gently at the leash, the cord ratcheting out, clicking loudly.

"That man in those pictures on the wall. The pictures you talk to."

He meant Jacob, of course.

"Yes?"

"Is he dead?"

My throat tightened.

"Yes. He and the little boy in those pictures died in a car crash several years ago. The man was my husband. We were married. The little boy was my son."

I felt the tears start to form, and I fought to hold them back. I did not want to wander through the dark, my eyes fractured like stained glass from salty tears.

"I thought so. You get sad when you look at them. But I wasn't sure. You never told me. I thought I should wait to ask you about them."

"I do get sad sometimes. I miss them very much."

We walked on a short distance, Rufus's nails clicking on the cement sidewalk. They would need to be clipped during his next visit with the groomer. He did not like the groomer. Too many dogs, a shampooing at the hands of a stranger, rattling hair clippers. It was an unnerving experience for him.

"I think you should date." Rufus had the speaking part of conversation down. His timing was not as solid. A kind and caring person would most likely have waited longer to give me that opinion—especially following on the heels of my unburdening about my husband's and son's deaths.

We turned the corner onto Western. It was uphill until Hawthorn. It wasn't steep, but I never liked this part of the evening route.

"Really? Why? Why do you think I should date?"

Rufus could not shrug, of course, but he nearly shrugged just by using his tone of voice.

"Aren't people supposed to be together? I see that on television all the time. People together. A man and a lady. People talk a lot about getting together."

"But I don't have to be with someone. I have you. I can talk to you."

"That is true. You do."

We walked in silence, the empty branches clacking together in the breeze, like mute, cold, wooden fingers drumming on a desk in another room.

"But I'm pretty sure you need to be with another person."

"Pretty sure?" I asked. I was debating with a dog.

Good grief.

"I think that's what is supposed to happen. Isn't that what he says it should be like?" Rufus asked.

Of course this conversation was already semi-crazy and totally delusional—talking to a dog, carrying on a normal face-to-face, or face-to-muzzle, as it were, asking the dog his opinion on what I should do with my life.

Perfectly normal, right?

"Who? Who says?"

Did he have a secret life that I did not know about? Did he talk to the black lab next door—that stupid, pushy, knuckle-headed beast? What kind of advice could that animal provide?

Rufus stopped to sniff at a leaf that skittered in front of him. When his investigation stopped, he lifted his head and replied. "Why, God, of course."

5

Rufus clammed up for two days. He didn't say a word during our walks, even though I asked him repeatedly about his communication with God. I suspect he meant the God of all, and not some canine deity that I was unaware of. But I couldn't be sure. Could there be a dog god of sorts that all dogs knew about, and about whom humans were clueless?

I did not allow myself to become fixated on Rufus and his talking. I mean, what if his speech was really just my delusional thinking—a manifestation of my repressed desires and grief and doubts and whatever other mental hobgoblins lived in my gray matter? I felt certain it was not. I told myself that I was certain that I had actually heard what I heard, and that Rufus talks. . . . I guess most delusional people are sure that they are sane and rational. But I *was* sane and rational. Or rather, I *am* sane and rational. I have continued to write, and my prose is generally sane and logical. My plots have not begun to include little creatures from the planet Xerlon. I manage to feed myself and find appropriate, if not stylish, clothing. I pay the bills when they come due. I do not hoard aluminum foil or wrap it about my head to keep the federal government from scanning my brain during the day.

So Rufus didn't talk on command. I would wait. And if he never spoke again, I would simply keep his talk a secret and never tell anyone about these episodes. Ever.

Perhaps what complicated my thinking or my receptivity was my wrestling with Ava's question . . . or, rather, demand.

Dating.

I know. I had considered dating, a few times, and only to myself. In the aftermath of the accident, I was too grief-stricken, too paralyzed, too numb, too angry, too bitter, too anguished to even consider the option of trying it all again. Like a small child who takes his first ride on a two-wheeler only to have a terrible accident, ripping a knee apart in the process—well, that young child is not too keen on mounting a bicycle ever again. I was the same as that small, scarred, scared child.

As the months passed, the concept of another man remained horridly strange, but I guess I knew dating did not lie out of the range of distant possibilities—really distant possibilities.

And now, I have to face that fact. If I do not want to die alone, or at least die without human companionship, I have to consider that distant possibility.

Dating.

That night, a cold wind hastened in from the north. I usually pay little attention to the weather. It is what it is. My mother-in-law would watch The Weather Channel for hours on end, letting us know that rain would be coming in four days. The weather forecasters, always helpful, would warn her of impending doom at the hands of the weather. A stretch of below-zero weather? Stay home, make sure that the furnace operated properly, have firewood, stay in contact with family. A stretch of one hundred-plus degree days? Stay home, go to a cooling center if needed, drink lots of water, stay in contact with family.

Weather forecasters did not predict the weather. They wanted to scare people into staying at home, cowering in the basement, watching The Weather Channel all the while—or at least until the dangerous weather passed.

And you know what? The dangerous weather never passed. In Chicago, there are perhaps a couple dozen perfect days during the year. On those days you could safely venture out—but only if you had slathered on sufficient sunscreen to blot out the evil sun. And there is great consternation among the sunfearers that no sunscreen in existence could prove effective at blunting the sun's evil rays. It was a terrifying, never-ending pattern of threatening weather, followed by terrible weather, followed by downright dangerous weather.

But I digress.

Tonight, well, the weather tonight grew cold enough that my mother-in-law would have stocked up on groceries and ammunition, if she had been in town. No snow yet, but biting wind. I slipped into my well-puffed down parka, tightened the hood around my face, grabbed my bright yellow gloves and Rufus and I headed out into the iced air.

I wear calf-high, superinsulated boots, no lacing required, and a thick, faux sheep-fleecy interior. In fact, I seldom wear socks with these boots, they are that warm and comfortable.

We both walk briskly, movement being the key to staying warm.

We turned a corner. Rufus stiffened and pulled at the leash. Another dog approached, being held on his leash by an older gentleman. Rufus and I pass a number of other dogs and owners during our walks. I know none of their humans' names. We humans know each other by our dogs' names. Gus is a fat yellow lab, who waddles rather than walks. Sometimes Rufus will bounce around the older, fatter dog, both of them offering fake barks of challenge. Sometimes just a sniff and a growl will do.

The other man greeted Rufus by name. I do the same to Gus. We act as our pets' spokespeople. We both comment on the sudden drop in temperature. The other man said it is time to move south.

"Eighteen months and I retire. I'll be out of here in eighteen months and a week."

"Where to?" I asked.

"My daughter lives in Orlando. That's where Gus and I are headed. It will do his old bones good to get out of the cold."

No mention of a wife. Divorced or widowed. I think divorced. There are subtle clues that only the single man or woman can interpret. Rings, of course, are the biggest hint. But it also has to do with how questions are answered. A single man talking to a single woman states things differently. Not suggestive, by any means, but differently. Why? Because he knows he has no one to correct or advise him otherwise. Making an appointment is another clue—married people will always hedge, saying he or she must check with his or her spouse to make sure the date is open. Single people or divorced people never do. And theirs is also an element of need—not pathetic neediness—but a single person often really wants to connect. So conversations are quickly deeper. Married people already have a connection, so dialogue with them often remains superficial.

Rufus and I bid our farewell and continue. The moon has been lost to us, behind a thickness of iced clouds. Despite the streetlights, the night seemed darker than usual, darker than most.

"Do you like Gus?" Rufus asked me, his breath coming in puffs with each word. Out of the blue, he spoke again. I wish it had been a more explanatory statement—preferably about his divine communication skills.

"I guess. He seems like a nice dog. He is very calm. But he is fat."

"That's fat? Really? Gus is fat?"

"He is, Rufus. Maybe twenty pounds more than he should be."

We trotted along. Our chatting felt so right, so calming, the cold disappeared.

"Where is Orlando? What is that?"

"It's a city, Rufus. We live in a small city. Wheaton. A city is a group of people living in the same place. Orlando is bigger than here. And it is a lot warmer. They don't really have winter there. It never gets really cold. Never gets this cold, that's for sure."

Though I could not see his face, I was sure Rufus tried to digest this information. We do watch television together. Maybe he gets some of what he knows from TV shows and news programs and The History Channel and whatever else it is that I watch when I zone out some evenings. It would be a sporadic source of information, for sure, and incomprehensible at times. I mean, how would a stranger, a dog, interpret *Days of Our Lives*—not that I've ever watched it . . . that often. Recently.

"Gus would like the warmth. He says his back legs hurt all the time."

I almost asked Rufus how he would know that. But like taking a watch apart to see how it works would surely render the watch useless, I simply took Rufus at his word, that Gus had arthritis in his legs or hips and yearned to be in a warmer climate. It made sense to me.

Instead of asking him how he and Gus communicate, I decided instead to confront Rufus on his apparent shift in allegiance the other afternoon.

"When I asked you if you thought I should start dating—you said I should . . . right away. Why?"

Rufus did not hesitate. "Because you are ready. To date. I think. If *date* means to be with a man. Then you are ready."

"And you know that how?"

"I can smell it. You are lonely. You need to be with someone. People should be in pairs—like swans. That is the way God has it planned, isn't it? I know it's different with animals, sometimes, but people, well—doesn't God want them to be in pairs?"

I tried to figure out how to respond when Rufus posed another question. "Swans . . . those are those big white things that float, right? The ones we saw at that big water? The ones that wanted to chase us, right?"

We had gone to Herrick Lake in the spring, a bigger lake, and had watched two swans, a husband and wife, I guess, swim closer and closer to us as we walked along the shore.

"They didn't chase us."

"I said 'wanted to.' I could hear them. Another step closer and they would have charged. They scare me. Like that big other bird on the smaller water."

The egret from last summer that had swooped by us, so close I could make out the colors of the underside of its wings.

"So God told you that?" I asked.

"Sort of. Not really. I mean . . . I sort of know what he has said. Instinct, I guess. And you know what he has written—that men marry women, right? Mostly. Not always. But it's better if they were. You are not a pair. And now that I know what dating is, you should try it. You would be a pair, then, right?"

"I guess so."

We walked in silence.

"So God wants me to date?" I asked.

"I guess. That's what's in the Bible. Isn't it? I can't read, but that feels true."

We turned onto our street. "How often do you talk with God?" I continued. For me, well—I prayed, sometimes. Less now. I used to pray a lot. I sort of . . . gave it up for all the good it did me and all the answers that never came. I wanted to know how this dog came to have a direct line to the Almighty.

"Once a week. Like all the animals."

"Only once a week?"

"It's enough for a dog."

Ava's insistence wore me down. I guess I had been ready to be worn down. Her doctor friend—"He's a podiatrist, not a doctor"—had a friend, a few years older than me, divorced, and ready to "get back on the market."

His words, according to Ava.

I was already wary. Like I'm some vegetable on display in the produce aisle? I am pretty sure Ava liked to torment me some, in a good way, in a way that would keep me a bit off balance and unable to retreat into my safe, Christian isolation again.

"So what does he do for a living?"

She shrugged. We were ensconced in two, large, people-enveloping leather chairs at Starbucks. I wondered about bedbugs, since recent infestations were a staple of the twenty-four-hour news shows these past few months. Maybe bedbugs don't like leather. I had no idea if it was true or not, but I felt better for thinking it.

"I'm not sure exactly. Something in sales. Maybe."

"But he does have a job, right?" I said, not fully leaning back into the plush leather.

"Oh, sure. I'm sure that he does."

We both sipped away.

"So what do I do now? Pass him a note in study hall?"

This made Ava laugh so hard that she nearly spilled her triple-named coffee concoction—I only get lattes—and she pushed her napkin at her nose. Once recomposed, she glared at me.

"Stop being funny. I could have choked to death."

"Sorry," I said, not feeling sorry at all. I liked it when I made others laugh. It had not happened all that frequently over the past few years.

"No notes. I'll call the podiatrist and he'll call his friend and he'll call you. Very neat and tidy."

I sat back, the import of what I had just agreed to negating all my bedbug fears.

"So what do we do? Dinner? Dancing? Movies?"

Ava smoothed the folds in her skirt. It was much shorter than the type I would wear. I wore sensible jeans. "It won't be dancing. I've seen you dance before. Better coordination I have seen in marionette shows. So that's out."

I scowled in displeasure. My dancing skills were . . . good . . . adequate. *Uninhibited* would be a better word. Untrained and uninhibited.

Better than a marionette, for sure.

"And a movie is no good either," Ava continued. "Too much time not talking. And if you do eat afterward, it will be late, and you'll be sleepy and yawny."

"I will not," I countered, then remembered almost falling asleep at Denny's, the only restaurant we could find open after a late showing of the what seemed like a five-hour-long movie,

Titanic. Ava had to nudge me awake after she surreptitiously chowed down half of my Grand Slam breakfast.

"So it's just dinner?"

Ava wiped at her mouth with the back of her hand.

"Yes. But you have to pick the place. Don't depend on the man to do it. If he picks, it will probably be at some stupid and loud sports bar that sells 'dynamite wings.' I learned my lesson with the podiatrist. All he eats is fried-somethings. And the fry-ier the better. Sports bars are his default choice. Disgusting venues, and unashamed purveyors of bad American food."

My head started to hurt with the plethora of new—and not welcome—choices this "dating thing" had brought into my life.

"What sort of restaurant, then?"

"How about that Greek place across the road. Carols?"

"I guess that's okay. But the sign out front needs an apostrophe. C-A-R-O-L-S. No apostrophe. I've told the owner and he just smiles at me."

"He's Greek," Ava said. "Maybe he has three sisters, all named Carol. Or, more likely, he probably doesn't speak English."

"He does too."

"Like a dog understands English, Mary. He knows restaurant English."

"Restaurant English?"

"You know. He understands what a hamburger is and what 'chef's salad' means—and that's it."

"You are so jingoistic," I replied. I didn't think she knew the word and I liked using such words when I could—my only edge in our relationship. She had me beat in every other category—looks, skinniness, vivaciousness, and the ability to make me laugh. But I was smarter.

Book smarter, anyhow.

She did not rise to the bait.

"Listen, I know you're not going to do Starbucks. You've already told me the story of when you and Jacob first went out—like a hundred times—to a Starbucks. So that whole chain is out. Caribou is also out, probably, because it sells coffee. As for restaurants, you go upscale and then it feels like you owe him something afterward—and I know you won't be going there."

"Ever."

"We'll see," she said, almost as if she could determine my frustrations on the intimacy front from looking at my face. She couldn't, let me assure you of that. "The flesh can be weak, you know. So Carols is good. The place is nice and safe and well lit. There can't be any unexpected expectations from that sort of meal. And it would be best if the date is just for coffee and dessert, rather than dinner," Ava said, swallowed some coffee, took a deep breath, and continued. "I'm not real fond of the podiatrist's eating habits. How a man can get through elementary medical school eating like an eight-year-old is beyond me. So dessert and coffee is safer. No twenty-five-minute waits for the Greek-style pork chops. No need to chatter away if he turns out to be . . . taciturn."

She used that word in triumph. I had used it on her a few weeks ago and she must have looked it up afterward.

"Or phlegmatic," she added.

I waited a moment, then replied. "That has to more do with attitude, not wordiness."

And for that, Ava punched me in the arm—hard enough to hurt—and maybe to bruise my most sensitive flesh as well.

———— ∞ ————

We had agreed to meet at Carol's . . . or rather, Carols. This saved us both any uncomfortable car rides home in case we thought the other one was a complete jerk, or a stalker, or a terminally mousy woman with no sex appeal.

I waited in the small front lobby. The owners had recycled a few booth seats that they turned into a waiting area. In this restaurant, it was totally unnecessary. A waiting crowd never formed. Not because it was a bad restaurant, but because they turned tables over quickly. I think. Well, to be honest, no one would call it a gourmet place, but it was okay. Dependable. Always edible.

A man came in to the small vestibule. His eyes darted around, so I imagined he was my potential date. Or, now, I guess, my actual date.

"Mary?" he asked.

He sounded nice, his voice a little deeper than on the phone. If Rufus asked me to describe him later, the first word that came to my mind was *average*. And not in the bad sense of the word—I don't mean that I wouldn't call him good or bad, just average. He stood a little taller than me. I found that out when we couldn't decide to shake hands in greeting or exchange an air hug. That's like an air kiss. A hug without really touching. I had my hand extended; he was expecting a hug. We met in the middle of both.

"Brian?"

His grin at the sound of his name grew wider than it should have been—by my standards. But he didn't do it in a Labrador sort of ear-to-ear grin.

"That's me. You ready?" he asked and turned to the Greek owner who obviously understood it when Brian held two fingers in the air, indicating the size of our party. I thought our numbers were pretty obvious without the hand gesture, but that was just me.

I might have guessed that Brian was a few years older than me. I'm a terrible judge of ages. Ava said he was older by a bit. His face looked older than mine, I think, with a few more wrinkles around his eyes. Maybe he had had too much sun. He looked like a golfer.

(I don't like golf much, either. Jacob golfed sporadically. He would watch hours of the game on Sunday afternoon when the Bears weren't playing. Watching golf on TV was akin to watching curling on TV. Why do it? Then he would yell at the screen, for both good and bad shots. Anyway, Brian looked like a golfer. He wore a golf shirt—though that didn't mean anything, I guess, but it did have a little shark on the sleeve. I imagined only dedicated golfers would spend extra money to get sharks on their sleeves. His hair had thinned, was blondish, and, while he didn't do a complete comb-over, it wasn't cut short to expose the thinning, either. He had nice eyes, sort of brown. He was a few pounds heavier than he should be—but who wasn't at our ages? He wore khakis and sneakers.

He waited until I slid into the booth. For a moment, I thought he might slide in next to me. Actually, I think he would have if I had made room, but instead I parked myself in the exact middle and did not move. He waited half a beat, then took the other side.

He smiled. That was a good sign.

"You're not like I pictured you," he said. I thought I heard a hint of relief. "I mean, when I got word that I might be meeting, like, a famous author, I went right to my Apple computer [yes, he said "Apple computer"] and looked your books up on the Internet. And they had your picture on the back. At least on Amazon, they did."

I also had a website. It wasn't all that fancy. My publisher made me do it. And there were a number of photos of me there. I guess his Web search couldn't find my name listed. Or perhaps he stopped after the first hit.

"So how do I look different?"

"I dunno. You're taller than I thought."

The photo on the books was a profile, head-and-shoulders shot, making it hard to tell height.

I am being horrible here. . . . I could only describe him as a nice man. He may have been just as nervous as I was.

"And your hair is different. It's shorter now, right?"

He scored points for being observant. I had it cut into what my stylist called "a cute little bob," which I hated and could not wait until it grew out.

The waitress sidled over.

"Ladies first," Brian said.

After hearing my pie and coffee order, he followed suit. I had hoped the instructions about "not dinner" had been passed along. I immediately became worried about it and asked.

"You did know that . . . well, this was just going to be a dessert-and-coffee affair tonight, right?"

I watched his eyes. I think he might have been formulating some sort of feigned surprise, then saw me watch him, and decided against it. Perhaps he was more perceptive than I gave him credit for.

"Sure. I got the word. I mean, that's a good thing," he said. "I bet we're both a little nervous and all. An entire meal is a long time if things aren't clicking."

He was perceptive. And good-natured too.

Maybe I would warm up to him.

Fifty minutes went by quickly. In that time I learned that Brian had been indeed divorced ("We're not friends exactly. We both made mistakes—so I don't spend time saying bad things about her. It's bad for karma. And no kids, which is good, I guess."); had a job selling some sort of medical stent (not the latest technology, but "the cheapest—so a lot of doctors go that route. If you ever have open-heart surgery, let me know and I can get you a deal on medical devices."); that he sold his house after the divorce to handle all his legal bills and divorce settlement, and now lives in the basement of his mother's house—only temporarily ("until I find a good investment-grade real estate place—like a house or something"); and that he has been friends with Dr. Tom for "a gazillion years."

It wasn't horrible.

There were no emotional sparks, not that I expected any, to be sure. There were no sudden flashes of growing old with this man, like there had been with Jacob. I had disabused myself of thinking that this experience would match—or even come remotely close to—the day I met my late husband.

I did feel as if I had been cheating on Jacob and tried my best to smile and push that thought away. Not an easy task—and I was not actually all that successful. I figured, however, that time would make the process less strange and easier to bear.

I ate my cherry pie—with ice cream, the pie not warmed—with coffee, four smallish cups start to finish. He ordered toast. And tea. Only two cups of tea. I didn't understand the toast part of the order, but I desperately wanted to avoid being too critical this evening, or reading too much into insignificant matters.

Brian picked up the check, without hesitation, and put down two dollars as a tip on a ten-dollar tab. He was generous with the waitress. That's a very good sign.

He escorted me to my car. We both said we had a nice time—a pleasant conversation.

He would have kissed me good-bye if I had leaned into him. But neither of us expected that to occur, so neither of us was disappointed. We did the same handshake-air hug like when we met. Maybe that would become our private joke.

I didn't think so—but it could happen.

He told me he would call.

I told him that would be nice.

Perhaps we were both lying. Perhaps we were both telling the truth.

I had no idea of who had done what, or why.

Dating.

Go figure.

That night, Rufus seemed eager to talk. We had barely gotten to the sidewalk outside my house before he started peppering me with questions.

"Did you date well?" he asked.

I had decided that I would not spend a lot of time correcting his syntax. If I could understand him, that would be sufficient.

"The date went well, I guess. He seems to be a nice man. We talked. It was pleasant."

He did not ask me all that many questions—Brian, not Rufus—as if he had learned enough about me from the two paragraphs on Amazon.com to satisfy all his curiosity. Jacob had been eager to learn every detail about my life and my past and what I thought about the debate between cell phones and smart phones.

But . . . Brian was nice, and he was a man, and it was so comforting to speak to a person with a deeper voice than mine.

"Will you mate with him now?"

"Rufus!" I snapped back, in my best shocked schoolteacher voice. "That's rude."

"Rude?" he replied, the hurt in his voice obvious and palpable. "But . . . how long does it take people to mate? I know dogs don't wait very long. Or so I'm told."

I wondered if Rufus knew what I had done to him as a puppy, to remove all those sexual complications from his life. I didn't need one more thing to feel guilty about. But . . . maybe he lacked the awareness to know what "intimacies" he no longer could enjoy.

And talking to Rufus was like talking to a precocious five-year-old who knew the names of every dinosaur that ever walked the earth but couldn't tie his shoes or make it to the bathroom in time every time. Rufus, like that child, was remarkably poised, and terribly articulate on some subjects, and then, much like the average American five-year-old at times, speaking in baby terms. I could be like that as well. I knew how to write a novel, but balance a checkbook? Well, for me, that seemed as difficult as speaking Russian . . . underwater. In the winter. "Rufus," I said, my voice now under control, "humans have to know each other a long time before they do . . . that. Most humans, I guess. At least, the humans I know. Some go faster. But that's not normal. I guess. At least to me, it isn't."

One of my guilty pleasures was my three-year subscription to *People* magazine. Hollywood types, it seems, bedded and moved on to the next person at an alarming rate. How would any of them keep it all straight, I wondered. And how discouraging it seemed to me to read that a pair broke up because "it wasn't fun anymore." One Hollywood actress in a failed marriage had actually said that. As if it was noble to leave the other person because you stopped laughing and the sex became normal.

Don't get me started.

"I would never do that with someone if I wasn't married to him." I explained to Rufus.

Rufus did not appear to hold onto his hurts or slights much longer than a moment—and he may not have taken any offense to begin with. After sniffing a browning geranium, he looked up and asked, "What is 'married'?"

Well, what is that? How does one explain it to a species that does not mate for . . . well, for any length of time?

"'Married' means saying the other person is so special that you make a promise that you will be with him forever and never be with another person. You get married to someone with all your friends and family watching. So they can share in your happiness."

Rufus gladly accepted a tossed treat.

"And then you mate?"

I sighed.

Rufus wasn't being prurient at all. He was just trying to figure out humans using dog perceptions.

"Yes, Rufus. To me, to people who believe and follow God, marriage comes before mating."

Rufus snorted once, then once again.

"Does God say that is the way it is supposed to be?" he asked.

"He does."

"Okay."

And with that our conversation for the evening had ended. I believe we both had a lot to think about.

6

The next morning, Rufus and I went out for a short walk. He had never talked in the mornings and I did not expect otherwise today. I didn't really pay attention to what went on around me—nothing, I am pretty sure—and Rufus became the beneficiary of my lack of awareness as I thought about the night before.

Dating.

How perfectly weird and abnormal is that? For a forty-plus widow woman, that is.

And here's the rub: I didn't consider what I had done as dating. I had seen one man, for less than an hour, over not-a-dinner. So this had been a semi-date. No on expected anything to follow after the semi-date. There would not have to be any second meetings with Brian, unless we both thought that it wouldn't be horrible. He could call, he might not call, and the world would continue to spin on its axis.

Did I want him to call me?

I don't know. I knew I would have to have an answer before Ava called me the following morning, so I actually had set the alarm an hour earlier and had my first cup of coffee at

5:00 a.m. It was so early that Rufus did not even follow me downstairs. A few minutes later, he did stumble down, but only after he heard the refrigerator door open. That meant his chance of a snack increased exponentially.

I had hoped that the quiet and the early hour and the night's sleep would help me sort things out and put things into perspective.

It did no such thing.

Brian had been very nice . . . and while I did not expect there to be fireworks, they would have been nice.

Maybe it is different the second time. Maybe there can be no fireworks. Maybe it is a different form of attraction, of affection, and perhaps, even a different form of love . . .

I must have tossed a dozen treats to Rufus during our six-block walk. The tossing—done purely out of habit.

Once home, I made a second cup of coffee. I resisted the urge to check e-mails. I could be sure that Brian had not e-mailed me, but . . . there I felt that deep desire to be desired. Like accepting a job offer for a job you really don't want, but you accept it anyway because they wanted you and that felt really, really good. I tried to sort out my feelings, but nothing sorted. Ideas and thoughts flashed about.

The phone rang and nearly knocked me off the chair. Even Rufus jumped up in his crate in surprise.

It was 5:45.

In the morning.

Who calls this early? And it better not be him. Or Ava.

I have this nifty phone system that announces who is calling in a weird, sort of French-accented computer voice.

"Arizona call," the voice announced, with a chopped, dispassionate French tone. "Arh-a-zonuh cahl."

Arizona? Who do I know that lives in . . .

I shut my eyes.

Oh, Lord, no . . .

I walked over to the desk. Rufus cowered in his crate, perhaps thinking I was going to lock him in or something.

I picked up the phone and pressed TALK.

"Hello?"

"Mary? Is that you?"

It was my mother-in-law, or, I guess, legally, my former mother-in-law.

"Bernice? How nice to hear from you."

"Mary?"

Who else would be answering my phone at 5:45? A burglar?

"Yes, it's Mary. How are you, Bernice?"

"What time is it there?"

Bernice is a well-enough educated woman. She always asked the same question when calling from Arizona. Her son, her late son, explained the time difference perhaps a hundred times to her—even making her a map with the two cities listed: Wheaton and Mesa—and what time it would be in both of them.

It made no difference. It never had.

"It's 5:45, Bernice."

"In the morning?" she said shrilly, her tone incredulous. "Are you sure? I called early because I didn't want to miss you."

I never go out. Once, and only once in the past three years, I had missed one of her infrequent calls. She had grown frantic that time, imagining that I lay dead at the bottom of the stairs.

"I didn't wake you, did I?" she asked. Jacob's parents were early risers, but I would have bet that she set her alarm for extra early this morning.

And then I realized why she might be calling.

Lord, please let me be wrong. Please. Oh, please, please.

"Who was that man you were with last night, Mary? You were on a date? Is that it?"

It is why she's calling. Good heavens above, she knows. She already knows.

A thousand thoughts swirled about, as if I were trapped in a windstorm of neuroses—and I could not assemble my thoughts into a string to produce a rational response.

"He was . . . I mean, he is . . . the friend of a friend."

I could hear her sharp intake of breath.

"So you're dating now? Is that it? Already?"

I sat down on one of the stools by the counter. I could feel my face begin to flush, my fingers tremble, guilty over something that I hadn't done, guilty over sinning against my dead husband.

"I wouldn't have called it a date, Bernice. Honest."

"That's not what Lena said. She was there. She saw the whole thing. And Lena does not lie, Mary. She goes to church. She's as honest as they come."

I used my free hand to massage the already-tightening muscles in my neck. If I didn't work on them now, they would start to spasm, and I would have to take to my bed with a heating pad. Or would I need an ice pack? It didn't really matter. When the tightness happened, nothing would help—except time.

"Bernice, all I did was have coffee and a piece of pie with a nice gentleman. And how does Lena know that he's not my insurance agent or financial planner or . . ."

"Is he either of those things?"

"No," I replied, feeling guiltier, like I was trying to find an acceptable alibi.

"Well, then, it's not very Christian to tell fibs like that."

"I'm not. But Lena didn't see . . . what she saw."

"She did too. She's a God-fearing Christian woman, Lena is, and if she saw you on a date, then you were on a date."

I had no reply. I had been on a date. A semi-date, but it would have been too hard to explain the difference.

"Okay, Bernice. I admit it. It was a date. It's been three years. It's been a long time."

Bernice remained silent. Not quiet, but silent.

"We just talked. Honest. It felt good to talk."

Bernice drew in a sharp breath. That I could hear.

"You can't talk at Bible study? Which you don't attend anymore, either. Lena goes. You don't."

I tried to place Lena. The name was familiar, but I could not recall an image. I would have guessed mousy hair, brown, done in helmet style, with longish dresses that could only be the product of a Sew-Rite pattern book, hand-sewn with a few crooked seams—but only where they don't really show.

Stop being so mean, Mary. You're horrible.

"I know, Bernice. I'm struggling with writing a book. It's hard."

I did not like lying to my former mother-in-law, but if she could throw guilt around, so could I. "Sales haven't been as good as they have been in the past. Keeping up with all the expenses is a real struggle. I'll . . . I'll probably have to sell this place eventually. Too expensive for me to maintain."

Actually, I was doing mostly okay, I guess. There had been insurance and all that. Eventually, I would probably sell this house—more because it had become way too big for me, rather than purely for financial reasons.

"Well, if you're running out of money, running to a new man is not the answer. We could afford to send . . . I don't know . . . maybe a hundred dollars a month. We don't need to eat out as often as we do."

We were playing a tennis match of guilt.

"No. I wouldn't think of it. I've been thinking of looking for a job. Have a steady income—rather than wait on royalties."

"Well . . . Mary . . . I guess it has been a while. It's just so hard. You know. It's like I don't want to admit that they're gone."

She is good. She really is.

I bucked up, pinched my cheek, refused to cry.

I am terrible.

"I know, Bernice. It is hard. But we only had coffee . . ."

"And pie. You said pie."

"And pie, yes. I don't think he'll call again. But it was nice to talk. You have George, after all. You have companionship."

I would have sworn Bernice snorted. A derisive snort, at that.

"Sure. We talk. All the time. He's a regular talking machine, George is. Yak, yak, yak. That's all he does is talk. Can't get him to shut up."

I recognized her tone as sarcastic. George, at his most gregarious, was no more than monosyllabic. I never understood how the two of them produced such a wonderful son. Sometimes the acorn gets carried off by a fast-moving squirrel and planted in some other, entirely different, and more humane garden plot, tended to by kind and gentle farmers who till the earth with grace and love.

"I'm glad you called, Bernice. I'll keep you posted on the news. I'll send an e-mail. You are reading e-mails, right?"

Another snort.

"George says there's a virus and I tell him to call that Greek Squad place and he won't because they charge money and George swears he'll get it fixed himself." She drew in a breath, as if she had emphysema, which she didn't. "So no, we're not getting e-mails. Print it out and mail it to me, Mary. Mail, we get."

I promised I would and clicked the phone off, and then stared at Rufus, who had slept through the entire conversation.

There would be no asking him questions about it this evening, that's for sure.

———— ∞∞∞ ————

Ava called ten minutes later.

At 6:15 a.m.

I don't think she ever woke up that early for anything else.

"So . . . ," she said, drawing out the word long enough to color it up with several sexual innuendos, if I had been that type of person—which, of course, I was not.

The early hour, the odd subject, guilt, an already jittery, caffeinated nervous system—I mean, that all takes its toll on logic, reason, and *The Chicago Manual of Style*.

Blast you, Strunk and White.

"So . . . what?" I responded, feeling all clever and witty.

I am being sarcastic. Or is that ironic? Too early in the day for either, I imagine.

Ava was many things, but she was not a fish that took the shiny, easy bait. She would wait in the cool, deep shadows, before snapping.

"How uncomfortable were you?"

"Not at all, really. That is . . . until Bernice called this morning."

"Bernice? Your Bernice?"

She had snapped at the bait, the shiny lure with a barb.

I related our conversation, and despite the early hour, Ava laughed heartily, not just from the absurdity of it all, but from picturing Bernice in her tattered housecoat—worn because of parsimony, not poverty—and a set of curlers from Woolworth's in her hair. She still had curler sets that dated back to the Eisenhower administration.

After we both stopped laughing (and I admit that I felt guilty for laughing, though I am sure Ava did not), she asked me again, "So?"

"The date went fine, Ava. I liked being out again. I felt grown up and not in a bad way. But I don't know if I'm feeling what I'm supposed to be feeling. I know it can't be like it was, but what happens now? There's no fireworks—that I get. But what should there be, then?"

Ava didn't have any answers for me. I didn't expect them. She once admitted that there were no fireworks with her first husband, and there weren't any with Dr. Tom, either.

Maybe Ava was just not the fireworks sort of woman.

I wonder if Rufus knows what fireworks are.

Oh, that's right, he does. He hates them. Last Fourth of July, we spent most of the evening walk spastically lurching into bushes every time another bottle rocket whizzed up into the warm summer night.

I guess I shouldn't ask him about expecting fireworks then.

I spent the day sitting at my computer, straightening up my desktop, moving Word documents into folders and folders into other folders, getting thing uncluttered. I even spent nearly an hour just eliminating old e-mails, like the video of the surprised kitten in the shoebox and the monkey that plays the piano. I know I'm too sentimental. It is hard to get rid of the past.

Not that my organizational frenzy extended to my real office. No, the office stayed an undisciplined mess. Jacob had pushed me to be more ruthless. "You use most of your office for long-term storage, sweets. You have an open space on your desk the size of a postcard—and not one of those big ones, either. I don't see how you can produce anything clear and pithy in such disorder."

Of course, I laughed when he said *pithy*. I mean, how many people use the word *pithy* on a regular basis, if ever? I had heard Jacob use it more than once, for sure, and laughed every time.

Okay, so I am an arrested adolescent.

Pithy.

You have to admit it's a funny word.

And the office was a mess. I had scrapbooks and photo albums on the top shelf of the closet, which no one could access to because you had to remove the shelf below to get at it. They were lost in plain sight. And the other closet, I filled with all manner of paper that I would never, ever use—like thick, yellow card stock. Why in the world did I buy that in the first place? Might have been for a potential school project by my son. School remained out of the question, but I could not get rid of that thick, yellow paper. It was perfectly good— just not usable to me.

Maybe if I held a garage sale, I could get rid of all the odd bits and pieces that were clogging up my life.

Who am I kidding? That will never happen. It'll take a bomb or something.

───── ∞ ─────

That night, after a totally unproductive day trying to plot out the second act of a book that I hoped some generous publisher might buy, Rufus and I went for our walk. The book, in the Amish genre, was a stand-alone novel about a beautiful Amish girl . . .

Wait a second. Didn't I already write this one?

Of course, the plot felt similar to an earlier book, but not identical. In this one, the beautiful Amish girl actually had a twin who had been separated at birth from her sister. The worldly sister gets involved in drug smuggling . . .

I don't know. Maybe it doesn't make any sense at all.

But my desktop was neat and tidy and I felt a small wave of accomplishment lap at my feet.

And now, in the cold, in the dark, with Rufus almost bounding about, I felt normal again, at peace. No books. No dates. No Arizona phone calls. I sucked in great gulps of the coldness, exhaling great clouds of breath into the night air. The air was cold, not too cold, just gloves-cold, not yet mitten-cold with a scarf.

Brian had not called. I truly and honestly did not expect him to call. I knew he would wait at least a day. I am sure both Ava and Dr. Tom counseled him on not acting too eager, not wanting to scare the skittish fawn off into the deep forest.

Fawn? Who am I kidding?

They probably told him not to make the old, grizzled, arthritic doe skedaddle out of the cornfield and into the next cornfield. They were being honest.

So he would not call today, and probably not tomorrow. The third day—that's when he would call. If he called. There were no guarantees. He may have felt no chemistry either. He may not have felt any fireworks.

I may not be hideous—like that actor in *The Elephant Man* who wheezed, angrily, "I am not an animal!" No, my appearance would not be placed in that panic-inducing category, but neither could I be considered a knockout. I could be classified as pleasant looking. I believe I told you how Jacob described me—pretty, not beautiful. Most of what he said still applied. Of course, I was older than that now. There were more wrinkles around my eyes these days. I think, if anything, my face is thinner, more detailed now than it has ever been. My eyes are still clear and focused. My face still lights up when I smile— that is what people tell me.

Yet perhaps the sum of all of me—all of my face and my fig- ure, such as it is (normal, not bosomy, nor svelte, but normal, thank you very much)—had not been enough to get Brian's pulse ticking upward. I could have dressed more . . . pro- vocatively, but that would have been like a butcher slipping his thumb on the scales: cheating. (Do butchers still do that? Did they ever do that?)

No, if Brian called again, he would do so because he saw something inside of me that attracted him, not because he saw down my blouse and saw something there that attracted him.

So how do I explain all of this to a dog? Dogs don't look down blouses.

Unless they think that you have hidden dog treats in your bra. Which I have never done.

"Rufus," I said.

Rufus slowed, then stopped, and looked back up at me, over his shoulder. (Is it called a shoulder on a dog? Well, yes, it is. Dogs have disconnected shoulder bones (lacking the collar- bone of the human skeleton) that allow a greater stride length for running and leaping. Thank you, Wikipedia.

He waited. I think that maybe talking proved difficult for him—difficult for him to make the proper vocalizations—so he didn't spend a lot of time chitchatting.

"So, now that I've been out on a date with Brian, what do I do?"

Rufus stared at me, nearly immobile, as if trying to see my eyes.

"Are you asking if you should mate with him now? You said that you don't do that."

I had my hand on my hip in my best "peeved June Cleaver" imitation.

"Rufus, that is not my question. You don't have to worry about me . . . mating with anyone before it is the proper time."

Rufus looked away. A rustling occurred in the tree to our left. It might have been a squirrel, but there were no warning chirps from the branches. And I thought most squirrels were already hibernating—or in their winterized torpor state. (That I knew without looking at Wikipedia.)

"Okay," he responded and began to walk.

"If he calls me, do I go out with him again?"

Rufus did not break stride.

Then I found myself voicing the question that made me sound even more like a lunatic than ever before. "Do you think I should go out with him again?"

Even that question did not break the dog's stride.

"I don't know," he said. "I haven't met him."

"Do you need to meet him?"

Rufus snorted. "What does that funny man say on that funny show—the one with Santa's Little Helper?"

"*The Simpsons?* Homer Simpson?"

Santa's Little Helper is the Simpson family dog.

"Is he fat?" Rufus asked. "That's him, then. What does he say?"

"D'oh?"

I don't think Rufus laughed. Or at least I never heard him laugh. I am pretty sure that he found some things amusing, or funny, or worthy of a smile, if he could smile, which he couldn't. He did like to watch *The Simpsons* with me on Sunday nights.

"D'oh," I repeated and I saw his shoulders, even though they were disconnected, lurch a notch, like he might have been silently laughing.

"So I need to bring him home?"

Rufus did not answer, for the question answered itself. Of course I would have to bring him home. Rufus would have to meet him. And Rufus would tell me if Brian was an honorable man.

Yes.

And now, who sounds like a total and complete lunatic, the grand sort of lunatic who has lost all tethers with reality?

I do, of course, and Rufus and I remained silent on the remainder of our walk. I even stopped tossing dog treats to the poor animal, even though I think he stared at me over his disconnected shoulder, wondering why the treat supply had suddenly gone dry.

On the third day, I was ready.

I admit to having practiced some lines and responses, speaking aloud to the empty rooms, as if he had actually called. I made sure not to do it near any of the Jacob pictures. I would not want Rufus to think I had gone off the deep end again.

Who am I kidding? I had been there and back already, right?

The phone rang at 11:00. I didn't think he would call at 11:00, since he had a job and all. Hard to call for a second date in the middle of a workday, I imagined.

The call came from California.

The only person I knew, or at least knew well enough to be calling me, in California, was my literary agent. It would be either really good news, or really discouraging news. Middle ground seldom existed with Marcella.

Who in their right mind names a perfectly normal child Marcella? I suppose it was unique and memorable. Maybe the odd name became her ticket to being a profitable agent.

"So how is my favorite Amish pro doing these days?"

I was her go-to writer of all things Amish. Over the years, I had pitched a number of different story ideas and different plots and settings and characters and religious backgrounds—from histrionic Presbyterians to gum-chewing Catholics to secular humanists to normal, everyday Christian people like Ned Flanders on *The Simpsons*. But hardly anything other than your standard Amish novel, and the occasional Quaker and Mennonite novel, had sold. I had written two non-Christian books that were published by a small press in Kansas. Both received good reviews yet they both suffered from lack of sales and distribution. Talk about an actor who is typecast—or branded by one role. I became a "branded" author. I didn't mind, mostly, since I was a writer, a working writer, who actually had books published. That is more than 99 percent of the writers in America can say. And I had more than one book published—again—more than most writers can ever hope to say. But I am now typecast as the nice writer who doesn't talk about sex or write about violent things in her books (other than the weather). I had grown tired of it. I wanted to branch out, but no one had given me the opportunity.

"I'm doing fine. And you?"

Marcella did not need a large conversational opening. We didn't talk that often because Marcella talked so much. I let her go on and on, about the weather, her cats, her in-laws, the crazy California politics, and the threat of the next big earthquake.

Finally, she arrived, in a very circuitous way, to me—and to my literary efforts. Marcella had not gotten rich off of me, but she probably made her car payments for the past several years through my book sales.

She did not wrap bad news in gay ribbons and bows.

"No one is buying Amish anymore, Mary. I hate to tell you, but your last proposal received no interest from any of our previous publishers."

"No one?"

This was the bad, drug-dealing twin sister of the good Amish girl who stayed home.

"Nope."

Her reply sat there, like a fat goose in a hunter's crosshairs.

"You have any vampire books? I know that a vampire who believes in God is sort of a contradiction in terms, but they are buying vampire stories."

Vampire stories? I don't do vampires.

"Or werewolves, maybe. They're not quite as sexy as vampires, but I might be able to sell one of those. You have anything like that?"

Usually, I would have snapped at the chance to try something new—but vampires? Or worse yet, werewolves? I just couldn't see how I could make that work.

"Well. Think about it. Maybe you'll come up with an angle on that."

"What about the New York houses?" I asked. "Are they buying Amish? I could make it less . . . less religious, I guess. A little sexier, even."

Marcella laughed, though not pleasantly.

"New York isn't buying anything unless your name is Rowling or King or Turow. Or Clancy. They are playing safe and no one is paying for unknowns these days."

I took a breath. It felt as though my literary career had entered a new phase: dead.

"I know you're not an unknown everywhere, but you are in New York circles. If you lived under a bridge for a while, then I could sell you as a new writer. An unknown primitive, who has a unique voice that no one has heard yet."

I didn't want to live under a bridge—or even a secluded viaduct. How would Rufus adapt to living in a cardboard box by the freeway?

"No. I don't think that will work," I answered. "Let me think about the werewolf idea, though. Maybe I can come up with something."

"You do that," Marcella replied. "You think about it. Let me know if you can whip up a proposal for some sort of super-natural thriller. I think I could sell that for you. If it's the right concept."

We exchanged some pleasantries and she said she would "keep beating the bushes, but don't hold your breath." She suggested that I might benefit if I took a few months off to think about where I might be heading as a writer—as if it wasn't a concept that didn't occupy all my thoughts anyhow.

She gave me a cheery good-bye and said that I should stay in touch.

I hung up the phone and sat there, almost totally dumbfounded.

Rufus sat in his chair watching me, his eyes narrowed as if he was sleepy, which I knew he was not. I think he felt bad for me and realized that he had no answers either.

Maybe Brian is fabulously wealthy and desires me so much that he'll help me self-publish my next effort—whatever it might be.

Yes, and dogs can talk, right? That will be the day.

I would have to do something. I needed to sell another book. Or find a job. Or have something remarkable happen in my life.

Like maybe my dog could tell me what to do next.

Right?

7

Brian called later that day, at 5:15. At first, I imagined that he had just finished work, and rushed home to call me. He didn't, since he called from a cell phone.

The French-sounding voice on my answering machine said: "cell-uuu-larh cahl."

I was still in a funk about Marcella's call. I spent most of the afternoon wandering about the house looking for direction.

"Hi," he said. "I wanted to tell you that I had a good time with you . . . over coffee. Or tea, I guess, in my case."

I told him that I did too.

"Would you like to try a real dinner? Maybe Saturday?"

"Saturday would be good."

"That's great," he said, his voice full of relief. "I could pick you up this time, okay?"

At least Rufus would have a chance to meet him.

"How about Ki's?" he asked.

Ki's has a reputation as a pretty good restaurant—sort of an older person's place, complete with a bar and not-completely-awful lounge singers, Barbie Jean and the DelMontes, with their glossy eight by ten photos thumbtacked to a wall in the lobby.

Yes, I made that up.

"Okay," I replied. It would be a real date and we could see how things would work out.

"We'll go Dutch, if that's okay with you. No pressure that way."

I wouldn't have felt any pressure if he wanted to pay for my food, but I guess I understood. His "going Dutch" request was not an automatic penalty, not a red flag, but I admit that the ref made a motion to pull the flag from his pocket and hesitated at the last moment and let the infraction slide—just this once.

You don't live with a football fan for all those seasons without some of it rubbing off on you.

No penalty, but the ref would keep a close eye on the game from that moment on.

"Ki's?" Ava asked, cradling the phone to her cheek. "Seriously? Well, it is better than Hooter's."

"He wouldn't have ever suggested Hooter's," I responded, defending Brian for no good reason, shuffling about my kitchen, wearing Jacob's old, too-big, yet luxurious, lamb's wool slippers that I bought for him the Christmas before . . . before the accident. I would have donated them to charity, but I hadn't done that with any of his other clothes, and I didn't have a pair of slippers of my own. His were sufficient. And warm.

"Don't kid yourself, Mary."

"I'm not. But not all men are like Dr. Tom."

"Thank God," Ava replied. "Grease would be our national food if he had anything to say about it."

"But he looks healthy, Ava. You're always on him about his diet—but he looks good."

"Freak of nature, that's all. If I ate what he eats, I'd be like one of those women on *The Jerry Springer Show* in a few months."

I poured a third cup of coffee. I suspect people think I obsess about coffee. I really don't. I just happen to drink way too much of it. Some days—maybe twenty cups. I know, I know—but most of them are small cups. And I'm not overly jittery. Honest.

"Anyhow, Ki's is a good place. Older crowd."

"I know. But you can talk there. I went to that new Italian place in Glen Ellyn with Beverly and her husband . . ."

"You went out with a married couple? How kind of them," Ava said.

"Don't be mean. They are nice people," I replied. Ava waited a beat, then added, "Did she wear gingham?"

I would have spit out my coffee laughing, had I just drunk a mouthful—which I hadn't.

"She did."

"With lace at the collar?"

"All of her dresses have lace at the collar," I said and then hated myself, just a little, for being mean and gossipy. But the truth is the truth. Beverly dressed as if she stepped out of a J. C. Penney's catalog, circa 1953. She did have an unmistakable style about her. I would have said pre-Beatles, premodern, pre-style. "But I'm talking about the restaurant here. It's too loud, and we had to actually shout at one another to be heard. Most uncomfortable."

"Yep, Ki's is much better. You will call me afterward to tell me all about it, right? I have a vested interest in this love match."

"It's not a love match, Ava. It's just a date."

She waited a second.

"That's not what I'm going to tell Bernice," she said coolly, and then promptly hung up—all before I could shout at her, in mock anger, that if she breathed a word of this date to anyone, I would stalk her down and break her arm.

Keeping secrets. Sheesh.

What am I? Sixteen?

Rufus stared up at me from his pet bed—his usual spot during my morning coffees—narrowed his eyes, and rolled onto his side, evidence of his desire to be left alone and absolved of answering any of my foolish morning questions.

Later that morning, I looked in my wallet. I don't make a habit of looking in my wallet. I guess looking there sort of happens in the course of a day—like when I buy something. But I wanted to check on my cash supply. I tried to pay cash for most of my smaller purchases. It gave me a better feel for where my money was going. That's what the lady financial guru said on her finance show on cable—the woman with the big teeth and even bigger grin. It's easy for her to tell people what they can buy and what they can't; she has millions of dollars and two homes and who knows what else. Even if I did everything she said, I would never become rich. Unless I wrote a financial book like she did. Which I can't, because I'm terrible at finances. Yet I did follow her advice about paying in cash. I think the advice came from her. Maybe it might have been from that other guy, who looked like he dressed in clothing from a Goodwill store. Not that I am anti-poor or anything. Or anti-charity. But if you're on TV, even if it is cable TV, wear something else other than striped polo shirts that look too small on you.

I had nineteen dollars in my purse and way too much change. I took the change out, more pennies than anything else, and dropped it into the large, clear jar, half-filled with mostly pennies, on the far kitchen counter.

One day, I'll take that to the bank and have it counted.

Even though the last time I did that, I got more than a few semi-angry glares from the teller. They count money all day. How hard is it for them to pour a jar full of coins into that machine that does the counting for them?

I would need to go to the bank for actual cash before my date . . . my dinner at Ki's. It would be easier to put down cash on the table—since we'd be splitting the bill—than it would be to figure out how much the waitress should assign to two credit cards.

I knew I should check out my bank balances then. Maybe my checking account needed additional funds . Maybe I would need to transfer money from the larger savings account. I sat at the computer, Rufus followed me back into the office, of course. I am sure he thought that there might be food involved somehow. There wouldn't be, of course, but a dog can hope, right?

I typed in my impossibly long user name and even longer, more complicated password. The password had to be eleven characters long and include at least two numbers. Who can remember all that? I used the state of my birth—Pennsylvania—and the year of my birth. (If you're a hacker, please ignore what I just wrote.) The bank's cheery website came up and welcomed me by name.

The balance in my checking account stood at $783.53. No big bills were coming, so that should be sufficient for a while. I clicked back a page to check the savings account balance. I didn't often look at the number, but when I did this time, the amount shocked me—sort of. It was smaller than I remembered. Much smaller. *Dwindled* is the word that popped into my head. I did have Jacob's insurance money deposited in a separate account—some $200,000. I still had a mortgage on the house. Jacob had taken out a policy that paid off maybe half of the outstanding mortgage when he . . . when he . . .

How do I describe to myself what happened? "Passed away" seems too much like a funeral director's euphemism. "Died" seemed abrupt—and he didn't die. He was killed. Both he and our son suffered the same fate. I guess I seldom mentioned it to myself, so the few times it came up, I stumbled.

So the house had a mortgage. Rather, I had a mortgage. I have more money than many widows, I am sure. I had some retirement money, maybe $50,000, in a 401(k) account that I couldn't get to until I turned sixty-two. But I didn't have all that much cash in savings.

In the western suburbs of Chicago, where I lived, real estate taxes were high enough to feel onerous, and I wrote a check out for just over $10,000 in real estate taxes last year alone. That would be enough to deplete most of my savings—that's how little remained.

All of a sudden, I began to feel afraid again, nervous and anxious—just like I was the days after the accident. At first, I imagined that my royalties and advances from my books would be enough to maintain my lifestyle. But thanks to Marcella's assessment of my literary future—well, that may be wishful thinking at best. The writer's newsletter . . . I enjoyed doing it, but in reality, it broke even at best. Unless I could come up with a way of doubling or tripling its circulation, I suppose I would have to consider shutting it down. I hated to see that eventuality on the horizon. Looming on the horizon would be a more apt description.

So how much money would I need for my date with Brian? Fifty dollars would be the maximum. I would order the chicken, drink water with the meal, eschew dessert, and have more than enough for the rest of the week—provided I didn't do more than a half dozen runs to Starbucks.

Rufus sat up in his chair and sort of snorted and barked, as if asking me to go outside. He did this often. I would let him out the back door, he would run down the steps, run around the bottom deck, then run back up the steps. I blamed myself. I always gave him a treat when we came back home. He didn't have to go out. He simply cadged treats from me.

So we walked to the back door. I went outside with him. The air was cold, bracing, and it helped clear my head. I heard his nails clicking on the bottom deck, shuffling through the leaves that weren't raked from this fall. I looked out over my smallish domain and felt an inordinate wave of sadness, or melancholy, wash over me.

I'll have to give all this up. There's no way I can continue to live here and have enough money to live on. If I stay, I'll have to work. And I don't know if I can do that.

Even now, I hesitated. Not that I was reluctant to work—far from it—I simply didn't want to have to tell my story over and over again. And I would be branded the "widow lady" of the office. I just didn't think I could do that. Not yet, anyhow.

Rufus scrambled up the steps. I gave him his treat and I sat in the sunroom, Rufus beside me on the sofa, staring blankly into space, wondering what was to become of me.

Maybe Rufus might shed some light on my dilemma.

Maybe I should ask God what I should do.

I would ask him—but he and I aren't really speaking these days.

<hr />

That night, a full moon rose over a very chilled landscape. It had not snowed in Illinois yet, or at least not in DuPage County, but it was cold enough to do so. I bundled up and checked The Weather Channel before we left. No wind. That meant I could make do with just the hood of my coat and not ruin my hair with a thick wool cap.

Not that I had much of a coiffure to be ruined.

Rufus snorted a few times. I should take him to a dog allergist, probably, but after reviewing my finances, odds were good that he would have to learn to live with it.

"Rufus," I asked, well aware of the absurdity of it all, "should I think about selling the house?"

We lived in a big house: four bedrooms—five, really, if you counted my office, which could be legally called a bedroom since it had two closets—and four bathrooms (one in the finished basement, which had its own small kitchen and bedroom.) Two-and-a-half-car garage. Way too much space, of course, for just me and the dog. Big square footage meant higher tax bills and higher utilities and higher insurance.

By selling, would I be admitting some sort of failure?

If the house sold for what I thought it might, I would have maybe . . . I don't know . . . another $50,000 profit? Or does the Realtor take more than 5 percent?

"I dunno," Rufus responded. I have heard that tone before. Dispassionate, maybe. Or uncaring.

I didn't like it.

"So God doesn't care if I need to sell the house?"

Rufus did not break stride.

"I don't know much about houses. You do need shelter, right? We both do."

I nodded, then realized that Rufus could not see me nod.

"But is this a good time to be selling a house? Will I make enough money on it? Doesn't God claim to provide?"

Now, my tone grew snippy. I didn't think Rufus was all that savvy when it came to someone being snarky or mean or insolent. But, then again, maybe he was.

"Doesn't God care?" I asked again, this time nearly to mostly impatient. "Isn't he supposed to care for the sparrows? Isn't he supposed to care for the least of them? Am I not as important as some stupid, insignificant sparrow?"

Why should I have to give everything up? I didn't allow some crash to take the only two people whom I really loved. I certainly did not ordain the accident—for some stupid greater good.

Rufus stopped in his tracks and stared up at me as if he was trying to gauge my mood, looking at me with those dark, expressionless eyes, trying to decipher what I thought. I think I was being pretty transparent.

He bent to nip at an itch on his front paw. Then he spoke.

"I don't think this is a question for a dog. Or God. It seems wrong. Like you want God to help you make money. You need shelter. And you have shelter, don't you?"

I didn't want to answer him. I didn't want to talk to him. And I didn't. And he didn't get another treat during the walk and only one when we got back.

I'm not sure if he knew whether I was mad at him or someone else.

It didn't really matter.

I spent all of Saturday morning cleaning the house. When Jacob was still alive, we hired a cleaning lady to come in once a week for half a day. It felt marvelous to come home to a recently cleaned house—mopped floors, dusted blinds, scrubbed bathrooms, gleaming appliances.

Now, all that cleaning was my responsibility.

Rufus followed me from room to room as I worked, often laying down in the doorway, his eyebrows moving back and forth, as he watched me work. Most of the house did not get that dirty. My bedroom and bathroom were the only two rooms upstairs that I used, but I felt obligated to vacuum all the other rooms, and dust when the dust became so obvious that I could no longer ignore it.

Rufus complicated the act of vacuuming. He had determined, early on, that the vacuum cleaner posed a threat as an evil machine, and he did his best to try and protect me from its nefarious ways, barking and lunging at the head of the unit, trying to bite it, or gnaw at it, as I maneuvered it along the carpet. If I stopped and took the head off and approached Rufus with only the silver tube, as the machine inhaled great whooshes of air, he would run off to another room, cowering. But as soon as I put the head back on, he would begin to stalk.

I could just shush him away with a hard word, and he would stop. If I was in a hurry, or feeling unfriendly, I would do exactly that. Otherwise, I would let him feel heroic and a noble defender of our home and hearth.

I dusted the empty rooms upstairs.

John's bedroom was not empty, exactly. The bed remained there, and the desk, the nightstand, the bookcases. But soon after the accident, I could no longer bear to see all the reminders of his short life, so I went to a self-storage facility, bought two large bundles of medium-sized storage boxes, and packed up virtually everything in his room, and—sweating and crying and cursing—had carried each taped box up the rickety, pull-down stairs into the attic. And there the boxes remained, unseen and untouched. I had remade his bed with a neutral set of sheets, and a neutral bedcover. I left his camp picture on his nightstand.

Even now, when cleaning, the room nearly empty and devoid of personality, I would sit on the bed and weep, missing everything about him, missing his smile and his scent and his odd, off-kilter humor.

Today, I just hurried through the room, vacuuming whatever dust had settled on the floor since the last time, Rufus growling and snorting at the vacuum cleaner, making the house a safer place.

I spent nearly an hour in the kitchen; cleaning out the refrigerator required most of that time.

My refrigerator is food purgatory. I make too much of something, or bring home half a sandwich from a lunch out, or deliberately make enough for two meals. What usually happens is that food stays in the cold and dark until I throw it out. I should save a lot of anguish and chilled space by tossing it out in the beginning. I seldom eat leftovers.

I know, I know, I'm not rich and I should use up all that I have. But I can't. Something about the congealed nature of old food.

Rufus would gladly eat it all. I tried that once with three pieces of fish that I had left over from an all-you-can-eat fish fry. (I didn't get extra to take home, honest. They brought me seven pieces on the first go-round, and I had that many legitimately left over.) Anyhow, I fed one to Rufus that first night, which he ate with great enthusiasm. I repeated it the second night; same Rufus result. The third day told another story. I am sure his canine stomach had not been designed to handle processed fats, and the result caused me to scrub floors for another two days. Rufus looked terribly chagrined at his malady, and slunk into his cage after each episode. Of course, I could not be angry. I had been at fault. And he graciously only got sick on the hardwood floors, rather than the few area rugs on the main floor.

Today, I tossed out a bunch of white containers and some condiments whose expiration date lay two years prior to the current year, and disposed of the contents of a few Tupperware containers whose surface had become a seventh-grade biology project on mold growth. I tried not to inhale while doing so, thinking that I may have concocted a lethal strain of blue bacterium that the world has yet to experience.

I'm sure I didn't, but "squeamish" is my middle name.

It isn't, of course, and mold was about the only thing I really find to be disgusting.

That and spiders.

Rufus doesn't like spiders, either. Some bugs he would chase and eat if I didn't yell at him to leave them alone. Not so much with spiders, though.

Then I sprayed all the stainless steel appliances with cleanser, wiped, and sprayed again with Windex. My cleaning lady, when she worked here , said the two-step process was the best technique for doing away with all streaking.

I put the vacuum cleaner away, straightened up the pillows and throws in the family room and the sunroom, and squared up the several piles of magazines that I would one day go through and clip out all the really good recipes, as well as make notes on all the wonderful places to travel to, books to read, and music to experience.

I knew I was kidding myself, but one's ability to delude one's self is infinite.

You know who said that originally? Sandy Koufax, the star pitcher of the . . . . I don't remember what team. Out in California. A Jewish ball player. And he said that about pro athletes hanging on too long. He quit at the top of his game. Yes, I know I said I wasn't a sports fan, and I'm not, but my father and Jacob were both rabid fans. It connected them.

And now I saved magazines that I would never read, and cleaned a house to impress a man whom I would not invite inside.

Crazy, isn't it?

I'll be honest here. I am not sure about that. I did not think that I would invite Brian back to the house. I told Ava that. I would imagine that she told Dr. Tom and he may have relayed the information on to Brian for me.

There would be no "Would you like a cup of coffee?" at the door.

Not now. Not after this date.

But a question remained: why am I cleaning like a madwoman? If he's not going to see the house, who cares if it's dirty or not?

Rufus followed me as I put the bucket of cleaning supplies back into the laundry room closet. He also expected a treat, because that is where I kept them and he had begun to expect a treat every time I went into the room.

I can be a sucker for a sad face.

I looked at the clock in the kitchen.

It was 2:15.

Brian said he would pick me up a little after 5:30. I had told him that would be fine. I had more than three hours to obsess about getting ready.

I hoped that the early hour was not because he wanted to take advantage of the early bird specials.

But I had an uneasy feeling that it was.

The next morning, Ava forced her way into my house.

That may be a harsh description, but it is what she did. She used her emergency key to let herself in before I woke up. Rufus barked and squealed. I heard that from upstairs. Of course I remained in bed. Or rather, had remained back in bed. I had been up at 5:00, had taken Rufus for a walk, came back, and crawled back into bed. That did not happen often.

Never, actually.

And not because I was tired from the night before.

Ava rattled around in the kitchen, making enough noise to wake me again. She called up after a few minutes.

"It's me, the burglar," she said. "You're almost out of cream."

I figured she could navigate the kitchen fine on her own for a few more minutes and I took a shower—a quick shower— but I wanted to be awake for her interrogation.

And I knew that I would be getting an interrogation. Thankfully, I had not seen any church ladies at the restaurant, nor did I see anyone who would have been likely to have known Bernice. Most of the ladies there were much more stylish.

But now I'm being catty.

The hot water on my skin, pulsing against the bare nape of my neck, felt particularly delicious this morning.

Perhaps I was regaining a bit of my sensual side . . . hidden for these last few years.

Who am I kidding? I was never that . . . sensual.

Was I?

Jacob and I had a rich life together, if you know what I mean. Jacob could be so gentle and patient, and . . . well, at times, adventuresome. I mean, I am a literate, literary-minded person who likes words. Jacob could use words with devastating effect on me. Whispering in my ear all sorts of intimacies.

I spun the faucet to cold . . . or less warm, actually.

I was allowed myself to be carried away, and I did not want that to happen.

I dressed in shorts, despite the cold. Longer shorts, and a baggy, thick sweatshirt from the University of Pittsburgh, my alma mater—not an original sweatshirt; that one would have faded to tatters years and years ago. This was a replacement model. And I am pretty sure it was at least one size up from the one I wore back then. Time does take its toll.

I brushed my hair back, still wet, put on Jacob's slippers, and padded downstairs.

Ava held her coffee cup up as I entered the kitchen, as if saluting a returning hero.

I did not speak, but busied myself making my first cup of instant-brewed coffee. I had one of those fancy one-cup-at-a-time coffeemakers that was really expensive, with the little tubs of individual coffee that cost ten times as much as my cup of standard grocery store instant. (The fancy machine had been a gift from my agent, when literary fortunes were apparently much better than they are these days.)

Ava remained remarkably poised and patient, sipping little bated-breath sips as I bustled around. Only when I sat in the chair opposite her did she find her voice.

"So . . ." she said, drawing out her words to an almost leer, "how was it? Or should I say, how was he?"

I could have risen to her bait. I knew what she meant, to what she implied. And I know that she liked to grab my dainty, prim, golden chain and give it a hard yank now and again, just to see what I would do.

Nothing, apparently, this morning.

"I had a nice time," I replied. "Brian was very nice. And Ki's was very nice."

I watched as Ava's eyes narrowed, like a snake looking at a frightened baby bird abandoned on the ground. Only Ava's tongue wasn't forked.

Ava meant well, I think. She did like prodding and poking. Maybe it made her feel better about herself in some unconscious way. Maybe she needed to feel superior.

"A nice time . . . hmmm."

"I did. We had a very pleasant dinner."

I figured I could derail her train of thought.

"When he picked me up so early, I imagined that he meant to get there for the early-bird specials."

"And he didn't?"

"The waitress offered the early-bird menu, but he said he wanted to look at the 'real' one. He said that if I wanted to see what the specials were, I should feel free to."

"Really?"

"You sound surprised," I replied.

"I am, sort of. I mean, he's buddies with Dr. Tom, and Dr. Tom can be the world's biggest cheapskate at times. Like when he asks for two senior citizen tickets at the movies. I may be older, but I am not that old."

"Really? He does that?"

"He says that what sixteen-year-old ticket seller is going to challenge him on it?"

Rufus rolled over in his cage, snorting twice, rustling and readjusting himself on his stack of cushions. Every day, at least once, I would have to get down on all fours and square up the stack of mattress layers in his cage, so he wouldn't have to endure a thick roll of foam rubber under his rib cage. He would grow immediately nervous when I did this, and try and force his way back into the cage—as if he was trying to prevent me from entering his den.

"And so the date went well? No spinach stuck in your teeth for the entire evening?"

"Not that I noticed."

And in order to circumnavigate any more of Ava's inquiries into the exact nature of the evening, I went ahead and gave her a five-minute synopsis of the date.

Here's my recap: we sat for awhile. He had a glass of wine. I stuck with coffee. We chatted about the weather and the Bears' chances this season (which were not so good; I still listened to the news, so I could be conversant as to their status, on a superficial level), the last movie we saw, the last book we read—and he charmed me by saying he went to the Lombard library and checked out one of my early books. It was an Amish story, and he said he read it only at home so no one would see him reading a romance book. He said the first couple of chapters were quite good.

I would have been happy if the evening had stopped at that compliment. Being complimented was heady stuff. Almost better that having people feel sympathy for you.

And then we ordered. He had the small steak and I had the chicken. (I was being cautiously frugal.) We both agreed that our meals tasted quite good. And they did, really. They make fabulous roasted chicken at Ki's.

He had a second glass of wine after dinner. We both passed on dessert. I had more coffee. He told some funny stories about working with doctors and having to watch actual operations, to see how the stents get placed.

I told Ava that I appreciated his sensibilities. Most men (and maybe this is unfair) would relish the opportunity to make the stories horridly graphic with blood and spurting veins and arteries. But Brian did nothing of the sort. He kept the blood aspect to a mere trace—we were at dinner, after all.

"And you know what?" I asked Ava.

"What?"

"He actually let me talk. He asked me about writing and I talked for a long time—and he listened. Maybe he only acted interested, but if he did, he did a wonderful job of faking it."

"Really? He listened? And there's actually a man who does the faking? Unheard of."

"Ava, you can be terrible at times," I said, trying not to sound like a prudish scold, but letting her know that I sort of mostly disapproved. "He did listen. And asked . . . like follow-up questions and everything. I liked having someone to talk with—and not simply be talked at."

Ava took a deep breath.

"Do you mind if I date him as well? He sounds like . . . like a nice guy."

I smiled, knowing that I had an edge here somehow.

"No," I replied. "You already have one. And that's enough."

8

The following day, Sunday, as cold as it had been all year, dawned with a wind that yowled across the open field behind my house. Winter robbed nearly everything of its color; only browns and grays remained in the muted sunlight, struggling to knife through a thick stratum of bleak clouds, the color of old oatmeal. I nearly froze by the time Rufus and I returned home from our morning walk. There had been no time to talk. The previous night had not been not much better. When the wind howled, Rufus often remained mute. Maybe he found it hard to talk over the noise of the wind and weather.

He had his returning-home snacks. I realized I was wide awake and, after seeing that it was only 7:00, I decided to shower, dress, and go to the early service at church. Most of our old friends went to the middle service. Attendance at the first service ran on the sparse side. I could sneak in late and sneak out early and not run into anyone I knew.

I'm not sure why I decided to go that particular morning.

Maybe my date got me thinking. Maybe things were changing in my life. Maybe I wanted . . . I don't know. Maybe I wanted some sort of sign, some sort of divine affirmation.

Where better to get a sign than at a church? Or a mountain-top? We're in Illinois, remember? There are no mountains in Illinois.

I parked down the street, being charitable to those who would arrive later, and the wind, now stronger, whipped and cawed as I clutched my too-thin-for-this-weather coat around my throat. I must have been a sight when I entered, my hair streaming in all directions, my face red, my eyes watering.

I prayed that I would not see anyone that I knew.

I did not. Attendance, by my estimation, stood even lower than I expected, because of the harsh weather most likely. My church's, or any church's, numbers suffer in the cold and nasty conditions.

I took a bulletin and sat in the back, on the right side (not my usual spot, but out of the way). Our church . . . my church . . . or this church, I guess, leaned right and backward when it came to style. Hymns, yes, we still sang them—with a pipe organ as well. Bulletins, yes, we still used them—instead of a projection screen or a Facebook update, or whatever the hip churches are doing these days.

Tweeting, maybe.

I could never do that—Tweet—simply because it sounded stupid to me. Not communicating, but the word itself. Tweeting. Please. It is what birds do.

The first two hymns sounded reedy and fragile as the congregation struggled to match the volume of the organ, whose organist appeared oblivious to the overpowering pipes.

The pastor today, the one delivering the sermon, was not the senior pastor. I was momentarily displeased because I liked the senior pastor's messages. This new guy—well, I couldn't be sure. And then I thought that I may never have heard him before. He was newish, and I had not been attending that regularly in recent months . . . or years, I guess.

Maybe he would surprise me. Maybe this specific conflu-
ence of times and events and temperatures and all the other
auguries would fall into place in a perfect alignment to bring
his message to a needy ear.

Wasn't that what I expected? Wasn't I looking for a sign?

I was. I have been heeding the words of a fifteen-pound dog
for the last few months. I wanted to hear from a man of God.
Not that the dog of God was leading me astray, but maybe I
needed more.

And just how ludicrous do I sound? I am eternally grateful
that my thoughts do not become visible, in little cartoon bal-
loons over my head.

The pastor strode to the pulpit. He had a lean and hungry
look about him, which I did not immediately embrace. I suspect that I never immediately warm to anyone who is whippet
thin and looks as if he has run twelve miles a day—before
breakfast.

He was that sort of person.

Isn't it telling about the frailty of humans that I have, within
seconds, dismissed this fellow human being as being cold and
inconsiderate? I hope that other people don't do that to me.

He began to speak.

He read a long passage from the book of Job.

And my heart sank.

If you haven't read it, that part of the Bible talks about Job, a
rich man who had everything he could possibly want, and how
he lost everything—or rather, had it taken away from him.

"Suffering makes us better." I think that's an accurate quote
from the skinny pastor. He went on to read: "The LORD gave
me what I had, and the LORD has taken it away. Praise the name
of the LORD!' In all of this, Job did not sin by blaming God."

He went on, but after only a few moments, I stopped listening. Not because I chose to, but because I grew angry, the weepy kind of angry that stops all cogent thought.

I fought back tears as well as attempted to quell the anger ascending in me like a helium balloon. The tears acted as ballast, I guess.

I couldn't hear, because of the internal bedlam in my head.

Yes, everything I had belonged to God. And maybe he had the right to take it away.

But why? Why would he do that? Was I not good enough for God that he had to "refine" me in some horrible fire? And after he snatched from me the only two people who were blameless in my life, he wants me to thank him for it?

Well, he has another thing coming if he thinks that will happen. Because it won't. Not now. Not ever. There is no good that can come out of my husband and son being torn apart by a drunk driver and a semi-truck full of blasted, stupid, unnecessary flat-screen televisions from China. There is no good in that. They're gone and I am here all alone.

I came as close to swearing in church as I had ever in my life.

There is nothing that will ever change that in my life.

I tried to use a tissue and stanch the tears. I was not too successful.

"Job did not sin by blaming God."

And that's it then? That's the sign? That I've been sinning for the past three years? That I haven't been as darn magnanimous and accepting as a "good" Christian should be, smiling bravely in spite of my loss? Well, God, if that's what you wanted to tell me, then message received.

I couldn't stay. I just couldn't.

And I had used angry, almost-swear words inside a church, if only in my head, though that would be marked against me as a sin, too, I imagine. I would have sworn—a lot—if I was a person who used profanity. I wasn't, and wished that I could have been, for just this moment.

I pretended to cough, stood up, and slipped out the back doors, not looking left or right, not hearing anyone call to me, pulling on my jacket as I almost stumbled down the stairs and to the sidewalk, almost running to my car, slamming the door harder than I have ever slammed a door, then pounding on the wheel a few times.

I wiped my face with the back of my hand, inserted the key in the ignition, started the engine, and wondered if I should drive through my tears and ire—though waiting until they passed seemed to be too much pain to endure motionless.

I didn't tell Rufus anything about church that day. When I returned home, he did stare at me for a long moment, as if he had noticed my red eyes. I'm not sure I had ever cried in front of Rufus before—I don't think so—but I imagined that he could not have truly understood the emotion or the reaction.

Dogs don't cry, do they?

Not according to Wikipedia, they don't. They lack the proper moral absolutes for understanding guilt and shame and remorse and unhappiness, the article said, so they have no reason to cry.

I guess that's correct. An animal can easily kill another animal and eat it—for survival—without even a momentary hesitation. I don't think I could do that. Not personally—though I suppose I did pay other people to do that for me.

My usual Sunday afternoon routine entailed reading the newspaper online, watching whatever old movie was featured on Turner Classic Movies, and napping on the sofa in the sunroom, under the thickness of a throw and blanket, with Rufus stationed at the top of the sofa, guarding against roaming packs of hooligan squirrels.

Today, I did none of that. I had two cups of strong coffee for lunch. I went downstairs into the basement, considered bringing up a box or two of Christmas decorations, and then decided against it (too early), went upstairs, opened the linen closet with the idea of reorganizing its haphazard contents, but didn't (too much work for a Sunday), then came back into the kitchen, made another cup of coffee, and sat in the uphol-stered chair, staring outside, over the deck, to the gray sky and bare trees.

It had not proved to be a productive day, by any stretch of the imagination.

The sermon stuck in my craw, being turned this way and that, my inner self trying to come to grips with it and not suc-ceeding in the least.

I know what the man said made theological sense and con-tained theological import—but to me, that was all it had.

I mentioned earlier that I wasn't sure if I still believed or not.

That's why. This is why.

I couldn't get it to make sense.

I just couldn't.

If Jacob had died of cancer or some horrible, agonizing disease—that I could have lived with, horrendous as it might have been. I could have held him and said good-bye. I could have shared in his pain. Even my son—I could have done that for him.

But there were no good-byes. We had no last hugs. The door to their lives had been slammed in my face.

Two closed coffins—that is all there ever was. Closed. Never to be opened. I had no chance at a good-bye. I had to suffer all alone. No one could understand or share that pain. No one. How do you say farewell to a wooden box?

If, in order to be a Christian in good standing, I have to accept, with grace and joy and long-suffering, that pain, then I am turning in my membership badge. I can't live under those rules. I can't be a member of a club that asks for too much sacrifice.

Yes, I am very aware that we live in a broken world and that believers and nonbelievers will suffer—but only the believers are told that they have to have joy in the midst of it. The non-believers can revel in their unhappiness and no one thinks they are weak or lack faith. They are deemed normal. Not me. Not as a believer. I need to put on a cheerful face in the midst of a crumbing, breaking heart. I can't do that anymore. I can't.

So . . . I spent the day, talking to myself and carrying on a very long, heated argument between myself and . . . I don't know . . . that new guy at church—the one with the lean and hungry look.

I ate two blueberry muffins at 4:00, although Rufus ate prob-ably a quarter of one of them. I know chocolate chips are bad for dogs, but I am pretty sure blueberries are okay. They have antioxidants in them, right? And he loves blueberry muffins, licking the floor to make sure every last crumb is devoured.

That was going to be my dinner. Being tied in angry knots left little room for an appetite to develop. And if I lost a pound or two, all the better.

Since I'm dating again, apparently.

And I didn't tell Rufus any of this, not in one of my out-loud monologues to the dog during the day, when I'm not sure he really paid attention to me anyhow. But I didn't tell him any of this because . . . well . . . I was pretty sure he wouldn't really understand. And I didn't want that to happen. And what would happen if he told God all about it. I didn't want that either. What God doesn't know won't hurt him.

That night, the air colder than it had been all fall and early winter, seemed even colder. I checked The Weather Channel before leaving on our walk—31 degrees. It felt icy. I didn't pay attention to the relative humidity—I don't think I really understand the term—but it did feel damp outside and that dampness seemed to have more penetrating power than just the cold.

I promised myself I would look it up on Wikipedia to find out the reason for it. Yes, I know you can't trust Wikipedia. When my son was alive, and in kindergarten, the teachers in the upper grades at grammar school forbade students from ever using Wikipedia as a source for any of their school assignments. What got me is that they would much rather trust a book as a solid, trustworthy source for a second-grade research paper on butterflies. But you have to remember this—I write books (or at least wrote books). I sounded very trustworthy and reliable as I described the cultural mores of the Amish community. I had never included a known falsehood in my books—but I am far from being an Amish scholar. All this to say, for my purposes, Wikipedia always worked fine.

Rufus hunkered down as we turned into the wind on Glencoe. A large open field lay to the south leaving nothing to impede the wind, as it bit and gnashed at us as we tucked into it that night. We both hurried to make the turn, to find some protection from the trees along the private, NO TRESPASSING pond area.

I was puffing when we got there.

"Cold," I said aloud.

"It is. I might need a jacket," Rufus said, "like the one Rusty wears."

Rusty was the schnauzer that might have been Rufus's legitimate cousin—the one from the same breeder. Rufus had scoffed at the idea of wearing a jacket like Rusty's—but he had snorted when it was September and 50 degrees. With the wind and the damp, opinions are easily swayed.

"I could get you one, if you want," I replied.

"Okay."

We walked a ways, and I tossed him a treat, which he chewed happily.

"Rufus," I said, "is my dating Brian okay? Is it okay for me to . . . want to see him again? Is it okay to want to be with him?"

I know. I know. It's crazy doing this. But if I asked any of my female friends or family—well, here's what would happen: Ava would claim that I need to be with a man—in more ways than one. Beth would want to know if he's a church-going man. Bernice would not want to even hear the question. Others would caution about going too fast, or too slow, or at all. Confusing, right? Rufus is the only clear, trustworthy voice I have right now. As they say, he doesn't have a horse in this race.

"Sure," he said quickly, as if he had been considering this question for a while before I asked it. "But I would like to meet him."

"Okay," I responded.

I waited until we got to the end of Anthony Street before I spoke again.

"Does God want me to be happy?" I asked, louder than I wanted, but I wanted the words to be heard over the wind rushing up Western Avenue.

Rufus responded quickly this evening.

"Being with a man is what will make you happy?"

I waited a half a block.

"I don't like being alone."

"I'm with you," Rufus said. And after another moment, he added, "And God is with you, right? I mean, you have asked him about it, right?"

I don't know why, but I immediately grew angry.

"Yeah, right," I snapped back. "I asked. But Brian is someone I can actually hold in my arms. I can actually feel him as he holds me back."

"And that's what you want?"

"Yes," I snapped quickly. "That is what I want."

I wondered what Rufus knew about God, really. He sort of knew what the Bible was—this book-thing that people look at. But he could not read—I felt pretty certain of that. So how could he know so much about God and what he stands for?

I guess I figured it out like this: when I pet Rufus on the head, in a kind, gentle way, more than just touch is communicated. Those gentle strokes must tell him that I care for him, that I will try my best to provide for him, that I will keep him from harm. None of that had been said in words—but instead, communicated through our shared touch. He knew exactly what it all meant.

Maybe good dog Rufus found the same sort of information emanating from God in the same way—nonverbal, but absolutely concrete and real. Maybe God reached down, somehow, and touched Rufus and from that divine touch, the good dog just *knew* God and what he was all about. Maybe that knowledge was all coded into his DNA and instinct.

He knew God because God knows him.

Or maybe I'm just a bit loony these days.

Both could be true just as easily as not.

9

Three weeks before Christmas, Ava and the podiatrist, and Brian and me. How weird is that? A double date.

Well, we did it. Dinner at one of the nicer restaurants in town—a faux French place. Actually, if I'm being uncritical, and I should be, it wasn't faux at all. I think one of the chefs had actually come from France. That's enough to lend an aura of European sophistication to a restaurant in a strip mall. And there's the rub.

The food was superb. The ambiance—well, they tried. My opinion that if you try to re-create some other locale, like a French bistro in DuPage County, then you will succeed in fooling no one at all. People will know that you bought the big French posters and other decorative pieces at Pier One down on Butterfield Road. It's the pretending I can't embrace. Jacob and I went to Epcot in Florida the year before John was born. At the end of the grand loop through a lot of "countries," I came away oddly dispirited. We weren't in Italy or France, or even Canada—we were sweating through an abnormally hot August in Orlando. And while the pasta tasted good at the Italian restaurant in Italy-land, and the waiters (at least ours) actually came from Italy, I still wasn't in Italy—where I wanted to be. "Don't fake it," I said at the time, "just be Disneyworld and try not to put a disguise on it."

I should not depart from my story for these tirades. I am sure you're much more interested in my evening with Dr. Tom et al. than you are of my anti-faux rants.

We had a nice time. The food, as I mentioned, was great. Anything loaded with butter and wine has to be good. And Dr. Tom, whom I had met a few times before, was charming and self-deprecating. I don't think he considered himself a real doctor either.

"But somebody has to do it," he said, "and it pays a lot better than selling shoes."

Brian acted kind and considerate that evening as well, as he had been on our previous few dates.

I should mention that Rufus had gotten to meet him. On our second real date, Brian stopped at the house to pick me up and I asked him to come in while I got my coat from upstairs. Rufus had gone ballistic again at the doorbell. He had calmed down when I greeted Brian with an air hug, and had stepped back a few paces to stare at this welcomed stranger.

"I'll be right down," I said as I hurried up the stairs. "Rufus, no more barking. Brian is a friend, okay?"

Rufus turned to look at me, as if to say that I should not be leaving him with a complete stranger like this. Who knows what the man might try to do to a defenseless little schnauzer?

If Brian was put off by a standoffish dog with an attitude, he did not show it. He knelt down and extended his hand, palm open, to the dog. Rufus, in turn, waited a long moment (I could see this from the darkened upstairs landing) then took a very tentative step forward and sniffed Brian's open hand. Brian did not move quickly, and spoke to Rufus in a low, calm voice, and brought up his hand to the top of Rufus's head, gently petting his head. The dog warmed a degree and took another step closer, sniffing and staring intently.

By then, I had my coat and came down the stairs.

"My, don't you look nice tonight," Brian said. He turned to face Rufus. "Doesn't she look nice tonight? I bet if you could talk you would say just that, right?"

For a moment, I grew terrified that Rufus might do exactly that: start to talk. He did not—and obeyed his speech-is-for-outside-only rule.

Later that night, after Brian had brought me home and left, following an air hug at the door, I changed into warmer clothes and Rufus and I went for our walk.

"Did you like him?" I asked.

"Who?" Rufus replied.

I could have easily gotten semi-infuriated at his passive-aggressiveness, but realized that Rufus may indeed not have known whom I referred to.

"Brian. The man who came over earlier. You sniffed him."

"Oh. Him. He seemed nice."

That's it? He seemed nice? That's all the divinely inspired discernment I am going to get?

I waited a half a block until I had to ask a follow-up question.

"But did you like him? Do you think he was a nice man? I mean, do you approve and all that?"

Rufus snorked a couple of times, I guess in an attempt to clear his snout.

"I don't know. He seemed nice. He had a nice voice. Do all men's voices sound that low?"

"Most, I guess. Men's voices are deeper, lower than women. It's the way we're made. Like the big black dog next door. He has a lower bark than you."

"He does? I thought my bark was . . . . deep too."

Maybe dogs are like people as well—where our own voices sound so much different in a recording than they do in our own heads.

"It's deep. Maybe he's just louder," I replied, thinking that Rufus might be sensitive to my unintended slight.

"Well, that man seems fine."

"So he's not God's choice for me?"

"I don't know. If you like him . . . But to be honest, I don't think God plans it so there is only one person that a human has to find in order to be happy."

"Really? I don't have to find the only person alive who might be my soul mate?"

Rufus stopped, chewed on his front paw for a moment, then continued.

"I don't know what 'soul mate' is, but I think there is more than one person for every person. I'm pretty sure, anyhow."

I kept quiet for the rest of the walk, trying to digest his take on dating predestination.

At the end of our date, at the end of the meal, thanks were issued all around, and Brian ran off to get his car.

Ava grabbed my arm and whispered into my ear, "Be careful, Mary," she said. I stepped back, trying to look peeved or shocked, or amused, or something. Something worthy of a strait-laced aunt whose purity and moral integrity had just been maligned in a backhanded way.

I waved off her comment.

"I'm fine."

Brian hurried around the car and opened the door for me. There was more waving and thank-yous in the cold night air.

Brian drove carefully. He walked me to my door. Before I could say anything, he volunteered, "I can't come in tonight, Mary. I have a super-early stent surgery tomorrow that I have to attend."

"That's okay," I said. "I'll give you a rain check."

That's when he took me in his arms and held me close, and I felt his face coming close to mine, and I tilted my head just so, like I had done a million times with Jacob (why did his name come up just now?). Brian tilted his head and then I felt his lips on mine and it wasn't unpleasant at all. Quite the opposite. It felt very nice, and I sensed that small electrical rush from the first touch. I found myself feeling the texture of his lips and the pressure—not pushy, but not fish-lipped either—and then I felt myself yielding my body into his, leaning toward him, him leaning into me, our winter coats muffling what might have been a more sensuous engagement, his arms and hands moving up my back and mine pulling him closer.

He was the one who backed away first.

It must have been the wine.

"Thank you for a really lovely evening," he whispered to me, his lips still only inches away from mine.

"No," I replied, "thank you."

And then he kissed me again—or did I kiss him?—quicker, a short press of lip to lip, and another one right afterward, like we had been kissing each other for years.

It felt really, really good.

"Unlock your door," he said softly. "I can't leave until you're inside."

He was quite the gentleman.

I did as he requested, all the while Rufus scrabbled at the other side of the door, hearing us on the front step, not barking, since he heard my voice.

I stepped inside. Brian bowed, not stupidly nor theatrically, but a short little quarter bow, as if he was placing a coda on this first evening between the two of us. The first real shared intimacy. I watched him as he got into his car, backed out of the driveway, and flashed his headlights as a second farewell. It was nice of him to consider the neighbors that way.

I watched him drive off. Rufus waited for me as I turned. I know the dog needed to go out—but did he have to stare at me that way?

———∽∾———

I didn't talk to Rufus anymore about Brian during our walk—and beyond. I anticipated what he would say in that regard—that if Brian made me happy, it was okay. Neither did Rufus ask if Brian . . . believed—in God and all that. In Rufus's world, everyone believed. I think they did anyhow. I never really asked him if all dogs believe. Maybe there are good dogs and bad dogs. Good dogs believe. Bad dogs don't believe. I should ask him about that. With good dogs, wouldn't they have to recognize their creation—and by default, their creator? People, well, they are a different breed. When things are communicated in shorthand, the possibility of miscommunication is probable and high. I mean . . . I believe, I guess. Yes, there is a God, a divine God who has put the universe in action, and who keeps it there. But he also can be a cruel God—take a look at my life if you want further proof. So I believe, in God, in a manner of speaking, but perhaps I am not what others might call a true believer. At least not now. Maybe I had been before, but not now. I couldn't say what might happen in the future. I mean, who knows what tomorrow will bring—in terms of people or opportunities or woe. Right now God and I are not speaking. Sometimes those "I'm not talking to you because I'm mad" estrangements become permanent. I couldn't speak for God, but that's how I felt.

And Brian might believe. He might be a believer—just like Jacob had been a believer. I don't know. We had not spoken about spiritual matters at all (although he had said something about "karma" during our first meeting). He was a kind man, and a gentleman, and despite his wearing sneakers too often, I found myself beginning to care for him.

Was God in this situation, in this unfolding, as it were? Rufus said he couldn't be sure. He once said he can't speak for God—but he was probably interested in what happened in our lives. He had said that there is more than one person out there who we can connect with on that deeper, more intimate level. So, if God didn't pull the strings, then he allowed me to muddle my own way through my own life. I think I already knew that.

And I had muddled onto Brian and, to be honest, it began to feel normal and good.

Instead of all that personal and intimate stuff, Rufus and I talked instead about vacations.

I had not been on vacation since . . . since the accident.

I have to stop that—tying every event backward to the date and time of the accident. It made me sad, reminded me of my loss, and did not allow me to move forward, to get on with my life. It was like an anchor, bearing both the good and bad aspects of being anchored—tied firmly to one place, and being held down and back from any forward movement.

But I hadn't been anywhere fun since that horrible day— not that I felt like going anywhere fun by myself. I had continued to make visits to my mother, twice a year, but those could not be remotely considered vacations. I drove from Chicago to western Pennsylvania, spent a night or two at the Wingate Hotel in Latrobe, visited my mother twice a day when I was there, then drove back, in a sour, picklish mood, eight hours alone in my car, filled with the echoes of recriminations and guilt.

A vacation? Please.

I had mentioned to Rufus some weeks earlier that Jacob had always promised me we would live on the ocean at some point during our life together. He never said when—just that we would. He loved the ocean, despite the fact that he spent very little time at the ocean. But those few times, he decided that he had been meant to walk in the salt air every day, with the roll and roil of the waves always a sound in his ears.

We had vacationed one week on Nantucket Island, with most of our time spent on the bay side of the island, yet it was enough to leave him permanently intoxicated by the proximity to saltwater. We had spent a week in Florida, on the water, near Vero Beach. Jacob would have chosen to spend every vacation on the coast.

I had mentioned once to Rufus when we walked past the pond that the ocean was so much bigger than the pond that you couldn't see to the end of it. I said that Jacob loved to walk in the sand at dusk, hearing the wind among the dune grass, and the salt spray stirring into the evening breeze. Rufus took that all in—but I could not be sure if the poetry of the words escaped him, or if their true meanings were not fully recognized by his canine abilities of interpretation.

I did mention to Rufus that night that I had been thinking of going to the beach this spring or summer.

Rufus thought it was a good idea.

Then I told him that I would either have to leave him at a kennel, or take him with me in the car for two days' worth of driving.

He had remained silent for the rest of that evening's walk. He did not like riding in the car, unlike most every other dog in the universe, and after I told him what a kennel experience was, he seemed to furrow his dog brow, as if deep in thought.

And tonight he asked about my plans for this spring.

"If I go to a kennel," he asked, "do I get to pick the dog I stay next to?"

"I don't think so. I think the kennel people put you where they want to."

He remained silent for a long time.

"I don't think I would like that," he finally replied. "What happens if that big, knuckleheaded black dog that lives in the house next to us winds up in the crate right beside me?"

I have to stop speaking ill of the big, stupid dog next door. Rufus is starting to be influenced by my poor evaluation of the beast, and I shouldn't force such bad attitudes on my innocent dog.

"How long do I have to stay in the car if I go with you?"

"It would take us two days. Each day, eight hours in the car."

We walked nearly a block.

"Could we fly there? I see those short stories on the television that say that it is very simple to fly on planes. And fast too. They feed you on airplanes, don't they?"

I did not want to get into a detailed denouncement of the current state of American air travel.

"They do, but, Rufus, if we fly, you'll have to stay in a cage, and be in the cargo hold of the plane—underneath the passengers, in the dark and cold. It is very noisy there."

That was even worse than being in a car.

"Oh."

We were in the driveway.

"I'll have to think about this some more," he said. "I may not like the ocean, after all."

Rufus knew a lot about a lot of things. From the barest sniff he could determine if the scent came from a mouse or a squirrel or a raccoon or a chipmunk, or another dog. And he was really good at the dog scent thing. He didn't know the names of all the breeds, but could describe them well enough for me to guess. And this all from a sniff. He wasn't as good with birds, but knew the difference between a big bird, like a crow, and a sparrow.

Other topics—well, he was not so smart. Things that he had not experienced—like the ocean—he didn't fully comprehend. He saw them on TV, but that's not reality to either him or me.

He claimed to know about God. But he had no direct, two-way conduit to God. He said he talked to God—he prayed. I believed that. But he did not ever speak for God. He knew enough to know that would be entirely presumptuous of him. He knew as much about God as I did. He knew there was a mystery there—as did I. He knew the basics of God and his character—as did I. He talked to God. I did not.

Rufus did not ever claim to be God's spokesman. He did claim to be a dog of God, like some people claim to be a child of God.

So I looked to him for advice. Rufus—not God.

And really now, how pathetic and, well, crazy is that? To trust a savant, a dog savant, with my life.

Pretty gosh-darned crazy if you must know.

But it also felt right.

I met Beth and Ava at the Good Apple Restaurant. I didn't particularly like the place, although they offered a prodigious amount of food for a very reasonable price. Each plate, heaping with eggs or fries, or whatever, besides offering too many calories, presented a dilemma: having too much food to eat at one sitting, meant taking the food home that would wind up in my food purgatory (remember?), or splitting an entrée with a friend, which smacked of weirdness. A husband or a parent could split a meal, perhaps, but not a friend.

So what do you do?

Beth loved the place; Ava was ambivalent.

We sat in a booth by the window and watched the large snowflakes swirl down. It was not yet frigid, just cold, and the snow fell in a most pleasant way, not serious; there would be no noticeable accumulation to worry nervous drivers—like me. That is what the weatherman said this morning.

Both Beth and Ava knew each other because of me—they had been introduced years ago. Beth, I am sure, saw Ava as an evangelistic and/or mission project—that if she could come up with just the right words or situation, Ava would repent and turn back to God.

I don't think Ava was ever "with" God, so walking away from him, or back toward him did not seem part of the equation. Beth always brought her Bible when we had lunch together, the three of us, just in case.

Ava liked to shock Beth.

Talking about sex became her de facto method of shocking Beth, and the best way to fluster her and make her blush. Just the mention of sex outside marriage was enough, which Ava could do because of her "relations" with Dr. Tom. But what moved sex beyond the pale, to Beth, I am sure, was that Ava told tales in greater detail than required, and with a greater emphasis on her satisfaction. Beth would blush bright red at some of Ava's escapades. Well, to be honest, so would I, but I suspect that I felt a little more inured from shock than Beth, a little less capable of being embarrassed by anything my worldly friend wound up doing with her podiatrist. She lived her own life, after all, and my morality did not have to be her morality for us to be friends.

I guess. I know it's not good theology, but at times I grew too tired to recast my worldview.

I ordered a half of a chicken salad sandwich and soup, and figured that I probably couldn't even finish that. I have been eating less recently. I would like to lose a few pounds before the holidays. Maybe Brian is also part of that desire. Not that I'm going to let him see the end result of any weight loss on my part. Well, I guess he could tell if my clothes fit better and all that—but nothing more than that, and I'm sure you know what I mean.

Ava ordered a hamburger and fries and soup and a salad. She claimed that Dr. Tom liked women "with a little meat on their bones." I hated Ava for having to consciously eat more to add a pound or two to her already too-skinny frame. I could accomplish the same weight gain by simply thinking about a milkshake.

Beth ordered a bowl of soup and a grilled cheese sand-wich—"hold the fries, please."

We all sort of settled into the booth, relaxed, leaned back, drank coffee (decaf for Beth, of course) and tried to empty the coffee mugs before one of the waitresses sloshed more coffee on top of a mixture that had been sweetened and milked to perfection. It was hard to keep them away from your cup at the Good Apple.

"So, Mary, does Beth know all about your new beau?" Ava asked, not with obvious nefarious intentions—well, maybe just a little.

I had told her about Brian, a little about him, rather than have her hear it from her mother, who had talked to my mother, or the keen-eyed Lena at Bible study. None of that would do, so I had told her straight out that I had seen Brian a few times, that he was nice, and that I don't think I was actually dating him, just seeing him as a friend.

Beth took the news without visible alarm, or even arched eyebrows, but she had looked as if she had been expecting such news for some time. She reacted like you would when a parent goes into hospice—that it's just a matter of time before the inevitable occurs—so you're not really surprised, just taken a little bit aback by the timing of it all.

"I do," Beth answered, nibbling on a bialy. She may not order much food, but she also made good use of the free bread basket. "I think it is fine. It has been some time, you know—a respectable amount of distance and time. Dating a nice man is not inappropriate at all. It is nice to have a man to talk to."

It was interesting to watch my two friends talk about me as if I had just happened to slip away to the restroom, or had been kidnapped by Australian terrorists. Maybe I could learn something. (Please, I am not disparaging Australia. It was the first country that came to mind. It could easily have been Armenia. Now I'm stuck wondering what Australian terrorists might look like. Would they carry boomerangs? Or didgeridoos, like Scots marching into battle with bagpipes?)

"I know for sure that Mary needs a man to do more than just talk . . . if you know what I mean," said Ava.

I am sure Beth knew what Ava meant and didn't like her implication one bit.

And I know that I have, up to this point, been just as adamant about abstention and morality as anyone else when it came to men and dating and sex. Up until Brian, I had no reference point. In the linear path of my life, at first there had been no one, and then there had been Jacob, and now there was no one again. I definitely liked the Jacob part of my life the best, but he was gone. And now I had Brian, sort of. And now temptation entered my life—again. Before, when it was Jacob and me, temptation existed, but I did not know what I was avoiding. Jacob knew a bit more than I did, but had never risked being drummed out of the church or anything. But now I know. I am aware. I knew full well what was missing from my life. I keenly felt the absence of being close to a man . . . in more ways than one. Now it became harder. Now the temptation loomed, more real, and visceral, and, well, alluring and tempting.

I remained steadfast. I told myself I would remain steadfast. I told others that I was steadfast. But . . . maybe I wasn't so steadfast. Or maybe the gates were weakening. Maybe the flesh was becoming more willing.

I was fascinated to see how the discussion before my two friends would end up.

"A woman doesn't need that . . . like a man needs that," Beth replied, crossing her arms lightly.

Ava appeared to be in pain.

"That's just not true. There's the same desires and needs for both. It is for me—as you well know. And our Mary is not getting any younger."

"So? And since she's a little older now, that means that she should have more self-control, more power to resist things that she shouldn't do. And she knows to avoid putting herself into situations where she might be too tempted."

Ava bit into her hamburger, the size of a small house pet, and chewed with great gusto.

"And how is that accomplished? Does our poor, sex-deprived Mary join a monastery?"

"You mean a convent," Beth inserted.

"Whatever. But she's a normal woman. With normal desires. A woman needs to be with a man. For completion. For satisfaction."

Beth chewed at her grilled cheese like a rabbit with a carrot, nibbling at it as if it were going to be pulled from her hands by some unseen force.

"Perhaps. But Mary knows that would be wrong. Outside of marriage, all that is wrong."

Ava slashed a fry through a large puddle of ketchup and inserted the entire piece into her mouth.

"So, tell me, how far can she go without risking thunder and lightning from above?"

Beth almost wandered into the trap, but at the last moment, backed away from providing a list of what I could and could not do with a man. At least in my unmarried state. I wish she hadn't stopped. I would have liked to learn what my parameters were to maintain my "good girl" status.

"That's not the point. Mary knows full well that without a wedding ring, all such . . . shenanigans are off limits to her."

Yes, she used the word *shenanigans*. I never once considered any of "that sort of thing" as shenanigans. Maybe it depended on the way "those things" were done. That I had not considered. I know that I never once pictured Beth and her husband, Todd, as engaging in shenanigans. And I sure did not want to start today.

Ava chewed another large bit of her hamburger, which was rare, with raw onions.

Perhaps the red meat infusion caused it. Perhaps a nearly full stomach had mellowed her. Ava softened, at least a bit, and pulled back from the confrontation.

"Okay. Mary knows what's good and bad."

Beth's face showed a small smile of triumph.

"But if she knows what's good for her, she'll be bad. It does the heart well to exercise that way every once in a while."

Beth's smile turned flat. I saw her hand reach toward the Bible in her purse, but she hesitated, and brought her hand back to her grilled cheese sandwich. I saw it in her eyes. She had no hope for Ava's soul, but would be praying, in earnest, for mine.

And perhaps she had good reason for her fervency.

Ava drove me home after our lunch. She didn't talk much, not until she pulled into my driveway.

"Mary, I know you're a good person."

"A good little girl?" I asked.

"You know what I mean."

I did. I was a good person. I followed the rules. The rest of the world didn't, for sure, but I stuck with the rules.

"I just think you deserve some happiness . . . after everything that's happened in your life. I just think it's time to loosen up a little. Have some fun with Brian. He seems like he would be really kind and gentle and considerate. There aren't many men who I could say that about."

I couldn't be sure how she expected me to respond. I guess I didn't know how I thought I should respond. So I just listened.

"You've suffered a lot these last few years. You've lost so much. You've been alone. You deserve some fun. You deserve to have a good time. Relax, Mary. Have a good time with Brian. You'll be amazed at how much better you'll feel once you get over that hurdle."

She looked like she might be close to tears, and she reached over and gave me a hug.

"Have a good time, Mary. Of all the people I know, you most deserve to be happy again."

Again, how do I respond to that? Or should I even try?

I didn't. I waved as she backed out of the driveway.

I looked up to the sky. A thin wind knifed in from the west—not bitter, but still cold.

I shuddered.

It felt a lot like snow.

And all of a sudden I have become a shaman and sooth-sayer, predicting the snows based on my feelings.

It made me happy to think that, and I went in and gave Rufus an extra serving of dog biscuits.

"So, Rufus, what I am supposed to do? I really liked kissing him. I never thought I would. I mean . . . I thought that hav-ing been married to Jacob would prevent me from ever feeling . . . you know . . . sexual with a man, ever again. But that's not true now."

I was pretty sure that Rufus did not really understand kiss-ing—or the reasons behind it. I tried to explain that to him a few nights ago. He understood the mechanics, but I do not think he grasped the implications that lay beneath the action.

And sex, well, he understood that—in the basic, mechani-cal way—but was pretty much in the dark to all the layers and levels of meaning that accompanied the physical act between humans.

And why did I talk to him about sex and kissing in the first place?

It wasn't like I was going to do anything about it. After all, I am a good girl, and despite the urgings of Ava, I intend to stay a good girl—regardless of the deep and powerful urges that have begun to sweep up and down my body, like miniature tsunamis, hormones and urges and desires, roiling along with no breakwater or dikes to stop their mad rush onto my sometimes willing, sometimes not-willing flesh.

"What do you want to do with him?" Rufus asked. He had stopped to chew out a clump of snow from his front left paw. He did not like snow all that much. I tried to keep his paws closely trimmed, but to no avail. He still wound up with clumps of snow between his paw pads that I would sometimes need to remove by placing him in a few inches of warm water in the laundry tub, which he hated because then I he thought I would be forced to give him a bath—despite the fact that I never did and reminded him every time.

"What people do with other people, I guess. I mean what a woman does with a man. Be with him. Hold him. Kiss him every once and while."

"I don't think dogs have the same sort of warm-up activities, do they?" Rufus asked.

"They do not."

He watched several Cubs games with me this past summer and afterward asked why the one man threw so many balls to the other man when no one was swinging that big stick. I told him it a new pitcher had to "warm up" before he started to pitch for real.

Rufus understood warming up.

"Do you think God has some say in this? Dating and all that, I mean," I asked Rufus when he finished chewing at snow on his other front paw. Some snows—wet and damp—stuck more tightly to his fur. This snow fell quickly, wet and damp. "Or do you?"

"I'm sure he does," he replied. "I don't. I don't have any dog sense about this."

"Nothing in your dog DNA or instinct that speaks to this?"

Rufus stopped a moment.

"I don't know what DNA is. Instinct I know. They talked about it on that show with the big dogs. Remember? The white ones that swim."

"You mean the polar bear show we watched?"

"Yes. The big white dogs that eat seals."

The narrator had spoken about the bear's powerful instinct for survival. We walked in silence for a moment.

"What does seal taste like? Could we get some of that?"

"I don't think we can. I don't think people are allowed to eat seals."

"But big dogs can?"

"I guess. Nature takes care of nature, Rufus."

"Oh. Okay."

Maybe I should go on my instinct as well. Maybe. Since there isn't just one special person available to me. Maybe I should muddle through this situation on my own. Maybe I should listen to my body and my heart and my head.

"Don't bother asking God about Brian on my behalf, Rufus."

"Brian? Who's that?"

Rufus had never been good with names. He called Ava Beth sometimes and vice versa.

"The man I am dating. The one who stopped at the house. With the deep voice."

"Oh, him. Was I asking God about something?"

"No, you're not," I replied. "I think I've made my own decision."

"Okay. Instinct?"

"I guess," I replied and we walked the rest of the way home without talking.

After our walk, Rufus stretched out at the corner of the bed. I had the TV on mute with the subtitles on. I disliked the incessant chatter that TV provided, but I did like the company.

I would not talk to God about Brian. Really—what would be the use? To let him snatch away someone else who I cared for? I think I would try and figure this one out on my own. I'm an adult, capable of making my own decisions with my own life.

Ava is right. I do deserve some joy and happiness . . . and excitement in my life. Some satisfaction. I lived by the rules in the past. And where did all of that get me? Pain and loss.

What could be worse than that?

A little guilt?

I could handle a little guilt. I could definitely live with a little guilt if I had more moments of pleasure and joy.

I suspect I stood at a crossroads. When the time came, I wondered what road I would find myself on.

Time would tell.

10

Two weeks before Christmas was a tricky time—for both Brian and me.

Do I buy him a Christmas gift? Will he buy me a gift? How much do we spend? Neither of us could be considered rich, with unlimited capital, but we probably both needed to do something for the other in this time of gift giving and gift receiving.

And what do I get a man whom I don't know all that well? Cologne? Seems like a pretty adolescent gift selection. A shirt? Too intimate. Some electronic gadget? Too expensive—and geeky. A book? I know he reads some, but what genre? I could give a gift card to a bookstore, but that presents two problems: one, he knows how much I spent, and two, I don't like giving gift cards. They're just like money, only a lot stupider. They have to go to the store where you bought it, and I have no idea why a piece of plastic with money on it is more personal than actual money. The gift card industry did a great job of selling a concept.

All that to say, I had no idea what to do. I seriously considered a nice, small gift book of some sort, and a tin with homemade cookies. I wasn't Martha Stewart, but I could make a good batch of chocolate chip cookies.

We had had dinner—at Carols—and afterward had returned to my house. Snow began to fall as we ate and snow made me a nervous driver—almost as nervous as being a passenger in a car in the snow. So this evening, I asked Brian if he wanted to come in for coffee. The snow did not seem to bother him, and he owned a large four-wheel-drive car—as big as two of my small Toyotas put together. It seemed asking a man in for coffee could be considered a symbol or a subtle request for more than just coffee . . . but we were both older, both wiser, and both a bit more removed from snickering innuendoes that the request to "come in for coffee" carried.

This time, Brian had no early operation or doctor's appointment to keep him from saying yes. As I entered the house with Brian, Rufus barking for a moment or two until I scolded him to stop, I felt something new, something not exactly electric but I felt something. A charged atmosphere, for sure.

It was weird. I never really expected to feel that way again . . . since the accident. Rats. I said I was going to stop that. And I mean it this time. I had felt that way with Jacob—a lot. Before we got married, there were some snuggling sessions that left me jangled and frazzled for hours. And after we were married, the same thing happened. Only then I was jangled and frazzled for different reasons. Better reasons, but still . . .

And the nervy, jumpy feeling was like a warning siren being sounded well before the tornado struck. I could feel the charge in the air, a faster heartbeat, a slight dilation of the eyes, a general tightness in anticipation.

I liked the feeling. I liked being almost electrified.

I made coffee. We talked at the kitchen table. It was early.

He saw the fireplace in the family room. He asked if I had wood. I said I didn't, but I had a box of fake logs in the closet that I have had for over a year because I was too lazy to light a fire on my own, or did not want to appear to be indolent, enjoying a fire all by myself.

Brian laughed at my sweet neuroses, took two logs out, opened the flue, set the logs just so, and lit them with the long-necked lighter I kept on the fireplace mantel—just in case.

Soon enough, the logs were burning nicely, crackling like they were real logs. I poured a second cup of coffee for each of us and brought them into the living room. I turned off the lights in the kitchen. The fire filled the room with flickering, romantic light. Brian sat at the end of the sofa. He would allow me to adjust my seating to him. Did I mention that he acted the perfect gentleman?

I took a seat close to him—not on his lap or anything, but close enough. I could barely feel his leg against my leg. We were both wearing jeans, as if that offered some insulation from the electricity.

Rufus positioned himself five feet away from the fire. He looked at the flames, then at me, then back at the flames. They may have made him nervous. I don't think I've had any fires in the fireplace since Rufus became a member of the family last year.

Brian moved his arm—the one closest to me—out and around and it came to rest behind me, above me, not really touching me, but it was there, nonetheless. For a long moment, I didn't know what to do. Then I gave up thinking about it. I would enjoy myself tonight. I would experience things. I would just go with my feelings. I would just . . . let myself do what I wanted.

I leaned into him, just a little. Not much. But touching, we were, more or less.

I really liked it. My heart beat like crazy. How's that for a literate metaphor? *Like crazy.* The words, the good ones, were all locked up tight in my head, and the electricity prevented any of the smarter, fancy words from escaping.

He kissed me—a kind and gentle kiss. I expected it, and I wanted it. It felt so nice. I put my hand around his neck, offering my silent encouragement.

I felt his hand on my side, and I did not object or move, or try some manner to avoid it. His hand remained there, on my ribcage, and I enjoyed the delicate and tentative pressure on my body—a place where no man had touched me for years now. At the moment, I felt pretty sure I knew where his hand was headed and I was pretty sure I was not going to do anything to stop him. Kissing him was just too pleasant to think of objections or reasons to slow down. Here I am, a widowed lady in her mid-forties, and I had no reason to slow down. If not now, when?

I liked his hand there on my body. I hadn't been touched there for years. My doctor, maybe, but she didn't make a habit of placing her hand flat against my side like that. I am pretty sure I would not object if Brian moved his hand farther afield on my personal geography.

Good heavens, what terribly infantile metaphors . . . or similes . . . or whatever they are.

Stopping, just for a second, and looking at myself as I sat on the sofa, next to a man I hardly knew, his hand in a more intimate place than any other man other than . . . Jacob . . . I . . . decided to just relax. I had been starved for so long—I could see that now. What harm could there be to finally get to enjoy life, to feel my heart race again—because of pleasure, not terror.

I would let him do with me what he would. Sort of.

And his hand moved, just a millimeter, and I felt fireworks. Well, maybe not fireworks just yet, but as if someone held a match closer and closer to the fuse.

Our actual fire in the fireplace sparked loudly, and I could see, even though I had nearly closed my eyes in pleasure, Rufus jump a bit, and then he turned to me, to the two of us, I guess, and stared hard. I tried not to see his eyes or watch his inscrutable expression. He stood up and ran at us, actually ran the few feet. He sort of threw himself at my leg, his front feet on my knee, his back feet bouncing up and down, like a small boy needing to go to the bathroom.

I knew what he wanted. Either a treat or to go out.

"Rufus," I hissed, not wanting to break the mood, "go away. Later."

That would often be enough to stop him. He would get back down on all fours, stare another moment, then slink away, his task unfulfilled.

But this night, he kept dancing, bobbing and weaving, and making almost inaudible "wuff" sounds, nearly prancing, his nails, which needed trimming, digging into my knee.

"Rufus," I hissed louder. "Later!"

His dance went on undiminished.

I heard Brian chuckle.

"Ignore him," I instructed Brian. "He'll get tired of it and leave us alone."

We both waited, neither of us humans moving. Just the dog moved, bouncing up and down, wuff, wuff, wuff, a breathless sort of bark.

"It's not working," Brian whispered.

"He'll stop," I insisted.

Brian moved his hand.

Don't move your hand! Please! Keep it there!

"If he has an accident, that will be worse," Brian said. I had to agree with him.

"He needs to go out." I sat up, smoothed my blouse, and watched with pleasure as Brian watched me smooth my blouse. "I'll take him to the end of the block. That should be enough."

Brian sat up straighter and looked me in the eye.

"And I should wait here, in the warm house, by the fire, waiting until you bring the dog back? No man worth his salt could agree to that. I will take him out. You stay all warm and toasty."

"No," I replied. "I couldn't impose on you like that."

He placed his fingertip on my lips, a gentle touch, turning my words into silence.

"Please. Just give me the leash. I'll be back in five minutes."

I snapped the leash in place, gave Brian a plastic bag and a few dog treats, a quick recap of instructions, and closed the door after the two of them. As the door closed, Rufus turned around and looked at me. I read his look as nervousness—after all, he stood there, waiting, with a new walking partner. Or maybe I saw something else, something more nuanced than that, a look more akin to weariness, or surrender, or divine acceptance. I was put off for a moment, trying to find an interpretation that fit the dog's appearance.

Divine acceptance? Where had that come from? Yet that is what his furry little face displayed.

I could never have been prepared for the terror I would face in ten minutes.

How could anyone be prepared?

Five minutes passed. I sat on the sofa and watched the fire, contemplating if I should add another pre-fab log to the flames. I closed my eyes and imagined Brian's hand on my side again and wondered if he would resume the position when he returned with Rufus. I wondered what he might do next and if I should rehearse my whispered response.

Good heavens, I had become a seventeen-year-old again, out on her first date.

But with a lot more knowledge than I had at seventeen.

Now seven minutes passed. Then ten. And I became worried. Did Brian lose his way in the neighborhood? I told him to go to the end of the block and come back. Obviously, Rufus had led him off that course. Maybe Rufus had become shy, or obstinate, or fussy that night. I don't know what criteria Rufus used to select a spot. He presented no discernible pattern as far as I could tell.

Perhaps Rufus got loose and ran off. If he quickly backed away from me, his leash could slip off his neck. He never did it intentionally, and when it happened, only once before, he stood there, surprised, not the least bit aware that he had broken free. He simply waited until I slipped the leash back over his head.

What would happen if Brian fell and broke his ankle? Was he carrying a cell phone? He did not always carry one, which I found charming. But he could have gotten hurt.

I got my coat and walked to the front door. The snow came down—great, fat, wet chunks of snow that sounded like a moist kiss as they landed.

Rufus would be soaked when he returned.

I squinted into the snow and looked up the street. No cars were out, the streetlights were nearly hidden in the glittery snow, the neighborhood hushed and still. Then I saw them, coming down Glencoe, from the north. I seldom went that way. Rufus might be scared from the new route.

I saw Brian wave broadly. I think he grinned. I waved back, happy now that my two men have returned safely. Then Brian bent down to Rufus.

Why would he do that?

I think he was unsnapping his leash.

"Go ahead, boy. Run back to Mary," he said, his deep voice catching and faltering through the falling flakes.

I would never do that. I had never done that. Rufus would never run off, but still . . .

Rufus did see me, and broke into what I thought was a grin. Maybe it was my humanizing the little dog. Rufus had said before that schnauzers do not grin, or could not grin, I'm not sure I remember which. I'm not sure why my head filled up with such prattle when I should be terrified instead.

Too many bad things happen when people are untethered from me.

Of course, Rufus saw me, heard me, recognized his home, and took off at a run toward me, down the block.

As he passed by the Turners' house, I saw the faintest of lights, of headlights, and I began to process a terrifying geometry of coincidences, of fate, of God's hand in the rustling and turning of the world, down to the mundane life and death of a dog, his dog, God's follower here on earth.

The car came down the hill, off Wakeman, and did not slow at the stop sign. A driver could see for the entire block in either direction, and if no one was coming—why stop? I did it myself more than once, though I usually slowed a little—a little safer that way.

The snow prevented any rumble of tire on pavement or asphalt; sounds were muted to just the hushing whisper of a car gliding over a thick, wet pack of snow. No sound, just a whispered deathly swishing hush as the car bumped onto Glencoe and continued straight down Wakeman—my street, our street—windshield wipers clacking at the snow.

The car was at the end of the block. Rufus was mid-block, on the other side of the street. Just as small animals and squirrels have no concept of a fast-moving vehicle, neither did Rufus. Maybe some dogs knew of the danger of a speeding car, but if some dogs were aware, Rufus was not. He jumped over the snow-packed curb, a swell of snow left by the snowplow's visit an hour earlier, and slid onto the road, his small black body lit by the harsh swing of the car's headlights.

Oh, God, it was happening again.

I screamed. I think I screamed. I don't know. My world began to crash before my eyes, those eyes already welling up with tears, my throat already swelling shut by grief. It was all so familiar; it was all so foreign.

Rufus had not looked. He had no reason to look. I had always kept him from harm. I had always tugged his leash tight to me when a car approached our path. I had always kept a lookout for the blister of headlights on our path, from behind, from our side.

Rufus had not looked.

Maybe he did, once, a slight turn of the head toward the danger, but he did not stop.

The driver of the car, a neighbor, a nice neighbor with children and a good job at a food brokerage house, slammed on the brakes. But that would do no good—even with the automatic braking systems now in cars. It would slow and eventually stop, moving in a straight line, but even a computer could not override the elementary laws of physics and mass and inertia and slick roads glazed with a thickness of snow.

No, nothing could stop the events about to unfold.

My hand went to my mouth as I screamed and I shut my eyes. I could not bear it.

I heard the yelp, the terrified squeal of a dog, my dog, my sweet and helpless Rufus, as the three thousand pounds of metal and rubber and plastic hulked over the poor, doomed animal.

The car slid into my mailbox with a crunch, the mailbox canting to the parkway, my neighbor jumping out of the car, shouting that he couldn't stop and he didn't see the dog until the last minute and that he's sorry and so very sorry and Brian is sliding and running toward the car and the death and the snow and me screaming and sobbing and sliding down the driveway like a woman possessed and hysterical and Brian running up to me saying he is sorry and that he didn't see the car and that he would never have done that if a car had been nearby and that he would get me another dog to replace Rufus and that I could start over with a puppy for Christmas . . .

And that's when I balled my right hand into a fist. I don't think I have ever struck anyone in my life. I grew up as an only child, so no sibling fisticuffs ever occurred. I was a nice girl and nice girls do not get into catfights at school. I did not excel at sports, so there were no competitive squabbles over a field hockey game.

No, I was nice and gentle and understanding and accepting . . . until this very moment.

Brian, now at my side, prattled on about a new dog, something white and fluffy, and I made a tight fist, so tight that later that evening, I saw little crescent slice marks, complete with half-moons of dried blood, in my palm, caused by my newly manicured nails. With that tight fist, I coiled back and threw the punch. I aimed for his jaw—just to shut him up—to prevent him from already forgetting about Rufus and moving on—but I missed. He stood taller than I thought, and my punch hit him square on the throat and he fell backward from me, maintaining his balance for a moment, then stumbled and tripped, like a pratfall in a movie, onto his backside, and then slid backward several feet.

I turned to my neighbor, who had sprung from his car, his face torn by guilt. "It's not your fault, Mike," I said. "The dog . . . Rufus . . . he ran out in front of you. I know. You couldn't stop. It's not your fault."

A wash of relief came over him, almost like an angel had forgiven him of a sin he did not know he had committed, providing absolution to an innocent man.

Perhaps I could find solace in his peace, in his forgiveness.

But maybe I couldn't. Now I had to retrieve my sweet dog and . . . plan for a burial in the hard frozen ground. I began to sob again.

I gasped for air. I saw Brian struggle to his knees, coughing and holding his throat. I hoped I hurt him.

Then, oh my Lord, and then, I heard it.

A yelp. A whine. And a rustle, swish, rustle, like a broom being dragged from under a car.

I saw his eyes first, wide and scared, but open and responsive.

Rufus was dragging himself out from under the car, on the passenger side, toward the rear. Dragging and whimpering and looking and searching for me.

I dived down into the snow and slush despite the fact that I wore new, expensive wool pants. I dived down and a trembling, greasy, wet, bedraggled dog managed to limp into my arms.

It was the single most clear, pellucid moment of joy I have ever experienced. Giving birth was different—better—and longer. That moment of joy came after ten hours of nasty labor, and the outcome entirely expected.

Being married was joyful—but again—the outcome all but assured.

This moment seemed to transcend all of that and more. I fully expected to retrieve a mangled dog carcass from under the bowels of the car.

And I didn't.

Rufus was alive—injured but alive. If he died, at least it would be in my arms. He would be held by someone who loved him, cared for him, and would mourn for him after he was gone. But Rufus did not seem like he was about to die. His body was unmangled, uncrushed. He was alive.

Mike came over beside me.

"I must have missed him. I mean—the tires—he didn't get run over. I didn't run him over. He must have slid under the car."

Brian stood up now, coughing and trying to speak. He croaked, froglike, whispery and thick. I paid no attention to him.

I unwrapped the coat from my shoulders, wrapped it around Rufus, and cradled him to me. He whimpered loudly when my hand touched his right front leg, but that was all. I saw no blood. His eyes remained clear and focused. His breathing seemed normal.

I stood up and hurried to the garage door, punched in the code and the door clattered up.

"Get your keys, Brian, and go home. I'm taking Rufus to the vet."

"Nonsense," he croaked. I think that's what he said. "I'll take you."

"No," I replied, my voice steady and clear, angular and ice sharp. "I will. You go home. Get your keys and go. Now."

He must have seen my eyes—the deadly, cold resolve in my eyes—and nodded.

"Help Mike get his car off my mailbox and go home," I said sharply, and laid poor Rufus on the front seat, bundled thick into my coat. My keys were already in the ignition. That's where I leave them. I know—it may not be the safest place, but in the last three years, I have never once misplaced my keys. So who's the foolish one now?

The car rattled to a start, Brian came out of the house with his car keys, I backed out of the driveway, and opened the window.

"You'll be okay, Mike?"

He shrugged. "I don't think I even dented my bumper. I'll come back tomorrow and try and fix your mailbox."

"Thanks," I replied, and did not look at Brian. I pressed the gas and slowly left the scene of my Christmas miracle.

———

The wonderful thing about living in a metropolitan area is that your choices in services were multiplied. Not only did I have a hundred vets to choose from, I also had two vet hospitals within ten miles that were open all night and offered emergency walk-in services.

Forced to drive slowly because of the snow-packed roads, I found it easy to put a hand to the face of the scared dog, trying to reassure him.

"It'll be okay," I said. "We'll be at the vet's in a few minutes."

I could not watch Rufus. The snow made it imperative to really, really pay attention to my driving.

"Dr. B?" Rufus asked.

This was the first time he spoke in an enclosed space. His voice, richer and deeper than I could hear at night, out in the open, surprised me a little.

"No, not Dr. B. I have to go to the all-night emergency vet up on Roosevelt Road."

"Is she nice?"

"I'm sure she is," I replied, not knowing if it was indeed a she, or if the doctor was indeed nice. Regardless, though, Rufus would be tended to; he would be repaired.

He would not die! He would not die!

"My leg hurts," Rufus said.

"It might be broken."

"Is that bad?"

"Lots of kids break arms or legs. Doctors fix them all the time. Does anything else hurt?"

Rufus must have run a quick check on himself.

"My neck hurts a little. Not much. My leg hurts a lot."

"The doctor will fix you up," I replied. "Hang on. We're almost there."

I pulled into the vet's driveway. Before I undid my seat belt, Rufus spoke again.

"Is the ocean a warm place?"

I could have told him about Maine and Canada and the snowstorms there, but I didn't. Instead, I replied, "Yes, the ocean is warm."

"Then, okay. We should move to the ocean. God says I should move."

I saw his jaw move. I did not imagine his speech. He talked. He talked to me.

"God said to move?"

Rufus couldn't lie—or at least, not well. And why would a dog lie?

Rufus looked away. It was a guilty turn of the head.

"No. I made that up." His words were thick with apology.

"When? Why?"

165

"While I lay under the car. I wanted God to say that I needed to be warm."

"Why?"

"Because my leg hurts and I want to be warm."

"And you think we should move?"

Rufus licked at his injured leg and whimpered.

"Now I do."

"Rufus, why did you run out in front of that car?"

"Mike's car?"

Sometimes, even in moments like this, Rufus could drive me batty.

"Yes, Mike's car."

"You were going to make a bad mistake. You said that you would never mate before being married, because God says not to, and you're not married and I knew I had to stop it. So I did the only thing I could."

"Get run over by a car? You did that to stop me?"

"It stopped you, didn't it?"

My eyes filled with tears again. I had grown tired of crying, but these tears felt different.

"You risked death to save me?"

"I guess. That's what members of the pack do, don't they? You're in my pack, aren't you?"

I placed my hand on his head, as gently as I could.

"I love you, Rufus."

He did not need to reply.

"The ocean? Really?" I asked.

"If it's warm."

I parked right out front of the vet's office. I hurried around to the passenger side of the car. Just as I scooped the dog up in my arms, I heard him ask, "It is warm at the ocean, isn't it?"

"It is, Rufus. It never snows at the ocean."

Dr. Bartles was on call that night.

"Like Bartles and Jaymes," he said when he entered the examination room. "The wine coolers—remember?"

Everyone under thirty has no idea of who either of those people are, and I only had a vague recollection.

Dr. Bartles gently prodded and probed Rufus. His temperature was normal. "That's good. Sometimes an internal injury will cause temps to spike."

Rufus yelped when he touched his front leg.

"This is broken. No doubt about that," he said. "We'll X-ray the leg, and the rest of him too. But he looks in good shape. No cuts. No lacerations. Eyes are good. No spinal damage from the looks of it. That's what kills most of the animals hit by cars—the spine is broken and then that's that."

He poked a bit more.

"You have one lucky dog on your hands. Went right under the front wheels, you say?"

"Yes. He crawled out from the side."

"Well, he's a bit greasy, but let's get him X-rayed. You can wait in the lobby. Shouldn't be that long."

A sleepy technician came out with the news.

"It's broken. The right front leg. A clean break. The doc is setting a cast on it now. Everything else checked out fine. That's okay, right? You do want to keep the dog, right?"

"Of course."

The technician shrugged. He had the name Tony stitched on his shirt pocket, but he did not look like a Tony.

"What else would I do?" I asked.

Tony waved it off. "Some people hear that it costs $400 to set a leg versus $50 to put a dog down . . . well, they opt for the cheaper choice."

I could have said that such a dilemma posed a terrible and inhumane choice . . . but I didn't. I just nodded. What if you didn't have $400 or what if $400 was all you had to support your family for the next month?

Animals caused tough choices. I guess people did as well.

"The doc will call you when he's done."

———— ✸ ————

Rufus stood on the exam table, his right front leg encased in a white cast. His face glowed with relief. The leg hair had been shaved up past the cast. His skin had a pinkish color at the top of the cast.

Dr. Bartles held what I know is called an Elizabethan collar.

"He'll chew the cast off if we don't use this," he said.

Rufus looked at the collar, then at me. We had both seen the movie *Up*, where a bad dog had to wear a collar like that.

I looked at Rufus. I could read his eyes.

"He won't chew at it. He promises. I promise. If he does, I'll bring him right back."

The doctor did not look assured.

"You won't chew on the cast, will you, Rufus?" I asked him.

The dog looked up at the vet and offered him the most convincing face I had ever seen.

"Okay. If he does, you bring him back," the vet replied.

The doctor turned away, then back again.

"I almost forgot. His leg will hurt. I gave him a localized shot while I put the cast on. Do you think a few pain pills might help?"

I looked at Rufus.

"Yes. He would like enough for a few days," I replied.

"Okay, I'll give him one now. Help him sleep tonight. Could you hold him and I'll get the pill down?"

"I don't have to. Just give him the pill. He'll swallow it."

"You're kidding, aren't you?"

"No. Hand him the pill."

The doctor took one pill out of the bottle and held it out to Rufus, who lapped it up and swallowed a second later.

"You have one special dog there, Mrs. Fassler. Most dogs will fight a pill like that."

"I know. He is special. Very special."

Late that night, near midnight, I heard Rufus rustle and stir in his crate. I sat and watched him from the comfy chair in the kitchen, with a thick blanket over me, thankful that he had been spared—and that I had been spared. He had to sleep in his crate, since climbing stairs would be out of the question for some time.

I tried to push the me-and-Brian-what-might-have-happened-if thought from my mind. I would think on that later.

I saw Rufus's eyes as he struggled to stand.

"You have to go outside, don't you?"

His answer would have been yes. I could see that.

I carefully picked him up and carried him to the front lawn, placing him down on the snow as gently as I could. The mailbox canted backward. The tire tracks and the skid were obliterated by the freshly fallen snow. Snow had continued to fall, in dusts and fits, the wind gone, a quiet blanketing of the area.

"I don't want to do it here," Rufus said softly, almost in a whisper, as if he did not want any neighbor to hear him. "I live here."

"I know. But until your leg heals and the cast comes off, this is where you'll go. Understood?"

"Okay," he grumbled.

He slowly walked through the heavy snow when he finished. He managed to get to the small wall that separated the lawn from the driveway and stopped.

I had been watching the snow and did not see him standing there.

"You're sure the ocean is warm?" he asked again.

"It is. Always warm and it never snows."

He nodded.

"That's good," he said. "The ocean. Where it's warm. He didn't say anything about the ocean. But he did say we need to trust him."

Trust?

"God said that? Trust? In what?"

"I don't know. I mean, I think he said that. That is a good word, right? Even if I said it?"

"Yes," I replied. "It is a good word."

I picked Rufus up from the snow.

Who am I to argue with a dog?

11

I know. I shouldn't have punched Brian in the throat. I know that physical violence is never the answer. And, yes, I did take his call early the next day—the morning after the accident. His voice, hoarse still, was audible enough. He inquired about Rufus. His rasp—it made me feel good. I know, I shouldn't have felt that way, but I did. And I forgave him for letting Rufus off his leash. I apologized several times for hitting him. He apologized many times to me. But, a few minutes into the conversation, I knew that I had to tell him that we had no future together. At this point in my life, I think honesty trumps feeling awkward.

He took it well. . . . I guess he took it well.

After all, it would probably be difficult to remain involved with a woman who reacted as I did. And how many men would feel good about getting punched out by a mere slip of a woman? (I may be more than a mere slip—but you know what I mean.) And I was not still mad. I did forgive him. I did. Holding grudges and anger is a cancer on the soul. I think that's sort of a famous quote by someone noteworthy. Nor was it an issue of Brian being spectacularly negligent. I'm sure he didn't see the car or understand the implications of what could—and did—happen. But to react so cavalierly, so indifferently to what could have been a horrible tragedy—well, that I could not abide. How do you simply pick up and move on after the death of someone—even a dog—whom you loved with all your heart? Did he expect me to do that?

At that moment, I knew that I could never "be" with Brian. He might be able to move on from tragedy and loss with nary a second thought. I could not. And what may look like a small fissure to some would always be a chasm, an abyss, to me— always dividing us. It was a gulf that could not be bridged by desire or good intentions.

So I thanked him for all he had done, and for being nice to me. And I told him, in no uncertain terms, that we had no future together.

And, after wrapping up that entanglement to my life, I set about unwrapping and then cutting every other entanglement that tied me to this place and this house and this life.

The neighbor at the end of the cul-de-sac was a Realtor—a very good one if you trusted her signs posted all over town. I called her and told her that I intended to put the house on the market and would appreciate her advice on what to do to make the place more attractive to buyers. I sent an e-mail to all my subscribers to the writer's website, stating that I would be closing the newsletter and website and I would promptly refund any unused subscription liabilities. (It was not a huge sum—somewhere just over four figures.) I made a list of all the people I would need to call to inform that I planned on moving, all the things I would need to accomplish before a move could take place.

I gave Rufus his pain medication, which I am sure he had begun to associate with his pain relief. He took it gratefully, hobbled over to his crate, scooted around as best he could, laid his head down, and easily shut his eyes.

I knew he would sleep for several hours.

I made a quick trip to a self-storage place near where I had once worked, and bought four large bundles of medium-sized boxes, three bundles of book boxes, and one bundle of larger, lamp-sized boxes. The empty boxes filled the back of my car.

"Moving, you are?" the self-storage person said, very Yoda-like.

"Moving, I am," I replied and immediately regretted it, since the young man's expression did not change, indicating he was totally unaware of being in on the joke.

He hesitated a moment.

"Where to?"

I shrugged.

"I have no idea," I said, feeling at that moment a huge chasm of liberation open up inside of me.

"Really? Most people know. I'm pretty sure most of them know. Don't they?"

I imagined that most people did know. So did I, I guess, in a very generalized way—a macro-knowledge of my moving.

"Well, someplace near the ocean."

He nodded, sagely, as much as a clerk in a self-storage facility three days before Christmas can be sage.

"That's nice. I like the ocean."

Validation.

I let the phone go to voice mail that morning.

Ava called, asking about the date. Beth called. Brian called again and left a long message saying that he understood and there were no hard feelings and that we could still be friends.

Mike called asking about Rufus. That call I picked up in the middle of his taped message.

"He's okay, Mike," I said, and explained the doctor's diagnosis and the cast and how grateful I was that the dog had been spared.

"That makes a lot of us. The whole family worried themselves sick. My kids would have been crushed if Rufus had been really hurt."

I once again gladly offered Mike absolution.

I tried to be quiet as I assembled boxes, but there is no way to dispense packing tape quietly. The tape squeals and protests at being unrolled. Yet even the adhesive squallings did not wake Rufus. Those pain pills must be pretty potent.

Soon after, I had assembled every box I had purchased—at least the bottoms of them—using three rows of packing tape along the bottom joints. (I tend to over-tape everything.) The pile became unmanageable in the kitchen, so I started tossing them into the dining room and then the formal living room—two areas that I seldom used. I imagined that I would fill up the boxes with all the "important" material from my life. When I was finished with the taping, I switched on the coffeemaker, and made a cup of instant-brewed coffee—strong, with two sugars this time. I tried to unwrap a package of Girl Scout cookies (Trefoil shortbread cookies) silently. Even the slightest crinkle of cellophane would normally get Rufus excited, charging toward me from wherever he had ensconced himself. But he slept on.

Powerful pills, those pain meds.

Maybe I could use them when we traveled to the ocean. Rufus would sleep—a blissful, unworried sleep—and would arrive at our night's destination in peace.

But then he would be up all night, unless I gave him another pill, and that seemed to put us on the slope of dog drug addiction.

I discarded the plan as quickly as I reviewed the potential downsides.

I ate my four Girl Scout cookies, drank my coffee, then decided that I should call Ava back. She may now have heard about the accident. She may be frantic with worry. Maybe. I looked at the clock. It was only 9:45. I would have sworn it was later.

"Ava," I said calmly, "I'm leaving."

She sputtered, not really offering a cogent response.

I launched into my story, tragic and miraculous, marked by my epiphany, an exclamation point, as it were, summing up my life to date, and the necessity of my forward movement to some oceanfront, or near oceanfront, somewhere.

Really, I have gotten paid to write words in succession. People paid me to do that.

So I finished my story (not telling her about Rufus saying that we should move to the ocean where it's warm) and said that I was now beginning the process of packing up my life.

"And starting over?" she asked.

"No. Not that. I loved what I had. Before I lost everything. So it's not a negation of that. But it is a new beginning. Or a rebirth. Or . . . well, okay, starting over."

I heard her inhale. She did that when she was thinking.

"I'll miss you," she said, her words calm and matter-of-fact, as if she had been expecting this sort of news all along. "But it will take a while, won't it? You will wait till the house sells, right? We'll still have time for lunches and coffee, right?"

I assured her that nothing was going to happen quickly.

"Have you told Bernice?"

"No. I'm going to send a letter. I would e-mail, but I think her computer is still down. She'll get the letter, be able to process it a bit—then we'll talk. I mean, it is not like we live close now."

I heard another inhale.

"I can help you pack, right?"

"Sure, I would love that."

"It also means that I get everything that you're leaving behind, right?"

I laughed—the first time in the conversation that either of us laughed.

"Sure. You're welcome to the detritus of my life. What you don't want, I give to charity."

I heard Rufus stir. His eyes were slits. He stared for a moment, then slowly lowered his head again and closed his eyes.

Those were some wonderful pills.

I wonder if they come in human dosages.

I'm sure they do.

<hr>

My Realtor neighbor came, gave me a checklist of things that I needed to repair, repaint, toss, moved clean, close, or hide. The list ran two pages long.

"But nowhere near as long as most, sweetie," she said. "Your house is hospital clean in comparison to most of my clients." She had emigrated from Israel and called everyone "sweetie."

She did not mean it as faint praise. I have been in other people's homes and while I was cluttered, at times, and only in a few rooms, other people's clutter made me look obsessive and manic, in terms of cleaning and organization.

I had a roll of contractor's fifty-five-gallon trash bags—thick, green, huge bags. I discovered them tucked away in Jacob's basement workshop. Inhabiting many of the dark nooks and corners of the basement were items that no one would want. Broken things with cords. I read somewhere that people find it very difficult to throw away an item—even if badly broken—with an electrical cord on it. I admit to that problem. I found radios, iPod speakers, alarm clocks, irons, waffle irons, mixers, camcorders more than a decade old, VHS tape players that would eat any tape that was inserted, fans, heaters, frying pans, toasters, and lamps—all broken, all never to be repaired, at least by me. There were more, and I felt more and more like a hoarder as I assembled my dusty, broken finds. Those I stuffed into the big green bags, trying to keep the combined weight under forty-five pounds. What does forty-five pounds feel like? That was the limit that our garbage collectors set on any single bag of debris. I didn't think they carried scales with them in their trucks, but nonetheless, I attempted to stay vigilant to the limit.

Speaking of scales, I found three scales under the bed upstairs. I had forgotten all about them, the three of them unhappily living with a thickness of dust bunnies.

I also stuffed bags full of clothes—my husband's, my son's. These I would give to the church's resale shop. Someone would make use of them. I tried not to think about much at all as I packed them into bags. I did not caress or hold any item to my cheek. It would serve no purpose other than making me very sad.

I would make a clean break, and this was no time to hold up a diminutive T-shirt of my son's and begin to weep. I had his memories, and they were better and more powerful than any swatch of fabric. I had wept enough over the size and scents of old clothes. No more. Not now.

I'm not sure why it felt easier to do this today when I hadn't been able to do it for years—packing up the remains of my old life, that is. Perhaps I had to come to that "clean break with the past" time. And now, here it was. Time to move on.

I'm not sure why today felt different from a thousand other days—but it was—and I began the process of moving on.

I packed a bag full of men's shoes—just shoes. I had no idea that my husband owned so many shoes, and all very well cared for, albeit dusty at the moment. These items would provide money to the church's charity, and good attire for someone less fortunate. And not one of them would grow teary-eyed when looking at an old T-shirt from a Cubs game. (I was more a Sox fan—but not a very faithful one. I only followed them, barely, if they were in contention at the end of the season.)

I emptied the drawers in the kitchen desk. Of course, I tested every pen to see if it would produce a legible line. Maybe a third of them did. The rest made me feel so wonderfully free and alive when I tossed them into a discard bag. I should have started this process much earlier. I had no idea that throwing away worthless things could bring about such contentment and . . . well . . . joy. Maybe that's true in life too. Get rid of the worthless things that tied you down and held you back. That's what I was doing. That's what was making me feel whole for the first time in a long time. Well, perhaps not totally whole, but closer to whole than ever before.

Ava came over later that afternoon. She made a big fuss over the injured Rufus, who appeared to revel in the sympathy, rolling onto his side, displaying his broken leg like a toddler holding a scrawled crayon picture to his mother. She made herself a cup of coffee, and wanted to go through the bag of useless pens I had already discarded. I refused to let her do that, insisting that I could tell if a pen had indeed run out of ink.

178

What is it about pens that resist tossing? In the old days a pencil became short or it wasn't. A fountain pen had ink or it didn't. You could tell when things were done. Now, no one could tell if there was still some recalcitrant ink left in the barrel of the pen. Life is more complex and ambiguous these days.

—— ✑ ——

That night, after a long day of packing and discarding, and sharing a few tears with Ava when she left, Rufus clumped about in the front yard, his cast protected by a plastic grocery bag held up by a small strip of duct tape. I did not turn the front porch lights on, knowing that Rufus did not like doing what he had to do in full view of the neighbors. He stood out there, in the cold, sniffing the air, obviously, I thought, wishing he could take one of the normal routes on our walks. He could not, of course.

I huddled in my puffy coat, hunching deep inside the folds, trying to stay warm. The weather felt so different when we were not walking—colder, more boring, actually.

"Rufus," I asked in a soft winter voice, "why did you decide so quickly that going to the ocean was the right thing to do?"

"Gus said it was warm there. He went there once. He liked it. I like warm. I'm tired of being cold."

I nodded, then added, "I am too," not certain if Rufus understood the meaning of a nod.

"Will that man come back?"

"What man?" I asked, pretty sure who Rufus meant. After all, he did not know that many men.

"The man who let me off my leash."

"Brian."

"I guess, if that's his name."

"It is. I don't think you will ever see him again."

Rufus snorted in the cold, a puff of breathy vapor visible in the frigid air. "I never liked him."

That, of course, was a revelation to me. The most I had gotten from Rufus was that he "seemed nice."

"Why didn't you tell me?" I asked, the wonderment, or better yet, bewilderment, hopefully, apparent in my voice. "You could have said maybe God didn't like him or want us to be together or something. Then all of this could have been avoided."

I bet Rufus would have shrugged, had he been able to shrug.

"I don't know. I didn't ask God about him."

I furrowed my brow as visibly as I could to show this dog that I was getting close to being exasperated with him and his reticence.

"Why not?"

Rufus snorted again, this time, I thought, in a nonverbal way of answering me. Rufus did not do ironic or cynical well.

"People have free will. Right? I think I heard you say that. Or maybe it was God who said it."

"Free will? Really?"

"Yes," Rufus replied, frustratingly calm. "So it was not my place to say anything. And I'm not a biter. So I couldn't very well bite him . . . that man. And a dog in the pack does not bite the leader of the pack."

"But Brian wasn't the leader."

Rufus paused a moment, then spoke softly. "Oh. Yes. I guess he wasn't the leader, was he? Him, I could have bitten, couldn't I?"

"You could have. Maybe you should have."

Rufus turned back toward the front door, snow already clumped about his three good legs.

"But . . . Then, I'm not a biter. I said that already, didn't I?"

"You did."

"So the decision was up to you."

Sometimes knowing who was ultimately responsible for a bad decision was not all that comforting.

Not at all.

———∞———

The next morning, still dark and cold, we stumbled outside, Rufus stretching and yawning. I never feel quite civilized during our early morning walks—but no one in their right mind is out at 5:00 a.m. in the dead of winter. Other than the lady who delivers the newspapers.

I stopped getting the newspaper a few years ago. Up until then, I could be counted among the most loyal of readers, scanning every headline, reading nearly all the opinion pieces and editorials, feeling virtuous at remaining a solid citizen and dutifully informed over everything that was happening in the world. Then my eyes started to go. Not that they were great before. I had begun squinting years earlier, but newspapers were using such tiny fonts. Seriously. And it became harder and harder to read the newspaper in the faint light of morning. Plus, I could get the same material—for free—on the Internet. What are those editors thinking? "We'll give the news away for free and expect people to pay for it as well." Like that makes a lot of sense.

Anyhow . . .

So Rufus and I were out in the cold, and I was obsessing about packing and when to hold the estate sale to sell all the material that I didn't want, couldn't use, or didn't know what to do with.

"Do dogs pack?" Rufus asked, looking up from a dark corner of the front yard.

"No, Rufus. They don't."

"What about my bed?"

"Well, that I will bring with us. And your crate. I'll take both of those things in the car with us."

Rufus snorted as if he was in agreement.

"And what about my crunchy treats? Do you pack those? Will you remember to pack those?"

"Of course, I will."

"That's good," Rufus replied, and began to hobble toward the front door.

"Can you buy crunchies at the ocean?"

"Yes. They sell them everywhere."

How wonderful to be a dog with such simple needs, so few necessities.

12

The days surrounding Christmas were somewhat of a blur to me. As usual, at least usual for the last several years, I did not go anywhere on Christmas morning. In the past, Bernice had begged me to fly to Arizona.

"Being alone on Christmas . . . well, that's just not right," she'd said. "Only communists ignore Christmas."

I didn't think she was accusing me of being a secret, suburban communist, but she meant well. The first Christmas alone had been terrible, but it would have been more terrible had I been around people who were enjoying it. The second time became easier, and I actually did agree to go to a friend's house for dinner, later on, late in the afternoon on Christmas Day.

This year, the holiday came and went, and I had reheated Chinese food on Christmas day, amid a flurry of boxes and packing and feeling overwhelmed.

Beth came to visit two days before New Year's Eve. If there was one day worse than Christmas to be alone on, it was New Year's Eve. This year, I thought, would be easier. I would be busy, not watching a cadaverous Dick Clark announcing the ball drop in Times Square. I mean—really—what kind of person goes to Times Square on New Year's Eve? Any sane or rational person? I don't think so.

Beth arrived with a plate of homemade cookies. Call me a scrooge, but I don't like homemade cookies. I mean, I know how dirty my kitchen can be, and I'm a clean person. What happens in other people's kitchens is best to remain a matter of conjecture. But these were lemon bars and I like lemon bars and Beth said she made them herself and I usually trust Beth to maintain a modicum of proper sanitary procedures. So I made her a cup of decaf coffee. I made a cup of real coffee for myself and we sat in the cluttered kitchen.

Rufus did his now-usual dance with a broken leg, seeming to revel in the sympathy it aroused. And Beth gave him a bite of her lemon bars. He likes lemon bars too.

I nudged a box, half-filled with plates that I would not be bringing with me. Why anyone needs five versions of dessert plates is beyond me. Yet I had five sets. I would bring with me only two.

After a long pause, Beth drew in a deep breath, pushed the hair from her eyes, and tucked it behind her ears—again. It was a habit I would not miss.

I knew she was working on the best way to broach the subject, and I even knew what the subject was: am I making a rash decision?

"Mary . . . You are one of my oldest and dearest friends . . .".

I don't think I am, but it still made me feel good, in a weird sort of way, to be valued by someone. I mean, I knew that we were friends and had been friends for nearly a decade now. But I would have sworn there were other people in Beth's life who were dearer to her than I was. Still . . .

"I know what you're going to ask," I said, preempting her, and saving her a bit of anguish of bringing up perhaps a touchy subject. "And I am not being rash. I've thought this out pretty thoroughly."

Beth looked both surprised and relieved.

"Are you sure, Mary? I mean, really sure? I know that God doesn't want us to do foolish things just because of our emotions. Or just because your dog got hit by a car."

Beth might have been the only person who made that connection, and in a sense, she was the only person with the right answer as to my reasons for going. Or partly right, anyhow.

"Doesn't God seem to reward people who move slowly and cautiously?" Beth asked. I would bet that she had no evidence from the Scriptures, but slow and cautious reflected her take on the proper evangelical path to heaven.

"Emotions can't be trusted," she went on. "They can make us do things that we maybe shouldn't do. You have to be careful."

"But don't emotions help us do the right things sometimes?" I asked.

"I don't think so," she responded. "Well, maybe sometimes. But not usually. We sort of tell ourselves what we want to hear and the more we do that, the more we begin to agree with ourselves—and maybe get fooled into thinking what is wrong is actually right."

Beth is a wonderful person, but not a student of logic. Yet Beth, like so many other people in my life, did not truly understand my life, and just who I wanted to be. So now I felt like a teenager again, complaining that my parents didn't understand me, since neither one of them, obviously, had ever been a teenager. In one sense, though, I was correct. None of the people in my life right now had suffered as I had suffered. Sure, people lost aged parents, and aunts or uncles or grandmothers passed on, but no one I knew had suffered as I had.

And that suffering allowed me to act in a way that made sense to me—even if it did not make sense to others. Not only did it allow me to do so, it forced me to do so.

"Maybe . . . maybe you're running away. A little. From the past, I mean." Beth grew more uncomfortable, as if she were accusing me of using the death of my husband and son to rationalize my irrational desire to leave this place and head to an ocean. With my talking dog.

"So what if I am?" I replied. I was not angry, not at all. I simply wanted to know how she viewed this decision as a bad decision.

"Well, I'm not sure," she said, a little flustered. "But maybe you leaving is . . . well, I mean . . . maybe you have to stay and face the past. Face it rather than run away. That's what I'm saying."

I still did not get angry, and am not angry even now, even though I could have been. I could have let the ire rise and snap back at her and slam my palm on the table scaring both her and Rufus. It might have felt good to me to do that, but it would serve no useful purpose. Instead, I remained calm and collected. Impassive, almost.

"Beth, I know you mean well. I do. But . . . I have lost everything. I have been alone these past years and people still think I am not facing the past. What have I been doing all these years? I have faced it. I have dealt with the loss. I know what it is to be alone. I have lived with that reality every day of my life since the accident. There is not a single hour passes that, somewhere in my thoughts, that terrible day intrudes on my reality. I am done facing it. I can't face it anymore. I can't deal with it anymore. It has been dealt with. I am ready to move on. And I don't think I need to prove anything to anyone. Or even explain it. I know that I am doing the right thing."

Beth offered me a half-sideways pickerel smile, looking like a fish that bumped into the unseen glass wall of an aquarium. "Well, I don't want you to do anything rash. Patience is a godly virtue. It is. Make sure what you're doing is God's will."

I looked around at the small mountain range of boxes—some packed and taped, some half-filled—that littered my interior landscape. It was too late to urge caution against making rash decisions. The die had been cast. The page had been turned.

And my dog wanted to go to the ocean.

"Beth, you are a dear friend, but moving to the ocean, I think, is the first positive thing I've done in my life . . . since they died. It's right, Beth. It is."

She kept her wary smile.

"Are you sure? Have you prayed this through?"

I lied to her. Lied right to her face.

"I did, Beth. I really did."

Lying about praying. How far I had fallen.

"I have prayed so much about this it's not even funny."

———✺———

February clumped over Chicago, cold, gray, windy, bone-chilling, marrow-draining, and filled the weak with the numbing dread of an endless winter. I inured myself to the brutality of the midwestern variety of winter, hoping, praying (not really) that it would be my last. Snow fell and stayed, fingers of drifts edging onto homes and streets and mailboxes. Snippets of snow clutched about Rufus and me as we walked. His cast had been removed, his leg was healed, his pain was gone (so he said), and his hair became scraggly and withered, as it slowly regrew on the shaved portion of his leg. Because it did not have protection from the cold, I cut off the end of a child's sock and slipped it as a legging over his foreleg, and held it snug, not tight, with a length of Velcro. His paw remained exposed to the cold, but his pink and wrinkled leg remained warmer.

Both of us had had enough of winter.

Bernice called me several times. She never once tried to talk me out of moving. In fact, she said that she wondered why it had taken me so long to decide. "Our house back in Wheaton had become much too big for two people, Mary. I get winded just thinking about vacuuming the place."

She asked one important question: "can we visit you when you find a place and get settled? I do like the ocean."

Of course I said yes.

Validation.

And then I decided to buy a new car. Or a car that would be new to me. I had been driving around in a small, nondescript car for years. There was nothing wrong with it, but if I was going to head east, and be on the road for weeks and perhaps months, I needed something bigger.

After all, Rufus would be with me. He needed space.

I decided to buy a used Volvo station wagon. They are safe cars, right? Volvos are for thinking people. Right? Nothing flashy or pretentious. But bigger. Roomier. I could carry with me enough stuff to start over again—once I found a place. Until I could have the rest of my furnishings shipped to me.

I had some money set aside that I could use. Plus I'd have the trade-in dollars, even though that wouldn't be all that much. A car could not be considered a luxury, but a necessity.

I found a Volvo wagon at that used car franchise that has locations all over the country. It was eight years old, a XC something or other, with low mileage and a luggage rack on top—not that I would use it, though it might come in handy. One huge plus: it had cruise control—a luxury I had never enjoyed on any of my previous cars. And leather seats. With seat warmers. What decadent people we have become, needing our tender bottoms gently warmed as we make our way through a frigid environment.

I felt rich.

And the Volvo had plenty of room for Rufus's crate.

February slipped past, a blur of gray and cold.

I began to get nervous about the selling of the house. Only a handful of potential buyers had visited, and none of them had been interested enough to make an offer.

Maybe God, if he actually got involved in petty matters like house sales, would use this as a means to get me to stay put. Maybe that's what the Divine wanted of me. Open doors and closed doors. Isn't that what people often include in their prayers? Really now—some people boldly pray for open doors, and some people are too polite or righteously humble to come out and ask for them directly.

I hadn't asked God about this—or anything else. I had felt guilty about lying to Beth, but it stilled her concerns. And that's what our "pretend" prayers often do—offer a balm to the nervous and timid. And make us look more spiritual than we are.

I can be terrible, can't I? I am sorry for being such a horrid person at times.

But I needed to get out of this cold and this bleakness and this avalanche of memories that kept threatening to engulf me, to bury me forever beneath the suffocating folds of the past.

I would have asked Rufus to speak to God about the lack of buyers, but he already said that house values were not a subject he felt like addressing with the Almighty. So be it. I did not press him. He appeared to be very interested in the daily temperature at Hilton Head. He had no idea where that was; he had no knowledge of distances and geography. He knew that Hilton Head lay on the ocean. I told him that it was one of the places we would explore. I would have showed him a map, but it would have had no meaning to him. I could trace our intended route to the ocean, but it would be all but gibberish to him—funny squiggles on paper that had no meaning. He remained happy to know that I knew the way and how to get to our Eden. He found contentment in that. But he did seem to like the sound of Hilton Head. I think he liked things with two names. He would ask if I saw the weather report on my computer for Hilton Head.

"What is the temperature at Hilton Head today?" he would ask.

I would relate what I had found . . . let's say it was sixty-five degrees. It was often sixty-five degrees in the dead of February. How delicious that would be—to wear a sweater instead of a full-length parka with Everest-level insulation.

"What is the temperature here?" he would then ask.

"Fifteen degrees." It was often fifteen degrees in Chicago in February.

"Is sixty-five better or worse than fifteen?"

"It is much, much warmer," I would say. "I wouldn't need gloves or a coat. I could just wear a shirt outside."

Then he would almost smile. As I said, schnauzers are not physically equipped to do much smiling, but I think he tried. It appeared that his steps were a bit bouncier when he discovered that it would be so much warmer.

"And when will we move?"

"When I sell the house."

"And when will that be?"

"When someone decides to buy it from me," I would say.

"Oh. Then I hope that person decides soon. We are missing out on warm weather, aren't we?"

We certainly were.

———— ∞ ————

During the first week of March, my Realtor brought me the news of an offer on my house.

"That young couple from a couple of weeks ago. They really liked the house, but were afraid that they couldn't afford it. They're going to make an offer."

I wondered if that meant they would be making an absurdly low offer, hoping that I would be desperate.

I wasn't. Not yet, anyhow.

The offer came in lower, but not absurdly lower than my asking price. I know, I know, I should have negotiated tough, played hardball with these people. But I wanted it sold. I wanted to start my life over. And the offer was close to what I wanted.

My Realtor neighbor brought the offer in for me to sign that afternoon. I signed it.

That night Rufus and I stopped by the pond, still a thin, reflective slab of ice. He stretched his front leg. The broken bone had healed, and the fur had grown back, yet he remained a little tentative at times, as if his muscles were still adjusting to the repaired bone.

"You sold the house, right? Is that what that lady from across the street said?"

"I did. I signed the papers. Unless something happens, I move out by the end of the month. We can move out."

"Did you make money like you wanted?" he asked as we started walking again. He limped now, ever so slightly. I could see the hitch in his step. No trauma goes forever unnoticed.

No break or injury goes away without leaving a scar, a limp, a hitch, some reminder of the pain in the past. Perhaps the poor dog would always limp a little. I suspect we could never enter any dog agility trials in the future. We hadn't done so in the past, so it was no great loss. Limping is better than disabled— and much, much better than dead.

"Did you make money? You talk about money a lot."

I scowled. I did not talk about money all that much. Maybe it just seems that way to a dog. Money is a worry—especially for someone now no longer gainfully employed.

"I sort of broke even, I guess. I didn't make any money. I didn't lose any money."

We went another block. Then he asked one more question that night. "But will you have enough money to buy my crunchies?"

Early the next morning, my Realtor neighbor returned with a book's thickness of papers, all relating to the contract and the expectations of sale and liens and taxes and mortgage approvals and who knows what else. I signed them all, thinking that no one reads any of it. Or do they? Perhaps I should have. But I didn't.

"Listen, sweetie, I know that I shouldn't ask . . . an inconvenience, but . . ."

"Ask what?" I replied.

"Well, the couple who are buying your house are outside in my car. They wondered if they could come in and take some measurements of the rooms. To plan out furniture. That sort of thing. You don't have to say yes. They can come back later."

Mounds of boxes still populated most rooms. I had packed up three-quarters of what I needed, but that was all. There remained a shambled, hillbilly-ish, as-seen-on-the-*Cops*-TV-show quality to the house. I remained a shambles as well, in well-worn sweatpants and a mismatched sweatshirt, my hair pulled back with a band, no makeup, a loose fuzziness of slippers on my feet.

I know what I would have said two months earlier.

"Sure. Let them come in. They do know I'm packing, right?"

"They do. They have their little boy with them. Rufus is okay with little people?"

I stopped for just a moment, just a fraction. I felt a cloud over my heart. I felt the familiar, and almost welcome tightness about my heart and throat.

"Sure. He's fine with them. He may bark some when they come in."

Rufus did not bark once. He did not jump or bounce or get excited at all.

The young couple—a pretty couple, or should that be a handsome couple?—came in, excitement and fear and joy and anticipation radiating from them, like the northern lights.

"Are you sure it's not an imposition us being here?" the wife asked. "We don't want to intrude." I had been told their names, of course, but I did not want to know their names. I had been introduced, but I did not want to know who these people are or were or will be. This would be easier. "No problem," I said. I smiled. "I hope you can overlook the packing supplies and the mess. It'll be cleaned out when I leave—that I promise."

She was blond, tiny, with deep-set blue eyes. Like a perfect Swedish princess, her eyes wide, her smile quick. He was darker. Taller. Handsome.

The little boy . . . "This is Tyler. He's four."

"Four and a half," Tyler said, holding up four fingers.

He had perfect blond hair like his mother's and had her eyes and her easy, welcoming smile. He had tiny, little-boy jeans on with a sweatshirt and tiny, perfect black sneakers. He had his hands in his jean jacket pockets, as if his parents had instructed him not to touch anything and keeping his hands involved would help him obey.

"I'll stay in the kitchen with Maya. We can talk about the neighborhood and who's putting their house up for sale. Take your time measuring."

"It's really just the bedrooms. We don't have that much furniture and . . . well, we want to figure out where it goes."

Tyler saw Rufus standing in the kitchen. The dog just stood there. This was most unlike him. He usually reacted vigorously, energetically, to visitors. Today, he remained impassive. He just stood there, like a perfectly positioned statue.

"They have a dog," he said, pointing to Rufus.

"That's Rufus," I said. "Would you like to pet him?"

Tyler remained solemn, but nodded in earnest. His mother said, "If it's okay with you."

Tyler sat on the floor with Rufus, in the kitchen, as Maya and I sat in the two upholstered chairs and chatted about inconsequential things, like snow removal and lawn services and where I might be heading.

Rufus had never been a fan of small children. He tolerated the few he had met, but would quickly make himself scarce after only a minute or two. Not so today. Tyler carefully and respectfully patted him, stroking his back and head, very gentle for a four-year-old. He was smiling, and I think Rufus might have tried to smile as well.

It took my buyers nearly twenty minutes to do all their measuring. I was happy to let them have the time. The woman glowed with expectations of the future—here at this house, inside these walls, expecting to build a future, holding onto a golden promise of a shared life.

"Tyler, are you ready to go?"

Tyler obediently rose, patted Rufus once more, then walked to his mother, who took his hand. He leaned up to her and she leaned down to him. He whispered into her ear. She stood up, offered an odd smile, and said, "No, honey, he doesn't."

She must have seen my expression.

She looked at her firstborn son, with his perfect blond hair and blue eyes, and then back to me.

"He wanted to know if the dog comes with the house. He loves dogs."

I saw the look in Rufus's eyes—as if he had been afraid that he might have been a condition of the sale.

I knelt down to Tyler and looked him in the eyes.

My heart was breaking and I could not show that pain to anyone.

"Tyler, Rufus and I have to stay together. Rufus has been with me since he was a little puppy. And he tells me things. We need to be together. But maybe, when you move in here . . ."

I looked up at his mother before continuing. She shrugged as if to say "maybe—go ahead."

". . . when you move in here, maybe you can get your own little dog."

Tyler brightened.

"Really?"

"We'll see, Tyler," his mother cautioned. I already knew the answer. So did Tyler, I am sure.

I asked the perfect little boy one more question before I stood up.

"What would you call your dog?"

Tyler scrunched his face, deep in thought. Picking a name would be a big assignment for a perfect little boy.

"I would call him Johnnie."

"That's the name of his best friend at preschool," his mother explained.

I took a deep breath, then another. I would remain composed. I would. I looked square in the young boy's eyes.

"That's a very good name, Tyler. A very good name."

Validation.

13

Estate sales should be held in the summer, when doors can stay open and no one tracks mud into the house. But I had to move now, and we were in the gray month of March—sleet in the morning and the air grew raw and angry by noon. The good thing about an estate sale in the winter is that you have so little competition. All the estate sale and garage sale addicts out there—and you know who you are—have been inactive for months and months now, at least in the north. Down south, I don't think you face the same deprivation, but in Chicago, only the insane hold garage sales in the winter. So I knew I had a lot of pent-up demand going for me.

I sold virtually everything that I had decided not to take with me. Two weeks earlier, I rented a pack-it-yourself storage container that a nice man dropped off in my driveway. I filled it with boxes, one sofa, two chairs, one table, four kitchen chairs, one bed frame, one relatively new HDTV, a few end tables, a wardrobe of clothes, and not much else. I would buy a mattress and box spring wherever I ultimately landed.

People bought everything else that made up my previous life. Old framed artwork. Desks. Odd tables. Two complete silverware sets. Dishes. An overflow of books. Rugs. A leather sofa. Three televisions—one an ancient analog model. A display cabinet. A full set of furniture from the basement. Tools. Cans of old paint. (Really—a nearly full gallon of off-white sold for a dollar.) Wrapping paper. Towels. Sheets. Pillows. Bed frames. Bookcases. Candles. Lamps. A large dining room table. Fans. Another desk. Tell you what: walk through your house. Everything in your house was something that I sold in one form or another. Mixers. Mixing bowls. Measuring cups—I had collected three sets somehow. Place mats. Napkins. Candle holders. Vases. (I did keep one vase for myself—a Mother's Day gift.) A box of scarves. A box of mittens and gloves. More glasses and mugs and plates than I could count. A full set of Waterford tumblers and wine glasses (which I had used perhaps six times in ten years). Serving plates. A toaster oven. Three coffeemakers. (I kept one.) A huge bag of Tupperware and Tupperware-like containers. Five plastic bins filled with Christmas decorations. An old camp stove that I had forgotten I had. An artificial Christmas tree. Three Christmas wreaths and one springtime wreath. Three bicycles. Two animal carriers—now too small for the adult schnauzer in the family. Shovels. Rakes. An electric tire pump (which I did not know how to use). Two garbage cans. Two large armoires. An exercise bike (which I never used). A treadmill (which I used once last year). An old cedar chest.

I am certain that I have forgotten more items than I remembered.

My head spins at trying to remember why I bought these things, when I bought them, and if I ever used some of them.

I made enough money in two days of estate selling to pay for my new-to-me Volvo wagon.

I began to feel lighter and more unencumbered as each person walked out of my house clutching some new addition to his or her life—and a subtraction from mine.

Rufus had been sent to the Realtor neighbor's house for the sale. It would do him no good to have to face the hundreds of customers who tromped through the house.

That night—the second night, after the estate sale had ended, and after the house had been emptied, and after I got Rufus's leash and supply of crunchies—he stopped at the corner as we walked and asked, "What happened to all your things? The sofa thing that I sleep on in that sunny room is gone. What do I do now?"

I had explained to him earlier how an estate sale worked, but I am pretty sure some of our human endeavors were simply beyond him.

"I sold them all. We're moving, remember? I don't have room in the car for a sofa."

He walked along for a while, obviously digesting the information.

"My bed is still there, isn't it? I didn't notice."

"It is. We're taking that with us."

Another long pause.

"Okay, then."

I gave him a treat, which he crunched up happily.

"But where will I sleep in the sunny room? The sofa is gone."

"On the floor, if you want to sleep in there."

The room stood empty.

"The floor? Really?"

We turned the corner of our street.

"Yes, Rufus. The floor. But we are leaving in a few days. Then everything changes."

He remained silent until we arrived at the driveway.

"I don't like change," he said. "Change is bad."

———∞———

Walking through the empty house was not as painful or emotional for me as I once feared. Stripped of all the mementos and trappings of my previous life, empty rooms were just that: empty. There were no ghosts of memories, no emotional trauma from seeing a reminder of my husband or my son. It was simply architecture, simply shelter. Nothing more than walls and floors and ceilings and windows and doors.

The people who conducted the estate sale had come in and done a thorough sweeping and cleaning job as part of their process. They even filled all the nail holes in the walls with Spackle. Both the cleaning and spackling were codicils in the contract. (How often have you heard the words *Spackle* and *codicil* in the same sentence? Never, I bet.)

Rufus and I walked through every room. I felt like I was leaving a hotel room and making one last sweep to ensure that I had not left a sock under the bed or my cell phone charger still plugged into the wall.

I hadn't done any of those things.

Rufus sniffed about, checking corners and windowsills. I knew he would not talk to me during the day. (I kept promising myself to ask him why he remained silent in the sun, and I kept forgetting. Perhaps it is not important.) Yet I knew he could listen and understand most of what I said.

"So that's it, Rufus. Everything is gone. The car is packed up. The things I am keeping will be shipped to us once I . . . when we find a place to live."

He looked up at me.

"And yes, I have a bag of your crunchies in the car. And your bed."

I knew that satisfied him.

A door had been closed on what had been my life. It was a door that I had chosen to close and not one that had been slammed in my face. I had some control over this, some degree of personal choice. It had not punched into my gut in the middle of the night, leaving me without breath, without hope, without a real life for so long.

Now, I got to do the inventing. I got to do the creating. A new life, my new life, would rise from the ashes of this one, like a phoenix of sorts, a great bird arising from the detritus of an old life that no longer worked.

The car was packed. I had two large duffle bags filled. I had a smaller computer bag—I now owned a very small laptop—which also held my cell phone charger and e-book reader. I had a small, unimpressive digital camera. Perhaps I would need to document some of this trip, but I didn't plan on making it a scrapbooked adventure. There were three boxes, taped securely. I carried a set of sheets and towels, a minimum of dishes, cups, plates, spoons, forks, and an open box containing a toaster, an electric kettle, and the ingredients for making coffee. I had stayed at . . . well . . . less-expensive hotels in the past and the "coffee service" that is often included with the room is coffee in name only. There is always too much sugar, not enough coffee, and the "coffee lightener" only changed the coffee from a mud-black to a mud-brown. From the first moment, I knew I would bring my own coffee accoutrements with me. I would have packed them in their own suitcase, but I had sold all the rest of my luggage in the estate sale. A cardboard box would do just fine.

I debated what to do with Rufus in the car for what might be weeks of travel. There are some who say a dog should be put in a halter and fastened to the seat belt, ensuring the animal's safety. There are others who argue against it. Whenever he rode in the car before, Rufus would lie on the front seat, his head down, his eyes nearly closed, looking as if he expected to die at any moment—not from a crash or my terrible driving (which wasn't true) but from his general heightened anxiety over being in an automobile in the first place. I did not want to put him in a harness and fasten him to the seat belt. I am pretty certain he would not have liked that. Instead, I placed his crate in the back of the car. Since it was only the two of us traveling, I had folded down the back passenger seats. I placed his crate snug up against the back of the front passenger seat and used a cargo belt to secure it to the floor, so in the event of an accident, the crate would remain secured. Rufus could see me from the crate, and I could turn and glance back to him as I drove. I hoped that being slightly confined would ease his anxieties. There was more than enough open space for a bowl of food and water to be placed down when we stopped.

I laid a road atlas on the front seat, a traveling mug for coffee in the cup holder, and my iPod securely plugged into the car's audio system. I had sunglasses in the door compartment, a baseball hat to wear if I rode with an open window, and a bag of hard candy hidden in the glove box. (Rufus has long ago decided that he expects to taste whatever it is that I am eating. I don't think he should be eating candy—and if I keep it out of sight, so much the better.)

I had filled up the gas tank the day before, had the oil changed a few days before that, had all the fluids checked and filled, and had the tires properly inflated. I had the owner's card and the insurance card in a little leather-like folder in the glove box. I had the emergency kit my husband had given me years ago—flares, signs, a flashlight, tools, bandages, blanket, jumper cables, tow rope—tucked away in a small storage nook at the rear of the car.

Every item on the exit list had a "go" status attached to it.

I put the key in the door. I had my hand on the key. I looked up at the house that once held my hopes and dreams and my life and my husband and my son and I could not stop it—the tears began to flow. I sobbed and sobbed. My heart tightened. My throat tightened. My cheeks grew wet. I began to sniffle as I sobbed, the tears just flowing, unexpected, unbidden. Rufus had been lying down in his crate, his head nestled between his front paws. He raised his head, startled, I imagine, at my outburst. Then he stood up and pressed his little snout between the thin bars of his crate. His impatience or anxiety was marked by his slight movements, shifting his weight from side to side, raising one paw, then another. Then he growled. And then he barked. I am pretty sure I mentioned that he did not tend to bark, so his bark came as a surprise to me. Then he barked again, more emphatic this time, and again, trying to get me to pay attention.

What if I was doing the wrong thing? What if all this turned into a huge mistake? My friends are here. My life had been here—is here still, right? The remnants are still here. Why am I running away from it all? I should find a small apartment here. I could stay here. I could do freelance editing work again. I could go back to church again, and I could join the singles group. I know people here. I have a history here. What am I doing, really? Maybe Beth was right that I am simply running away from my past. Am I doing that? Have I not accepted what happened yet?

All this raced through my thoughts at a million miles an hour, amid my sobs and wailing and tears.

Rufus barked again, louder this time, more heartfelt, if a dog's bark can be described as heartfelt. I turned to him and placed my fingers through the opening. He stuck his nose against my flesh. Then he backed away a little and just stared at me. His eyes were worried, but not really. Concerned, perhaps. Wondering what had upset me so much.

Then he did something he rarely does. He licked my fingers. Rufus, unlike other dogs, other slobbery and obnoxious dogs, did not lick much. He just did not do it. Maybe people tasted bad to him. He would sniff, but not lick and slobber, like the big knuckleheaded dog we were leaving next door. But this time he did, gently, delicately, as if he were trying to reassure me somehow by doing something completely out of his character.

I sniffed loudly. I wiped at my face with the back of my hand. I took a deep breath.

At least I wore no mascara that would run and make my face look like a zombie-woman.

"Is it okay, Rufus? Will it be okay? We are doing the right thing, aren't we?"

Rufus pushed his forehead against my fingers, still wrapped around the bars of the crate.

I took another deep breath.

"I guess we're doing the right thing. We are."

I switched the engine on and backed carefully out of the driveway. As I began to drive away, an unfamiliar car approached. The car held the handsome couple and their son. The boy saw me, I guess, and pressed his face to the window and waved. I waved back. I could see the excitement and happiness radiate from his parents.

This adventure I embarked on, this exit and entrance—it was the right thing to do.

In the rear view mirror, I saw little Tyler jump from the car and literally hop toward the front door. He was home.

Validation.

Note to readers: you can skip the next six thousand words or so. Really. I won't mind. And maybe you should. The next few days in my life are a pitiful, wallowing, depressive maelstrom, awash with doubt, anxiety, seller's remorse, mover's remorse, self-recrimination, depression, and more regret and self-pity. I became paralyzed, certain I had made a mistake. I was certain that I would or should move back to Illinois. The only amusing and interesting event that occurred during these few days of gypsy-like travel is that Rufus became terrified by a horse, and then became fixated on the potential threat of horses invading our new home. For a dog that once stood nose-to-nose with a barking Great Dane, that surprising streak of fear surfaced in my good dog. But other than that, it was all bad. But I have to write those words. I really do. It's the only way the story is complete. But skip ahead if you like.

Things get better. They really do.

14

From my childhood, I remembered Bedford, Pennsylvania, a stop on the Pennsylvania Turnpike, being advertised on billboards beside the highway as the "City of Motels." As I neared the exit, I wondered why that would be so. Bedford appeared like a pleasant small town, with a fort or a tavern or something or other dating back to before the Revolutionary War. But that would not explain the plethora of motels in the middle of that state. Perhaps, back when cars went slower, when people traveled slower, a few hundred miles out of New York City brought you close to evening and a need to stop and sleep, and by then, you were in Bedford. Traveling times have diminished over the years. I could leave Chicago early in the morning, stopping only for coffee and gas, and be in Pittsburgh in time for an early dinner. If I pushed, I could make Philadelphia while restaurants were still open for dinner. I had never done that, but knew that I could, if pushed, and if I didn't get too nervous at setting cruise control at seventy-six miles an hour. Or maybe seventy-nine, and taking a chance at being stopped for speeding.

So, I imagined, Bedford did not have the same stopping power it once had. But still, there were a lot of motels right off the turnpike. I had Googled the place before I left and found one motel that advertised itself as "pet friendly." I had made reservations, just to be safe, just for the first night. From then on, I would be fancy-free and let the highways take me—us— where they would.

Rufus made a show of stretching and shaking when I opened the crate door. I carried his food and water into the motel room, and told Rufus I would be right back, since I feared he might get nervous in the new surroundings and start to bark, then I went to retrieve my smaller suitcase and cardboard box with coffee-making supplies. I went back to the car for my pillow. I have always found it difficult to use strange pillows. They were either too soft or too hard or smelled odd.

I led Rufus out of the room and down the hall and outside, to the large field behind the motel. One could hear the muted rumble of the turnpike only a block or two away. Perhaps that's why this motel was more than reasonable.

"Is this our new house?" Rufus asked as he sniffed a thicket of tall grass. "It smells funny out here."

I anticipated his question. He had no frame of reference. He could live in a hotel room, as long as he got daily walks and crunchies.

"No, Rufus, this is just for tonight. We have a ways to go to get to the ocean."

"The ocean is far."

"Did you mind the ride? You slept for a while, didn't you?"

"I don't know. Maybe. The car wiggles . . ."

"Vibrates."

"Yes, that. It makes me sleepy."

"So the ride isn't as bad as you thought, was it?"

He scratched at the dark Pennsylvania soil with his back legs.

"No. Since I'm in my crate and all."

We walked back to the Johnson Motor Court and Lodge in silence, the hum and thrum of the turnpike just audible as the breeze carried it along, a constant backdrop. Rufus stopped more often to sniff and examine. It was all new to him. Every morning and every night for a while would be new to him.

I looked up at the stars, only a handful visible through the ground clutter of neon and sodium vapor illumination that pocked the area around the turnpike exit. And I tried to prevent the soft, insistent rise of a nameless dread that slowly unclenched its fist under my heart.

I am doing the right thing. I know I am.

We walked across the parking lot, Rufus's nails clicking with each step.

Then why am I so terrified?

I used the keycard to unlock the hallway door. A faint odor of disinfectant and cigarette smoke lingered.

I'm making a mistake. I am making a mistake. I should have never sold my house.

I attempted to push the thoughts from my mind, but the more I tried, the louder their thump and drumbeat became. Rufus circled around a dozen times at the foot of the bed, sniffing and nosing at the orange blanket. He looked up at me several times.

"I know. It smells funny. But it is only for tonight. We keep going right after breakfast." He settled in a small coil of blanket, rested his head on his paws, and stared at me.

I knew what he was thinking. Or maybe . . . I just projected my fear onto him.

Why did you bring me to this terrible place?

⚬⚬⚬

I felt certain that I could not bring Rufus with me to the motel's breakfast room, though I bet some owners do, their yappy, fussy, scrabbling mini-dogs tucked in their purses or coat pockets. I had a yogurt, a glass of what might have been orange juice, a banana, a toasted bagel with two packets of strawberry jam, and two cinnamon rolls (they were on the small side). I had two cups of coffee, which actually tasted quite good, surprisingly. I toasted one slice of white bread and layered on two slabs of butter. Rufus liked toast. I took a third coffee with me in a cardboard cup and presented the toast to Rufus, torn in four pieces on a small paper plate. He ate it eagerly.

The sun had already risen when I took Rufus out for our morning constitutional. He may have questions or observations about the trip or the motel or my rising anxiety, but he did not speak, as is his norm. Just as well. I didn't think I could answer any of his questions without developing a hitch in my voice, some tremor that would lead him to other questions—and further worry for both of us.

No, silence was good. Especially for today, for this morning.

We got back on the turnpike and headed east. I planned on turning south at Harrisburg, toward Baltimore and then Washington, D.C. From there I would drive to Richmond and perhaps a little further for today. Then I would stop somewhere for the night. It wasn't that far, but much of the route went through or around populated areas with lots of beltways and route changes and decisions to make every few miles. A spiderweb of decisions. Decisions made me nervous—or at least driving decisions did. My new Volvo had a built-in GPS system that I programmed first for Baltimore. I would stop there and tap in a new destination. The problem lay in the fact that there were multiple ways to arrive at my final destination, perhaps dozens upon dozens, and the GPS may have picked the short-est, but not the easiest or the one with the fewest turns. All I could do was select the option for "Maximize Freeways."

I suppose if I were being an astute, observant writer, I could use this GPS method as a metaphor for my life—multiple paths to one specific goal—without a clear "Best Route" as an option. There are many ways to reach paradise. Not the Christian par-adise—there's only one way there—but a temporal paradise . . . you know what I mean, right? Find personal satisfaction and self-worth through working—or not working. It's the same destination, satisfaction, but there are two very different routes to take to get there.

To get to Baltimore and beyond, I had reviewed the route I intended to take on my road atlas and marked down, on a four-by-six card, every highway I thought I would need to be on to get there.

South from Harrisburg, it would be I-83, into Maryland, and to the north side of Baltimore. Then take 695—either west or south—around Baltimore proper, to 95 South. A second road paralleled that route that didn't seem to be a labeled as an interstate, but was marked with 295, and a different color than 95. Was this route faster? It might be, since it angled more to the east of Washington.

How do you know what's best? Unless you live there, there is no telling what route works better.

Like life. That's the GPS metaphor again. Maybe I could write an article about that for some magazine. Maybe. I would need to remember all the nuances I was considering now, yet at the moment, I was getting more nervous about my choices, even though they were miles and hours distant.

From Washington, it would be 95 around the city and on to Richmond.

Rufus had settled into his crate nicely, hardly stirring when I took the ticket at the start of our turnpike segment. We drove on, into the sun, into a chilly but clear day in Pennsylvania.

I wondered when it would be warm enough to drive with the window down.

———— ∞∞ ————

I stopped for lunch at a McDonald's somewhere west of Baltimore. Rufus stirred and stretched as the car came to a stop. He sniffed the air. I am sure that he could smell the grease, thick in the air around the fast-food restaurant. I know I could, and I'm not a dog with a sensitive nose. I put some water in his bowl, a handful of kibble in his dish, let him out of the crate, and left both front windows open a crack. It was still very chilly and quite cloudy—so, please, no hate mail from readers telling me I am a negligent pet owner for leaving poor Rufus in a sweltering car. Besides—I was going to eat quickly, keeping the car in full view the whole time. It's probably not enough for my more militant readers, but when you're alone and with a dog, you do what you have to do.

I ordered the two cheeseburgers meal. I bought a third burger on top of that, which I would share with Rufus. I timed my lunch. From start to finish: fourteen minutes. I know, it's barbaric to wolf down any meal that quickly, but when they hand you your food even as you finish ordering it, that's not a fast time.

I came back to the car, split the third burger with the good dog Rufus, and then took him out into the field behind the restaurant.

"We are not going to live here," I said, knowing he would have asked if he were to speak, which he wouldn't do—that I could be sure of. "We're going to get back in the car and drive a few more hours until we stop for the night. Okay?"

Rufus looked up at me like he understood.

Even if he didn't, it was what I intended on doing.

I reset the GPS for Richmond, studied my road atlas for a long time, got gas, and continued on my trek.

∽∾∽

In the past—while a widow, not when I was with Jacob—I liked driving to Pennsylvania to visit my mother. I had a destination, I knew the route, I knew where I would get radio reception for the NPR stations along the way, I knew to wait to stop for lunch until Ohio. So the drive to Pennsylvania—some ten hours in length, depending on the weather and how fast I felt like driving—was . . . like going on a silent monastic retreat for me. No talking. No arguments. No instructions on the proper technique of passing or staying in the right-hand lane. There was no one who would look askance at my stopping for Starbucks every forty-five minutes or so. And since the route and all the environments were so well known, I could switch off my conscious thoughts and set my mind to autopilot. I loved that feeling of letting my mind go free, reliving incidents from the distant past. (Like my senior prom. That came up often. Go figure.) Solutions and options to current situations would appear in my thoughts, almost miraculously. I could daydream a hundred different scenarios and no evil inner voice would interrupt, saying that I had a deadline to meet, or a floor that needed vacuuming. No, I really enjoyed the long, desolate stretches of driving alone. A solitary road trip became great therapy, and inexpensive—only dependent on the price of gasoline, I guess.

I looked forward to that same carefree drive this trip.

It was not happening. Not in the least.

At first I blamed the newness of the route, then the newness of the car, then the fact that good dog Rufus traveled with me.

None of that mattered, I decided, somewhere to the southwest of Baltimore.

The unsettled feeling, the dislocated feeling, I think, all stemmed from the fact that I had nowhere to be. I owned no home now—no more home base. I had no real destination waiting for me. I had become a ship adrift—and even worse. Eventually, even a wayward ship is blown by the prevailing winds into some place, some rocky shoal, some barren island. I was not like that ship. I could go anywhere and everywhere. Yes, we headed toward the ocean, but the east coast of America is like . . . well, like one long piece of possibilities. I could spend years looking and never find a home. True, I had narrowed the choices down—a little—by starting in Virginia Beach and heading south. I may not have mentioned that decision before. I did tell Rufus, I think, even though Virginia Beach meant nothing to him. It did have two names, which he liked.

If one went further north from Virginia Beach, one could experience real winters, with gales and blizzards and snow tinted with salt. I wanted to escape all that, I think. Going south would not make one immune from storms, just the low temperatures of the dreaded nor'easters.

But after eliminating a long swath of northward shoreline, I had a still-too-large path of potential waiting for me. How would I find the "right" place to live? How would I find a house in a nice neighborhood? It took living in Wheaton for years to know what areas might be considered less than desirable. Now I would have to make a decision in the matter of a few hours or days.

So my thoughts remained jumbled and unfocused, unable to rest on any topic, any event, any incident for long.

I did not like the feeling.

And every moment that I remained unsettled became another moment when I had time to almost regret the decision to leave Wheaton and head into a much more unsettled future. I mean, I could be making things worse by moving, rather than better.

I suppose I could go back to Wheaton. I mean, I could tell people that I just didn't like the East Coast. They would welcome me back. And they wouldn't think ill of me for returning. People do it all the time—admit that they made mistakes. It's not irrevocable.

Then those thoughts would leave me for a while.

Bet never for good. At least not during these first few days.

We made it to Williamsburg, Virginia, that day. I was tired of driving. Baltimore and Washington were like one big sub-urb with lots of traffic, all the time.

Rattled would be a good descriptive term for how I felt. Just rattled—emotionally as well as physically. Rufus seemed none the worse for wear. That evening, as we walked around the hotel, he admitted that he had slept most of the day.

"I liked that place with the food," he said. "We could stay there."

He meant the McDonald's. He was trying to be helpful.

We were staying at an Embassy Suites Hotel, a few miles from Williamsburg. Rufus appeared impressed when we entered the suite, sniffing it very carefully.

"No, we are not living here," I explained again. "We are only staying for one night."

I had room service deliver a hamburger. Room service can be expensive and I wasn't all that hungry. Rufus had a third of my burger. These were not great dog-feeding habits, but my stressful situation made it hard to keep to a healthy routine. For some reason, in a hotel, I lose the willpower to deny him a bite or two when he stares up at me while I eat. I'm a wimp, I know, but I was also tired. Very tired.

<hr />

The next morning, I felt much better. I helped myself to a very large breakfast. I brought Rufus back a small serving of scrambled eggs, which are supposed to be good for his coat.

Since we were only a few miles from historic Colonial Williamsburg, I decided to stop and walk the grounds. I had never been there before. Apparently, you have to buy a ticket to enter some of the locations, but you can visit the stores and restaurants without a fee—other than facing the lure of souvenirs.

I packed up the car, parked in a city lot, snapped on Rufus's leash, told him to be on his best behavior, and began to walk down the main street of Colonial Williamsburg—a terrifically impressive collection of old homes and shops and government buildings from the time of our nation's founding. I had already explained to Rufus that we would just be visiting and we would drive to the ocean later in the day.

Early April brings about a beautiful spring in Williamsburg, I observed. A scattering of trees and shrubs had begun to blossom and I could smell the early sweetness of bayberry bushes. Their scent feels historic. The skies were clear and the sun warmed my shoulders.

Then, all of a sudden Rufus stopped cold and scurried behind my legs, almost tripping me in his haste. A half a block away, turning the corner, and coming toward us was a roan-colored horse, his rider in Revolutionary-era garb. As they came closer, Rufus pulled away further, and found himself at the farthest limit of his retractable leash. Rather than risk his slipping out of his collar, I went toward the side of the street and bent down to the frightened dog, putting my arm around him, and held him as best I could.

"It's a horse," I whispered to him. "I bet it's a real friendly horse too."

Rufus would have none of it and tried to claw his way out of my grasp. I held tighter and the horse and rider slowly walked past us. Rufus's eyes were wide in fear and his heart thumped, almost audibly to the unaided ear.

"He won't hurt you. He won't step on you. I promise."

He eyed the animal as it made its way down the street and turned a far corner.

I hadn't expected encountering any horses today, but since this was a historical site, I suppose I should have expected it.

We walked around for another thirty minutes or so, Rufus never more than a foot or two away from my legs. His closeness made walking difficult, and nearly dangerous.

I enjoyed what I saw in Williamsburg. But when something is not shared, it is never as poignant, or as meaningful, or as beautiful as it might have been if it were shared with someone.

I gathered Rufus, still apparently nervous and concerned about the possible reappearance of the big animal, and got him into his crate in the car. He did settle down somewhat, protected in a familiar environment.

I headed south and east, and plotted the route so I would come into Virginia Beach from the north side. There were some bridges to cross to get there. I did not like long bridges. I never have. Consider it an unnatural fear. I suspect I was afraid of twisting the wheel of the car and launching myself into space. Unnatural, I know. But the fear lay there, hiding deep in my subconscious.

I managed to find the route through the city that roughly ran past the ocean. I tried to rouse Rufus to look at the water, but he didn't want to stand up as I drove. Maybe it made him feel unsettled as well. Virginia Beach is probably a lovely city, but I wasn't sure where I was going, and between the ocean and me was a wall of condos that only let me see the ocean in short gaps as I drove. On the other side of the street were restaurants, stores, and jungle mini-golf places with volcanoes and wrecked pirate ships with Jolly Roger flags fluttering in the afternoon spring breeze.

This isn't what I wanted. Not at all.

At a red light, I stopped to turn around and look at Rufus. His head was resting on his front paws, and his eyebrows went up as I turned. I tried to read his eyes—always a difficult task. I thought I saw discomfort, or some sense of impending doom. He looked like he did whenever I had to take him to the veterinarian or groomer: scared, resigned, dark, and morose.

I didn't want to see him this way.

A horn behind me sounded. The light had turned green. I drove farther down the street, hoping that as I left the city behind, I would find something that resembled home.

I didn't.

We made it as far as the south end of the city, several miles from the main drag of hotels and condos. I saw a Holiday Inn on the other side of the street—meaning it would cost a lot less than if it were really on the ocean. Still only early afternoon, I felt more tired than I had been in months and months. I didn't ask, as I checked in, if the place considered itself pet-friendly or not. Rufus would be a quiet guest, quieter and cleaner than many human guests. I asked for a room away from the street on the first floor. When it's not summer at the ocean, hotel guests can be more selective.

I carried Rufus into the room, dragged my suitcase in, pulled the decorative bed cover off the bed, and lay down, feeling most exhausted. Rufus clambered up onto the bed and lay down beside me, his head on one of the pillows. He didn't look all that comfortable that way; maybe he simply mimicked what I did every night.

When I woke up, the sun had been down for a long time. I looked out and the darkness had descended. I hurried outside, retrieved my box of coffee-making supplies, and made a large mug of very hot coffee, with three spoonfuls of powdered creamer. I sat in the lone upholstered chair and sipped. Rufus sat close by me, closer than he ever did when we were back home—the home I no longer had or could ever go back to.

I had imagined all those validation points, hadn't I? None of them were really validating my stupid choices right now.

I had three packets of cheese crackers "Made with Real Cheddar Cheese." (How much real cheddar cheese could there be in these tiny snacks?) I ate those, sharing them with Rufus, who didn't seem to like them any more than I did.

I was so tired already. Tired of traveling. I felt sure I had made a mistake, but did not know what to do to rectify it. Do I simply go home and look for an apartment for me and Rufus? But what of my . . . our plans to find a warm place to live? Do I turn my back on that?

I gathered up the leash and Rufus and I walked down the well-lit sidewalk that ran along the street. A cluster of lights glowed farther south. Maybe there would be a soft-serve ice-cream stand there. I felt a desire for a chocolate cone dipped in chocolate topping.

"What was that big thing? This morning. The big thing that scared me."

"That's called a horse, Rufus. I told you that already. Before people had cars, they rode horses everywhere."

"Do horses live at the ocean?"

"Some do, I guess. But no more than anywhere else."

"There weren't any horses at home. I never saw a horse there."

"I am sure there were horses in barns nearby—we just never went to any of them."

"If there are horses at the ocean, I'm not sure I want to live there," he said, more firmly than usual. "I don't like horses at all. They smell funny. And they could step on me."

"They wouldn't step on you. I promise."

"I don't like them."

We walked on another block. The lights grew brighter. I think it was a 7-Eleven and a gas station. Maybe I could get a Slurpee instead of a cone. I wanted something bad for me, something unnourishing. I wanted . . . I don't know what I wanted. I didn't know what I wanted at all.

Rufus stopped and sat down.

"I want to go home," he said.

I could have asked him if he meant home as in Illinois, or back to the hotel, or back in the car and his crate. I didn't want to ask him. I didn't want to know what he meant, even though I was pretty sure he meant home in Illinois. I hope he knew that we couldn't go back to that life. That life did not exist anymore. We needed to find a new life.

"Did you ask God about this?" I asked Rufus. "About wanting to go home?"

Rufus remained sitting.

"No."

"Are you going to?"

"No."

"Why? I thought you talked to God a lot."

"I do."

"Then are you going to ask him?"

"No."

"Rufus," I said with a note of exasperation in my voice, "Why not?"

"I don't like horses. Not at all. You said that some of them live at the ocean. I don't want to go there, then. You never told me about horses before. Trusting has nothing to do with horses. Nothing at all."

I bent down to him. Both his sitting and talking and my bending close to him were unusual. We always talked as we walked. Neither of us made a fuss about the process.

"Rufus, there are a lot of big animals out there. Cows, for one. They're almost as big as horses."

"Do cows live at the ocean?" He looked over his shoulder, toward the ocean, toward the muted sound of the waves.

"I don't think so. Maybe somewhere, but not around here."

"I don't want to be here. I want things the way they used to be. I want my bed down by the kitchen. We don't even have a kitchen anymore. Nothing is like it was. I don't like that. And now, you tell me about horses and cows. I don't like surprises like that."

I stood back up. Talking to Rufus at close range felt abnormal.

"I'm sorry, Rufus, but we can't go back to the way things were. We can't go back to the old house. A new family lives there now. We have to find a new place, with a new kitchen and a great place to put your bed—where maybe you could lay in the sun during the day."

"What about the horses?"

I sighed. Rufus made me sigh often. How do you calm the heart of a dog—an intelligent dog—but one that just can't grasp enigmatic complexities of the world, like horses and cows and the threat of being stepped on.

"Rufus," I said in my best parental voice. "We have to keep moving. Maybe we'll find the right place tomorrow. Wherever it is, there will not be any horses around. I promise you that. But we can't go back. We have to go forward. We have to give up what we can't have anymore. I think you can understand that. You said we have to trust God. Right? You said that."

Rufus stared at his front paws.

"I guess. Maybe. But I don't like this change. I liked the way things were. Except for the cold. And the snow. And getting run over by cars. Other than that, I liked it. And there were no horses there at all. None at all."

This time I bent to him, not to hear him, but to hug him tight to me.

We were both lost and alone and dislocated and we wanted what we had before and would never, ever get back.

"God did say to trust him," Rufus added, his voice soft, almost a whisper. "I don't know what that means exactly. But I think he will show us what he wants us to do. Right? He does that sort of thing, right?"

"He does, Rufus. I'm pretty sure he does."

I was too tired to tell Rufus that I am still not on speaking terms with the Almighty. Once you stop talking, starting up a conversation is all that much harder. Silence begins to solidify, like concrete. Once it is set, it is terribly difficult to break up. But Rufus talks with him. God will protect Rufus, right? And if Rufus is safe, doesn't a little of that spill over onto me? I think it might. I hope it does. I guess we'll see . . .

I stood up, and then we walked back to the Holiday Inn, both of us quiet. I felt better. I felt tired, but I felt better.

Just before we got to the hotel parking lot, I said to Rufus, "Tomorrow will be a better day. And there won't be any horses at all. I promise."

It was a promise that I hoped I would be able to keep.

15

I had to drive back west, toward Norfolk, to go south again, into North Carolina. A very thin, red line ran down the sliver of land—the Barrier Islands. At the end of a very long stretch of land, a dotted line crossed a blue expanse of Pamlico Sound. It indicated a ferry, and I checked with the desk clerk at the Holiday Inn and asked if that ferry ran all year. He assured me it did. It had better. If it didn't, it would mean a long ride back north, to get to a bridge that crossed the sound as it narrowed, close to land.

I guess it really didn't matter. I had nowhere I had to be. But I sure hoped that the ferry was operating.

I wonder how Rufus would take to a ferry voyage—even a short one. Would he treat it as an unwelcome surprise—like horses?

Using my handy road atlas, I found my way to the two-lane road that ran down the center of the barrier islands. I passed Kill Devil Hills and Nags Head and the site of man's first powered air flight. I drove past lots of small towns with homes that I knew, without stopping or asking, were so far out of my price range—multistory places with lots of glass and cedar siding and swimming pools and a great expanse of seashore and palmetto grass and endless views. I suppose if I was rich, I might have stopped and looked at some of the places that featured FOR SALE signs, gently clapping into the strong Atlantic breeze.

But I wasn't rich. Not even close.

I drove through the Cape Hatteras National Seashore. My stomach reminded me of the time—lunchtime—but there were no McDonald's along the pristine seashore. Nor had I expected any. I arrived in Ocracoke and found the ferry.

It did operate, and the last ferry of the day would be departing in less than a half hour. The ferry, the brochure claimed, would hold fifty-three cars. Upon departure, there were twelve autos and one small truck on board. The very nice young man who took my ticket said I could take the dog out on deck, as long as he remained on a leash.

I decided to let Rufus decide.

"Rufus, we're on a boat that will take us across the sound, which is sort of like the ocean, but not quite as wavy or bumpy. You can walk around with me out on the deck if you want. I'll open up your crate. If you want to come out for a walk and look at the ocean, come out. If not, you can stay in your crate."

He looked at me, then peered out the side window. He looked at me again.

"It's very safe. No horses. No cows, either. And all the cars are stopped."

Gingerly, he stepped out of the crate. I snapped the leash on him and led him from the car. The ferry started with a loud whooshing sound, as the propellers bit into the water. Rufus snugged himself against my leg, but did not try to retreat to the car. He tried his best to be brave, I guess.

I led him up the steps to the top deck and an open deck space, with a scattering of benches that looked forward, facing the wind and the sun. The ferry rolled and swayed a bit, even though the waters of the sound were calm—at least to my non-nautical eyes.

"Rufus, the boat will bounce a little bit. The water is not as smooth as a road. But it is nothing to be afraid of."

We walked a little closer to the rail, Rufus sniffing loudly.

"That's salt water you smell. And maybe some fish."

He snorted once, then again, then he sat down, facing the wind, his ears slightly back, half-flapping in the breeze. I could plainly see he enjoyed it. At least that is what it looked like to me. His eyes were half-closed as well, as if he were deliberately sunning himself.

You could see where we were heading: a small green thickness of land some miles to the south. From there we would continue south, past Morehead City and on to Wilmington. From there we would travel on to Myrtle Beach. I knew people who disparaged Myrtle Beach as the "Redneck Riviera," but perhaps there was a patch there of cute little houses, and a home waiting for us.

Perhaps. That would be validation . . . right?

I am not a gypsy. I don't like traveling. I just decided that I don't like this at all. I've been in three hotel rooms . . . and I don't like it.

So if I find a place . . . how will I know that I found the right place? How will I be able to tell?

I pulled my sweater a little tighter. A sliver of crispness in the air kept everything fresh and clean smelling.

Maybe there'll be some sort of sign.

Rufus snorted again.

Yeah, that's what I figured too.

<hr>

We made it across the sound. Rufus appeared to enjoy the ferry ride. I know I did. We got into the car and drove on, now into the early afternoon. We had skipped lunch today. Well, I had skipped lunch. At home—which doesn't exist anymore, I know, I know—Rufus had food available to him all day. He would nibble on it now and again. But I needed more definitive and better-timed feedings than that. I wanted food. Rufus had already eaten a few bites from his bowl of kibble in the car.

After a short distance, I noticed a sign that read WELCOME TO ATLANTIC BEACH. (Weren't all the beaches I had been seeing Atlantic beaches?) Under that was listed a population count of just over 1,800. I liked the sound of that. Pretty small for a town, but the idea just appealed to me. I pulled over for just a moment to check my map. A larger city lay across the sound—Morehead City—connected by a long bridge. That meant a place for grocery stores and merchandise all well within reach.

Hmm . . .

I drove slowly. There would not be a lot of impatient beach traffic this early in the year. No wall of condos faced the ocean. Just homes. Some duplexes, I think. The tallest building I saw could only have been two stories high—three if you counted the parking area underneath—since most of the homes were up on pilings or stilts or whatever they were called. Spider leg construction. To be honest here, I felt certain that I could not afford oceanfront regardless of the number of stories . . . but a street or two back from the water? Maybe. The houses were smaller, more modest—some obviously rental units, some looking lived in, with current residents.

Hmm.

Okay, this was the first possibility I had encountered so far on my trip. I know I was anxious to find a place I could label as a "possibility." I turned down a street a block off the ocean, a street of modest homes—some on stilts, some not, some cottages, some more substantial places. And a few with FOR SALE signs in front as well.

But my stomach growled again. That always proved to be a very bad influence on my decision-making abilities. Never go grocery shopping when you're hungry, right? I never did shopping of any type hungry. I would buy things just to get out of the store so I would be able to go elsewhere and find food.

A few blocks further on, I saw a sign for the Shark Shack. There were picnic tables out front—a restaurant perfectly suited for a dog if I've ever seen one.

I sat at an outside picnic table, under an umbrella, and ordered the grouper bites and the shrimp. Rufus sat on the ground beside me, sniffing and squinting in the sunlight. For April, it was nearing T-shirt warmth. I liked that. A lot. Rufus liked the grouper bites. I know—I'm a bad pet owner. But he was hungry. And I am sure he had never tasted grouper before.

The waitress—Cindi, her name tag said—came out and asked if I wanted anything else.

"Coffee, please, with cream and sugar."

"What about the dog?" she asked and smiled.

"I think he's had enough for today. And he doesn't drink coffee."

She returned with a large, thick mug.

"Do you live around here?" I asked. I seldom engaged in conversation with strangers. But here, well, I played the role of the stranger.

"I do. Well, across the bridge. Over in Morehead City."

"Is it a nice place to live?" I asked. Then I added, "I'm thinking of moving . . . well, I am moving . . . and wondered about what this place is like."

I didn't want to appear like a stalker or anything weird. I wanted to sound normal.

"Yeah, I guess it's okay. I've only lived here for five years. My husband is a drill instructor at Camp Lejeune. You know—the marine base."

I had heard of it, but I didn't really know where it was—until now.

"You don't live on the base?"

"No. Base housing is pretty awful. We rent out a condo over there. That's why I'm working here. Help pay the bills and all. But this is a nice place to work. I'm outside a lot. Get a good tan in the summer. People are nice. It's pretty much okay. For now."

I smiled back. Not a ringing endorsement, but she didn't say it was terrible either.

"What about hurricanes?"

She put her hand on her hip. "Well, the way I figure it is that every place has something terrible about it. We lived in Kansas when we were first married. Really hot. And flat. With a regular sprinkling of spring tornadoes. My sister lives in New York City. There you have . . . well, New York City to deal with. Rude people—or maybe they're all just in a hurry. And it's really, really crowded. Here . . . I guess we get hurricanes every now and then, but doesn't every place get something? And if it doesn't, it's either too expensive or there's too many stuck-up people that live there. Everyone around here is pretty normal, you know. Some pickup trucks and all that. But otherwise normal. I like normal people. So, I guess this place is pretty much okay."

I thanked her, sipped at my coffee, and stared out at the street. Not much traffic in April. I am pretty sure that during the summer it would get really jammed. But then again, there weren't any huge resorts for people to come to. Even if all the houses filled up, it wouldn't be that bad.

Hmm.

Validation? Sort of. Maybe a little.

I drove down the road a bit further south. Rufus fell asleep. I passed another Holiday Inn—this one on the beach. I stopped, reserved a room, and then continued my drive. I doubled back and drove down the side streets. Atlantic Beach was not more than five or six blocks wide and a few miles long, with the standard beach resort apparel and accessory stores along the way. I need to ask someone just how many bamboo beach mats could one place possibly sell?

It was late afternoon by now. I went back to the Holiday Inn, and Rufus and I settled into our room. Standing on the balcony of our third-floor room, I could see the ocean. When I left the sliding glass door open, I could hear the ocean. I liked that. The beach wasn't a mile wide, but neither was it a narrow strip of sand. Fifty yards across? I'm no good at distances like that. But the distance was comfortable. With sort of a sand dune-like area, spotted with shrubs and sea grass, dividing the beach from the houses, I'd call the view pretty. Not Hawaii pretty, but . . . well, I liked the view. Very pretty. The beach, flat and level, would be good for walking. Some beaches have an extreme slope to them, so you need to have one short leg and one long leg to walk comfortably—but that would only be good in one direction.

I lay down on the bed. Rufus jumped up and snorted around, moving the pillows with his snout. He does that a lot. It's not like dogs had pillows way back when; his behavior is just instinctual—like he was moving grass around with his nose and wallowing out a place to lay down. After a moment or two, he felt settled and flopped sideways on the bed. He stared at me, looking like he wanted to talk. He didn't. I surmised what his conversation might be: he wanted to know if we would live here and that he had grown tired of traveling already, and do any horses live here.

I knew the answer to one of his questions—the horse question. And I had grown very tired of traveling too.

When I began planning for this trip, when I made the decision to uproot Rufus and me from everything we had known and loved, I thought it would be easy. I thought it would be fun. I thought that I would spend a month or two or three exploring all the small seaside towns between here and Florida. I thought it would be enjoyable. I thought I would be okay with traveling—like that guy on the public broadcasting channel who is always traveling all over Europe. He seems to enjoy it. I thought I would too. But I didn't. Not at all. And what made it more uncomfortable is that I thought that this is probably what Jacob would have wanted me to do—after he was gone, that is.

Now, less than a week into it, I wanted it to stop. I am sure Rufus wanted it to stop.

What could I have been thinking? Did I really think that I would be magically shown where I was supposed to settle? Did I think that God would have neon signs pointing out MARY'S NEW HOUSE? Did I really think that life worked that way? And I sort of expected, at least a little bit, that the Almighty would swoop in like a superhero and point me to my new Eden? After all, isn't he in the business of protecting Rufus? If Rufus had protection, wouldn't that mean that I would be protected by default? I can't believe how stupid all this now sounded. I can't believe I had listened to a dog. How could he really help me now? And what alternative do I have, now that I started in on this journey?

I switched on the power on my cell phone and dialed.

Ava picked up on the third ring.

"How are you? Where are you? I miss you so much."

I explained where I had landed for the day. I told her about Rufus and the colonial horse.

"That is just so adorable. It really is. Poor Rufus. You should have been filming it. Doesn't your camera have a video record option?"

As if I knew. And if I had known, as if I also would have figured out how to use it.

And then I told her of our drive down the barrier islands and our ferry ride.

"I am so jealous. It snowed here last night. In April. Snow. Can you believe it? I can't stand it here any longer. Find a place quickly, so I can visit. Some place where college boys go to for their spring break, okay? I could come down for spring break. We could have a really good time, if you know what I mean."

I knew what she meant.

"Spring break is over, Ava, isn't it? I think it's already happened this year."

"Well, then find a place with a college nearby. That will ensure a beach filled with potential."

"I don't think there is a big college anywhere near Atlantic Beach."

"I bet there is a branch of some big school nearby. That'll be good enough for now. When can I come?"

I took a deep breath. I tried not to sigh.

"What's the problem?" she asked. Ava knew me well.

"I don't know. I'm tired of traveling."

"Already? It's only been a few days."

"I know. I'm not a gypsy, I guess. I want to be somewhere already."

Ava did not answer.

"I shouldn't have done this."

No response.

"Maybe . . ."

No response.

I had to pose the question. I had to have her take on my situation, on what I felt "Maybe I should come home. Back to Wheaton."

No response.

"It would be the sane thing to do . . . right? Back to my friends."

No response.

"Ava, are you there? Can you hear me now?"

I heard the sigh. I think she practiced at sounding exasperated—perhaps more perturbed than exasperated.

"Listen, Mary. I gave you a going-away party three weeks ago. You don't get a welcome home party until you've been gone . . . I don't know . . . two years. You're not coming home."

"Why not? If I made a mistake."

"You didn't make a mistake. You're just scared. And maybe a little lonely. Maybe that's a good thing. To be lonely for a while. By yourself lonely. Without friends to supply you with the drug of sympathy. Sympathy is the most addicting drug there is. You need to be away from that. And you've never been on your own."

I wanted to shout at Ava to shut up. But I didn't, because I was too nice. And, in that moment, I sort of realized that she might have been telling the truth. I had been alone—but not by myself. Maybe I needed to be alone. And by myself.

I did like sympathy as well. How did she know that?

"So, is this Atlantic Beach a nice place?" Ava asked, changing the subject, having given me all the advice she had to give.

"I guess," I said. A little tacky in spots, but mostly nice."

"Hey, every place by the ocean is a little tacky. Unless you move to Hawaii—and you can't afford to move to Hawaii. I am right, aren't I? You can't afford a place on Wakawakawaka Beach, right?"

"Yes. I can't afford Hawaii. But I think I could live here. I think. I picked up one of those free real estate catalogs at the Shark Shack."

"Shark Shack?"

"A restaurant that I had lunch at. Fish bites. They were good."

"See, what did I tell you? Every place by the beach is a little tacky."

I scowled at Ava and ignored her snideness.

"If I buy a few blocks off the beach—then I can afford it. A small house. It would cost a lot less than what my house in Wheaton cost."

"Are there places to eat there—besides the Shark Shack?"

"Yes."

"Is there a Walmart nearby?"

"Yes. I saw the sign for it on the highway. Three miles, it said."

"What's the beach like?"

I described it to her.

"Then buy a place there already."

I swallowed.

"Really? Here? Just like that?"

"Mary, you picked up and moved. You were my best friend. Still are, I think. But I knew you had to go. It was time. You need to start a new life. I don't think you could do that here. Too many people thinking that they had you figured out. Thinking that they knew what you needed. Thinking that you had to fit into some sort of preconceived idea of a person—like go back to church and marry a deacon."

"Elder."

"What?"

"They are called elders at the church. The church I went to."

"Former church, then. And I don't care what you call them. It wasn't who you were. Trust me."

"Then who am I?"

"I don't know. But you don't know either. I love you like a sister." She laughed. "I take that back. I have a sister and we don't get along at all. But I love and care about you, Mary. You need to do this. You do. Forge a new life. You have to trust me. Atlantic Beach sounds like a good place to do that. If you look up and down the coast, looking for a more perfect place, you will never settle down. Make a choice, Mary. Make a choice and live with it. Your new life will find you there. In Atlantic Beach. It will find you."

Is that validation? I couldn't tell anymore.

"Okay. I'll look around some. But if I don't find the right place . . ."

"You'll find the right place. A little cottage with a picket fence and a screened porch, and when the wind is right you'll be able to hear the ocean. Trust me, Mary. You have to do this—even if you don't want to."

"Really?"

"Yes. Really. And call me tomorrow. The good Toe Doctor is due here in five minutes and I'm not dressed—which he would like, but not tonight."

"I'll call you."

"Trust me, Mary. Things will look better in the morning."

I hung up and listened to the ocean.

What's up with all the "trust me" stuff. Is that some sort of sign?

———— ∞ ————

That night, I drove down to Mosquito Amos's for take-out ribs and chicken. I got the ribs, which I brought back to the hotel. Rufus danced about once he got a sniff of the meat—the puppy-food dance, I called it. The ribs were excellent—huge and juicy, with amazing barbeque sauce. The coleslaw just sweet enough, and the baked potato was as large as Rufus's head. Everything tasted great.

Maybe this is a good place.

I gave Rufus two rib bones. He thought they were delicious, too.

After darkness had settled in, and after I washed the barbeque sauce from my fingers and hands, I snapped on Rufus's leash and headed to the ocean. A small wooden walkway led over the sand dune, through a thicket of brush and sea grass and down onto the beach. The moon was full, and the beach as well lit as any of our walking paths back in Wheaton. The heady salt air washed over us as we climbed down the steps and onto the sand. The wind had gone soft now, the waves a gentle lapping at the shore. Rufus stopped at the edge of the beach and looked out over the water, a million stars reflected in its calm surface, like diamonds dancing on slow-moving Jell-O. (Yes, I used to be a writer. Slow-moving Jell-O? Please.) The moon hung at my shoulder, nearly full, gibbous, offering enough light to read a book—if the type was large enough, that is.

He looked down at the ground.

"What is this?" he asked.

"Sand. It's what beaches are made of."

He took a few tentative steps.

"It feels funny on my paws. Like warm snow."

We walked north along the beach. A trio of pelicans came by, flapping more noisily than I thought they would be.

Rufus stopped and stared.

"What are those?"

"Pelicans. They eat fish."

"Not dogs?"

"Not dogs. Just fish. They scoop them up from the water in their beaks."

He turned to watch them fly on, courting the edge of the sea and shore, glistening in the moonlight.

"I don't like them," he said with finality.

I walked us closer to the water's edge. We stood, just beyond the farthest reach of the waves.

"Does it always do that?" Rufus asked. "The water at home never did this."

He meant the pond behind our house.

"They're called waves. I think it has something to do with the moon and the wind."

Rufus looked up at the moon, and then back at me, as if I was toying with him, trying to make him feel stupid or foolish.

"But I'm not sure," I added. "Sometimes the waves are bigger. Sometimes smaller."

Rufus took one step forward. At home, or, rather, back in Wheaton, he avoided puddles. Some dogs seemed oblivious to casual water. Not Rufus. He didn't like it. He let the wave roll in and wash over the edge of his front paws.

"The water is warm."

"Because of the Gulf Stream, I think," I said, then realized that it would be too much of an explanation for a dog.

He bent down and nosed at the water. I guess he stuck his tongue out.

He snorted.

"This tastes like those pretzels you tried to feed me once. I didn't like those pretzels at all."

"That's okay, Rufus. You don't have to drink this water. You shouldn't drink it. There is salt in it."

"Why?"

I hesitated. I might have known that once, in eleventh grade Earth and Space Science class taught by Mr. Riggens, who had just graduated from Indiana University of Pennsylvania. He was . . . Mr. Riggens, that is . . . how shall I put this politely? He was a pompous jerk.

"I . . . I don't know there is salt in there, exactly. But it is salty. Most of the water on the earth is salty."

We continued our walk, at the water's edge, where the sand felt firm and the walking became easy.

Twenty minutes later, and perhaps a mile from the hotel, I stopped.

"Time to turn around and go back."

Rufus looked up at me. At home . . . back in Wheaton, I mean . . . I guess we never turned around. We always walked in a long, loopy circle, bordered by blocks and streets. We never just stopped and reversed our course. I wondered if I had to explain this as well, but Rufus only slowed a minute when he turned, then continued walking.

"I like it here," he said. "It smells good."

"I like it here too," I replied.

"Are we going to live here?"

"Well, not at the hotel."

"I know that," Rufus said. Even he had the exasperated tone down. "I mean . . . here."

"I don't know. Maybe. It is warm. And we are by the ocean."

"I like the ocean."

He stopped and looked over his shoulder, a furtive glance.

"There aren't any horses here, are there?"

"I am almost positive there are no horses on the beach."

He snorted again.

"I like the beach too," he said. "We could live here."

Maybe I should pray about this. I hadn't prayed about it. That was not unusual. I hadn't prayed about anything for so long. I didn't think it would be appropriate to start praying now. That would feel disingenuous and hypocritical—like I would call on God only when I found myself in trouble or confused or both. He and I weren't talking and I felt pretty certain that that silence was fine with both of us.

But not so much with Rufus. God and Rufus still talked. If you could believe Rufus, that is. I had a sudden rush that Rufus might merely be making a pretense of his piety and spirituality. But then again, he was a talking dog. No, that had to be something special, something out of the ordinary, something ordained . . . or something like that.

"Did God say anything about this place? Did you ask him if this would be a place that we could live in?"

Rufus bent to sniff a large clamshell, wedged into the wet sand.

"That's an empty clamshell, Rufus. Or oyster. Of some sort of shelled animal."

Rufus sniffed again and looked out over the darkening expanse of ocean.

"I did ask God, actually. I didn't think I would, or should, I guess. But I did."

I waited. I don't think Rufus knew the power of a long, pregnant pause. But this pause proved most effective.

"And?"

"Well, he said it was a nice place. He said there are nice people here. And he said something about being victorious. Something like that."

"Victorious? What does that mean?"

"I don't know. But I am sure that God likes the ocean. He made it warm and salty and beautiful. I like that. I think we should live here. He said we need to trust him again."

"Does that mean I need to trust you who is trusting him who said to live here?"

Goodness. I do sound delusional, don't I? But you know what I mean.

Rufus hesitated, then snorted.

"I guess. If that means we should live here, then yes."

"Really?"

"Sure. As long as there are no horses."

"They don't allow horses on this beach, Rufus," I said. I had looked it up on my phone earlier. "And no ATVs either."

Rufus snorted in affirmation.

Victorious? Validation?

16

The next morning, after our early stroll on the beach, both of us enjoying it even more than the previous evening's stroll, we came back to the hotel room. I took a shower and at 9:00 a.m., I called a local Realtor, Janet Stout, from "The Star Team." Janet might have been the senior member on the team. She had silver hair in a very sophisticated, upswirl flip, and looked every bit like a woman who stepped out of *Southern Living* magazine—at least as much as much as I could tell from her one-inch-square photo on the back of the free real estate listing catalog.

When you are absolutely new in town, how do you start? I took a chance on a postage-stamp photo. Seemed like a plan to me.

Janet's accent dripped southern honey—the accent that northern people make fun of—but on the phone, it sounded natural and welcoming, and sounded just perfect.

I took that as a sign.

I told her I wanted to buy a house . . . today.

Music to a Realtor's ears, I would imagine. A symphony would be more like it.

She had several properties in Atlantic Beach that could work for me, she said, and all in my price range. She would meet me at Robin Avenue, just a block off the beach. She gave me directions. It lay no more than five minutes from the Holiday Inn.

Janet drove up in a black Lexus, I think. I'm not that good with car makes. She must sell enough houses to keep her in nice cars. And she wore a very stylish outfit, out of *Town & Country*. A Peck and Peck woman. Is Peck and Peck—or would that be, *are* Peck and Peck—still in business? They sell stylish, expensive outfits, from what I recall. I had never read a copy of *Town & Country* either, but her outfit is what I imagined them featuring. Fine, aristocratic women on a fox hunt. Or planning the charity ball at the country club, sipping frosty mint juleps. She extended a hand and the warmest of welcomes. Her entire face turned into a smile, her eyes almost vanishing when she did.

"And what a darling dog," she exclaimed, bending to Rufus. He turned his head, just a little, and sniffed, then allowed her to pet his head, which she did enthusiastically (for a well-dressed woman) for a long moment. "My lands, he is such a gentleman. A real sweetheart, he is. Terriers aren't known for their sweet dispositions, now are they? He is a sweetie."

She stood back up, straightened her blouse, and grew taller somehow, then grandly gestured with her left arm. "This is it."

I loved her accent. I wished my mother had had that accent. No, I wished I had that accent.

"It's been a rental unit for two years," she said. "The couple who own it moved to a condo over in the city and . . . well, the husband passed on last winter and she wants to sell both properties and move to California. She has a daughter there."

The address had a Cape Cod cottage located square in the middle of the lot. I think it's Cape Cod. I'm not an expert on

architectural styles. The Amish had simple homes—no ornamentation, no frills. Their houses were easy to write about.
Amish styles . . . well, they didn't have any. I mean, none that
changed over time. They had bonnets and long dresses and I
had their fashions down pat. But—back to the task at hand—
the house on Robin, a small Cape Cod, faced east, with two
dormer windows, a screened porch, green shutters on the windows that looked like they really closed, and a picket fence
around the yard. The house and fence were mostly white, but
faded white, and chipped. It all needed painting—but I knew
that painting was a comparatively cheap fix. (I watch home
improvement shows on TV. A can of paint and voilà!—a new
look.) From the front of the house, you could actually see the
ocean peeking through between the oceanfront properties.
Perfect.

We walked up a half-dozen steps to the screen door. It
squealed a welcome as the Realtor shoved it open.

"The listing sheet says that the roof is four years old, and
the mechanicals, furnace and air conditioning, are five years
old. That's good." She looked around. "You'll have to paint, for
sure, and repair the screens, of course. I'm not sure if I remember what it needs on the inside. TLC for sure. Maybe it's the
bathrooms that need gutting. I think that is it. But that's not
too bad."

We entered the front room.

"A bit musty. I don't think anyone has been in here since
the fall, other than the rental company's caretaker. I called him
before I came. Just to make sure that the place was in showing
condition. No raccoons taking up residence without paying
rent," she said, enjoying herself.

The front room ran the width of the house, and appeared
more than spacious with lots of large-paned windows and
hardwood floors. One side featured two mismatched sofas; a

few end tables; a coffee table; and a huge, old, analog television set. On the other side, was a dining room table and chairs. I liked the openness of the space.

Janet sniffed, but not an entirely dismissive sniff. My mother could dismiss an entire year's worth of writing with a well-timed and well-toned haughty sniff.

"Not horrible. You could do something with it."

She assumed that I had a sense of style. Sheer flattery—and it worked so very well.

Rufus walked at my side. He sniffed discreetly, perhaps to spare me any anxiety.

The rest of the first floor consisted of a kitchen—smallish, but quite serviceable and in need of new counters, new cabinet doors, and appliances; a nice-sized bathroom, which did need gutting—ancient tile and fixtures, clean as a whistle, but not "good" old, not good retro old, just plain old and ugly; and a master bedroom, a large airy room big enough for a king-size bed, dresser, and sitting area.

"There's hardwood floors under this old carpeting," Janet said.

The upstairs was one large room, with wide, pine planked flooring, that had eight single beds lined up in it, and a second bathroom.

"Snow White could have lived here," Janet said, laughing as southern ladies are reputed do, with a sense of decorum and grace. I loved this woman already.

I lifted windows, tested doors, flushed toilets, turned on the water, switched on the gas range, flipped light switches, stood in the kitchen and tried to imagine if my cooking style would adapt to the new layout.

"Does it flood? Has it ever flooded? Like during storms. Or hurricanes?" I asked and tried to sound neutral. Rufus looked up at me when I said the word *hurricane*. His eyes showed a new level of concern. We both watch The Weather Channel. He knew what hurricanes were. Darn that all-knowing Jim Cantore. Now, besides horses, Rufus would have to contend with the threat of hurricanes. "That you're aware of, I mean."

"Sweetie, if a hurricane hits here, everyone floods. You just pay your flood insurance every year. Get good insurance. I can help you get the right coverage. You live near the ocean, you have to live with what the ocean brings you. But you can be victorious over Mother Nature, if you've a mind to, and if you plan ahead."

Victorious?

"I've lived here my whole life. We've had a few hurricanes over the years. Topsail Beach down the way gets washed away because they built it on a sand dune. Atlantic Beach has always held its own. They built it on higher ground. On the ocean, a few feet makes all the difference. But here is what you have to do: you listen to the radio. If they send out a warning, you pack up your sweet dog, make certain that your insurance policy is paid up, and drive to Raleigh to wait it out. Do some shopping while you wait. Get a manicure. Go to a spa. That's what I do."

That's the most sensible response to a hurricane evacuation that I had ever heard. Even the good dog Rufus seemed to be assuaged by her answer.

"Now, let me show you the yard."

The house sat on a quarter-acre lot, which Joan said was large for this size house. The grass, such as it was, was flat sea grass, she called it, and didn't need mowing much.

"You can get a service to do that for you."

The fence ran the perimeter of the property. It was bigger than my lot back in Wheaton.

"Of course, the fence needs to be repaired. Or taken down— your preference. A thousand dollars should be enough to get it fixed. Add some painting costs, of course. Fifteen hundred. Two thousand, tops."

Labor must be less expensive in the south.

We had made our way back to her car. I looked at the house from there. I could imagine myself on a porch swing, on the screened porch, with an iced tea in my hand, listening to the surf. I could just hear it, if I listened. And there were patches of blue water visible from the porch. The sun would be behind me in the evening—no squinting. A sidewalk ran the length of the block. I could see people strolling by, offering a genteel wave, perhaps. Rufus could keep guard from there. We could take our walks under the glow of streetlights, walk to the ocean, only a block away, stand in the breeze and put the day to rest—or greet the dawn.

It felt right. I looked at Rufus. He offered his best, and most practiced, serene, untroubled look, as if he foresaw no problems or concerns with my decision.

"What about the neighbors?"

She nodded. "The houses on either side are owner-occupied. They're full-time residents here. Maybe half the homes on this street are full-timers. That's good for home values. There are a few summer homes, used all summer and some weekends the rest of the year. And a few rentals. Nothing too rowdy. Families. No swarms of boisterous college boys from Duke, if that's what you're concerned with."

"A little."

I wondered what the right decision would feel like. In the past, I had a husband to ask. In the past, I had prayers to offer. I could wait, back then, for divine revelation, divine reassurance. I didn't have those options now. Neither of them. Rufus may have. Perhaps that's why he appeared serene. I could take a chance on my own human free will. Rufus said I had free will, right? Rufus said God wasn't all that concerned with my housing situation. Something like that.

"Is the price a fair one?" I asked.

A serious look came over Janet, a member of The Star Team. She pursed her lips and leaned closer to me, conspiratorially.

"I would offer 10 percent under the asking price. Maybe even 15 percent. Trust me. The market is slow here. I think she would take it."

I waited a moment, waited to feel something. Trust? Victory? I don't know anymore. Trusting in a dog to help guide me on my odd pilgrimage?

"Okay. Let's write up a contract. How soon could we close? I'm staying at the Holiday Inn and let's just say that the charm is wearing off quickly."

We met later at a Starbucks on Highway 70 in Morehead City. "They have an outside patio so your sweet little dog doesn't have to wait in the car," Janet had said.

I signed the paperwork for the offer, and asked about a home inspection, suggestions for contractors, and where to change my driver's licenses—all manner of Welcome Wagon queries. (Do they still have Welcome Wagons?)

"As for a closing date, the owner is very flexible," Janet said. "I called her agent on the ride over. She also said that since the place is a rental, and if the closing gets held up for any reason, well, you could move in today and pay rent until the closing date. I'm sure whatever the rental amount is will be less than the Holiday Inn charges."

I could move in today.

"Do you have enough supplies to do that? Sheets and towels and things like that?" Janet asked.

"I do. What I don't have, I can pick up at the Walmart. Does Morehead City have a place that delivers mattresses?"

Trust. Is that what all this was? I couldn't be sure, but I simply moved forward and that felt right.

―――∽∞∾―――

My offer was accepted twenty minutes later—no bargaining back and forth. I signed the paperwork—lots of paperwork—and met the owner's agent at Janet's office for the keys to the house.

"Listen," the seller's agent said. (She wasn't anything like a southern belle. I would have guessed a Boston accent, if any.) "The owner is just glad to sell it. She's not going to charge you rent or anything like that. She just wanted to be sure you weren't bringing in any Picassos or rare art since she said her insurance wouldn't cover that."

I assured her that there were no Picassos under the dog crate in my car.

While at the Star Team Realty office, I called for a mattress delivery, trash removal service (since I wouldn't keep any of the house's furniture), a contractor to remove the old carpet in the master bedroom, a cleaning service to do a thorough cleaning (including windows and gutters), and two contractors—both recommended by Janet to meet me at the house later that day for estimates on painting, redoing the bathrooms, updating the kitchen, refinishing the wood floors, and replacing the screens on the screened porch. While there, I took some quick measurements of the windows and ordered wide white wood blinds for all the windows.

By the end of the day, everything had been arranged. Janet had been right when she said that contractors in the area are really hungry for work. Thanks to a bad economy, I would have a livable house in seven to ten days, bathrooms and kitchen included, if everything went as planned. I could camp out at the Holiday Inn for seven to ten more days and enjoy the beach.

I stopped at Walmart and bought enough towels and two sets of king-size sheets, a four-piece dish set, and soap. I stopped at an appliance store and priced washers, dryers, and kitchen appliances.

I kept a running total in my head for all my purchases and potential purchases and scheduled services—and it added up to tens of thousands of dollars less than I had estimated spending on a new home when I had done my original budgeting back in Wheaton.

I would still need to get a job. That I had anticipated from the outset. I guess I could apply at the Shark Shack. I had spent two months as a waitress between high school and college and in all honesty, I was terrible at it—shy, insecure, with a bad case of jitter-induced short-term memory loss. I forgot to return to tables with water, or ketchup, or more napkins, or the check.

Perhaps since I've matured, I might do better.

Perhaps.

That first night I told Rufus about buying the house. I had been pretty sure he understood what I had done. But I could never be sure how much language he had paid close attention to during the day. He became a regular dog during the daylight hours. He became sort of a literate vampire canine by night.

"I know. I paid attention today. You seemed excited," he said, as we walked, skirting the edge of the night's waves. The wind grew a little stronger, a bit more robust this evening, so the waves charged at us a little faster. Rufus would jump out of the way when they got too close. I think he took my admonition about not drinking the water to heart.

"What about hurricanes?" he asked right off. "That lady with the silver hair said there were hurricanes here. I don't think I like hurricanes."

I told him that he needn't worry, that hurricanes don't sneak up on anyone. I told him that if one comes, The Weather Channel knows about it days in advance and we could get out of the way. I said hurricanes are not at all like horses that sneak up on dogs.

"Then, that's good," he said, his words firm and solid.

I wanted to ask him if he had spoken more with God, if he had prayed about this house, or this town. I wanted him to tell me that I made the right decision. I wanted God to pat me on the back and tell me that I had passed the test and my life would be getting easier from here on in. I wanted Rufus to tell me that everything would be fine and I would no longer feel alone and abandoned. I wanted to feel whole again and I wanted God to tell me that I was whole again, that he would heal the split in my heart, that he would patch the terrible gash that felt like a permanent affliction on its muscles.

I wanted all that, and none of it came.

I didn't ask the poor dog any of these questions. I knew what his answer would be, or at least surmised what his answer would be. He would say something about free will and us making our own choices and trusting God—providing that we prayed to God and had a relationship with him.

I don't think I had that. No, I take that back. I know I didn't have that relationship with God. Even now. Even after moving halfway across the country on the merest nudging of the Divine—as interpreted by a dog, of all creatures. I hoped for a symbiotic spiritual relationship—that the person, or creature that I now lived close to . . . that he lived, spiritually speaking, close to God and in order to bless and protect him, I would gather at the edges of that protection and be protected myself. I figured this was a logically foolproof plan. In order for Rufus to have a stable home and environment, I would have to have the same things. I would warm myself on the edges of Rufus's celestial protection and blessing. How could it not work? If I were to have made the wrong choice—and everything here went horribly wrong—then Rufus would suffer. God wouldn't let that happen, would he? He sees the sparrows fall . . .

Like a wayward husband basking in the spiritual strength and calm of a believing wife. That is the way it works. At least, that is the way I hoped it would work.

17

Ten days later, the house stood complete and ready for occupancy. Well—almost complete. The granite countertop for the kitchen hadn't been cut yet. The granite people planned to install it in a week, and promised they could do so with a bare minimum of disruption and hardly any mess.

The house turned out glorious. The newly refinished floors gleamed, and the bathrooms, all fresh and white, with new tile and fixtures, smelled of adhesive and grout. The paint on the wood trim glistened, the walls were renewed, and the new stainless steel appliances in the kitchen shined in the afternoon sun. I purchased one small sofa at a warehouse store, one area rug for the bedroom, a pair of chairs for the eating counter in the kitchen, a wicker sofa and chair with summery-striped cushions for the screened porch, and an antique wooden bed frame from a consignment shop in Morehead City, and filled my car with groceries.

The cable people came and installed my Internet connection and I sent an "all" e-mail to every friend and relative I could gather on my e-mail list, telling them of my new address and phone number. I sent a postcard to Bernice, just to be sure she got word. Their e-mail might still be down.

I left the upstairs empty. With just one large room, I could eventually place a few beds up there. I might, come summer, when guests arrived. But for now, I just loved the barrenness of the large, empty, clean space. I made a vow with myself never to allow this house to become cluttered with anything. "Keep things sparse and simple" became my new mantra. Or motto. "Mantra" may imply some oddball Eastern religious sect—and heaven knows, we can't have that.

I called the moving/storage company in Wheaton and told them where to ship my crated possessions. I almost wished I could have said to simply dispose of them all, that I intended on starting over from scratch, that I wouldn't need three boxes of sweaters and winter coats anymore. But I couldn't do that. There were some possessions—pictures and mementos—that I wanted to keep. That I needed. A good thing about living in Atlantic Beach is that the cost of taking away unwanted furniture and assorted detritus of life appeared to be very inexpensive.

Rufus and I sat on the screened porch that first night, enjoying the warm spring evening. The screen door allowed Rufus to lie down on a new sisal rug I'd bought, and watch the street. He'd never had that opportunity back in Wheaton. Most of the windows in the front of our old house were blocked by furniture, or the view obstructed by bushes. Here he had a clear sight line to the street and the sky over the ocean beyond.

I felt settled. Mostly settled. Mostly to partly settled.

That night, Rufus said again that he liked the house, he liked the beach, and he liked the warm water (he once walked in up to his knees). His happiness made me happy—though I was not completely settled. Almost.

I dialed a number on my cell phone. Ava answered on the first ring.

"Congratulations," she said. "Now, I have a place on the ocean to stay at for free."

"You do. And you're welcome anytime."

I gave her the rundown of all that had transpired—the work on the house, my purchases, my being pleased with what had occurred, being happy that I found an affordable place so quickly.

Ava waited.

"Then what's wrong?" she finally asked.

"Nothing's wrong," I countered. "Everything is hunky-dory."

I thought I had learned how to lie well, to hide my true emotions behind a mask of cheeriness. A few years of widow-hood and you get good at it.

Ava would have none of it.

"Don't lie to me. There's a hitch in your voice. Something's going on. Rufus hates it, right?"

"No," I replied. "He seems to really like it. He likes walking on the beach. He wades in the water and looks happy."

"Then you hate it, right? Like those $400 shoes you lusted after for months and then bought and when you wore them for the first time on a date, they hurt your feet and made your calves look misshapen."

"I never bought $400 shoes."

"Oh, yes . . . that happened to me, didn't it? But the principle is the same. You want it until you get it, right? Then you don't want it."

I sighed. I don't like sighing.

"I don't know. I think everything is fine. But I don't feel like all the pieces are in place. Like I'm still missing something. I can't explain it."

"Well, when you start making friends, maybe get a job, things will be better."

"I don't know. Maybe. But I don't think friends and a job are what I'm missing. I don't know. Maybe you're right. Maybe it will pass. It has been a pretty hectic few weeks. Things will get better, right?"

"They will. Trust me on that," she said.

I didn't trust her at all.

⚬⚬⚬

My granite guy/kitchen contractor made arrangements to install the countertop—mostly black, with some greenish-gray veins—on Friday.

"You'll be there Friday morning to let us in, Miss Fassler?" asked Billy B.

"I will. I get up early, so any time after seven is fine with me." I was eager to have everything totally done. I don't understand how anyone could put up with months and months of interior remodeling while living in the house. I had one item left to do and it bothered me to the point of distraction.

Billy B proved himself a man of his word. He and his crew showed up at a few minutes past seven. Rufus made a point of barking loudly, bouncing up and down at the door to the screened porch. I opened it, and it still squealed.

"I'll put some oil on the hinges, Miss Mary. Or sand off the bottom sill a bit. Fix that for free, if you'd like."

"I would. Thank you so much."

He touched the brow of his baseball cap, which had Billy B William Interiors stitched on the crown.

His team of workers heaved and strained as they carried in the massive, polished sheet of granite. It looked spectacular, if I have to praise myself for a fine job of selecting interior finishes. The old countertop came off with a minimum of fuss, and the new one slipped into place. A new stainless steel sink with new faucets was installed.

Half the crew took off, and the remaining three workmen tidied up while Billy B supervised.

I stole a glance at him. I had to—he wasn't married—and I gathered that he and I were about the same age.

I'm pretty sure he wasn't married. He wore no ring. But perhaps he wore no ornamentation because of work hazards, like getting the ring caught in some sort of machinery.

"Looks very nice, Miss Mary," he said, as the crew packed up.

"Thank you."

Billy B stood thin as a whippet. Maybe a middle-aged whippet. A few pounds north of a whippet. But sinewy. Like he worked hard all his life. He was blond. He might have been bald, but I had never seen him without his company baseball cap. He had features . . . I want to say chiseled, but that is such a cliché. Yet they were chiseled. Prominent cheekbones. Angular jaw. Warm, green eyes. Broad shoulders . . . for a whippet. And a permanent grin. He may not shave every day, but when you're hauling five hundred pounds of granite countertop, you don't really require a close shave, do you?

"I wasn't sure when you picked this stone at the yard. I thought . . . well, I thought it might be too dark for a small kitchen. But no, you were right. It just works in here with the white cabinets and stainless steel appliances, doesn't it? You have a flair for this, Miss Mary."

"I think it does work well, doesn't it?" I replied, proud of being praised for my immaculate sense of design, my flair.

Billy B took off his cap. He was not going bald. Not at all. He had a thickness of blond hair, appearing as if it had been styled under his cap, askew in just the right way, tufts and peaks, looking very, very chic.

"Miss Mary, I hope you don't think I'm being too forward here . . ."

How do you answer a statement like that?

"But I was talking with Miss Janet over at Star Team Realty. Well, she did tell me a little of where you all came from. And why. And all that. Sorry to hear about your loss. I know that must have been hard on you."

He said it, not in a sympathetic manner, but simply acknowledging the truth of my past. I liked that. It hadn't happened quite this way before. Not that I could remember, at any rate.

"Thank you, Billy B. I appreciate that."

He gave me the wryest grin in return, like he knew that it had been the right thing to say, and that he said it just at the right time, and that I would be almost charmed by his down-home charm and innocence.

And, darn it, he was absolutely right.

"Can I ask you a question, Billy B?"

"You can ask me anything, Miss Mary."

Again, his answer did not sound smarmy, or sexual, like some men would sound, leering ever so slightly to see if I reddened at all, seeing if that flirt . . . worked.

"What does the *B* stand for?" His company name appeared as Billy B William Interiors. I had already figured that it might have been a family name. If Billy was a nickname for William, then he would be William B. William. Odd. His lead carpenter was named Ransom.

"Well, funny you should ask, Miss Mary. Folks usually ask right off, or they never do. You waited a good while before asking. Polite, you know. I like that in a woman."

I wanted to blush, just a little, but I don't think I did.

He likes that in a woman. Well . . . he noticed. That's a good sign.

"Well, Miss Mary. I could drag this story out. But I have another job to head to after here. The *B* is a nickname for William. You know, Billy gets turned into a *B* because a *B* is simpler for a baby sister to say when learning to talk."

I nodded, as if I understood, but I didn't.

"So . . . why Billy B?" I was confused.

He looked down at his shoes.

"The first Billy is for William. The *B* is for William as well."

He looked up, and he waited.

I suspect he saw my face drawn up tight in confusion, then slowly open, like a flower blossoming.

"So . . . you're William William William?

He grinned again. This time it was knowing and playful. He must have been used to it.

"Yes, ma'am. My parents had one odd sense of humor, I guess. My mother joked that she always had to call me three times until I listened to her. So that's another reason for their choice. But all my life, I've been Billy B, so no one has paid much mind to it."

I could not help laughing. A little.

"It is funny, in a weird southern gothic way, isn't it, Miss Mary? Something out of Faulkner. Or maybe James Dickey."

"It is. But I love it."

He obviously is well read. And very intuitive. I like that in a man.

He waited a short moment.

"I know this might not be all proper and everything, Miss Mary, but would you like to have dinner with me sometime? Maybe next weekend? I know a great shrimp place up by New Bern. Off the beaten path, as they say."

I tried not to look surprised. Or pleased. I was both. A lot.

"Billy B, I would like that," I replied. "I would like that a lot."

He slapped his hat back on his head.

"Well, capital then, Miss Mary," he answered, in the best North Carolinian interpretation of an English accent I have yet heard. "Capital indeed. I shall call you midweek with details."

"And I shall wait, anon," I said, wondering if I used the word *anon* in the right way. I probably didn't, but Billy B was too much a gentleman to pay heed to my possible gaffe.

The shrimp tasted fantastic. They must have caught it that day, or even as I ordered them. I don't think I have ever tasted shrimp quite as fresh as these.

And Billy B had been right. The restaurant, Captain Ratty's, was a place I never would have gone to—probably from the name alone. But it proved to be delightful. Billy B seemed to be a well-known customer. At least they all treated us with great charm.

I took easily to calling Billy B just that. It sort of rolled off one's tongue, didn't it?

Yes, I was on a date. With a man. After Brian, I thought in my darker moments, that such things would never happen to me again. But within a few weeks of moving to Atlantic Beach—well, there was a man.

And I liked him. He was funny and self-deprecating and very, very intelligent. He said he had graduated from North Carolina State University here in New Bern with a degree "in nothing useful" and started working on remodeling to pay off his student loans. And twenty years later, he surprised himself to still be doing remodeling, still enjoying it, and doing "pretty good."

Of course, I told him a little of my own story as well. You already know it, so no need to repeat any of it.

After splitting a piece of Key lime pie (I would have preferred the whole piece for myself, but I tried to look like a lady) Billy B drove along the coast, on some back roads, toward Atlantic Beach. Much of the drive went through the Croatan National Forest. Billy B remarked that this was the only coastal forest park on the East Coast, and magnificent stands of pine lined the road. I would have called it romantic, but romance remained a bit farther away. We would have time to get there . . . later.

We pulled into my gravel driveway. I could hear Rufus from inside the house, scrabbling up on the one chair that faced a front window and afforded him a look at the street. He barked—not an angry, warning bark, but one of recognition.

Billy B escorted me to the front door, the door to the screened porch.

Do I turn and face him here . . . or at the inside front door?

"Well, it is late, Miss Mary."

He called me Miss Mary. I think southerners have a thing for two names. I liked his calling me that. Respectful and playful at the same time.

"Are you sure? I could make coffee. I am good at making coffee."

He smiled.

"I am sure you are good at lots of things," he said, and I did not read even the remotest reference to sex into his comment. How does he do that?

"But I need to get up early. Church and all tomorrow."

"Oh, sure. I understand."

I hoped he did not read into my response that I had no intention or plans to get up early tomorrow and look for a church.

"I had a real nice time. I'll call you this week. Wednesday, probably. Not too soon, and not too late, right?"

I laughed. That is what I was thinking.

And then, as natural as can be, he bent in toward me, loosely slipped his left arm around my waist, and kissed me. It didn't last long enough to be considered a long kiss, nor a short peck. It was just long enough to leave me wanting more, and beginning a mental countdown to Wednesday evening.

"I would like that Billy B. I really, really would."

And I meant that.

Rufus stayed mostly quiet during our walk that night. He asked me if I had a good time, and I said I did. He always asks me what I ate. I told him shrimp and Key lime pie. And he asked me if I brought any home to him. I had to tell him I didn't.

"Have I had Key lime pie before? Is it sweet?"

"It is sweet. And I am pretty sure you haven't ever eaten it."

We walked along, and just as we returned to the house, he asked, "The next time you have Key lime pie, could you bring me some? I would like to try that. It has three names. I don't think I have eaten anything with three names before. It sounds really tasty."

And I assured him that I would.

We fell asleep, in our tidy, snug little home, white with green shutters and a picket fence, and the faint hissing of the surf as it rolled into shore and receded back again.

I think I was happy.

18

True to his word, Billy B did call on Wednesday. He proposed a Friday night date. Dinner, he said. Someplace local. Since I hadn't been here all that long, he suggested that I might appreciate going someplace I probably wouldn't go by myself.

He seemed to be intuitive that way. Maybe he faced the same single person problems that I did. Maybe not, since men can get away with a lot more than women can in that department. No, I am not being a feminist, but a man can more comfortably go into a restaurant by himself. A woman by herself—well, I just think that some people will have the wrong idea of what sort of woman she is. For a woman to walk alone into a tavern, let's say—people will think she's on the prowl. A man does it and no one thinks it odd or unusual at all.

It's the way of the world. And no, I'm not angry about it. I'm not going to picket taverns here to raise the consciousness of the culture. And besides, I never go to taverns. Unless they have really good ribs.

Since a second date was planned, I asked Rufus what he thought about Billy B. We were on our nightly walk along the ocean. We walked down a block to a public access point on the beach, and walked down a small wooden walkway and up the beach for about a half mile, where another public access point cut through the dunes to the beach. So Rufus and I were back on our large circle-walking pattern. I liked walking by the beach. The sound of the waves simply washed any cares from my mind—at least while we were walking. The hush and flow of the waves would be great therapy, if doctors could make money on prescribing it. Perhaps when the weather turned stormy, I might have a different opinion. But now, in the calm, in the warmth, I loved it.

Rufus did too. He treated the narrow spit of sand at the edge of the water as the only probable route. He still avoided water when he could, but if it washed onto his paws, he made no complaint. "I like it here," he said more than once. "I'm glad you moved us here."

Back to Billy B.

Rufus must have trouble with remembering men's faces, because at first, he could not recall Billy B. I had to explain the baseball cap, the man who brought the large piece of stone, and he still could not place him.

"The man who ate the Key lime pie with me," I finally said.

"Oh, that man. I know him. Will you have Key lime pie when he comes next?"

"I don't know," I answered. "But do you like him? Is he a nice man?"

Rufus stopped and walked very deliberately around the small carcass of a jellyfish. I told him to avoid the blobby things because they could sting him. He had been stung by a wasp back in Illinois. He had yelped at that, and had licked the bite area incessantly for two days. I told him it was like a wasp, only that jellyfish didn't fly. After that, he kept his distance from all beached jellyfish.

"Well, I don't have special dog ability to tell if someone is nice or not. I don't think I do, anyhow. He is nice to me. He bends down to pet me. And he's careful with my ears. Some people are not. He is careful. He smelled okay. A little like sweat."

I took that as an endorsement. And it made me feel a little giddy at the same time. I could imagine myself with this man. And that, in itself, felt like something entirely new. Perhaps Brian, back in Wheaton—the man who I punched in the throat—had opened the door a bit to the possibility of another man in my life. After the accident, I couldn't even imagine being with a man. I felt I could be accused of cheating, or committing adultery. Now, time had passed, and distance. I could now think of a future in which I did not live alone. And not just with Rufus. With another human being.

And that made me giddy, a little. Sort of.

Egads, to think I once made a semi-pro living at using the right words in the right way. Perhaps that skill has vanished as my ability to think of men arose, like a phoenix, in my life.

———— ✿ ————

The rest of my possessions arrived from Wheaton, placed flatly in my driveway in a large blue-and-white container. The delivery service offered assistance in unloading. I knew furniture had been packed inside, so I took advantage of strong men who knew how to heft a sofa up stairs and through doors.

I set up a second sitting area upstairs. The sofa from Wheaton went there, along with the two upholstered chairs that had been in my kitchen. That was the big stuff. I had them pile all the boxes in the dining area of my first-floor living room area. The stack intimidated me. Having only a smattering of possessions had felt liberating, and now this influx of stuff seemed constricting. It made me feel claustrophobic almost.

They emptied out the container in less than thirty minutes. Now I faced the task of either finding a place for everything or reducing the pile through giveaways.

I hung the pictures in short order. The few photos of John and Jacob were hung in the master bedroom. Somehow, I didn't want them more shared than that. The lamps were really needed. This house did not have recessed lighting as did my house in Wheaton, so dark here was darker than there. I quickly went through the clothes, and filled three medium-sized boxes with items that I knew I would never wear again. The next-door neighbor had told me that she has one pair of long pants, and the rest of her wardrobe consists of shorts. I would recycle five of the six pairs of wool pants I had packed.

Rufus sniffed and nosed about the boxes, as if he was look-ing for some item misplaced. He did find his favorite squirrel plush toy. He did not destroy toys like some dogs. He chewed off the eyes, but the rest of the animal remained intact. For the rest of the afternoon, he sat on the sofa, watching me, with his head resting on his old squirrel.

A few boxes were filled with personal items, photos, and memories. I did not want them on display, nor did I want them discarded. Upstairs, I had access to an enclosed attic area, about the size of two large closets. I had that filled in short order with all the too-meaningful-to-toss items, which I could close the door on.

After I finished, I had marked for charity perhaps one-third of the items I brought with me to North Carolina. I felt a bit more burdened, but not overwhelmed. I called the Salvation Army and asked if they would be interested in picking up my unwanted items. They were, and two days later, my place returned to being clear and sparse again.

And then Billy B called and the world was a good place again.

∞

Friday evening came and Billy B arrived, on time, in a button-down shirt, a very well-fitting blue sport coat, and slim-fit khaki pants. He had warned me that he would be dressed in "business casual."

"I know women get nervous if they feel over- or under-dressed. And I don't ever want to make you uncomfortable."

He had made reservations at Shepherd's Point, in Morehead City, across the sound—another restaurant I would not have gone to by myself. Too nice, too romantic, too much a couples place.

They had Key lime pie listed as their signature dessert. Rufus would get his wish after all.

As I had the waiter box up a two-bite section of the pie, Billy B stirred his coffee.

"It's for the dog, right?" Billy B asked.

"Maybe. If he's lucky. If I don't eat it on the way home."

"Don't worry. Every once in a while I have to stop at McDonald's and get a cheeseburger for my old basset hound. He loves their cheeseburgers. And fries. But not often. He's old and you have to watch their cholesterol."

The dinner was so nice, the conversation so natural, it felt as if we had known each other for years and not weeks. Billy B seemed to have friends all over town. Three people stopped by our table to say hello. Of course, he introduced me, as a proper gentleman should.

"It's a small town, Miss Mary. You live in one place long enough and you're bound to know a whole lot of people."

265

I decided to ask the question that had been at the back of my mind since the first time I had considered accepting a date with Billy B.

"So tell me—how come you're not married? I know, I know, I don't have to know . . . and you don't have to tell me anything . . . but when you pass a certain age, that question sort of sits out there, waiting to be asked. You know what I mean?"

If the question rattled him, he appeared adept at hiding it.

"No. I mean, I do know what you mean. And no, there's no problem answering it. I guess I am surprised that you didn't hear about it from someone else."

I braced myself—mentally only, I hope.

"Who would I have heard it from? I'm new here, remember?"

"Your next door neighbors. The Phillipses. They knew all about it."

Alarm flags were flapping in the storm, but I forced myself to remain dispassionate and calm—on the outside.

In jail? Arrested? Embezzlement? Something really horrible?

"I was married. To my high school sweetheart. We were great for fifteen years."

I waited. I didn't want to seem like I was prying. But now I was desperate to know. Not desperate. Well . . . maybe a little desperate. And more than a bit scared, I guess.

"We had a wonderful marriage. We did. Everything was great. Never had children; that bothered both of us. But it didn't overwhelm us."

He took a sip of coffee.

I really wanted the express version of the story.

"Then, five years ago, she fell in love with the pastor of the church we were attending. I didn't suspect a thing. I really didn't. Then all of a sudden she left. Packed up all her clothes and moved out. While I worked on a job. She called me that night and said it was over. She planned on starting a new life with him. She said he was her true soul mate. And she wanted a divorce."

I started to breathe again. A divorce, I could handle.

"I didn't want to let her go. So I put up a fight. And this went on while the pastor still preached at the church. The congregation started to take sides, and some blamed this one or that one. Some of them thought I should accept it and move on. Some wanted me to leave, like it was all my fault. Some wanted the pastor excommunicated—or whatever Bible churches do. But I didn't want any of that. I wanted my old life. I liked my old life."

The waiter came to our table, a little reluctant to break into our conversation, though he did have the bill in his hand. I apologized, and ordered coffee, after declining it before. It is not that I needed to be awake, but I needed something to do with my hands.

This isn't a deal-breaker. It doesn't sound like it was his fault. I mean, every relationship has ups and downs. Is any divorce absolutely one-sided?

"It went on for six months. Finally, I had had enough. I knew she was never going to change her mind. I relented and allowed the divorce to happen. Fighting costs a lot and doesn't change the way people feel."

I added three sugars to the coffee, two more than I normally do.

"Is the pastor still there—at that church? Did they get married?"

He sighed—a painful sigh. I didn't enjoy watching him relive what must have been a horrible time, but I did want to know.

I had a sudden and small epiphany. I understood why people wanted details of my husband and son's accident. Not because of morbid curiosity, but because they needed to feel some manner of closure as well.

"He is still at that church. And they are married. The church almost fell apart. Went down to a handful of supporters. But the man is a good preacher. Very charismatic. Very dynamic. I hear people say that the building is almost full again on Sunday mornings. I guess a sinner attracts sinners. People can empathize with him. Maybe that's it."

I didn't know what else to ask. He must have been devastated. Disillusioned for sure.

It seemed as if he had heard my thoughts.

"The funny thing is—you would think that my faith in God would be challenged or shaken. But it wasn't. I came through this all feeling more protected and more loved than I ever had before in my life. God provided for me when it mattered."

He leaned across the table.

"What about you, Miss Mary? We haven't talked about church before. You know . . . the things you never discuss on the first couple of dates—religion and politics. I know you suffered a great loss. Mine was bad, nowhere near as bad as yours. How are you with God? Where's your faith?"

I tried to speak, but I couldn't find the right words. But I had to say something.

"Okay. I guess. I . . . God and me . . . well, we don't talk much anymore. After the accident. I didn't see why those two innocent people had to die. I still don't. If it is a lesson I am supposed to learn, I don't want to learn it."

Billy B did not look shocked or discouraged or anything. He simply listened, impassively. That was so kind of him. To listen without judgment.

"So . . . I don't really know about God anymore. I don't know if I still believe. I don't know if I want to believe."

Yes, I know all about Rufus and my pathetic attempts at thinking that he really talked to God, and my attempts at manipulating a Divine being that I was pretty sure didn't really exist, and if he did, didn't really care all that much for me. After all, he saved the life of a dog, but couldn't, or didn't, spare the lives of two innocent people.

So I decided then and there to be honest with Billy B.

"I'm not against religion, Billy B. But for me, it's simply caused a lot of pain. Promises never delivered on. So, as much as I might want to believe, I can't anymore. It's easier and safer this way."

He smiled at me. He understood. I know he understood. He cared about me. He took my hand in his, for the first time, and gently squeezed it. "I understand," he said. "I do."

He gave me a kiss when he walked me to the door, and a gentle, chaste hug. He again promised to call me.

I was sure that he would. I was sure.

And Rufus loved his pie with the three names. On our walk, he made me promise to buy an entire pie if they sell them in the big food stores. He made me promise twice.

I did. I promised.

And he asked me if I liked this man.

And I told him that I did. A lot.

I assumed that he remained silent during the rest of my walk because he was remembering how good the Key lime pie tasted.

I was wrong.

———⟨∞⟩———

Billy B called on Thursday. Not Wednesday. I worried a bit on Wednesday, but a day . . . well, that isn't cause for great concern, now, is it?

My optimism shows how wrong I can be. And was.

"Miss Mary . . ."

"Billy B," I said, cheerful and happy.

He called. Just like he said he would.

"Listen . . ."

I don't think I really paid attention to that word. Who starts off a conversation with the word *listen*? Wasn't I already listening? And besides, I now felt like this is the place I should be, that Atlantic Beach is just the place that God had in mind for Rufus . . . and me, by default. The perfect house, the perfect neighborhood, and now, maybe a perfect man. Of course, he was not perfect. Just like I was not perfect. But we seemed so well suited for each other. We had the same dreams and the same temperament. And he was wickedly handsome. Isn't that what kids today say? "Wicked good"? Anyhow, he called and now we would see each other this weekend. Maybe I would cook him dinner on Saturday. We could . . . you know . . . snuggle on the sofa as we listened to the waves. Or if it was warm enough, we could sit on the porch, in the new porch swing I would buy tomorrow, and we would swing gently and he would put his arm around me and the moon would come up over the beach . . .

Perfect.

"Listen . . . Miss Mary . . . I am not good at this sort of thing. But it has to be said. Even if I don't want to."

Well . . . that's not how this conversation should start. This doesn't sound perfect at all anymore.

"Listen. I can't see you anymore. After we talked last weekend . . . I rolled it over and over in my mind. And I just can't do it. You don't believe, Miss Mary. In God. You more or less said so right out."

Wait. This is all wrong!

"I sort of figured that after my wife and I divorced, that if I ever found another woman that I felt attracted to, she had to be a committed believer. She had to really know God. She had to be on the same page as me. I'm not a teenager anymore. I don't want to break anyone's heart—nor do I want to be hurt. Nor do I have the luxury of lots of time."

I sat down, the world around me gone gray. Not black, but gray.

"It was only a conversation, Billy B. I didn't really think about what I was saying. Maybe I was just mistaken."

I could hear him take a deep breath and probably run his hand across his chin.

"No, Miss Mary. I heard that certainty in your voice. It's unmistakable. I heard it in my wife's voice too. And faith in God . . . well, I may not pass out tracts on the street corner or raise my hands and yell 'Praise the Lord!' all the time, but God is real to me. And believing in him is a huge part of my life. When she left, I promised myself that I would forever remain true to God."

"But Billy B . . . "

That's all I could think of to say.

"I am sorry, Miss Mary. I truly am. You are a really nice person. You are. But if I keep seeing you, then I would be more and more tempted to forget that promise I made to myself and to God. It would be so easy to do that, and I would wind up hating myself—and you. Neither of us has the time to play games. Neither of us is good at charades. And both of us would have to do so much pretending if we stayed together."

"But Billy B . . ."

"I'm sorry. But I can't see you anymore. I hope you'll understand. If not today, maybe someday. I wish you all the best."

And then he hung up.

I had nothing to say, other than another mumbled, "Billy B?"

I sat on the sofa for a long time. It might have been hours, just trying not to think, hoping that that phone call did not really happen, that I had just imagined it, and pretty soon Billy B would call and life would go on.

Yet I knew that would not happen.

I cried some. I cried because I felt stupid about being too honest with him. I should have known better. I could have said that I was still searching. That would have been enough to keep him around. But I had to be honest, now, didn't I?

Stupid.

Stupid and honest. Maybe they go together.

After sniffling quietly for a long time, Rufus jumped up onto the sofa and stared at me, wondering what was wrong. I did not cry often. Hardly ever with Rufus watching.

I might tell him about what happened during our walk tonight. But somehow, I had the feeling that he already knew. I knew I didn't want to talk to him now. I just wanted to hug him and feel something live close to me. He was only a dog, but that was all I had, and that would be enough.

I did not speak a word to Rufus on our nightly walk. It had started to drizzle, just a little, and we hurried along. This was no time for explanations or conversations.

Tomorrow would be time enough.

I woke up early and had three cups of coffee before 5:00 a.m. It remained dark and the beach was windswept as Rufus and I took our morning walk. His ears kept getting lifted up by the wind. I wondered if he disliked that feeling. The surf crashed higher than it had been since we arrived. We stayed farther back from the water on the beach. A low, gray scud of clouds hung over the waves. Even the cawing gulls were all but lost in the overcast. The wind was not cold, not even chilly. Storms and threatening weather were almost always cold back in Wheaton. Here, warm could threaten, just as easily as could cold. Perhaps even more so, because a warm threat was more unexpected.

I thought again about telling Rufus what happened the day before, that Billy B said he would not see me again. But he is a dog, and dogs don't have the same romantic impulses as we humans. He understood loyalty and respect, and love, of a sort. But I don't know if he could understand what I had been feeling for Billy B, nor did I think I could adequately explain it to him. So I didn't really try. I steeled myself and swore that I would learn something from this. I don't know what.

Instead, I asked him a question.

"Does every dog know God?"

Rufus sniffed at a shell.

"Yes. I think. I don't know every dog, but the dogs I know, they know God."

"Did Gus know God?"

Rufus perked up, almost jumped.

"Why, yes, he did. Gus lives near the ocean. Could we visit Gus? I would like to see Gus again."

I couldn't tell Rufus that I never knew Gus's owner's last name—or his first name for that matter—and had absolutely no idea of how I would find that information. I decided to take the coward's way out.

"We'll see Rufus. We'll see. It depends on how close he lives. Florida is a big place."

"He said Orlando. Is Orlando big?"

"It is, Rufus. And very far away. But I will try to find out where he lives."

"Okay," Rufus said, walking with a jaunty air now, even in the wind and sputtering rain. "He is a good dog. He knows who God is. Gus is a good dog."

I thought for a moment.

"Did the big, black, knuckleheaded dog next door know God?"

Rufus stopped when he heard my question. If he was pondering some deep question or working through some deep thought, he would often stop or slow, as if the thinking and contemplating part of it became so intense that walking could not continue while he engaged in the other two actions.

"I think so. I think all dogs know God. But not all dogs are good dogs. If a dog is a good dog, that means they know who God is and do good things. Some dogs that do bad things do bad things because they have bad people around them. But, deep down, all dogs know what is good and bad. Good dogs do good things. Bad dogs . . . they do bad things, even if they know better. But all dogs know what they're doing. I'm pretty sure of that."

Now it was my turn to remain quiet, trying to understand what Rufus said. It sounded clear and concise. It sounded logical. It almost sounded divine.

But that would mean that I knew right from wrong and if I had been doing bad things, the bad things were being done on purpose. Of course, I am not a dog, so perhaps the rules for dogs and people are quite different—at least to God, that is.

"Do all dogs talk to God?"

Rufus did not slow, or even turn to me.

"The good ones all do. The good dogs I know all do. Maybe there are some good dogs that don't, but I am pretty sure that there aren't many of those. Good dogs talk to God. That's how it goes."

Rufus accepted a dog treat and chewed it with great gusto. I gave him another one, and we turned our backs to the wind and headed for home, the rain becoming more of a squall now.

Warm or not, neither of us liked getting wet.

I'm still not talking to God. I don't know how to break the silence. I don't know how to start a conversation. "Oh, by the way—the one responsible for the deaths of the only two people in the world that I truly loved—how are you today? Time to worship you and offer praise . . ."

I can't do that. I can't. And right now, I won't even attempt it.

And if God is using loss to teach me—well, he's doing a horrible job with the lesson plan. I know all about loss and pain—my husband, my son . . . Right now I didn't need a refresher course in feeling alone and lost and miserable.

19

Gray, windy, squalls, high waves, a thickness of salt mist in the air . . . it could not become any more dreary and depressing. I decided that this day would be a perfect day to start my job hunt.

What's a little more rejection at the moment? Can't hurt any worse. The day can't get any more bleak.

I would start at the county job center in Morehead City, just to get the lay of the land. I could probably do most of what I would do there on my computer at home, but I had to get moving. I had to do something, go somewhere. I could not stay alone in the house any longer.

———— ✿ ————

The job center was closed.

A sign had been taped, at an askew angle, on the inside of the front door, at waist level. Written in pencil were the words CLOSED DUE TO BOILER MANFUNCTION. WILL OPEN TOMORROW. NORMAL TIME.

That's what the sign said, word for word.

The rain picked up a bit, splattering big warm drops on the driver's-side window. I felt safe in my Volvo. It featured some magic traction device on slick roads. I never drove fast in the rain, but it felt good to know it was there in case I had to do so.

Going back home was not an option. Not yet. I didn't need groceries, or gas, or anything new for the house, or clothes.

I could use another cup of coffee.

I just saw a study on Google News that linked high coffee consumption—more than eight cups a day (which is me)—with a lowered risk of prostate cancer.

Oh joy. I found out that I am very well protected from a disease that I can never catch. Just my luck, I guess.

I stopped at a Starbucks, treated myself to a short latte, with one Splenda, and sat by the front window, ensconced in a comfortable leather chair, looking over a downtown block of Morehead City. It was not the quaintest old town I had ever seen, nor the best preserved, nor the liveliest—but it was still alive and attractive. That counted for something. A few good restaurants. A few antique stores. A few women's boutique shops. Two hair salons. A deli. Not bad.

I watched people scurry in and out of the rain. Some folks looked amazed that they were feeling raindrops, others perturbed that they ran the risk of getting wet, others all but oblivious to the rain. I liked those people the best—wearing slickers, or not, they walked slowly, window shopping, apparently not caring one whit about the conditions around them.

By the time I finished my coffee, the rain had slackened. I drove down the main street, only slowing when I noticed an old, two-story, brick building, with windows trimmed in white. I think the ornamentation might have been Victorian. But it could have been Federal. My readers would have known the difference. So let's just say they were Victorian frames. Simpler that way. An author's trick. The building looked old, but not decrepit—not at all. More like someone either had been keeping it up for decades, or spent a lot of money recently restoring it. In a sleepy town—I would have bet on the maintained-well-for-decades scenario.

The sign above the front door read CARTERET COUNTY HERALD.

I like newspapers. I always have. Putting together a publication with probably as many words as my first book—everyday—was a feat that boggled my mind. I liked to read them, peruse the ads, read over community calendars, figure out the Jumble, and do the crossword puzzle as well.

I think I knew that the county had a newspaper, but I don't think I had yet seen a copy. I don't think I looked for a copy either, so that may be why.

There was a sign taped to one of the two front windows. I wondered if there had been a rash of "manfunctioning" boilers in town that day.

No. The sign read HELP WANTED.

Really. A sign in the window of a newspaper office. Don't newspapers have classified ad sections for that? On a personal note, I had found all my jobs—remember that had been in the dark, pre-Internet age—through the Help Wanted sections of newspapers. Maybe the job market has come full circle. No, that's not the right term, but you know what I mean. (And I appear to be saying that a lot, as well.)

Downtown Morehead City in May was not the busiest place I had ever visited. An empty parking place opened up in front of the office. In fact, I could have chosen between a half-dozen empty parking places. I couldn't see a phone number on the sign from the street, so I parked and walked up to the front door.

On the sign, written in pencil, above the printed words HELP WANTED were penciled the words REPORTER/CLEAN-UP/ DELIVERY PERSON. Perhaps they needed someone to do all three tasks at once. Everyone knows that newspapers are having money problems these days.

I stepped inside the newspaper office, thinking that I could ask a receptionist for a job application or find out more about the jobs listed or get a copy of the most recent newspaper. Something.

No receptionist sat behind the counter. A stack of newspapers was on the counter. I glanced at the front page. The lead story covered the school board election. Not bad. They probably didn't do much national news on the front. They published the newspaper three times a week. Not bad. Publish once a week and a newspaper becomes easy to ignore.

To my left was a closed door marked with the words ADVERTISING DEPARTMENT.

Then I saw the small tent made from a folded four-by-six note card standing on the desk where the receptionist must normally sit.

"Gone. Be Back."

Simple declarative sentences tell a powerful story.

I felt better now. The caffeine jolt may have had something to do with it as well. I always feel better after an infusion of a couple of real, double shots of caffeine. Much more than a cup of instant-brewed coffee—no matter how strong I make it.

Off to the side, I heard someone talking loudly—a one-sided conversation—so I assume that either he was speaking to a mime, or was on the phone. I would guess it was a phone call. He spoke loudly, and maybe sounded a little upset. Maybe that is what newspaper people do on a regular basis.

In another moment, a large man—large, but not tall—came from around the corner. He was not bald, not yet, but on his way, and wore a rumpled white shirt, khaki trousers, and sus-penders. I would bet he was a man who woke up rumpled and stayed rumpled all day. He did have an inviting smile, though, and knowledgeable eyes—you know, eyes that indicated he knew . . . stuff.

Egads. Could I write or what?

"I thought I heard someone come in. Our trusty reception-ist, Lucinda, is out back having an affair with another cigarette. I'm often stuck doing her job. Curse the addictive qualities of nicotine. And I don't say that loudly, because tobacco is one of the area's big cash crops." He took a deep breath. "I'm Kistler Hibbs. I'm the editor here. Managing editor, if you want to know the proper title—which impresses no one except my mother. So I'm in charge. That's what they tell me, anyhow. You are applying for a job, correct?"

"I . . . I . . ."

"How did I know? Well, you look like you're not from around here. There's a look. I don't know how locals are dif-ferent, but they are. You're a recent move-in. I know you're not trying to sell anything or else you'd have a briefcase. You're not here to place a classified. You would use your computer to do that, since you are young enough to certainly have a computer and know how to use it. You're not related to anyone who works here—as far as I can recall. So . . . you must be applying for a job."

He was right. Must be a good reporter. Observant. A quick study.

"I saw the sign in the window," I said, hoping that I didn't sound enormously pathetic.

"Yes, I know it's odd that a newspaper hangs out a Help Wanted sign. But our publisher is like 150 years old. That's the way they did it back then."

I knew already that I would like Mr. Kistler Hibbs.

"He's not really 150 years old. More like 140. And you are inquiring about the job, correct? Please tell me that my parlor guessing game and prowess were spot-on today." He lowered his voice. "On occasion, I have been known to make a mistake in identification."

I told him that I was new to the area. I told him that I was applying for the reporter job.

"Have you written anything before?"

I should have brought a resumé with me. I should always travel with a résumé at the ready.

Do I even have a résumé? A new one, I mean. The last one I recall using had been written . . . a decade ago.

"I have. Well, yes. I have written . . . books."

Kistler Hibbs took a theatrical step backward, and clasped his hand over his mouth.

"You're Mary Fassler, aren't you?"

This time I was amazed. And I am sure that my face indicated just how amazed I had become. Very, very amazed.

"I've read some of your books. My wife loves you. I just read the one about the Amish cowboy. I wanted to head off into the West after I finished the last chapter."

"*Lariats of the Divine.*"

"Yes, that one! It was so marvelous. I loved it. Of course, I hated the cover. That ungainly man did not look at all like Stephen from the book. It didn't. I'm sorry. Horrid illustration."

I really liked Kistler Hibbs.

"I know. I didn't like it either. But a publisher has the right of way," I said.

He leaned toward me and looked around, to make sure no one listened in on us, in a most theatrical way.

"I hate publishers."

I went back to being amazed, after a short stint at being totally pleased at the recognition.

"But how . . ."

"Janet . . . down at The Star Team. She's our neighbor. She said she just sold a place in Atlantic Beach to a famous writer. And she mentioned your name. I anticipated sending a reporter over to do a story on you. I really did. If I had a good reporter, that is. Which I don't. Hence the sign in the window."

I remained amazed.

"Listen, Mary Fassler, Morehead City is a small town and we love our gossip, so be prepared to have no secrets here. Unless you do something really horrible. Then no one will ever talk about it—above a whisper, and behind your back to be certain, anyway."

I had no idea what to do next. It was one of the few fan encounters I have ever had—other than at poorly attended book signings, that is, or at conventions when one of my books was being given away for free. Free books meant that I had fans.

"Mary . . . may I call you Mary? I thought so. Listen. I know you can write. And I know you could do this job in your sleep. Human interest stories, mostly. Some news pieces. Beauty queens. Nurse of the Year awards. Political spotlights. Business stories—on business owners mostly, not business. Heavens. No one understands business. Or wants to read about it either. Odd collectors and their collections. Artists. Visiting person-alities. Spotlight on a teacher or some other unsung public servant. High-achieving students. A day in the life of someone or other in town. Maybe the odd county or city council meeting when someone is on vacation. People who are one hundred years old."

He scrunched his face into a prune, trying to think of other topics, but apparently had exhausted his mental list.

Then his features unscrunched.

"Maybe write a personal column or two whenever. 'Notes from a Newcomer' or something akin to that. What do you think? Do you want the job?"

My amazement knew no bounds. I am certain my jaw was slacker than it had ever been before.

"I know. The offer is out of the blue. And you may ask why. Why so quickly?"

"Well, that did just cross my mind," I replied.

Kistler Hibbs smiled. "Allow me to elucidate. First off—you can write. Your books are ample evidence of that fact. The value of that ability cannot be underestimated. I've had graduates of college journalism schools who could barely string three coherent sentences together. And heaven forbid you want the story done on time. They need time to think and compose—to find their muse. And when they do find it, they can't spell it. I hate spell check. It has ruined an entire generation of spellers. Now, as a writer of novels, you're used to deadlines. You must have a good work ethic or you couldn't have done all those books. And you're new to our pleasant town. A good way to meet people—and make a few dollars."

He stepped close to me and put his hand on my arm in a most fatherly way.

"Janet told me about what happened. I am so sorry for your loss. And I know that a few extra dollars—and work—is often what God wants for us. Keeps us occupied and focused on others, not ourselves. And the money can't hurt. What do you think? Start on Monday? The pay is adequate. Better pay than working at some horrid Quickie-Mart or an abominable warehouse store, regardless of what they sell. We offer benefits. Vacation time, 401(k), dental. Wait, do we have dental? I think so. Some dental, anyhow. Flexible hours. Mostly flexible. Work from home some of the time. You know, Mary Fassler, I have made the position sound so nice that perhaps I'll apply."

For twenty seconds, I tried to formulate a cogent reply, or consider different options, or think of questions to ask, or something.

Instead, I simply said, "Yes. I'll take it. I can start Monday. Can I bring my dog to the office on any day I have to work late?"

Kistler Hibbs smiled.

"As long as it doesn't have rabies—or at least as long as it doesn't show, then it is okay with me."

Before our walk, I treated Rufus to a half slice of Key lime pie. So far, his enthusiasm for the dessert had not waned a bit.

As we walked to the end of the driveway, I decided to turn away from the ocean this evening, and head toward the small retail area of Atlantic Beach. I had driven through the area a few times, but never seemed to really see what stores were there. Walking would let me really explore.

I turned toward the sound, part of the Atlantic Intercoastal Waterway, divided from the ocean by the narrow spit of land that Atlantic Beach had been built upon.

"You seem happy," Rufus said as we walked along a dark stretch of sidewalk.

"I am," I replied. "I found a job today."

I'm not sure if Rufus knew what a job really encompassed. I suppose I could have explained it to him, but it would have taken a long time. I cut it as short as I could. "That's a very good thing. It means that I will have enough money to buy a Key lime pie every week."

"Well, that is good news," Rufus said, his stubby tail wagging as much as it could, given its shortened arc. "Very good news."

The first time I took him to the newspaper office, he would have questions. I would wait until then to answer them.

We turned south, down the short business district. The area, bright and well lit, had several dozen pedestrians and walkers strolling about. An independent coffee shop stood on one corner—Sandy Sandy's Coffee Shop. As we walked past, the warm, enveloping, velvet odor of roasted coffee and steamed milk filled the night. Rufus lifted his head and drew in deeply. I would have stopped, but all the outside tables were taken, and I had had a lot of coffee today and I mostly didn't feel like sitting.

Across the street was a smallish beach accessory store—bamboo mats, swimming suits, Boogie Boards, suntan products, and endless rows of vacation stuff that no one needs but buys only when on vacation. A drugstore was part of the mix of stores, along with a convenience store with gas pumps, a restaurant that looked like a mom-and-pop affair, a real estate office (not The Star Team—think more modest), a resale shop that looked as if it sold higher-end items, and at the end of the block, a store with a neon sign that glowed RENT-A-SCOOTER.

We crossed the street and I looked in the darkened window. A row of scooters stood against one wall, lined up on the diagonal, looking all gleamy and polishy in the reflected neon.

(I really did write novels before this. Really.)

Rufus sniffed at the door.

"Smells like the smell your car makes."

"It does. But this store has scooters, not cars. They're sort of like motorcycles."

"I don't like motorcycles. They make a lot of noise. They scare me."

"I know, Rufus. But scooters are much smaller and slower."

"Like a bicycle?"

"More like a bicycle than a motorcycle. And not scary."

He sniffed again at the door.

"I think I'll come back . . . maybe tomorrow. . . . and rent a scooter for the day."

Rufus turned his head sideways and offered me a very odd look, as if he had just imagined the most ridiculous image in the world.

"Really? You?"

I didn't take kindly to being sneered at by a dog's preconceptions of what I could or could not do—or worse yet, what I should or should not do. I would bet that Rufus did not mean the comment in a snide way—but that's how it came out.

"Yes. I could ride a scooter. I did it in college. Once or twice. I liked it then and I might try it again."

I wanted to add a snotty "You have any problems with that?" but felt pretty certain that the sarcasm would go over the poor dog's head and he would simply think I was angry with him— which I was not.

Maybe I will. Maybe it's time to try out my wings . . .

This time I snorted.

Sounds like a bad country and western song title.

As we turned the corner on Robin, Rufus asked me the final question of the evening: "Can I have more Key lime pie when we get home?"

20

On Saturday—a warm day, not hot, not sunny, but pleasant—I walked over to Rent-a-Scooter. I had decided to show Rufus that I could be impetuous if I wanted to be, and that I could drive a scooter.

I hoped that I hadn't forgotten how to do it. College lay decades in the past, and I had forgotten everything I learned in freshman English composition, so maybe my scooter skills would be a little on the rusty side.

A bell tinkled above me as I walked in. Rufus had been right. It did smell of gas and motor oil, and car wax. Or scooter wax, I guess.

Some scooters in the line I had seen that night were gone—rented out, no doubt. It was still preseason, and the crowds had not descended on the beach yet. I wondered what that would look and feel like, and if I would begin to resent the tourists after a time, the traditional scornful native, wishing all these strangers and interlopers would simply go home.

After a moment, a door to the back end of the store opened and a tall man, about my age, with dark hair and dark eyes, wearing a gray mechanic's shirt, came out.

For a moment, his dark features reminded me too much of Jacob. I swallowed hard. As he drew closer, the resemblance faded, except for the coloring—I would guess Italian.

"Hello. Welcome to Rent-a-Scooter."

I smiled back. "I'd like to rent a scooter, please, for the afternoon."

He wiped his hands on a shop towel. "You've come to the right place. For a scooter, that is. We have them." The name Viktor was stitched above his breast pocket.

He, Viktor, I guess, asked me where I wanted to go.

"Just around town. I'm new here and I would like to explore the area a little."

He asked if I wanted to go fast. I gave him my best school-marm look and replied, "Do I look like I like to drive fast?"

He agreed with me, but added, "Looks can be deceiving."

He pointed to a blue scooter. "This Vespa is easy to ride. Not fast, but not slow, either. And I have a helmet that matches it. You said for the afternoon, right?"

"A couple of hours."

"Back by five?"

"Before then. More like two hours."

"We can do that. I need a driver's license. And you need to fill out a waiver release form. Once we do that, I can go over the controls. You'll be on the road in no time at all."

He smelled of oil and freshly laundered clothes—an odd combination. Intriguing.

The Vespa featured the simplest of controls. The right hand twisted the throttle for gas, and both sides had brake levers. It was like sitting at a desk, with both feet flat on the floorboard. Not much different from a bicycle, the Vespa was quick and responsive. It also ran quietly. Rufus wouldn't be scared. I felt much younger as I cruised about. Incongruous, improbable, and a little unnerved, but younger.

I drove past my house, and onto the driveway. I beeped the horn. It sounded like an Italian horn should sound.

Rufus's head popped up in the screen door. I waved. "Rufus, it's me," I shouted. He did not seem convinced. I would not go get him—he couldn't, nor would he, ride on the scooter with me. I pointed at the machine. "I like it. Can I buy one?"

Rufus took that opportunity to turn away from the door, like a parent obviously disgusted by an offspring's actions. I took it as his mild disapproval.

I so enjoyed my two-hour ride that when I pulled into the garage area at the rear of the store, I knew I had to have a scooter of my own. Viktor waved hello.

"Enjoy the ride?"

He was handsome in a down-home sort of way. Striking almost.

I'm not really obsessed by men. Honest. Viktor did not wear a wedding ring. I notice these things. That's all. And he was handsome.

"I really did. Like riding a bicycle. You don't forget. And I kept it on the slow side."

"That's good. Being safe."

I handed him the helmet. I am sure my hair looked like an exact impression of the inside of a helmet. Not my most striking look. Not anyone's striking look.

"Do you sell any of these scooters? Are any for sale?"

Viktor slipped the helmet over one of the handlebars.

"I do sell a few, Miss Fassler. But not until the end of the season. I buy a dozen new scooters at the beginning of the year, and at the end, I sell off a few that are a couple of years old. Still in good shape, but customers expect new models. Are you in the market?"

"I would love to have one. I had a blast."

"Can you wait until Labor Day? I'll have some to sell then. I'll make sure I keep a good one for you. A lot cheaper than buying new, that's for sure."

"I can wait. I'll come back at the end of summer."

At that moment, a young girl came through the back door, curly black hair a circular buzz around her face as she ran. "Daddy!" she shouted and leapt up at him from a few feet away. He caught her and swept her into his arms, where she snuggled against him. A horn sounded in the alley. Viktor waved and the car drove off.

"The end of summer will be fine," Viktor said. "I'll see you then, okay?"

Why are all the good ones taken?

I sat at the Shark Shack, enjoying my second order of grouper bites. Rufus had three of them, so I did not feel overly indulgent at the second order. I had french-fried sweet potatoes as well, another decadent southern delicacy. I don't know if it was really a southern dish or not, but a few restaurants offered them and they have since become my favorite greasy side dish.

Rufus sat, panting. He acted odd in the warm weather. Dogs pant when they are hot. We all know that. It helps dissipate heat, since they don't sweat. But Rufus gave the impression that he didn't like to pant, or found it undignified. He would pant for a short moment, close his mouth, swallow, pant, close his mouth, as if the act of panting made him self-conscious. He seemed healthy enough. I asked him during a walk if the heat bothered him.

"No. No. Not at all. Why do you ask?" he replied.

So I let the subject drop.

The waitress came out and sat next to me on the picnic bench. She patted Rufus's head, which he gratefully accepted.

"Thanks for the story on Marine wives," Cindi said. "Everyone on the base said it was one of the best stories they had read on the subject."

Cindi had been the first person I had talked to when we came to Atlantic Beach.

It seemed like a long time ago.

She was one of the Marine wives I interviewed for the story on military spouses—the trials they face, the separations, the anxiety, their often nomadic existence. She was a pleasant person to talk to—and very self-aware. That made for a good story. That made the paper as my first story. Well-received too.

"My husband usually hates things like that, yet he thought it was really good."

"Thanks, Cindi. I appreciate that. Sometimes stories turn out different from what you expected. But I liked working on that one."

"I've got another couple of tables to work. How about if I treat you to a Key lime pie for dessert?"

Rufus nearly fell over turning around and getting into position for a handout.

———— ∞ ————

A reporter for a newspaper in a small city was as close to a media personality as a person could get without being anything close to a media personality. Besides the newspaper, there was one local TV station that offered a local newscast. So together, we were "the media."

Armed with my clip-on name tag: Mary Fassler/Reporter/ *Carteret County Herald*, I could probably go anywhere, unchallenged, throughout Carteret County. I usually carried a large, older, digital camera with me as well, so I looked the part of a journalist. People assumed that you were on the job, and doors opened almost automatically. In truth, how often does the ordinary person's life show up in a newspaper? Rich and famous people might grow tired of their notoriety, but the average person never made it into print unless he or she was in a traffic accident, got arrested, or died.

Not the best way to get noted.

So when I, as a reporter, showed up at someone's office, or place of work, or home, I generally received a warm welcome. Maybe the fellow who covered city hall has a different take on the subject, but for me, the job proved to be an all-access key that opened doors and caused people to talk freely. Someone was interested in what he or she had to say. And, of course, I would not be going all "Mike Wallace" on them. I would write a nice story. That made a difference too.

I did a story on what public school teachers did over the summer. The pay in Carteret County is not the highest in the nation, so most of them worked: painting houses, running a Sweetie-Freeze soft serve stand (all the good names had been trademarked), tutoring, doing lawn service, serving as a life-guard, and the most unusual—pig wrangling. On a pig farm, someone has to get the pigs onto trucks and to market. Phil Kerl was the only pig wrangling I had ever met.

I did a story on a day in the life of one of Morehead City's oldest doctors who still made house calls. I decided then that he would be my doctor, only to find out that he wasn't adding new patients. "At eighty-four years old, I need to slow down a little. Smell the roses. Take Sundays off." He was a peach of a southern gentleman.

I did a story on a policeman who served on the New York City Police force for twenty years and retired to Carteret County. His was a typical story. He wound up bored stiff within six months, applied for a patrolman's job, and has been on the local force for twelve years. "I love it down here. It took a couple of years to get used to the pace. I found myself getting everywhere a half-hour early."

And now I was working on a piece about a local man, a twenty-four-year-old man, a rising star in the ranks of the world's top professional surfers. Atlantic Beach is not a noted surfer's beach, but this is where he got his start. I had to stop him at least twenty times to ask for a definition of one odd phrase or term after another. I mean, who knew what an "ankle snapper" meant or what a "rhino chaser" was?"

With this job, I even had my own desk at the offices of the *Carteret County Herald*—in the far corner, next to a window. I think other people used the desk in my absence, so I kept the personal effects to a bare minimum. I had a fake ivy plant, a picture of Rufus, and a clear glass jar filled with seashells. Hokey, yes, but I thought it looked pretty.

Kistler Hibbs entered the newsroom with a flourish. He did most things with a flourish, making it nigh onto impossible to ignore him. And everyone called him "Kistler Hibbs." Never Mr. Hibbs. Never Kistler. Never Sir. Just Kistler Hibbs—like it was all one word.

I liked him even more now than I did the day we first met. He was a generous man, a great editor, and a stitch.

Friday afternoons were empty times at the office. The Friday edition went to the printer the night before, at midnight. The Monday edition remained . . . like a week away. People who had the time, or the ability, or the nerve, made themselves scarce on Friday. Except for the sports department. Friday was a big high school sports night, but during the slow summer months, the Minor League Baseball team, the Morehead City Marlins, garnered some time, attention, and ink.

But all in all, Friday afternoons were quiet afternoons. I liked working in the office, more than I liked working at home. Rufus didn't seem to mind. When I asked him if it would bother him if I was gone for a few hours during the day, he simply asked if I intended to come back before our walk. I assured him that I would. "Okay, then. I can take a nap until you get home," he answered.

Working at the newspaper office gave me a new sense of belonging, of having a place that I could go to. I began to feel at home here—at the office, in Atlantic Beach, by the ocean. Despite the fiasco with Billy B (and that's how I began characterizing it—as a romantic fiasco) I started to feel as if this was the home and the job and the location that I was meant to have.

Could this have been God-ordained? Like I said before, he and I aren't talking. But Rufus seems happy and content. Maybe that's all the sign I needed. Or all the sign I will ever get.

Kistler Hibbs spread his arms wide when he saw me and shouted, in a nice, but very loud voice: "Mary Fassler—my Brenda Starr reporter!"

I waved back at him, and continued to type. In the old days, I imagine, a newsroom had been a noisier place, with clacking typewriters and paper being yanked out of the reels, and phones jangling, and the staccato tapping of hot-lead linotype machines in the back room. Now all you heard was the soft, nearly mute digital clicking of keyboards and the unearthly warble of cell phones.

I sound like a cranky old woman, don't I? And a little of me is cranky. But not old. Not yet.

By the time I finished the ninth paragraph, Kistler Hibbs had sidled up next to me and nearly reclined on the desk opposite mine. His proclivity to lie about was another reason the staff kept breakables and crushables off their desks. He propped up his ample head with his ample forearm. It looked so totally uncomfortable that it would make strangers wince when they saw him. But he could maintain the position for upward of thirty minutes. Maybe he did yoga in his off hours. Or Pilates. Yet he didn't seem to have off hours. He was always here when I worked in the office.

"Miss Mary Fassler. My soon-to-be award-winning reporter."

I must have appeared quizzical.

"I entered your Marine wife story in the North Carolina Newspaper Editorial Excellence Competition. Or contest. Or judging. I forget exactly what they call it. But it's a big deal if you win. The publisher comes out of his cave and hands you the award and grins at you like a Disney version of the crypt-keeper. You'll find it all so fascinating when you win."

All of this was news to me. That phrase takes on a new level of irony if you actually work in a news organization.

"But I never entered anything."

Kistler Hibbs waved me off.

"Of course you didn't. I did. You wouldn't have known about the competition, and probably wouldn't have wanted to enter even if you had. You're just too nice, Miss Mary Fassler."

Southerners seemed to have a predilection for things with three names.

"And besides, if you win, and I am pretty sure you will, that makes me look better—like a smart editor, rather than a slothful one."

He went on about the award ceremony two months away.

"It's up in Raleigh. At a deluxe hotel. Like a Ramada Inn. Big banquet with real chicken and real waiters and everything. No catering from the Waffle House for this affair. You can bring a date along. The paper would even pay for his entire $10 dinner ticket, I bet."

I must have made a face or looked like I intended to make a face. I thought that I kept most of my emotions—when it came to dating and all those romantic entanglement questions—under check. I remained impassive. I walked above the fray.

Apparently not, at least when it came to Kistler Hibbs.

"I'm sorry, Miss Fassler. I didn't mean to touch a sore point. Truly."

This time, I simply waved him off.

"It's no big deal. I've dated. Once or twice. But at my age, it's not easy. Things have a way of happening, I guess, that make relationships difficult. The older we get, the heavier the baggage."

We could hear Lucinda dealing with a customer out front. Her raspy, deep-toned growl was unmistakable. Something about a classified ad running for two weeks, which offered a much less expensive rate, or just one week. Lucinda was not our most skilled communications expert.

Kistler Hibbs unwound himself from his prone position.

"I am not one to give advice," he said, seriously, and then barked out his punchy laugh. "Oh, who am I kidding? I love to give out unwanted advice. It's my hobby, isn't it?"

I held up both hands, submitting to the obvious.

"Let go, Miss Mary Fassler. Let go of whatever holds you back from living now. I won't say that I understand how you feel, because obviously, I don't. But if there is something you're holding on to—a grudge, a hurt, unexpressed anger—then you need to let it go, or deal with it. It's a lot of work to hold onto hurt. Takes so much energy to keep hidden things cooking away at a simmer. Too many things simmering, and you don't have room to start a new meal. So . . ."

I widened my eyes, as if expecting more.

"So, I came close, right? I know I came close to the problem. Please tell me I did."

Kistler Hibbs behaved more like a clutchy, old, gossipy woman than most clutchy, old, gossipy women could ever hope to be.

And he was sort of on the right track.

I sighed. "You are close. I'll think about it. Maybe you're right."

And with that, he brightened as bright as a ballerina, and headed off to the front counter to undo whatever customer service damage Lucinda had done.

I won the award. I was surprised. Kistler Hibbs had been sure of my win all night. I heard others say that it truly is a prestigious award, and that I may even be offered a raise because of it. The banquet and the official presentation were not until the beginning of October, so I had time to not find a date for the affair.

Ava and Beth came to visit in August. I had invited them both to come at any time and they took me by surprise when they both agreed to come and decided to travel together.

Politics, as well as expensive rental cars, make strange bedfellows.

I set up two beds in the large room upstairs. The room filled up, much to my chagrin of my earlier impulse to leave it empty.

Since I had to work, at least some of the day, both women were happy to take their beach chairs, books, and suntan oil to the beach, only two blocks away. Ava won the award for the best and quickest overall tan. Beth's bathing apparel was much more modest. And she used up two full tubes of sunblock.

We had a wonderful time together. We went to the Shark Shack three times. Beth found the local grocery store and made dinner twice. Ava ordered pizza for our last evening together.

"They can't make pizza down here," Ava declared as she picked up her fourth piece.

"It's all right," Beth countered, thus ensuring that their point-counterpoint dialogue remained in place for virtually every topic we discussed during their stay. "It's actually quite good."

"Ketchup on bread dough," Ava countered, and claimed that Chicago, and perhaps New York, were the only places to find edible pizza in all of America.

Her disdain did not preclude her eating more than a fair share of the two large pizzas delivered from Luigi's Pizza and Subs down the road from Atlantic Beach.

Ava bought a six-pack of local beer from a small brewery in Beaufort, just up the coast. I knew of them only because I was scheduled to do a story on the two brothers who opened the business a few years ago. On my own, I seldom, if ever, partook. Now that Ava was here, perhaps I would relax—just a little.

Beth all but sneered at the offer.

"I'll stick with Diet Coke, thank you," she said, as crisp as starched linen.

Afterward dinner, we had some Key lime pie, and yes, Rufus had a small sliver. "That dog is getting fat," Ava said. "I like that in a dog."

Rufus looked hurt by the accusation. I knew he would ask me about it on our walk tonight, unless all three of us went, which is what had happened all week. Except for the morning walks. Then we were alone.

The three of us retired to the screened porch while Rufus slept on the sofa. Evenings could be warm and humid, but tonight, a breeze off the ocean cooled the air and kept the humidity at bay.

Ava brought it up first. I was surprised that the subject had not come up before.

"So, are you dating? What's the manpower situation like down here? There were a lot of cute beefcakes on the beach."

Beth responded as expected.

"Honestly, those boys were all in college. You're old enough to be . . ."

"You can stop right there, Beth. We were just talking. No one asked me out on a date."

"But you said you would have gone. That blond boy in the baggy blue suit looked to be only nineteen, right?"

She surprised me by paying such close attention. She surprised Ava too, apparently.

"Well, then, you seemed to be watching quite closely."

Beth blushed. She is not a blusher by nature, since she doesn't do anything to blush about. In a clam-sized voice, she said, "He was awfully cute. I'll give you that."

Ava all but slid off her chair. Beth hid her face in her hands, not really ashamed, but maybe a little. "Too much sun does that to me," she said aloud into her cupped hands. "I can't help it."

Later, after Beth had gone upstairs to pack (their flight from Raleigh departed early, and that meant leaving Atlantic Beach at 5:00 a.m.) Ava cornered me, figuratively speaking.

"Is there a man down here? You mentioned that one—the one who worked on your kitchen. Is he still around?"

I tried to describe, without emotion, the relational fiasco that Billy B had become. Ava listened, without comment, but her face did narrow, and her eyes grew harder, like a stern teacher, or a disapproving mother.

I knew that would be her reaction, and was happy that she had waited to the last day to scold me.

"Mary," Ava said, with some tenderness, "we love you."

I waited for the sympathy shower that had to follow.

"But you drive both of us absolutely crazy."

I'm sure I looked shocked.

Maybe a little hurt.

"Listen, Mary, I don't care about you praying, or not praying. I bet Beth does, but even she thinks all this is nuts. I don't care if you believe or if you don't believe. I mean that. I don't care if you talk to God, or if you never talk to God again."

I wanted to say something, to lash back at her, to be mean in return, but I couldn't think of how best to return her angry volley.

"Just get over it. Please," she said and crossed her arms over her chest. She winced. "Too much sun."

I broke ranks and smiled.

But she continued to scold. "Make a decision, Mary. If you don't want to talk with God, then don't talk to him. But don't keep agonizing over the fact. Don't drive the car while staring in the rearview mirror, trying to fix the past. You're going to get killed that way. You want to give up your faith, just do it. Give it up. If you want to believe in God . . . go ahead and do it. And that probably means that you have to pray. So quit feeling sorry for yourself. It's like you're wallowing in the mud pit of self-pity."

"I am not," I said, skillfully opposing everything she said and cleverly refuting her intricate denouement of me and my personality and my behavior over the last few years and everything I believed in. Or didn't believe in. "I'm not, either."

I am such a clever debater.

Ava snorted. "It's the fence-sitting that drives people crazy, Mary. And it drives men even crazier. Commit to one side or the other. You want the shoes? Buy the shoes. Don't expect me to talk you into the purchase."

Ava shook her head. "Now, I'm quoting the foot doctor as a relationship expert. But he's right. He said that to me after we got into a big fight at Nordstrom. I had forty pairs of shoes spread out all around me and I really, really wanted these wonderfully expensive, red, strappy things. But I couldn't pull the trigger. I wanted him to talk me into buying something that I wanted that he could not care less about. For a foot doctor, he doesn't care about shoes in the least. Go figure."

I hadn't followed her logic. I don't think she followed her logic either.

"All I'm telling you, Mary, is that you can't spend the rest of your life saying how bad God is, and then turning your back on him. If you think he doesn't care, then act like he doesn't care. If you want to 'talk' with him—then just do it. But don't play games with the process. It'll tire you out before it tires God out."

And then she did something that surprised me. She hugged me. Ava had never been much of a hugger. But she hugged me. And whispered in my ear, "Mary, you're miserable. Talk to him."

When she released me, she obviously felt better, relieved.

"I feel like I'm in sixth grade reporting to Bobby Deletora that May Ellen Fisher really does like him and that he should talk to her."

I sniffed a few times.

"Did Bobby talk to her?"

Ava grinned. "He did. They dated like forever. They eventually got married after college—and divorced three years later. What do I know about relationships, really?"

There were a lot of hugs, and a few tears, when the two of them left the following morning. Even Rufus seemed more animated than normal, bouncing about, nosing about their luggage.

Maybe he was making sure they weren't secreting away his favorite squirrel back to Chicago or concealing a stash of crunchies in their bags. We promised to call and to write and to visit. There were hugs all around, twice, and Rufus even got his share of hugs, though he did growl a bit when Ava squeezed him.

"Take care of her, Rufus," she said. "Bite her if she keeps on complaining about God not listening. Okay?"

I could have sworn that Rufus nodded. He later claimed that he didn't, but it sure looked like it. And then they were gone, driving off into the early morning dark. We were up, so Rufus and I decided to take to the beach before the crowds descended.

I could have let Rufus off the leash when we walked on the beach. I had tried it once. Rufus didn't like it.

"What if a wave comes in and sweeps me out into the ocean? How will you get me back to shore?"

I tried to explain that would not happen.

"I saw a big wave on television."

I believe he referred to the tsunami in Japan.

"So you want the leash?"

"I do. I am safer with a leash."

So we always used the leash. He seldom pulled on it, except for the occasional times when he saw a squirrel or another dog.

As soon as we reached the water's edge, Rufus turned to me and asked, almost confrontationally, "Am I fat? That lady said I'm fat."

I knew that question was coming.

"No, Rufus, Doctor B said you have big bones and are not fat. Besides we walk a lot. And she just said that because you had Key lime pie. I don't think she ever met a dog who likes pie like that."

"Are you sure?"

Rufus was certainly more insecure about his weight than I had ever imagined. I didn't think a dog would care. Maybe he thought fat was something else entirely, something all good dogs should avoid being.

"I am sure, Rufus. You are a good dog. And you are not fat. Not at all."

We walked along, the waves hissing a good morning, a few scats of gulls careening in the faint light of false dawn. I really did like the ocean. I really was glad that we had moved here. I really did think that this new life was the one I was meant to have.

Now, if I were able to dismiss Ava's comments as easily as I wanted to, everything would be perfect. I decided there was no time like the present to ask Rufus about it.

"Do you think I should start to pray again?"

Rufus looked up at me, confused.

"What? I don't understand."

"I mean, like praying. I sort of stopped talking with God . . . a long time ago. I told you about that."

"No. I don't think you did. That's not right—not talking to God."

"I did tell you that, Rufus. I am sure I did."

He stopped walking. He did that when confused or deep in thought.

Then he slowly spoke. "I thought you meant you didn't talk with him when we were walking. I think that's what I thought. I never once thought you stopped altogether. That is wrong. I think I already told you that, didn't I? Just now?"

"You did. So I should just forget about everything that happened and pretend that everything is hunky-dory and start including God in my conversations?"

Rufus made a wide half circle around a dead jellyfish, keeping his eyes focused on it in case it jumped at him. "Sure. You can do that."

"Just like that?"

"I don't understand. What is God supposed to do? Things are what they are. You start from here. You can't change what happened in the past, to what you want. I don't think it works that way. I know it doesn't work that way with dogs."

We walked on. The sun edged up onto the eastern horizon. I wanted to yell at somebody. Ava had been right. I think Rufus had been right, as well.

Rats.

The earth did not shake. The sky did not fill with lightning bolts. I had no soul-shaking epiphany. The logic piled too high for me to dismiss any longer. What could it hurt? No, that's not right. That's being snarky. I knew Atlantic Beach had been the right choice. Sometimes you just know. And there is no buildup, there is no crescendo. It just is. And that's what this was.

As we turned away from the ocean, I simply whispered aloud, my words carried off by the breeze, no doubt, "Dear God . . . it's me."

21

If I had been expecting rockets, or earth tremors, or a choir of celestial beings, all carrying amplified harps, I would remain disappointed.

Nothing happened.

I reintroduced myself to God, and said I hadn't talked to him for a while, then I ran out of things to say. And by that time, we were back at the house. Rufus took his early-morning nap, and I had to shower and fix breakfast. I had an interview at the office at nine.

Places to go, people to meet.

Maybe I felt a little looser. Maybe I felt a little less down.

I'm not sure. I once had a friend who first tried selling diet supplements, and then she tried selling dried blue-green lake algae, and finally, capsules filled with ginko biloba. She would insist that I try a week's worth, or a month's worth free of charge. Then she would call me every three days to see how much better I felt.

I hated to tell her that I never felt any better after taking whatever it was she was selling. I mean, I never felt run-down or fatigued or particularly dull-witted and forgetful in the past, so perhaps the effects of the drugs or algae or whatever were more subtle. Every time, I would have to tell her that I didn't think I felt anything. And she would respond with an ever-increasingly depressive, "Ohhhhh."

Maybe talking to God is similar to taking dried blue-green lake algae. Maybe it took a while to kick in.

The interview went well. Kistler Hibbs asked how my recent visitors "from up north in Yankee land" liked Atlantic Beach and my new house. I said they really enjoyed themselves, and I enjoyed having them, but if I told the truth, I was happy to see them go because I liked having quiet evenings.

"Don't get too used to the quiet, Miss Mary Fassler. Pretty soon you'll become that crazy old lady shaking your fist at the teenagers who walk down your street playing their music at all hours and much too loud."

I stifled a laugh. We had one of those ladies in our neighborhood growing up. We avoided her house, even on Halloween.

"I won't. I promise. But two people, all at once, all the time, expecting to be entertained—I guess I'm just out of practice."

Labor Day proved to be a bust in Atlantic Beach. I had been told there would be one big party up and down the beach, all weekend long. The rain started Friday morning, and by Saturday fell horizontally. To make things worse, thunder and lightning boomed and flashed sporadically all three days. The rain kept coming, but it was warm. I almost liked warm rain. It felt like you were taking a shower.

Thunder has a way of unsettling Rufus. At the first rolling boom, he runs to the front door first, then to the back, then, using his front paws, lifts himself up to stare out one of the windows. When it booms again, he heads off into the bedroom, coming out every few minutes—as if checking to make sure I am still there.

I had nothing planned for the weekend, so I sat on my sofa, under a throw, reading old newspapers, magazines, and a stack of books I had gathered for just such a time, drinking coffee, and eating shortbread cookies—the real good ones from Scotland. Eventually, Rufus came out and joined me on the sofa, nestling in close to me, lifting his head in surprise at every lightning flash, his eyes darting from the window to me and back to the window as if I had been causing all the terrible commotion. I had explained to him last year what happened during a thunderstorm, but all The Weather Channel explanations in the world did not settle his nervousness. It did not matter that I assured him that he would be safe inside. He even stopped begging for shortbread, a clear sign of his nervousness.

The weather settled down on Sunday. The air, because of all the nitrogen oxide released by the lightning bolts, smelled fresh and clean and wonderful, containing a thick layer of promise you could almost see.

I leashed up Rufus and headed toward the downtown area. The beach would have been strewn with washed-up seaweed and jellyfish and the occasional dead fish from the storm. Rufus loved the smell of dead fish and would roll on top of them if I didn't stop him. I learned that lesson the hard way, staring out to sea one day while Rufus coated himself in Eau de Dead Fish. Downtown would be safer. Despite the rain, a modicum of people walked about. Sandy Sandy's was filled. I didn't feel like coffee right now. We walked past the Rent-a-Scooter store. The "closed" sign hung on the front door. Rain is probably terrible for the scooter business. I looked in and saw the same row of polished scooters waiting for riders.

I had promised myself that I would buy one. And with my literary/reporting prize, a raise had been promised. So the purchase wouldn't cause a big dent in my finances—unless the scooters were really expensive. I had no idea how much they cost.

"I'm coming back this week and I'm going to buy a scooter, Rufus. Remember when I told you that?"

"I do. That's okay with me."

Then he stopped.

"I won't have to ride on it, will I? They look dangerous to me. Do they have a helmet that fits a dog? I don't think they do. Then it's even less safe for me."

"No, Rufus, you will never have to ride on it."

"Okay. Then everything is okay."

As we strolled east, toward the ocean, I realized that I did feel better. Not fabulous. Not on top of the world. But I felt lighter. More free.

Maybe my first steps back toward God were paying off.

Yes, I know that sounds terrible. I know that God is not some sort of cosmic, celestial gumball machine that starts to pay off after you put in a quarter's worth of praying. I knew that prayer and God do not work that way. And that's not how I felt inside, in my heart. These first few days of me praying— well, none of my prayers would be featured on the religious television stations. I didn't really know what to say at first. I still don't. I said I was sorry for being silent for so long. I said I felt lost. I tried to explain how I felt—lost and abandoned. I said I blamed God for what happened. I didn't hold back. I didn't try to fill the prayer with thees and thous. I can't say for sure that God had listened to the prayers of such a wayward one, but I can say for sure that it felt like he had listened. The dialogue was choppy and stilted and angry and contrite and apologetic and meandering and curt; it contained everything that I had held inside for all these years.

I prayed aloud, at night, as we walked. Rufus heard, of course, but did not say anything.

Except, at the end, when I stopped talking, he would add an emphatic "Amen."

His coda, his final word, felt so right—like he put the right postage on my awkward words, helping me know that the words were actually being heard by the Almighty, were actually being posted to their heavenly address.

It took a dog.

Go figure.

Tuesday at noon is when I decided to walk over to Rent-a-Scooter. Rufus fussed and bounced and whined more than normal. In fact, he hardly ever asked to come with me during the day. But today, he all but insisted.

So I leashed him up, and we set off.

The bell sounded as the two of us entered the store. Rufus sniffed the air like he was on the CSI investigation team.

"Hello. Welcome."

Viktor was as handsome as I remembered. Maybe more so. He had a touch of summer tan to him.

"Hi. Remember me?"

His face brightened and he greeted me with a wide smile.

Why are the good ones off limits?

"I do. Mary, right? The last name . . . starts with an . . . *F*. Right?"

"You are correct. Mary Fassler."

"Yes, that's it."

"So do you have a scooter to sell? We talked about you selling a few scooters at the end of the season."

"Of course I remember that. People rent. Not many buy."

He pointed to the last four scooters in the line. "These four, I'll sell. The blue one is probably the best one. Never had a problem with it. A few minor scratches here and there, but in the best shape of the four. Mechanically, it's A-One. You like blue?"

At that moment, the young girl I had seen at the shop some months earlier bounced out from the rear of the shop. She skidded to a stop when she saw us, her black hair a beehive halo around her face and shoulders. She stared at me, then really stared at Rufus. She looked up at her father.

"There's a dog in here," she said.

"Yes, Molly, that is definitely a dog," Viktor answered, smiling.

She looked at me, then back at her father.

"Can I pet him?"

Rufus had the gentlest of souls, but small children . . . well, they could give him a case of the willies. Sometimes. Not always. Once, back in Wheaton, when Rufus was younger, I had a visitor with a three-year-old son. I wasn't watching, but I heard a bark, a loud snippy bark, and the little boy started to cry in surprise.

At first, we thought Rufus had bit him—but he didn't. He just barked. That's what the little boy said. "He didn't bite, Mommy. He just barked."

Later on, Rufus told me the child had pulled on his ear, and added, "A bark is better than a bite, right?"

This little girl was older, and judging from her asking her father if she could pet him, better behaved.

"You'll be very gentle?" Viktor asked.

The little girl nodded solemnly.

"Is it okay, Miss Fassler?"

"Sure. I think he'll be fine."

The little girl took three very deliberate steps to Rufus's side and knelt down beside him, looking as if she had practiced the movements. Slowly, she reached out, and patted his head, then began to stroke him down the neck onto his back. He actually nudged closer to her and looked up at her wide face, his eyes clear and kind and accepting.

"So, do you like blue?"

Viktor's question snapped me back to the present.

"Sure. I guess. I mean, I never really had a favorite color. But the blue one is very nice."

Out of the corner of my eye, I saw the little girl reach around Rufus to hug him. With a hug, she might have been walking on thinner ice. But Rufus remained stoic and leaned into her as she hugged him. I could tell the hug remained loose, not tight, but soft and gentle and little-girl tender.

"His name is Rufus," I said.

"And her name is Molly. I don't think I introduced her before."

We watched the two of them for another moment.

"The blue one will be fine. Is it the one that I rented?"

Viktor thought for a moment.

"I think it was. Did you like the way it handled? Fast enough for you?"

I told him that it ran perfectly back then. I didn't try to go very fast, but it went as fast as I needed it to go.

"You can get it up to 60 miles an hour, but around here, you don't need all that speed."

"I would be scared, I think, going that fast. But maybe when I get used to it."

"Maybe. Getting used to something new takes time. But you just keep at it. Then it becomes second nature."

"Sure. How much will it be? And when can I come to pick it up?"

Viktor rubbed his chin, thinking. I could hear the rasp of his whiskered skin. He named a price, then said, "Friday. I'll have it ready by Friday. New oil. Cleaned. Buffed. All the paperwork. Would that work for you?"

"I'll see you Friday, then."

As we walked away, from a half block away, Molly ran out onto the sidewalk and waved good-bye. Rufus turned as she did, making eye contact with the little black-haired girl.

The Labor Day holiday meant a short week—except for the newspaper's sportswriters. Guy Wilson and Todd Grossman were "as busy as two cats in a rocking chair factory." That's how Kistler Hibbs described them. Kistler Hibbs's version made no sense and we all knew it, but it felt off-kilter yet deftly appropriate somehow. High school football had begun, and the *Herald* always did a feature on every local high school team in the county, complete with individual pictures of the players. I had nothing to do with any of it. And for that I was glad. As I mentioned before, sports is not my native language. I had been assigned to do a feature—a few weeks away—on how the wives of high school football coaches coped with the pressures of the game. I had been looking forward to that. It would be interesting.

Friday afternoon, I excused myself early.

Well, I didn't actually ask if I could leave early. I had no deadlines, so I sort of got up, sidled out of the newsroom and pretended to head to Starbucks down the street. Instead, I headed to my trusty Volvo, got in, and drove home.

I would pick up my scooter today. In the back of my house stood a large shed, complete with a cement floor. It had white siding that matched the house, with a green door, so it wasn't unattractive. I suspect that previous owners used it to store gardening equipment. Since I neither had any gardening equipment, nor planned on getting any, I could use it to store the scooter, out of the rain and out of sight. The shed had a large, very-secure-looking lock on it. No sense in tempting fate.

I parked the car, and ran in to change into jeans. I didn't think I had the élan to pull off riding a scooter in a skirt. I'm sure it could be done—just not done by me. I would hate to have it on my tombstone: "crashed while trying to hold her skirt down on a scooter."

The scooter store was only a few blocks away, so the walk would only take a few minutes. I planned on heading there by myself, but Rufus put up such a fuss, jumping and barking, actually barking loudly, and nosing at the door, that I relented finally, and took the leash off the peg in the back entryway. Once I had snapped on the leash, he settled down, as calm as a kitten.

That doesn't make sense either, as a metaphor. Kittens are not necessarily calm, are they? I think Kistler Hibbs and his nonsensical alliterations and metaphors had begun to corrupt my impeccable sensibilities.

The day was fine, bright, warm, with only the slightest breeze to stir the leaves. If this was the beginning of autumn, I knew I would learn to love the winter here.

My new scooter stood gleaming in the middle of the shop. Viktor must have waxed it, because it glistened in the sun. He greeted me with a warm "Hello."

I waved at him, then I asked him the question I had been meaning to ask him since the first time I saw him.

"Why Viktor with a *K*? Is it a family name?"

His pained yet cheerful smile indicated that it was not the first time he answered the question.

"You'll have to ask my parents. I did once and all my mother said is that she liked how it looked with K. I always thought it looked pretentious. I guess I could change it—but at this point in my life, I would have to relearn how to sign my name. And that seems like a lot of trouble."

I handed him the check—actually a cashier's check. He didn't ask for one, but I wanted to assure him that I had the money, and he wouldn't have to call in the check to the bank or whatever people do to check checks these days.

He handed me a thick packet. "Registration. Title. Owner's manual. Service record. Bill of sale. Everything you need is in there."

Molly bounced out from the back of the shop.

"Rufus," she said, loudly, with great cheer. "You brought Rufus." She hurried to his side, knelt down next to him, as before, and started petting him, just as gently and tenderly as she had done before.

Then it dawned on me.

"I don't know what I could have been thinking. I can't take the scooter now. I have Rufus with me."

Viktor realized it at the same time. "That's right. I don't think he would like the ride, would he?"

"He would hate it. Well, I can walk him home, then come back. Will you still be open?"

Viktor checked his watch.

"Sure. But . . . you don't have to do that. You take the scooter home. We'll follow you to your house. I'll take Rufus with us. It's almost closing time anyhow."

"No. I couldn't impose on you like that. You probably have to get home to dinner. Your wife will be worried."

Something dark crossed his face, just for a second, dark and foreboding.

"No. No one will be waiting."

He must have seen the concern in my eyes, or anxiety, or whatever flashed in my mind. I would be horrible at poker.

"My wife . . . I mean . . . she passed away four years ago. Molly's sitter is a college girl and she's gone back to school for the year. Molly doesn't start school till next week, so she's here with me."

I didn't know what to say. Now I knew why all the people I told about my husband were silent.

"I'm sorry," I finally said, soft as I could. I don't know if Molly was paying attention. "I didn't mean to pry."

Viktor did not appear angry or upset or concerned—just resigned.

"It's okay. Really. It's been four years."

We both were silent for a long moment. I could not tell you how long the silence lasted—even trying to remember it now. The time span is fuzzy, hazy, like a dense fog at the beach.

I have to say something. I have to.

"The same thing happened to me. Five years ago. My husband and my son. He was Molly's age."

I looked over at the little black-haired girl and felt that tightness in my chest and the heat in my throat and the wetness in my eyes. I turned away and wiped at my eyes with the back of my hand. I hoped I did it so no one really noticed what I had done.

"So . . . we both know how hard this can be, don't we?" Viktor said, his words at a whisper, not because of sadness, but to keep them from his daughter.

I nodded. I didn't trust myself to speak.

Molly spun around and lay on her stomach, put her head in her hands, and peered up at Rufus. He lay down on his stomach and stared back at the small girl. Rufus never interacted that way with me.

She was talking to him, her words only a whisper, her words only to be heard by Rufus and Rufus alone. He would be trusted with her words and no one else.

I sniffed loudly, then turned to him, with as big a smile as I could manage.

"Are you okay to drive?" he asked.

I sniffed again.

"I am. This sort of moment is old hat. Hard for a second or two, then it passes."

"I know. You get better at it as time goes by. Like shifting gears, isn't it?"

"Exactly. Sometimes you have to do it in an instant. That's when it's hard."

We both looked at the dog and the girl, and then we looked at each other. Neither of us spoke for a while. Again, I don't know how long we stared.

"Here's the key," he said, breaking first.

"I'll drive slow. I live over on Robin. Halfway down the block."

"The little white Cape Cod with green shutters? The one that was just painted?"

"Yes. I just moved here from near Chicago. Well, in April."

"I love that house. I've driven by it a couple of times. I like the picket fence."

I put the helmet on my head. I didn't snap the chin strap. That made me look like I was wearing a deranged party hat. And I only lived a few blocks away.

"Rufus, you will go with Molly and Viktor, okay? You'll ride with them and they'll take you to our house, okay?"

I knew Rufus understood perfectly. He followed at Molly's side, as they headed out to their red truck in the alley. Viktor pushed the scooter through the shop and outside for me. It started right away. I sat down and watched as Rufus slowly climbed up into the cab of the truck. Molly helped him at the last. It was a long stretch for a small dog, and Rufus could never really jump high. I heard the door slam, and I slowly pulled out and headed for the main street.

I thought back to what Rufus said about being victorious. Is that what he meant?

I dismissed it as crazy talk and made a long turn onto Robin, puttering along on my new scooter, happy. I pulled into my driveway and stopped at the back of the house. I switched off the engine, pulled the helmet off, then yanked the scooter up on its stand.

Viktor pulled up behind me.

"Ride okay?"

"Beautiful. I love it."

Molly opened her door and I expected Rufus to bound out. Normally he would have. He didn't take to cars well and the less time he had to spend in them, the better.

Molly kept petting him and whispering something to him.

I don't know what came over me. But something did. Some power. Or courage. Or foolishness.

"Listen," I said to Viktor, "I know this is really forward. But I have a big bowl of spaghetti planned for dinner. Well, I do now, anyhow. I'll tell you upfront that the sauce is from a jar. But it is good sauce—for being out of a jar. And the cheese is imported. That's what makes it good—wonderful cheese. Would you like to stay for a quick dinner? Molly and Rufus seem to be becoming fast friends."

I could practically see inside Viktor's mind. His eyes gave his thinking away. He wanted to, but did not want to be forward either. He wanted to, but he had to protect his daughter as well. He wanted to talk about his wife with someone who really understood, but was afraid to.

I was afraid too. When was the last time I invited a man for dinner? Like never, really.

I was thinking everything he was thinking. Do we have too much of a shared background? Am I—or is he—a nice person? Or perhaps quietly and dangerously crazy? Would there be too much pain?

Then he smiled. And I smiled back.

We both knew the answer.

"Sure. I would love that. I'm pretty sure Molly would love it too. She's a big fan of spaghetti."

"It's not gourmet spaghetti. It's just me doing the cooking."

He leaned toward me, speaking softly.

"I am positive that Molly's grandmother uses ketchup in her spaghetti sauce, so anything will be better than that. All the pressure is off, okay? Sauce from a jar, to me, is gourmet."

⁂

After dinner, Viktor and I sat on the screened porch. Rufus and Molly were inside. The music from the introduction of *SpongeBob SquarePants* could be heard through the screen door.

"Is it okay if she watches that show? It's been a long time since I had to monitor children's TV. I mean, I know what the show is, but kids' media is confusing."

Viktor held his coffee cup away from the sofa as if he was afraid of spilling.

"It's okay. Some of it is over her head. But I don't think any of it is bad. I don't think so. Maybe it's borderline, but it's hard to keep up with everything."

Dinner had gone well. I had the spaghetti done quickly. I had French bread slathered in garlic butter to serve with it, and I made a small mixed-green salad as well. The adults ate the salad.

Conversation flowed easily. I asked Viktor about his business. He asked me about my work. I didn't mention my book writing. I will, but to drag out books right now felt a little like bragging. He knew all about the *Herald* and had known Kistler Hibbs back in high school, though Kistler Hibbs had been four grades ahead of Viktor.

"That's what everyone called him back then too. He would correct people. 'It's Kistler Hibbs,' if you please."

I offered to make more coffee. Viktor accepted, but added that after the coffee they would go. Molly's bedtime during the summer was later, but they were getting into practice of going to bed earlier each day to get prepared for school hours.

We could hear the ocean tonight, a gentle thrumming, plus crickets. The occasional car drove down the street. I could hear music from my next-door neighbor's house. They were an older couple who were partial to classical music. I had no idea of the composer.

"Mozart," Viktor said. "Clarinet concerto in . . . something or other. B-flat, maybe."

"I'm impressed," I replied. Seriously. I was impressed.

"The result of a wasted childhood. I never played ball, just listened to classical music."

"Really?" I replied, already angry at his parents.

He laughed quickly. "No. My mother taught music. That sort of music filled our house. I grew up with it. I got to play ball too."

"That's good. I was ready to be mad at them—your parents, I mean."

We sat for a minute. Viktor sipped.

"This is nice," he said. "After my wife . . . I was angry for so long. Maybe still am, a little. Angry at the doctors. Angry at myself. Angry at God. You know—angry at everyone."

I knew exactly how he felt.

"I know exactly what you mean," I said.

"But I realized, over time, that it was nobody's fault. It happened. The world is a broken place at times. I guess we all want God to keep us alive forever."

"I know. I know what you mean," I said.

"Eventually, I found peace in the pain. I had to. I have a daughter to raise. That peace keeps me solid now. I thank God for that."

"So how did you get the peace?" I asked.

"I guess it came when I could finally acknowledge that God has a plan, that everything happens for a purpose, even if we don't like it and don't want it, and that he is still good—even when I don't understand it all."

I smiled at him, in the dark, and hoped that he saw me.

After a long moment, Viktor stood up.

"We have to be going. I don't want to, but Molly has to have a schedule. If not, she doesn't do well at all."

I took his empty cup.

"This was very nice, Mary. It was very pleasant."

We walked in on Molly and Rufus sitting on the sofa. Molly's arm wrapped around Rufus, who sat upright, as if he was absorbed in the SpongeBob cartoon. He might have been. He understood more on TV than I gave him credit for. But cartoons might be hard to explain to him.

Rufus and I stood at the screen door, waving as they left.

I felt both more solid than I had in months, or years, and more nervous as well. The nervousness I understood. The solidity, I did not.

Rufus and I walked the beach that night, the tiniest hint of cooler weather in the breeze. I must have had a hundred questions in my mind, but did not feel like giving any of them voice.

Rufus did ask me one question though.

"How old is that little girl?"

"Molly. Her name is Molly."

"Her name is hard for me to say."

"Not much different than Mary."

"I know. Mary is hard to say too."

"Molly is five years old. Maybe six. If her mother has been gone for five years . . . yes, she's probably six."

"Her mother died," Rufus said. "She told me she died."

"Yes. I don't know how. But she doesn't have a mother now."

"Oh."

And that was all.

I sat on the porch by myself that night, and wrapped a throw around my shoulders. Rufus gave up on sitting beside me, or else he wanted to leave me alone. He might have been that caring. I found it harder, sometimes, to process emotions with his sad face staring at me.

Maybe this praying has done something to me. Maybe it has torn down a wall.

I felt . . . I want to say free . . . but that's not it. I wanted to believe God is still good, like Viktor said. To feel lighter. And more solid. If God could do that for Viktor . . .

I looked up at the dark sky.

Dear God, I am sorry for being so . . . foolish. I am sorry for not talking to you. I am sorry for blaming you for what happened. Can you forgive me? I need your peace. Can you . . . ?

And that's when I felt something break inside of me, something bad and harsh and cold and saw-edged and raspy and mean. It broke, it snapped, it started to crumble and splinter and dissipate.

And that's when I started to cry. Not a sad cry, not a cry of pain, but a cry of release and relief. The tears fell for what I had lost, not only way back then, but in the years between then and now. I had lost me. I had lost my heart. My soul was damaged and broken and hidden.

And now, it felt as if light was entering into my very being for the first time in years and years and years. I sat there, my shoulders hunched and my lungs gasping for air, and then it was gone and then I felt . . . normal again. Like I felt alive once more. Reborn, almost. No, it felt really like being reborn.

And that's when Rufus slowly edged out onto the porch and stuck his cold nose into my calf and made me shriek like I had fallen into a vat of crystal-clear ice water.

We both jumped upright.

And I felt as good as I had ever felt in my life.

"Thank you, God. Thank you."

22

The next day, just after lunch, my phone rang.

I should have invested in caller ID, but I remained in my frugal mode when I signed up for local, landline service.

I picked it up.

"Hello?"

"Hi. This is Viktor . . . from the scooter shop."

How many Viktors does he think I know?

"Hi," I replied, as cheery as I could make a one-syllable word.

"I called to see how the scooter is running."

We both knew he lied. Not bad lying, but he didn't care about the scooter at all—at least not for this call.

I knew why he called, but I would not make him squirm.

"Great."

He paused. If we had been teenagers, I would have thought he frantically looked at his penciled sheet of handwritten conversation starters. I listened intently for the crinkle of paper. But all remained silent. .

"Listen," he finally said, ". . . uhh . . . maybe we could . . ."

I decided to jump in.

"Viktor, would you like to come over and have dinner here tonight? I know it's hard to get babysitters at the last minute. I would love to cook for someone other than just myself. I could make hamburgers. You could bring the chips and soda and maybe some potato salad?"

He paused again.

I prayed that I did not anticipate his positive response in error.

"I . . . I don't know how to make potato salad."

I managed to inhale.

"I don't think I can either. I always buy mine. And maybe dessert? Key lime pie is a personal favorite of mine."

I could see him smile through the phone.

"Mine too. Even Molly likes it."

I own a grill the size of a paperback book, but if you're only cooking four hamburgers, it works just fine. One each for the ladies, one and a half for the gentleman, and the remainder for the dog.

We sat around the kitchen table, passing chips and potato salad, Rufus going from Molly to me and back to Molly, trying to beg table scraps.

I only had to tell Molly once that Rufus should not be fed from the table. I know, I know, I do it all the time, and I would let Molly do it, eventually. But right now, she would probably give him her entire hamburger. My telling her once seemed to be enough. Every time Rufus sat beside her and stared up at her, Molly would slowly shake her head, her gloriously curly hair flowing like a cloud, and say, with great sorrow, "I am sorry, Rufus, I am not allowed to feed you."

I am not sure what we talked about that night. But I do remember Molly laughing, her little girl giggles making us giggle as well, which made her laugh even harder. Laughter of a child—I had forgotten how magical it can be. Laughter both wondrous and bittersweet at the same time. I hid the bittersweet part deep in my heart, like a hidden treasure that was only for me.

After dinner, Molly and Rufus were dismissed to watch television. Viktor and I cleared the table.

"It is so good to see her laugh," he said as he handed me a plate. "She doesn't laugh much. Or hasn't since . . . you know."

I waited. I waited a bit more. Then I decided to ask.

"Can you tell me what happened?"

He shut his eyes. Kept them shut.

Then he said, "This is the short version. Molly was a year old. Karen cut her finger while cutting Molly's birthday cake. Didn't think anything of it. Didn't heal quickly. Looked infected. Waited to go to the doctor. She was stubborn. A week later, I forced her to go. The wound developed a septic infection. She died three days later."

My hand went to my throat.

"I am so sorry. I really am."

"I know. I know you are, Mary. I could tell that the first time I met you."

I had to hug him then, and he hugged me back. And all the pain that I had carried for so long seemed to flow out of me. I rested my head on his shoulder. He stroked my hair. I felt his arms around me. He felt solid and muscular under my arms. And warm. And tender. And gentle.

After a moment, he relaxed and let me go.

He looked into my eyes.

"Can I call you again?"

"Yes, Viktor. You can."

The end of autumn brought some storms through Atlantic Beach, and a bout of chilly weather. Chilly in Atlantic Beach was T-shirt weather back in Chicago. At night, the beach felt nearly barren, save the lights of the homes that faced the ocean, and the occasional bonfire, with sparks flittering skyward and shadows dancing on the waves.

I had a sweatshirt on that night. I do not remember packing Rufus's coat. He never asked about it, since it had never been that cold.

We walked north along the beach. It was our favorite route, the beach access easier because of sidewalks. The air stayed still, the waves made small catlike lapping noises on the beach, and the moon floated above the still water.

Rufus spoke first that night.

"Are you happy?" he asked. I'm sure he knew, but perhaps he felt the need to make sure.

I tried to be as honest as I could in my reply.

"I am, Rufus. I am very happy. Thank you."

We walked up to the ruins of an old fishing pier. The city council had been discussing rebuilding it. Our newspaper reported that this round of discussion seemed to move the project much closer to a resolution.

Rufus stopped walking. He stared out over the ocean for a minute. A long minute. Dogs don't stare much.

"I'm going to stop talking now," he said, his words firm and solid.

I waited.

"You mean tonight? That's fine," I answered. Sometimes he talks a lot. Sometimes not much.

"No. I mean forever."

I didn't hear that correctly. I was sure what I heard was not what I heard.

"What?"

"It's hard to do this," he said.

"Hard to do what?"

"To talk. Most dogs don't talk, you know. I need to be a dog again."

"But you are a dog," I replied. "A very good dog. You're my best friend."

"You have a new best friend."

He was referring to Viktor.

"Are you going to marry him?"

I knelt down to Rufus.

"I don't know. He has to ask me."

"The little girl needs a mother, doesn't she? You would be a very good mother. She needs a mother."

"She does," I said, trying not to cry.

"I like her a lot. She is very kind to me and very gentle. She never pulls on my ears. She talks to me. She tells me secrets. You should marry him."

"He has to ask me to marry him."

"Will you marry him if he asks you?"

"I will," I nodded.

"He'll ask you. I think that's what the 'victorious' word was. It might have been Viktor. Maybe I heard it wrong."

We both stared out to sea.

"I'm going to stop talking now."

"But you're my best friend, Rufus. In the whole world. You're . . . I need you . . ."

"Not so much now. But I will always be your best dog, won't I? I'll be your best dog even if I don't talk anymore? I like being your best dog."

I hugged him with a fierce love.

"You will always be my best dog. Forever. I will always love you. You helped bring me back to God."

"And I will always love you the best," he said with a closing finality that broke my heart and healed my soul at the same time. "Forever."

"Thank you, Rufus. Thank you."

———— ✺ ————

And the breeze ruffled along the ripples in the sand, causing just the faintest hiss, and the moon glowed bright, lighting their way home. Rufus, a dog once again, a very good dog, walked home with his best friend, Mary.

23

Rufus stood to my side. It was early afternoon, in the spring, and the ocean reflected a gunmetal gray, quiet and gray, and the warm wind gently clattered the sea grass on the dunes. Clouds hovered above us, providing a white, comforting canopy.

Rufus wore a natty, striped bow tie around his neck, held there by a length of black elastic, which almost disappeared into his newly groomed coat. He did not want to wear it. That was obvious—even without words. He shook his head at first, trying to rid himself of the fashion accessory, until I took his jaw in my hands and stared into his eyes.

We were in my bedroom in my little house on Robin Avenue. He hadn't talked in a long time, and I'd stopped expecting it. But I still talked to him. A lot.

"Rufus," I said with some solemnity, "you have to wear this. Every member of the wedding party has to be properly dressed. That means bow ties on every dog in attendance."

Rufus would be the only dog in attendance, but that was beside the point.

He looked back at me, then slowly settled, knowing, understanding.

"I know you won't speak. It's okay."

He nuzzled into my neck.

"You listen to Molly, Rufus. You be her friend."

He pushed into me harder.

"I am happy, Rufus. Viktor and Molly are so very happy. And . . . I know you are happy too."

A small crowd gathered with us that Sunday afternoon. Everyone wore sandals or went barefoot. Ava had come. Beth had come. Bernice sent a beautiful bouquet. Viktor's mother-in-law was there, hugging, crying, and hugging more.

Molly and Rufus walked down the imaginary aisle together.

Viktor and I followed them.

Molly stood on one side, Rufus on the other, as we said our vows . . . before God.

Oh, yes—and God was there as well.

Discussion Questions

1. Come on now, a dog? Really? A dog talking to God? Seriously, though . . . do you think that God could, or would, use such a method to reach a person who was lost?

2. Mary shows her anger at what happened to her by turning away from religion, the church, and God. Do you think what happened to her when she finally returned to church and heard the sermon on Job could be an accurate retelling of the message—or was she just too hurt to hear the truth?

3. Besides her pain, what other obstacles did Mary face in finding her faith again?

4. Perhaps Mary's mother-in-law meant well when she called to find out about the new man in Mary's life—but she instead sounded scolding and accusatory. How might we be guilty of the same sort of attitude if we try to "exhort" someone who seems to be sinning?

5. Suppose Mary was only hearing Rufus's voice in her head—can that sort of inner voice be the sort of nudge we need to turn back to God? And could the nudge from an inner voice be of a divine nature?

6. Mary gave up her nice, sort-of-safe life in suburban Chicago—and that change defined the rest of her life. Is that sort of dramatic move ever required to effect change? Could she have, or would she have made the same changes even if she had stayed where she was?

7. Do you think Billy played fair when he curtailed his relationship with Mary because of her faith—or lack of it? Couldn't a case be made that he should have at least witnessed to her and tried to bring her back to faith?

8. Many people get stuck in a situation or an emotion because of a tragedy or dramatic event in their lives.

What sort of advice would you have given Mary about dealing with her tragedy? Would that advice change over time—would the advice you offer a month after the funeral be dramatically different than the advice offered a year after the funeral?

9. Mary knows what an intimate relationship feels like—and what it all means. Does that make resisting a new intimate relationship easier or harder?

10. If Rufus really talked, and really gave good advice, wouldn't it make sense for Mary to share that secret with someone else? Wouldn't a person want to tell others about something miraculous in their life? Does it make sense that she kept it private? After all, Rufus never tells Mary to keep his talking a secret.

11. The fact that Mary had insurance money and some financial resources made it easier for her being a widow. Many widows may not have such an easy time, comparatively. Does Mary having resources prevent her spiritual growth and maturity, or does it make it harder for her to come to grips with reality?

12. Do you think that Rufus will ever talk—really speak—to Viktor's young daughter? And how important is it for us to have someone to talk to who will never offer a judgment on what we are feeling and experiencing?

Want to learn more about author
Jim Kraus and check out other great fiction
from Abingdon Press?

Sign up for our fiction newsletter at
www.AbingdonPress.com/fiction
to read interviews with your favorite authors, find tips
for starting a reading group, and stay posted on what
new titles are on the horizon. It's a place to connect
with other fiction readers or post a
comment about this book.

Be sure to visit Jim online!

www.jimkraus.com

Abingdon Press fiction
a novel approach to faith

Plan your escape.

For more information and for more
fiction titles, please visit
AbingdonPress.com/fiction.

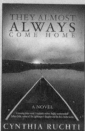